The Best
AMERICAN
SHORT
STORIES
1983

The Best
AMERICAN
SHORT
STORIES
1983

Selected from
U.S. and Canadian Magazines
by Anne Tyler
with Shannon Ravenel

With an Introduction by Anne Tyler

840716

 1983

Houghton Mifflin Company Boston

SC
BES

Shannon Ravenel is grateful to David Weems, who
gave valuable consultation on science fiction
and science fantasy.

Library of Congress Cataloging in Publication Data
Main entry under title:

The Best American short stories, 1983.

 Includes bibliographical references.
 1. Short stories, American. 2. American fiction—
20th century. I. Tyler, Anne. II. Ravenel, Shannon.
PS648.S5B42 1983   813′.01′08   83-10709
ISBN 0-395-34428-X
ISBN 0-395-34844-7 (pbk.)

Printed in the United States of America

V 10 9 8 7 6 5 4 3 2 1

"Hard to Be Good" by Bill Barich. First published in *The New Yorker*. Copyright © 1982 by Bill Barich. Reprinted by permission of the author.
 "The Dignity of Life" by Carol Bly. First published in *Ploughshares*. Copyright © 1982 by Carol Bly. Reprinted by permission of the author.
 "A Change of Season" by James Bond. First published in *Epoch*. Copyright © 1982 by James Bond. Reprinted by permission of the author.
 "Where I'm Calling From" by Raymond Carver. First published in *The New Yorker*. Copyright © 1982 by Raymond Carver. Reprinted by permission of the author.
 " 'Ollie, oh . . .' " by Carolyn Chute. First published in *Ploughshares*. Copyright © 1982 by Carolyn Chute. Reprinted by permission of the author.
 "My Mistress" by Laurie Colwin. First published in *Playboy*. Copyright © 1982 by Laurie Colwin. Reprinted by permission of the author.
 "The Count and the Princess" by Joseph Epstein. Reprinted by permission from *The Hudson Review*, vol. XXXV, no. 1 (Spring 1982). Copyright © 1982 by Joseph Epstein.

Contents

Publisher's Note

The *Best American Short Stories* series was started in 1915 under the editorship of Edward J. O'Brien. Its title reflects the optimism of a time when people assumed that an objective "best" could be identified, even in fields not measurable in physical terms.

Martha Foley took over as editor of the series in 1942 when Mr. O'Brien was killed in World War II. With her husband, Whit Burnett, she had edited *Story* magazine since 1931, and in later years she taught creative writing at Columbia School of Journalism. When Miss Foley died in 1977, at the age of eighty, she was at work on what would have been her thirty-seventh volume of *The Best American Short Stories*.

Beginning with the 1978 edition, Houghton Mifflin introduced a new editorial arrangement for the anthology. Inviting a different writer or critic to edit each new annual volume would provide a variety of viewpoints to enliven the series and broaden its scope. *Best American Short Stories* has thus become a series of informed but differing opinions that gains credibility from its very diversity.

Also beginning with the 1978 volume, the guest editors have worked with the annual editor, Shannon Ravenel, who during each calendar year reads as many qualifying short stories as she can get hold of, makes a preliminary selection of 120 stories for the guest editor's consideration, and selects the "100 Other Distinguished Short Stories of the Year," a listing that has always been an important feature of these volumes.

The stories chosen for this year's anthology were originally published in magazines issued between January 1982 and January 1983. The qualifications for selection are: (1) first serial publication in nationally distributed American or Canadian periodicals; (2) publication in English by writers who are American or Canadian; and (3) publication *as* short stories (novel excerpts are not knowingly considered by the editors). A list of the magazines consulted by Ms. Ravenel appears at the back of this volume. Other publications wishing to make sure that their contributors are considered for the series should include Ms. Ravenel on their subscription list (P.O. Box 3176, University City, Missouri 63130).

Introduction

EVERY YEAR, DOZENS of magazines drift across my doorstep. I leaf through them, and when a short story catches my eye I'll read it. Then I'll set the magazine aside, with a page corner folded down if I liked that story especially.

At every year's end, for various reasons, I am asked to list the stories that have impressed me during the past twelve months. So I hunt up the magazines I've saved, turn to the pages I've marked — and more often than not, find myself reading something I've completely forgotten. Oh, a few details may seem familiar, a line or two may echo back, but it's clear that I have not been carrying that story around in my thoughts all year. Just three or four stories, if that many, stay with me longer than a day or so. Yet in the same year, ten or twelve novels may have settled permanently into my life.

It bothers me that this should be true. I'm a firm believer in the short story, and in its special place as an art form all its own, not as a truncated, ersatz sort of novel. I am willing to allow that simply because a novel takes more time to read, it may lodge itself more firmly in my memory; but I would hate to think that a novel has proportionately any more substance, any more lasting effect, than a really good short story. Why is it, then, that so many short stories lose their bloom in the time it takes me to store a magazine on my closet shelf? Why is it that some few do not? What makes those few any different?

Well, this is the year I found out, more or less.

During 1982, Shannon Ravenel, who has been Annual Editor

of *The Best American Short Stories* since 1977, read 1379 stories published in 502 issues of 154 different magazines. At the end of that time she sent on to me the 120 stories that she considered the likeliest candidates for the 1983 edition.

I have never met Shannon Ravenel, but I notice that whenever I see her name I picture a pair of floating gray eyes — gray because it's my prejudice, evidently, that light-colored eyes take in more. But how Shannon Ravenel can take in over a thousand short stories each year and still retain her sense of appreciation, still pounce so unerringly upon those to which her guest editor should give closest scrutiny, and still choose, moreover, a balanced selection, with subjects ranging from baseball to the Red Chinese — that I can't possibly say.

At any rate, these 120 short stories arrived in the mail. They were torn from publications as diverse as *The New Yorker* and *The Threepenny Review*. Some I'd seen before; most I had not. A few — a very few — I remembered at once in their entirety.

John Updike's "Deaths of Distant Friends," for instance, reminded me at first reading of those tiny paintings that, when you examine certain details under a magnifying glass, appear to swell and take over the room. Minor losses stand for a loss much larger. The death of a golfing companion, not in himself of any deep importance to the narrator and certainly not to us, arouses a surprising ache when he's shown brightly colored and comfortingly cheery against the background of the narrator's own near-comic despair:

> His swing was too quick, and he kept his weight back on his right foot, and the ball often squirted off to the left without getting into the air at all, but he sank some gorgeous putts in his day, and he always dressed with a nattiness that seemed to betoken high hopes for his game. In buttercup-yellow slacks, sky-blue turtleneck, and tangerine cashmere cardigan he would wave from the practice green as, having driven out from Boston through clouds of grief and sleeplessness and moral confusion, I would drag my cart across the asphalt parking lot, my cleats scraping, like a monster's claws, at every step.

And as soon as I saw the first sentence of Diane Vreuls's "Beebee," I remembered that I'd already met the title character. "When he was six weeks old his mother gave him back," I read, and I felt a mixture of pity and affection as I recalled that clumsy, tough, unloved Beebee doggedly tending other people's babies and worshiping Stella McNult in her blue-flowered houseccoat. What will become of Beebee? It's a stroke of genius that his childhood is described not from the vantage of childhood but from adulthood, and through the eyes of the woman for whom he is understandably such an imperfect lover.

I remembered meeting Victrola, too, the title character in Wright Morris's story. Never mind that Victrola is only a dog. He's such an individual dog, so very much himself, with his slantwise style of sitting and the soiled spot on his head from too much patting; and he and his owner so hauntingly reflect each other, slogging through the tail ends of their lives. I'd spent an unforgettable morning with Victrola, even though it's true I'd sworn never again to read *The New Yorker* in the daytime.

And most definitely I remembered the heroine of Bobbie Ann Mason's "Graveyard Day" — funny, disorganized Waldeen, who has so much trouble adapting to change, even to a change for the better. Waldeen believes that a second husband would be "something like a sugar substitute," something like "a substitute host on a talk show," and the story takes its poignancy from the fact that although we see her point, we know she lives in a world where substitution is the name of the game.

Those four, then, were easy. I could say from personal experience that they were stories that would last. The trouble was, I needed a total of twenty. And when I tried simply riffling through the others, using an unscientific, just-because approach, I came up with forty-one.

So I was face to face with the question I'd been sidestepping for years. What are the qualities that separate a wonderful short story from a merely good one?

For one whole afternoon, I sat in the middle of a rug and rearranged tear sheets around me like so many parts of a jigsaw puzzle. Then I went off and left them. Some stories, I noticed, hung on in my mind while I was busy with other tasks. Some evaporated. Some I returned to the following day and found, when I picked them up, that they sprang back whole into my memory, all of a piece, as if carved from a single block. Those were the real successes.

Well, in the long run, this much emerged:

It seems to me that almost every really lasting story — *almost,* you notice — contains at least one moment of stillness that serves as a kind of pivot. This moment might occur anywhere, though it happens most often near the end. It may easily be closer to the beginning, however, in which case it can provide a frame through which the reader views all that happens afterward.

It may be part of the plot, as in "Victrola" when, amid the bustle and confusion surrounding the death of his dog, Bundy hears "Sit," and stands frozen, unable to bend his knees; or in "Graveyard Day" just after Waldeen's plunge into the leaf pile, when it's she who freezes the others. It may be outside the plot, an external comment, as when the narrator of "Deaths of Distant Friends" concludes his accounting of those deaths and reflects upon what they really mean:

> The world is growing lighter . . . The deaths of others carry us off bit by bit, until there will be nothing left, and this too will be, in a way, a mercy.

In "Beebee," the moment is a typographical device — that space break during which Beebee draws a breath (we imagine) to begin listing what he stole from Stella McNult.

Still moments, though, are not in themselves enough. They can be fabricated. Some popular fakes are many of those stories (but not all) composed of one-sentence paragraphs. These give an effect of stillness without having come by it honestly. And then there's the story with a punch line of an ending to which nothing has logically led up, so that although the ending briefly grips us, we realize a little too late that it's undeserved. No, something more is needed — which brings us to the second requirement.

All really satisfying stories, I believe, can generally be described as spendthrift.

The most appealing short-story writer is the one who's a wastrel. He neither hoards his best ideas for something more "important" (a novel) nor skimps on his materials because this is "only" a short story. (This may explain why Raymond Carver — a short-story writer and poet, but never a novelist — consistently produces top-quality stories, while those of his novelist contemporaries are more uneven.) A spendthrift story has a strange way of seeming bigger than the sum of its parts; it is stuffed full; it gives a sense of possessing further information that could be divulged if called for. Even the sparest in style implies a torrent of additional details barely suppressed, bursting through the seams.

The twenty stories in this collection are generous to the point of foolishness. Why didn't Raymond Carver save up his glorious lady chimney sweep and wrench a novel out of her? How come Laurie Colwin splurged that dazzlingly offhand mistress on a single six-page tale? Both writers spent their all on one toss of the dice, with uncommonly rich results: "Where I'm Calling From" almost physically transports us, settling us in the center of its sad little ingrown society and then, in one splendid leap, lifting us out again; while "My Mistress" is not so much a piece of reading as a personal encounter with someone at once hilarious and deeply moving.

For real profligacy, two other examples stand out at once. The first is James Bond's "A Change of Season," which begins with Buck Davaz's disapproving harrumph at the Yanceys — a shiftless lot, you figure, an airy bunch that stops work for the year when the first snowflake falls. But then there's a three-quarters turn by means of which we realize, suddenly, that the Yanceys are the ones who really know what it's all about. And after several of these turns (our own private still moments, each of them), we are joyfully certain that the ambitious and successful Buck Davaz, who makes no allowances for winter in any way, is the one to be disapproved of.

And if he didn't know winter how was he to know that after feeding cows you can go sit by the stove?
When did he hunt up his snow shovels? When did he fan his seed oats?
When did he think to check the braces in the barn?
And if he didn't know winter, how did he know spring? Summer? How did he know what to do and when if he didn't even know the season he stood in?

The other story that stands out is Louise Erdrich's "Scales." You think you won't much care about a gigantic, belligerent,

pregnant woman who weighs trucks for a living? Just wait. By
the time you see her violently knitting her orange and hot-pink
baby clothes, "pulling each stitch so tightly that the little garments she finished stood up by themselves like miniature suits
of mail," you'll care passionately. And the still moment created
by the last six sentences is absolutely deserved, absolutely powerful.

It's in the realm of character that the authors' generosity is
most clearly evident. The plot lines of the stories assembled here
tend to describe not simply what happened, but to whom —
exactly who, in the fullest sense, these people are. Guy Vanderhaeghe's "Reunion," for instance, tells an old tale — husband is
misfit at wife's family gathering, drinks too much, makes scene,
strains wife's loyalty — but it's elevated by the personality of the
husband. He is funny, original, and endearing, with special little
snags of attachment to his wife. At the end of the story, after
we've torn our hair and looked frantically in other directions
over various embarrassing forms of unpleasantness, we actually
laugh with relief at the husband's means of resolution.

In Susan Sheehe Stark's "Best Quality Glass Company, New
York," we start out wondering who the intruder in the cellar is,
as if this were any ordinary whodunit, but end up realizing
there's something else that matters more: the character of the
people intruded upon, the dark underside of family life. And
in Marian Thurm's "Starlight," the real suspense of the piece is
not — as Elaine's parents suppose — whether Elaine's children
will decide to come back to her, but why they preferred not to
live with her in the first place. What is wrong with her, exactly?
What did her children sense in her character that led them to
choose their father instead?

" 'Ollie, oh . . .' " could survive on plot alone — enough happens, surely — but without its meticulous characterization of
Ollie herself, it would be just another rural horror tale, conclud-
ing with the obvious still moment of violent death. Instead, Ollie's intensity of feeling — her obsessive lists, her self-centered
rages, her unexpected kindnesses — gives her story color and
presence. Why, even her husband's pickup truck has character!
(It's a "prince of trucks." It has "shoulders! Thighs. Spine. It
might still be growing.")

Moreover, there is something organic, built-in, about these plots. Events emerge with apparent inevitability from the quality of the characters' lives. Robert Taylor, Jr.'s "Colorado" is not merely a new version of "How I Spent My Summer Vacation." It's a glimpse of one family's internal workings, complete with a memorable image of the touchingly enthusiastic father splashing through mountain streams while his wife and children mope around the cabin. And Ursula K. Le Guin's "Sur" uses plot to make its statement in the deftest way imaginable. I'm ashamed to say how far I read before it dawned on me that all its characters were women.

In "The Count and the Princess," the whole point is the quality of Count Kinski's life as opposed to that of Mrs. Skolnik's, culminating in the dreadful stunned pause when the Count realizes that none of their differences matter more than being loved. It's intriguing, once we've reached the last page, to gaze off into space a moment and imagine what this mismatched marriage will amount to. We have all the facts necessary, surely. We know the couple's preferences in food, in music, and in evening entertainment, thanks to the wealth of information Joseph Epstein has so kindly provided.

A writer may be a spendthrift, of course, and still produce stories of the most elegant economy. By describing a single object in a household, Ursula K. Le Guin in "The Professor's Houses" speaks volumes about the passage of time and the ways in which we pretend we can foil that passage. This story is beautifully precise in style, with those "bright deciduous treasures" of the child and the "neat and amusing sound" of the little cat lapping milk. The last line is a supreme example of a still moment — almost an electric shock of a moment — created by the narrator's comment rather than by any physical event.

And Julie Schumacher's "Reunion," although it's lightweight and humorous, takes us deeper than we'd expected to go when it focuses upon a woman's stubborn denial of physical vulnerability. It's a particular pleasure to find that a moment in "Reunion" that seemed motionless only by accident — a chance photograph — is in fact motionless by design, reappearing at the end as something of much more significance than we'd understood the first time it was shown to us.

Carol Bly's "The Dignity of Life" is generous in two respects. First, it gives us a sense of a wide window opening onto a hitherto unfamiliar corner of the world, with its undertakers' lore and its "Casket Showing Room Lighting Plan." Second, it is not the slightest bit coy about the final confrontation between the funeral director and his teacher. A lesser, perhaps more fashionable story would have faded off into unspoken sadness and trailed away, but in "The Dignity of Life," Jack squarely challenges Molly ("What I want to know is, why did you ever do it? How could someone like you go and, go and, oh how could someone like you for the love of God go and spend the night with Marlyn Huutula?") and Molly gives him a straightforward answer. During the moment that results — one of the most naturally arrived-at still moments in this book, with the two of them tipping their heads at each other across the lamplight — you have to admire the author's courage. There are half a dozen ways she could have backed out of that scene, with all kinds of subtlety and grace, and she turned down every one of them.

Bill Barich's "Hard to Be Good" — another openhanded story — is so large and complete that you tend to look up at the end and find yourself surprised that it's still the same day. The story's strength is its care in dealing with someone the average reader might dismiss without a thought. "One more punk kid," we mutter, and start to turn the page; but something about the tone of the writing stops us. It *is* hard to be good, come to think of it. "It was circumstances, see?" Shane explains, and we groan and smile, both. Even his mother, whom we're prepared to dislike sight unseen purely on grounds of unmotherliness, turns out to be someone we can sympathize with, and his stepfather is a triumph: virtue made interesting and likable.

A story so rich that it's downright fattening is "Firstborn," by Larry Woiwode, who for a number of years now has been writing about domestic life in a grave, direct, deliberate voice that gives a sense of nothing held back, no issues evaded. "Firstborn" presents us with a painfully exact description of losing an infant, and then lifts off from the scene like some stately balloon to view what it means in the long run, in the history of a family. I like the fact that, by alphabetical happenstance, it is "Firstborn" that ends this book, with its abundance of detail and then that final paragraph — almost an aerial photo — fixing the father's image of his wife and children at the moment when he "began at last to be able to begin again to see."

It would be tidy, of course, to say that I'd picked an even twenty spendthrift stories each with a perfect still moment, and thrown out a hundred stingy stories utterly lacking in still moments. Unfortunately, it would also be wrong. One thing I hadn't sufficiently realized was the trickiness of making such a collection work as a unit. The reader should move from one choice to another without a jarring sensation, but with some change of pace. For this reason, many entries that I honestly loved are not included. I fall all over myself whenever I find a Donald Barthelme piece, to give one example, but none appears here, because I felt it would be something like fitting a poem into an anthology of prose. And although Carolyn Chute's "Olive and August" impressed me considerably, I left it out because, alongside her " 'Ollie, oh . . . ,' " it would have been too much of the same thing. On the other hand, I had no such concern about Ursula K. Le Guin's two selections, since they differ so that they might have been written by two separate people. She is a remarkably versatile and inventive writer, and I can't see denying a spot to one of her stories just because in the same year she happened to write another, totally dissimilar, that was equally impressive.

I would have preferred for these twenty stories to represent twenty different magazines. It didn't happen that way. The fact is that more good writers seem to be sending *The New Yorker* more good work than they send to other periodicals, and it would be unfair to all of us if I pretended otherwise. It does please me to see that without trying to, I have arrived at a fairly even balance between the sexes — nine selections by men, eleven by women — and that at least half of the writers are relatively unknown.

What we have here — with much rearranging and many second thoughts and more than a little blind luck — is a group of stories that I am confident of remembering for a long time to come. Probably there are others out there, just as deserving, that neither Shannon nor I happened to stumble across. Probably there are still others that I simply didn't understand, or

rejected out of unavoidable personal bias. I have no doubt at
all, though, that those I did choose have magnificent vitality,
and this in particular makes me happy. I like to imagine that if
you set this book on a table, it would almost bounce; it would
almost shout. It contains, after all, a 250-pound Indian who
keeps breaking out of jail, a mistress who mends her shoes with
electrical tape, nine women who live serenely in an ice cave in
the Antarctic, and a boy who hangs from high trees just to see
what's out there. All of these people have proved to be survivors, both in their own worlds and in my memory. I am proud
of them, and I am grateful to the writers who created them.

ANNE TYLER

BILL BARICH

Hard to Be Good

(FROM THE NEW YORKER)

SHANE GOT ARRESTED JUST BEFORE his sixteenth birthday. It was
a dumb bust, out on a suburban street corner in Anaheim, California, on a warm spring night. A couple of cops were cruising
through the haze and saw some kids passing around a joint, and
they pulled over and did some unwarranted pushing and shov-
ing, which resulted in a minor-league riot. Shane did not hit
either of the cops, although they testified to the contrary in
court, but he did break the antenna off their patrol car, so the
judge was not entirely wrong to give him a suspended sentence
and six months' probation. The whole affair was no big deal to
Shane, since he didn't feel guilty about what he'd done — the
cops had been *asking* for trouble — but it upset his grandparents, with whom he'd been living for some time.

His grandfather, Charlie Harris, drove him home after the
court appearance. Harris was a retired phone-company execu-
tive, stocky and white-haired, who had great respect for the
institutions of the world. "I hope you know how lucky you are
to get off easy," he said. "The judge could have thrown the book
at you."

Shane was slumped in his seat, studying his fingernails. "It
was a farce," he said.

"You take that kind of attitude and you'll wind up in the
penitentiary."

"I'm not going to wind up in any penitentiary. Anyhow, the
cops didn't tell the truth."

"Then they must have had a reason," Harris said.

After this, Harris made several secretive phone calls to his daughter Susan, who was Shane's mother. She lived in the redwood country north of San Francisco with her third husband, Roy Bentley. Bentley was some kind of wealthy manufacturer. Shane heard only bits of the conversations, but he was still able to guess what they were about. His grandparents were fed up with him. They'd been on his case ever since his school grades had started to drop, and it did no good anymore for him to explain that his math teacher failed everybody who wasn't a jock, or that his chemistry teacher was notoriously unfair — to the Harrises, teachers were in the same unimpeachable category as judges, cops, and ministers.

So Shane was not surprised when his grandfather broke the bad news. This happened one night when they were watching the stock-car races out in Riverside. They both loved speed and machinery. After the next-to-last race, Harris put his arm around Shane and told him that Susan wanted him to spend a couple of months with her during the summer. He used a casual tone of voice, but Shane understood that something irreversible had been set in motion.

"It's because of the bust, isn't it?" he asked. "I said it wasn't my fault."

"Nobody's blaming you. Your mother just wants to see you. Things are going well for her now."

"You really think Susan wants to see me?"

"Of course I do," said Harris, giving Shane a squeeze. "Listen, this Bentley guy's loaded. He owns a whole ranch. Your mom says you can have a separate cabin all to yourself. You'll have a wonderful visit."

"Not when all my friends are here," Shane said. "What's there to do in Mendocino?"

"Same stuff you do here. Don't be a baby, Shane. Where's your spirit of adventure?"

"It dissolved."

Harris moved his arm. "If you're going to take that attitude," he said, "we won't discuss it any further."

"It's always *my* attitude, isn't it? Never anybody else's."

"Shane," said Harris, as calmly as he could, "you just simmer down. You're not always going to get your own way in life.

That's the simple truth of the matter." He paused for a moment. "The important thing for you to remember is that we love you."

"Oh, sure," said Shane. "Sure you do."

Right after school let out in June, Shane got a check in the mail from his mother. She sent enough for him to buy a first-class plane ticket, but he bought a regular ticket instead and spent the difference on some Quaaludes and a bunch of new tapes for his cassette player. The drive to the airport seemed endless. At the last minute, his grandmother had decided to come along, too, so he was forced to sit in the back seat, like a little kid. The space was too small for his body; he thought he might explode through the metal and glass, the way the Incredible Hulk exploded through clothes. He watched the passing landscape, with its giant neon figures, its many exaggerated hamburgers and hot dogs. It appeared to him now as a register of all the experiences he would be denied. He would have a summer without surf and beer, without friends, and possibly without sunshine.

The scene at the airport was as difficult as he feared it might be. His grandmother started sniffling, and then his grandfather went through a big hugging routine, and then Shane himself had to repress a terrible urge to cry. He was glad when the car pulled away, taking two white heads with it. In the coffee shop, he drank a Coke and swallowed a couple of 'ludes to calm his nerves. As the pills took hold, he began to be impressed by the interior of the terminal. It seemed very slick and shiny, hard-surfaced, with light bouncing around everywhere. The heels of people's shoes caused a lot of noise.

Susan had enclosed a snapshot with her check, and Shane removed it from his wallet to study it again. It showed his mother and Roy Bentley posed on the deck of their house. Bentley was skinny, sparsely bearded, with rotten teeth. He looked more like a dope dealer than a manufacturer. Shane figured that he probably farmed marijuana in Mendocino, where sinsemilla grew with such astounding energy that it made millionaires out of extremely improbable types. He hoped that Bentley would at least be easy to get along with; in the past, he'd suffered at the hands of Susan's men. She tended to fall for losers. Shane's father had deserted her when Shane was ten months old, vanishing into Canada to avoid both his new family and the demands of his draft board. Her second husband, a frustrated drummer for a rock band, had a violent temper. He'd punched Susan, and he'd punched Shane. Their flat in the Haight-Ashbury came to resemble a combat zone. It was the drummer's random attacks that had prompted Susan to send Shane to stay with her parents. He was supposed to be there for only a few months, but the arrangement continued for more than three years. Shane still hated the drummer. He had fantasies about meeting him someday and smashing his fingers one by one with a ball peen hammer.

When Shane's flight was announced, he drifted down a polished corridor and gave his boarding pass to a stewardess whom he was sure he'd seen in an advertisement for shampoo. He had requested a seat over a wing, so he could watch the pilot work the flaps, and he had to slip by another young man to reach it. The young man smiled a sort of monkey smile at him. He was slightly older than Shane, maybe seventeen or eighteen, and dressed in a cheap department-store suit of Glen plaid.

Once the plane had taken off, Shane finagled a miniature bourbon from the shampoo lady and drank it in a gulp. The alcohol shot to his head. He felt exhilarated and drowsy, all at the same time. He glanced over at the young man next to him, who gave off a powerful aura of cleanliness, as though he'd been scoured with buckets and brushes, and said, without thinking much about it, "Hey, I'm really ripped."

The young man smiled his pleasant monkey smile. "It's O.K.," he said reassuringly. "Jesus loves you anyhow."

Shane thought the young man had missed the point. "I'm not talking bourbon," he whispered. "I'm talking drugs."

"I guess I must have done every drug there is," the young man said. He tugged on his right ear, which, like his left, was big. "I can understand the attraction."

The young man turned out to be Darren Grady. His parents were citrus growers. He was travelling to a seminary outside San Francisco.

"You're going to be a priest?" Shane asked.

Grady shook his head. "It's more in the nature of a brotherhood. Maybe you've seen those ads in magazines asking for new brothers?" Shane had not seen the ads. "I never noticed them, either," Grady went on, chewing a handful of peanuts, "until I got the call. You want to know how I got it? I was tripping on acid at Zuma Beach, and I saw this ball of fire over the ocean. Then I heard the ball speak. 'Judgment is near,' it said. I'm not kidding you. This really happened. At first, I thought I was hallucinating, but it wouldn't go away, even after I came down."

"So what'd you do?"

"Went and saw a doctor at the free clinic. He told me to lay off the dope. So I did. But I couldn't get rid of the ball."

"That's what made you want to be a priest?"

Grady frowned. "I can never tell it right," he said, picking through the peanut dust at the bottom of his little blue-and-silver bag.

Shane was moved by Grady's story. He'd had similar baffling trips, during which his mind had disgorged images of grievous importance, but he'd never ascribed a religious meaning to any of them. He felt foolish for bragging about taking pills. In order to set the record straight, he explained to Grady that he'd been exposed to drugs very early in life, because his mother had been a hippie; she'd named him after her favorite movie.

"It's not as bad as some names," Grady said. "I had a guy named Sunbeam in my class last year. Anyhow, you can go into court and get it changed."

Shane didn't want to see another judge, ever. "It doesn't bother me much now," he said, looking out at the sky. "When we lived in the Haight, Susan's husband, he was this drummer — he'd let me pass around joints during parties. Sometimes he'd let me have a hit. Susan knew, but I don't think she cared. I was so small, probably not much of it got into me. I don't know, though. I hate it when I see little kids smoking dope around school. You ought to be at least thirteen before you start."

"Maybe you should never start," Grady said.

"I wouldn't go that far. It helps to calm you."

Grady tapped his breastbone. "The calm should come from inside," he said.

It seemed to Shane that Grady was truly wise for his age, so he confided all his troubles. Grady listened patiently until he was done. "I don't want to downplay it, Shane," he said, "but I'm sure it'll be over soon. That's how it is with troubles. They float from one person to the next. It's bound to come clear for you real soon."

Shane's high had worn off by the time the plane landed. He and Grady took a bus into the city, and at the Greyhound station, off Market Street, they exchanged addresses and phone numbers. The light outside the station was intense, bathing bums and commuters in gold. Shane was feeling relaxed, but he got anxious again when Grady left for the seminary. He was nervous about seeing Susan; their last visit, down in Anaheim at Christmas, had been marked by stupid quarrels. He tried talking to a soldier who was also waiting around, but it didn't work. The soldier was chewing about four sticks of gum. Shane asked him to buy a bottle of apple wine, so they could split it, and when the soldier did Shane drank most of it, washing down two more pills in the process. He was semiconscious on the bus ride up the coast. The town of Mendocino, arranged on a cliff overlooking the Pacific, struck him as a misinterpretation of New England. "It's cute," he said, to nobody in particular.

From the lobby of an inn on the main drag, he phoned his mother, and then he fell asleep in a chair. Later, he heard somebody (he thought it was Susan) say, "Aw, Roy, he's wrecked," so he said a few words in return and walked wobbly-legged to a station wagon. The next thing he knew, somebody was handing him a sandwich. He took it apart, laying the various components — cheese, tomatoes, alfalfa sprouts, two slices of bread — on the table. It occurred to him that he wasn't hungry. He said something to that effect, and somebody said something back — Bentley, the guy from the photo. He followed Bentley into a black night. Moisture from redwood branches dripped onto his head. The air seemed to be eating into his skin. Bentley unlocked the door of a cabin that smelled of pitch and camphor, and said something about extra blankets. Then Shane was alone. The whirlies hit him, and he stumbled to a small, unstable bed. After he was under the covers, the whirlies subsided, and he was able to assess his surroundings. He thought they were pretty nice. The only thing that concerned him was that there seemed to be animals in the cabin — they didn't scratch or howl, but he was aware of them anyway, lurking just beyond his line of vision.

The animals were ducks, two of them, with bulbs inside glowing like hearts. Shane saw them when he woke in the morning. Gradually, he remembered where he was, along with the details of his arrival, and he felt disgusted and ashamed and yanked the covers over his head.

For some reason, he started thinking about Darren Grady. He was certain that Grady had never pulled such a dumb stunt. He wondered if Grady had made it to the seminary and if the other priests had shaved off his hair; he wondered, too, if Grady would recall their meeting or if all such mundane occurrences would automatically vanish from his mind, to be replaced by a steady image of God. Fifteen minutes or so passed in this fashion, helping to temper Shane's guilt and instill in him a new commitment to righteous behavior. He didn't pretend that he could ever be as wise and good as Grady, but he considered it within his power to improve. He got out of bed, examined the ducks more closely — they were lamps — and then, outside the cabin, he dumped his remaining pills on the ground and crushed them to dust. The act was like drawing breath.

Bentley's place was indeed like a ranch, fenced in and isolated from any neighbors. There were a few outbuildings, including a chicken coop and a beat-up barn missing boards from its siding. Inside the barn, Shane found birds' nests, rusty tools, and a broken-down old Chrysler with fish fins. Parts from the Chrysler's carburetor were scattered on a shelf, leaking oil.

Shane expected to be jumped on as soon as he opened the door to the main house, but nobody seemed to be around. He had no memory of its interior, except as a series of difficult-to-negotiate planes and angles. In the kitchen, he poured himself a glass of orange juice and sat down to read the sports page of a day-old paper. He heard his mother call to him from upstairs. "Is that you, Shane?" she asked. "Come up here right now. I want to talk to you."

He poured more juice and went up. "Where are you, Susan?"

"In here. I'm taking a bath."

The bathroom door was ajar; steam escaped from within.

Shane peeked and saw his mother in the tub, under a layer of froth and bubbles. Her hair was pinned up; it was thick, still mostly black, with a few gray strands. Shane thought she was immensely beautiful. He couldn't remember how old she was — maybe forty. The number was an ancient one, but he believed that it didn't really apply.

"Don't just stand there," she said. "It's drafty. Come in and shut the door." When he was inside, she said, "You look a little better today."

"Feel a little better," Shane said.

"How about a kiss for the old lady?"

He bent down, intending to kiss her on the cheek, but she lifted her arms from the water and embraced him. The sudden movement lifted her out of the soapsuds, so that her breasts were briefly visible. Shane had seen her naked before, countless times — in bathtubs and at nude beaches — but the quality of her flesh seemed different now, echoing as it did the flesh in the girlie magazines that he hid in his room in Anaheim.

"Oh, Shane," she said, pushing him away, "you were such a mess last night. What happened to you?"

Shane put his hands in his pockets. "Me and this friend of mine, Grady, we bought a bottle of apple wine and drank it at the bus station." He was quiet for a second or two. "I'm sorry I did it," he added.

"Well, you *should* be sorry. You gave us a real scare. When you behave like that, it makes me think you want me to feel guilty. I know I shouldn't have left you with Grandma and Grandpa for so long. You're my responsibility, and I've done a poor job of raising you."

Shane recognized this as therapist talk; Susan was always seeing one kind of counsellor or another. Left to her own devices, she would have sputtered and thrown something at him. Once, she'd almost beaned him with a ladle; another time, an entire needlepoint kit had whistled by his ear. "You can't *raise* me, Susan," he said. "I'm not spinach."

She laughed and looked directly at him. "No, you're not spinach. But you'd better be telling me the truth about last night. It better not be pills again."

"It's not pills."

"It better not be, because if you get caught fooling with them you could go to jail, you know. It's a violation of your probation. I don't understand how you got arrested in the first place. Who were those kids you were hanging around with?"

"There's nothing wrong with the kids," Shane said heatedly. "The cops started it. Anyway, Susan, since when are you so much against drugs? You used to smoke a joint every morning."

"I haven't smoked marijuana in years."

"Sure, Susan."

"Don't you dare talk to me like that, Shane," she said. "I'm your mother."

"I know."

"I'm not trying to be moralistic or anything. I just want you to keep out of trouble." She stood up in the tub; water dripped down her breasts, all down her body. "Give me that towel, will you, honey?"

He grabbed a towel from the rack and threw it at her, much too hard.

She pressed the towel against her chest. "*Now* what is it?"

"What do you *think* it is? Christ, Susan, don't you have any modesty?"

"I'm sorry," she said, embarrassed. "I forgot how old you are." She wrapped herself tightly in a terry-cloth robe. "Go downstairs and I'll make us some breakfast."

The eggs she fried were brown and fertile, with brilliant orange yolks. She served them on red ceramic plates from Mexico. The colors made Shane's head swim, but he still ate with appetite. He was glad the confrontation with Susan was over. Their future together no longer seemed littered with obstacles. As she moved about the kitchen, banging pots and pans in that careless way she had, he felt a deep and abiding fondness for her, even though he knew that she had presented him with a complicated life by refusing to simplify her own. Charlie Harris called her a "nonconformist," and Shane supposed that he was right — if you ordered Susan to do one thing, she'd be certain to do the opposite. He respected her independent streak, because he had a similar streak in him; they were joined in a bond forged of trial and error.

After Susan cleared the table, she gave him some towels to

put in the cabin and told him that she was going into town. He wanted to go with her, but she wouldn't let him.

"I don't mind errands," he said. He wanted to see what Mendocino looked like when it wasn't scrambled. "I could help you carry bags and stuff."

"We'll go tomorrow," Susan said firmly. "I'll have more time then. Today I've got my yoga class and a doctor's appointment." She came up behind him and hugged him. He could smell her sweet, fresh hair. Her breasts pressed against his backbone. "I love you very, very much," she said. "Now go get yourself clean."

Shane went dutifully out of the house, but he was worried a little. The word "doctor" had an awful connotation, like "teacher" or "cop." He had a terrible feeling that Susan might be sick. So a new thing began to haunt him — he ought to have been a better son. He remembered how in March his grandmother had reminded him to mail a birthday card to Susan, and how he had gone to the pharmacy and bought himself a candy bar instead. What possible use would candy be when Susan was in her grave? "You're so selfish," he said to himself, kicking at a pinecone. Every problem in the world, he saw, had its roots in some falling away from goodness.

That afternoon, around lunchtime, Shane was in the old barn, sitting behind the wheel of the Chrysler and staring at the bird-peopled rafters, when Bentley wandered in and interrupted his daydream, which had to do with driving at great speeds over the surface of the moon. In person, Bentley looked even more disreputable than he had in the photograph. He could have been a bowlegged prospector who'd spent the last thirty or forty years eating nothing but desert grit. His rotten teeth were like bits of sandstone hammered into his gums. "How's the boy?" he asked in a twangy, agreeable voice, leaning his elbows on the car door.

"The boy's fine," Shane said. "He's just fine."

"Well, I'm happy about that. I'd like to have the boy step from behind the steering wheel of the car so that I can have a chat with him."

Reluctantly, Shane got out of the car. His hands were balled into fists. Down in Anaheim, he'd decided that if Bentley was a puncher, he'd punch first.

"Take it easy," Bentley said. "I'm not going to hit you."

"Wouldn't put it past you to try," Shane muttered.

Bentley lifted an expensive lizard-skin cowboy boot and ground out the cigarette he'd been smoking against the sole. "I lost my taste for violence a long time ago," he said. "Course, if I needed to, I could still fold you up and put you in my pocket with the Marlboros."

"I'm warning you," Shane said, backing off.

"The trouble is, Shane," said Bentley, following him, "your mother and I got a good thing going, and I don't want some wise-ass punk from surfer land to come around and spoil it. You pull the kind of crap you pulled last night one more time, and I'll stick you into a Jiffy bag and mail you home to the old folks."

"You can't boss me around."

At this, Bentley chuckled a bit, revealing the stumps in his mouth. "Sure I can," he said. "So long as you're on my property, and living off my kindness, I am most assuredly your boss. And here's some more news, my friend — I'm putting you to work." When Shane protested, Bentley cut him short by jabbing him in the sternum. "I'm giving you two choices. Either you can work by yourself at the ranch, and do some painting and cleaning, or you can work with me at the factory."

"What's your business?"

"I'm a manufacturer."

"Yeah, but what do you manufacture?"

"What I manufacture," said Bentley, "is ducks."

They went to visit the factory in Bentley's station wagon, which smelled of stale tobacco and leather. "See that rise?" Bentley asked Shane, as they passed a sloping hillside off to the right. "If you were to walk to the top of it and then down into the gully, you'd come to another twenty-acre parcel I own."

"Do you have another house there?"

Bentley gave him a peculiar look. "No house, no nothing," he said. "It just sits. It's appreciating in value. We'll have a picnic there someday."

"My grandfather," said Shane, "he loves to barbecue."

"We don't barbecue," Bentley said. "What we do is eat that organic food that Susan cooks. The woman has a fear of meat." He turned on the radio; a country singer was singing about beer and divorce. "Listen here, boy," Bentley continued, "I want you to have a good time this summer. I'm not naive about dope. I've done my share of it. But you have to learn yourself some moderation. Moderation is the key. You keep on abusing yourself the way you're going, you'll wind up in a pine box."

"My grandfather said I'd wind up in the penitentiary."

"That, too," Bentley said.

The factory was situated at the edge of town, in a concrete building that might once have been a machine shop. Inside, ten or twelve young longhairs, both men and women, formed an assembly line at long wooden tables. As Bentley had said, they were making ducks — or duck lamps — by gluing two pieces of heavy-duty celluloid around a metal stand that had a socket at the top for a bulb. Once the duck halves were glued together, they were secured with rubber bands and left to dry for a day or two. The excess glue was later wiped from the ducks with solvent, and they were put in cardboard boxes and cradled in excelsior. The wholesale price was twelve dollars a duck, but they were sold in trendy stores for as much as forty apiece. The materials came from Hong Kong.

Shane was shocked. His mind boggled at the notion that somebody could earn a fortune on celluloid ducks. The arithmetic didn't seem right. Forty dollars? Who'd pay forty dollars? A movie star? Were there enough duck-loving movie stars to provide Bentley with the capital to own a ranch and forty-odd acres? Apparently so. But Shane remained suspicious — the scam was too good to be true. He wished that Harris, who was always harping on the importance of hard work, could be there to watch Bentley as he lounged around the shop, smoking cigarettes and joking with his crew. Harris would go right through the roof; he'd say the whole shebang was un-American. Shane liked the atmosphere, though. Nobody treated the craft of duck-making very seriously. Besides, a tall blond girl with ironed hair kept glancing at him from across the room; he fell into an immediate fantasy about her. He told Bentley he'd prefer to work at the factory instead of at the ranch.

"I'll start you in the morning," Bentley said. "You'll be a duck packer. You'll pack so many damn ducks, you'll be quacking in your sleep."

They locked up after everybody had quit for the day. On the ride home, Shane's thoughts drifted back to Susan, and he asked Bentley if anything was wrong with her.

"No way," Bentley said. "She's a fine, fine lady. Absolutely perfect."

"I mean, is she sick or anything?"

"Sick? No, she's not sick. She's just got some female trouble. When you get older, you'll learn that every woman has it sooner or later. They can't avoid it, and you can't help 'em with it. It's just something they have to go through on their own," Bentley said with a sigh. "We'll talk about it more when we get to the ranch."

But Shane didn't bring up the subject again (he was afraid of what he might hear), and Bentley volunteered no further information. Instead, they returned to the barn and played with the Chrysler until they were both covered with oil. They cleaned the points and plugs and reinstalled the carburetor. Bentley showed Shane how the engine had been modified to make it operate at maximum efficiency. "Let's fire up the sumbitch," he said, wiping his face on a polka-dotted bandanna. He let Shane sit in the driver's seat and try the ignition, but the engine wouldn't turn over. "Pump the pedal," he said. Shane pumped it and tried the ignition again. The engine roared. It sounded big in the barn, scattering robins and swallows into the dusk. Shane floored the pedal briefly and felt himself transported; energy ran through him as though he were a sieve.

After Shane had been at the factory for three weeks, he sent a postcard to his Anaheim pal Burt, the kid who'd actually hit a cop during the bust. He described his cabin, the redwoods, and the factory. "If you want to come up here," he wrote, "I can squeeze in another bed easy. And don't worry about me doing any you-know-what. I'm off that stuff for good."

Twice his grandparents called to see how he was getting along. He still felt estranged from them, and this was compounded when they told him they'd bought a camper and were

going to Joshua Tree National Monument until mid-August
unless Shane planned to come back before then.

"Me?" he asked, sounding wounded. "Since when do *I* have
plans?"

For the next twenty-four hours, he was sullen and depressed,
but he had to work at it, because he was having so much fun on
the job. Every morning at eight, he and Bentley headed off
together into a coastal fogbank that was always just beginning
to disperse. They drank coffee from Styrofoam cups and told
each other duck jokes while they watched the sky separate into
a confetti mist under which the town of Mendocino stood exposed, back from wherever it went at night. Shane packed boxes
with a ponytailed guy who was known as Eager on account of
his last name, Beaver. Eager was anything but — he had a meticulous nature, and he took pains to be sure that each duck was
nestled as comfortably as possible in its excelsior. He could have
been packing eggs or glassware. "C'mon, Eager," Shane said to
him one afternoon. "They're not alive, you know."

The tall blond girl was Emma King. She was nineteen, a college student. Shane followed her around like a dog. When the
weather was hot, Emma came to the factory in white shorts and
a red halter top, and Shane would monitor her every movement
from his packing station, waiting for her to reach down for a
tube of glue or bend low for the X-Acto knife she kept dropping
on the floor. She had a boyfriend she saw on weekends, but she
told Shane that she'd go to the movies with him before he returned to Anaheim. "I'm in love with this heavy girl, she's *nineteen!!!*" he wrote on another postcard to Burt. "We go drinking
together after work." This was almost true, or at least at the
outer fringe of validity. One Friday, Eager *had* invited him to
go to a tavern in the woods where anybody could get served,
but he'd decided against it to avoid trouble. Later, he heard that
Emma had been there, so in his mind they were linked.

He asked her for a photo, but she didn't have any, so he
borrowed Susan's camera and snapped her in different poses,
while she pretended to complain. The cutest shot was one of
Emma kissing a duck on its beak. Shane taped it to the dashboard of the Chrysler. He thought of it as his car now. Bentley
had promised it to him in lieu of wages if he could pass his

driver's test. Already, he was practicing. He did Y-turns and
parallel parking. Some evenings, he and Bentley took a ride to
the ocean, steaming down dirt roads that were dotted with
Scotch broom and beach poppies. Once, Bentley let him go by
himself, without any adult supervision, and he handled the
Chrysler with such authority and skill that he developed a stitch
in his side from excitement. It was a mystery to him how things
kept changing.

Another mystery was his mother. He'd never seen her so
happy. He could not reconcile so much happiness, in fact, with
scraggly, bowlegged, rotten-toothed Bentley. Here was a man
who could walk around for days with egg in his beard and never
even notice. The scent of nicotine was embedded in his clothes
and maybe in his skin. Could it be that love had nothing to do
with beauty? If Bentley could provoke love, then so could a
stone or a twig. So could a garbage can.

But there was no denying Susan's contentment. She thrived
on Bentley's generosity. She seemed to float around the house,
gliding barefoot an inch or two above the floor, dressed in
blouses and peasant skirts that showed off her bosomy fullness.
She baked bread, hummed romantic tunes, and filled all her
vases with flowers. She was constantly hugging her egg-stained
lover, patting him on his flat little prospector's ass. The affection
spilled over to Shane. Susan's arms were always grasping for
him, making up for lost time. She drew him to her for purposes
of both measurement and embrace. The very size of him
seemed to thrill her — he'd grown from almost nothing!
"Oh, Shane," she'd say in a husky voice, holding a hunk of his
cheek between her thumb and index finger. "You're such a dear
boy."

If Shane hadn't known better, he would have sworn that she
was stoned all the time, but he'd never seen any dope in the
house. As far as he could tell, the Bentleys had adopted a much
more civilized vice. They drank wine — a bottle or two every
evening, with Bentley leading the way. The wine burnished
their faces. It made them talkative, sentimental, occasionally
teary-eyed. After dinner, if the fog wasn't too thick, they'd put
on sweaters and sit on the deck and speak in conspiratorial tones
about the day's events, while bats sailed about overhead, like

punctuation. When there was nothing on TV, Shane sat with them, shivering no matter how many layers of clothing he wore.

"Thin blood," Bentley would say, teasing him. "Goddam thin Southern California surfer's blood."

"My blood's fine."

"It's *thin*, Shane. It takes six months for blood to adapt to a new climate."

Blood was yet another mystery. Sometimes Shane thought that he understood Susan better than Bentley did, simply because they were related by blood instead of marriage. Although he and Susan had often lived apart, had quarrelled and made mistakes, she was still his mother, and he was able, in a curious way, to anticipate her moods and know when something was bothering her. One night, as they sat outside, he saw that she was unusually quiet, removed from the conversation, and when Bentley went into the house he asked her if she'd got bad news at the doctor's office — she'd had another in her ongoing series of appointments that afternoon. The question made him tremble. Suppose she confessed something awful to him? Ignorance was a kind of protection. But she only smiled wistfully and patted his hand and said no, nothing very serious was wrong. It was just that the doctor had told her that she might need an operation — minor corrective surgery. She started to explain the problem to him in clinical terms, but it sounded indecent somehow to hear her describe her body as though it were an engine in need of repair, so he interrupted. "I know," he said, mimicking Bentley's sad resignation. "Female trouble." He put an arm around her, wanting to say more, but by then Bentley was back with full wineglasses and a word about the rising moon.

Shane's driving test was scheduled for a Thursday afternoon. Bentley gave him permission to come home early from work to practice. He backed the Chrysler into the barn several times without scratching it, and then he walked over to the house, hoping that Susan would make him a snack, but she'd gone to town for her yoga class. The phone rang while he was eating a boiled hot dog. Darren Grady was on the line, calling from Elk, a town south of Mendocino. Grady was upset, distressed, talking a mile a minute. He'd run away from the seminary. He was stranded, broke. Shane couldn't believe it. Where had Grady's wisdom gone? "Take it easy, Darren," he said. "Everything's going to be all right."

But Grady was blubbering. "I was trying to hitch to your place," he said, "but this highway patrol, he kicked me off the road. I cooled it in the bushes for a while and tried again, but here comes old highway patrol with his flasher on. I gave him the finger and split for town. I'm like a hunted criminal, Shane. You got to help me."

Shane glanced at the kitchen clock. He figured that he could get to Elk and back before he and Bentley were scheduled to meet the state examiner, so he told Grady to sit tight. The drive over there took about twenty minutes and gave him a severe case of paranoia. Every car that approached him seemed from a distance to be black and ominous and full of cops.

Grady was where he said he'd be, in front of a restaurant. He was sitting on the curb and eating a hamburger — some ketchup was on his chin — and drinking a can of beer. When he saw Shane, he waved wildly and let loose his monkey smile. Shane was surprised that Grady still had hair — there was no bald spot or anything. The only truly abused part of him was his Glen-plaid suit. All its department-store slickness had been rubbed away; there were holes in the knees of his trousers, as if he'd been on a long pilgrimage over concrete. Also, he'd lost his socks. The confidence he'd had on the plane was gone; now he was nothing but fidget. "I'll never forget you for this, Shane," he said, getting to his feet. "Is this yours?" he asked in wonderment, touching the Chrysler's fins. "It's a mean machine."

Shane eyed the half-demolished burger. "I thought you were broke," he said.

"I am, but I talked up the waitress in there" — Grady jerked his streaked face in the direction of the restaurant — "and traded her my Bible."

"She gave you beer for a Bible?"

"Just the hamburger. The beer I found."

This sounded fishy to Shane. "Where'd you find it?" he asked.

"Some guy left it on the seat of his car." Grady climbed into the Chrysler. For a moment, he seemed collected, drawn virtuously into himself, but then he fell apart and started bawling. "You're the only damn friend I've got," he said, blowing his nose in the hamburger wrapper.

Grady told Shane that he'd been on the road for three days. The first night, after he'd snuck out of the seminary, he hitched to San Francisco and slept in the Greyhound station, thinking he would catch a bus to Anaheim in the morning, but when he woke he realized that he'd have to confront his parents with the sorry evidence of his failure, so, instead of phoning them, he walked over to Powell Street and ate a breakfast of crab and shrimp at a place that was shaped like the prow of a ship, and then spent twenty-two bucks playing video games at an arcade. This left him with just one dollar to his name — his emergency dollar, which he kept folded in sixteenths and hidden in the secret compartment of his wallet. When he pulled it out, the slip of paper on which Shane had written Susan's address and phone number fell to the floor.

"You get it?" Grady asked, turning toward Shane, who was paying only a little attention, since he had to watch for cops. "It was a *sign!*"

"What about the ball?" Shane asked. His forehead was wrinkled in concentration.

"Ball? What ball?"

"The ball from Zuma Beach. Did it come back while you were with the priests?"

"It never did."

"Then why'd you leave?"

Grady shrugged. His fidgety fingers picked at his knees through the holes in his pants. "It's hard to be good," he said. From the pockets of his suit coat he took two fresh cans of beer and — before Shane could protest — popped the tops. Shane accepted a can and stuck it between his thighs. He hit a bump and got doused.

On the second day, Grady said, he'd reached the town of Healdsburg. He said it was the hottest place he'd ever been to — hotter than Hell, frankly. In the evening, when it got too dark to hitch anymore, he wandered to the town square, where there were palm trees and flowers and benches, and he took off his shoes and socks and dunked his feet in a fountain. The water felt soothing as it swirled between his toes, but a bunch of Mex-

icans who were hanging around the square kept watching him,
and he thought they might knife him or otherwise do him harm.
He knew this was an irrational fear, but it was fear nonetheless,
so he gathered himself together in a hurry, slipped his wet feet
into his shoes, and walked briskly down a side street that led
him to a vineyard, where he curled up on the warm ground and
slept the night away under cover of grape leaves. A flaming sun
woke him at dawn. He couldn't find his socks. Their absence
seemed to hurt him more than anything else. "Everybody knows
you're running away from something if you don't have socks
on," he said, biting his lower lip. "Who's going to stop for a
person with bare ankles?" With this, he finished his beer in a
gulp and threw the empty can out the window. The can rattled
over the macadam, bounced two or three times, and rolled past
the nose of a highway-patrol car that was parked in the bushes,
waiting for speeders.

"Aw, Grady," Shane said.

Grady swivelled around to look back. "That's the guy I gave
the finger to," he said.

Shane felt as though his body had been stripped of a dimension and then spliced into a deadly, predictable horror movie.
He tried to imagine that the cop hadn't seen the can — or, better, that the cop had decided to overlook it — but this didn't
work, since the cop had left his hiding place and was approaching the Chrysler at a steady clip. Shane gave Grady the half-full
beer he had between his thighs, and Grady dropped down in
the seat and drank it off, then shoved the empty into the glove
compartment. The cop came closer. Grady looked again, and,
panicked, said, "He's going to bust us, Shane. I know by his
face."

"You don't know for sure."

The cop's flasher went on.

Grady sank lower in the seat. "I'm holding, Shane," he said
morosely.

Shane didn't want to take his eyes from the road. "You're
what?"

"I'm holding some speed. I bought it at that arcade." He
showed Shane four pills. "Should I throw them out the window?"

The pills got swallowed — Shane couldn't think of any other

way to dispose of them. He and Grady ate two apiece, which lent a hallucinatory edge to subsequent events. The cop was wearing reflector sunglasses, for instance, so that Shane was able to watch himself react to the words that bubbled from between the cop's lips when the cop pulled them over. The cop spoke of littering, of underage drinking, of operating a motor vehicle without a license and without what he called a vehicular-registration slip. Eyeless, he led Shane and Grady to his car and locked them in the back seat behind a mesh screen. The pills really took hold on the ride to the police station, and Shane was possessed by a powerful sense of urgency and a concomitant inability to stop talking. He believed that he had an important message to deliver about the nature of goodness, and he delivered it ceaselessly — to the cop, to the officer who booked him, to the ink of the fingerprint pad, and to the cold iron bars of his cell.

Roy Bentley bailed out the boys. He came to the station with his attorney, a fashionably dressed man whose hair was all gray curls. The attorney seemed to know everybody around, and after a brief back-room conversation he reported to Bentley that the charges — except for littering — had been dropped. Bentley paid a stiff fine, then put the boys in his wagon and drove them to the ranch. They were amazed to be let go so quickly. "You must be important, Mr. Bentley," Grady said.

"You two are just lucky I've got some clout," Bentley told them. "A successful businessman is not a nobody up here. I'm a Democrat and I belong to the Rotary. But don't think it's over yet. You still got Shane's mother to face."

Susan exploded. There was no therapist talk this time. When Shane came through the door, slinking like an animal, she yelled and threw a potholder at him, and then, so as not to be discriminatory, she threw one at Grady, too. She grabbed Shane by the hair and held him in place while she lectured him. She said he was an ungrateful little bastard, spoiled, indifferent, snotty, rotten to the core. He refused to argue, but in the morning, when she was almost rational again, he explained to her exactly why he had done what he'd done, so that she would understand that he hadn't been frivolous or irresponsible. "It was circumstances, see?" he said, sitting forward in his chair and kneading his hands. "I couldn't just leave him in Elk, could I? How would you feel if you called some friend of yours for help and the friend said no?"

"What about Roy, Shane?" she asked. "You could have phoned him at the factory, and he would have gone for Darren."

"But it was an emergency, Susan."

"The only emergency was that you didn't think."

The next day she was more forgiving, taking into account his unblemished record, and also the fact that he had been (at least to some extent) victimized. She also agreed that Grady could stay in the cabin for a few days, provided that he let his parents know where he was. This Grady did. "Hello, Dad?" he said to his father, while Shane listened in. "It's me, Darren, your son. Remember about the seminary? Well, you were right. It didn't work out."

In the cabin, Shane and Grady lay on their beds in the dark and had long philosophical discussions. Grady said that when he got home he was going to forget about religion and enroll in a junior college to study biology, so he'd have a grasp of how the universe was put together. "Science today," he said, "it has the answer to mysteries that puzzled the ancients." Shane confessed that he was dreading his senior year in high school; he would be an entirely different person when he returned to that bleak, airless building, yet nobody would acknowledge it. "The system hates what's real," he said. Grady agreed.

On more than one occasion, they talked about how strange it is that sometimes when you do everything right, everything comes out wrong. Grady had examples. "I gave my sister this kitten for her birthday," he said, "and she was allergic to it." Or "Once when I was small, I washed my mom's car to surprise her, but I used steel wool and scratched up the paint."

Shane had other questions. "If it was me stranded in Elk," he asked, "would you have come and got me?"

"You know it," Grady said, with emotion crowding his throat.

Both of them took a solemn vow never to touch dope again, ever, in any form, no matter how tempted they might be.

Grady ended up staying for better than two weeks. Several important things happened while he was around.

First, Shane passed his rescheduled driver's test and celebrated by pinstriping the Chrysler and painting flames on both its doors. Then he asked Emma King to go to the drive-in with him. They went to a kung-fu double feature on a Friday night. She sat so far away from him that it seemed a deliberate attempt to deny his existence. He thought that maybe older women expected men to be bold, so after a while he walked his fingers across the seat and brushed them against Emma's thigh. She sneezed. He withdrew. Later, on the steps of her house, much to his surprise, she kissed him full on the lips and told him he was sweet. He knew it was the only kiss he'd ever get from her, so, driving home, he made a mental inventory of the moment and its various tactile sensations.

Next, on a Saturday afternoon, he and Grady took the Chrysler to the main town beach, but it was crowded with hippies throwing Frisbees to their dogs, and Shane suggested that they go instead to this great isolated spot even he had never been to before — Bentley's twenty undeveloped acres. They had to slide under a barbed-wire fence that had No Trespassing and Private Property signs plastered all over it. The trail down into the gully was steep and overgrown; the gully, in fact, was more like a canyon, with a stream trickling through it, and vegetation sprouting from the soil. The vegetation was so thick and matted that it was almost impossible for them to distinguish individual plants, but one of the plants they *could* distinguish was marijuana. A few stalky specimens were growing wild, like weeds. All Shane's suspicions were confirmed — Bentley *was* a grower.

"That's why he had the attorney," he whispered to Grady.

"Are you going to say anything?"

"Uh-uh. No way."

But Shane's conscience bothered him. In the eyes of the law, Bentley was a criminal. Did this put Susan in jeopardy, too? Would she be considered an accessory to the crime? So Shane spilled the beans to Bentley. He told him about the find and waited for Bentley to react.

Bentley tugged at the strands of his beard. "Well, you got me, all right," he said sheepishly. "I did grow me a few crops of Colombian down there a while back, before I met your mother, but the whole experience rubbed me wrong. I had a couple of brushes with John Law, and they made me real nervous. That's

why I took my profits and went into ducks. Ducks are as legal as
it gets."

"What about the plants we saw?"

"Must be volunteers. That happens sometimes. Stuff grows
from old seeds, leftover seeds. We'll go pull 'em up."

They pulled up all the marijuana plants in the gully, arranged
them in a pyre, and burned them. "It's sad," said Bentley. "But
it has to be."

Next, Susan went into the hospital for her operation. The
surgery was performed in the afternoon, and Shane was allowed to visit that evening. He was scared. Susan was in a private
room. She was still groggy from her anesthesia, and she had an
I.V. tube in her arm. He thought she was asleep, but she called
to him in a funny, childlike voice and asked him to sit in a chair
by the bed. "I'm in the clouds," she said, rubbing his hand.

"But are you O.K.?"

"I'm fine," she said. "The doctor fixed everything. He says I
can probably have a baby now."

"A *baby?*"

"You think I'm too old, don't you?"

"I don't know," Shane said. "How am I supposed to know
about babies?"

"Lots of women have babies at my age," Susan said, rubbing
and rubbing. "Roy and I want to try. Oh, Shane honey, I made
things so tough on you, I want another chance. Don't I deserve
another chance?"

"Sure," said Shane. "Of course you do."

But the potential baby confused him, and also depressed him
a bit. In his mind, it was rotten-toothed, bearded, and smelling
of tobacco. He wondered why Susan would want to introduce
such a creature into the world. "I'm never going to understand anything," he complained to Grady that night. "Not anything."

"What's there to understand?" Grady asked.

"Maybe you are wise, Grady," said Shane.

Grady left at the end of the week. Shane dropped him at the
Greyhound stop in Mendocino. They shook hands in a special
way they'd devised, with plenty of interlocked fingers and
thumbs.

"I never had a friend like you before," Grady said. "I'll never forget what you did for me."

"I'd do it again," said Shane. "Any time."

In late August, there was an unseasonal thunderstorm. It rattled windowpanes and made chickens flap in their coops. When it was over, the morning sky was clear and absolutely free of fog. Shane got up early and changed the oil in the Chrysler. He filled the trunk with his belongings and put a pair of ducks for the Harrises on the back seat. Susan was not entirely recovered from her surgery, so he had to say goodbye to her in her bedroom, where she was propped up against pillows. She asked him again if he didn't want to transfer to a school in Mendocino and stay on with them, but he told her that he missed his grandparents and his friends. "I might come back next summer," he said, kissing her on the cheek. "You'll probably have the baby by then." Bentley stuck fifty dollars in the pocket of his jeans. "You ain't such a bad apple, after all," said Bentley with a smile. Shane drove off quickly, without looking back. The highway was still slick and wet from the rain, and the scent of eucalyptus was in the air.

CAROL BLY

The Dignity of Life

(FROM PLOUGHSHARES)

TWO PEOPLE STOOD QUARRELING in the Casket Showing Room.
They were a sixty-three-year-old man named Marlyn Huutula
and his unmarried sister Estona. She was so angry that she bent
towards him from her end of the coffin.

"You really ought to keep your grimy hands out of that clean
quilting!" Estona told him in a ferocious whisper. "As if
you owned the place! As if Svea weren't lying dead this very
minute, right here in this very building, and you showing no
respect!"

Jack Canon, the funeral director, had been hovering near
them. Now he gave a swift glance over to see how grimy Marlyn's hands were. He would let this grown brother and sister
quarrel a moment; he meant to leave this end of the long Showing Room so that they would not feel self-conscious as they
whispered furiously about prices.

Marlyn and Estona were buying a casket, and the service that
went with it, for their aunt, Svea Istava, an old woman who had
come down in the world. Svea had died alone in her wreck of a
place just north of St. Aidan, Minnesota. From the time she
moved there in 1943, until she died in February, 1982, she had
always had a few faithful visitors. They would pick their way
through her sordid front farmyard, avoiding the wet place and
the coils of barbed wire. Her place was what was called "incon-
venient": that is, it had no water up to the house. But whenever
someone visited — Mrs. Friesman to leave her idiot son Momo,
or Jack Canon, the funeral director, or on Sundays during the

football seasons, her nephew, Marlyn Huutula — Svea filled
their cups with smoky coffee.

Her most frequent visitor, Momo Friesman, found her dead.
Next morning, people sitting around the Feral Café traded information about Svea, making her a kind of random liturgy.
They told one another how Svea had taken better care of that
dog, Biscuit, than she took of herself. They told each other it
was certainly hard to believe that Svea Istava had ever been the
wife of a Lieutenant Colonel in the 45th Field Artillery, whose
body had not been sent home because that was during World
War II, not Vietnam. Mrs. Friesman had seen his Bronze Star
and his European Theatre of Operations ribbon bar hanging
on cuphooks in Svea's smudgy cupboard. Finally, people in the
café settled to the most interesting thing about Svea: they said
she was worth $500,000. In one booth, the sheriff was talking
about her to the state patrolman who lived in Marrow Lake.
The Marrow Lake man went past Svea's place nearly every day
and had never seen such a dump. But the sheriff said that you
could tell the true class of a person, though, by how they treated
a dog. He himself had a handsome white shepherd bitch; that
Biscuit, now, originally was a runt from one of his litters. He
had taken it over to Svea because he knew she would make it a
good home, and so she had.

Everyone thought that Svea had left the whole $500,000 (if
she had any $500,000) to her nephew Marlyn instead of half
and half to Marlyn and his sister Estona. Marlyn visited her once
a week for years, whereas Estona talked mean about Svea. Estona, who ran the Nu-St. Aidan Motel, was always roping in
total strangers, finding out what they did, and then asking their
advice. With both elbows on the sign-in counter, her eyes trying
to read their bank balances when they opened their checkbooks,
her wrists supporting her cheeks, she would say, "So you're a
sales representative? As a sales representative, would you please
tell me if this sounds right to you? I mean, you're in a position
to know . . ." Then she would explain about Svea's money going
to her kid brother because he was a man and made up to her
on Sunday afternoons. Recently, she had said to the new Adult
Education teacher who stayed at the motel on Wednesday
nights, "You're a humanities consultant? Now that sounds like
something that has got to be about how people treat each other!

Fairly or unfairly? Well, would you tell me as a humanities consultant — would you call it fair that this old woman, who keeps
her place so bad it is amazing they don't get the countryside
nursing people in to spray around, do you think it is right she
would leave all that money to my brother and not my half to
me?" Estona regarded the humanities consultant as another
middle-aged woman like herself, who had to have picked up
some sense somewhere along the line. "I don't know if this is in
your field or not, but just looking at it humanly, can you tell me
that he is making any big sacrifices for his aunt when he can
check on his Vikings and Steelers bets as good on Svea's eleven-
inch black and white as he could on his own remote control at
home? Or maybe it's just me."

   As Marlyn and Estona stood around the Casket Showing
Room, Jack Canon thought of everything that had happened
since Svea's death. Her body had been discovered by Momo:
Jack had quickly gone out to fetch it. He knew Momo as well as
Svea, because Momo liked dead bodies. There was scarcely a
wake or visitation in the past ten or fifteen years at which Jack
hadn't had a word with Momo — that is, he had to take him
firmly by the elbow. Then, after he took Svea's body to the
chapel, twenty or more youngsters went out to her place, apparently, and dug great holes all over the yard. By the time the
sheriff reached the place, the boys had tipped over Svea's outhouse and were prodding the hole, looking for money. Another
boy and a girl had got hold of power augers and they were
drilling into the frozen ground, like mining prospectors, among
the stacked snowtreads and fence-wire wheels. The sheriff
pulled them all in on Possession and Vandalism and then let
them out again. He called Jack and said he was going to ask the
state patrolman to help keep an eye open these next days. "If
we are going to have any trouble," Jack told him, "it will be
during visitation days, not at the funeral itself." The two men
talked to each other quietly on the telephone, in the special,
measured way of people holding the fort for decency and dignity — while all the others give in to some horrible craze. The
sheriff said with a sigh, "Well, we'll manage! I've got to locate
that nephew of hers now, wherever he is!" Jack felt the respect
the sheriff had for him, a funeral director, and the disrespect
he felt for Marlyn Huutula, who never had steady work in the

wintertime if he could help it. Like half the men of St. Aidan, Marlyn kept a line of traps somewhere out east along St. Aidan Creek. Once he had tried to bribe the sheriff out of a speeding ticket while the sheriff stood at his car window, writing. Marlyn had picked up the rabbit lying on the passenger side and passed it up to the sheriff. The sheriff had been busy writing, so he didn't look carefully: all he saw was white fur and a little blood. At home, his shepherd had just had a new litter of white puppies, so he mistook this animal. It was a full minute before he saw it was a rabbit, not a puppy. He had been writing a Warning; now he tore up the yellow card and gave the man a Citation instead. All day, as he later told Jack, his stomach churned. Then he blushed. "I don't guess that would bother someone . . . in your line of work," he added.

"Yes it would bother him," Jack told him.

"I never had much tolerance," the sheriff said.

Jack Canon felt less tolerant every day now. He had started an Adult Education course two weeks ago; he thought it would give him perspective, but it was just the opposite. Now he minded remarks he heard that previously he would have passed off as "the kinds of things people say."

He frequently thought of his crimson vinyl notebook that lay on his office desk. It was labeled: HUMANITIES: ST. AIDAN ADULT EDUCATION PROGRAM — MOLLY GALAN, INSTRUCTOR. Jack had never been a man who took notes on his life as it went by. Yet now, several times a day, he said to himself, sometimes even aloud, since he was a good deal alone, "I ought to put *that* into the red notebook!" or "*That* ought to go into the red notebook if nothing else ever does!" And he looked forward to Wednesday night, the night of his class.

Tonight it was to meet in his office, as a matter of fact. That had come about because two weeks ago, on Registration Night, only one student had shown up to sign for the humanities course — Jack himself. His teacher was a spare, graying woman with a white forehead, who was unlike anyone he had ever known. He glanced over her head, her figure — her long hands with thin, unremarkable fingers, trying to say "It is in the eyes," or "It is the hands," or "It is how she *carries* herself" — but he knew all his guesses were wrong. She leaned against the second-

grade teacher's desk, and Jack sat cramped before her in a desk-
and-chair combination comfortable only for small children.
They waited for others to appear. Through the schoolroom
doorway, they heard shy voices, calls, remarks — people signing
up for Beginning Knitting Two, a continuation from the fall
semester.

No one else came at all. Presently, Mrs. Galan explained that
the guidelines of the course would allow the class to meet in
private homes, if the class so chose. The following Wednesday,
there was a blizzard, but Mrs. Galan made it on I-35 from St.
Paul to the Nu-St. Aidan Motel, and to the schoolbuilding. This
time she read off to Jack some of the course subjects approved
in the guidelines. They might choose among Ethnicity, Sources
of Community Wisdom, Ethical Consciousness in Rural America, or Longitudinal Studies of Human Success and Failure,
Attitudinal Changes Towards Death, or simply Other. They
agreed that the following Wednesday, since no one had shown
up again this time, they might as well meet in Jack's office. He
explained to her that she should walk round to the back of the
chapel, where the back door opened onto a concrete apron. It
was kept clear of snow, he told her.

In his years and years of single life Jack had noticed that
lonely people were either carefully groomed or remarkably
grimy. He himself had to be immaculate at all times. It was a
habit by the time he was fourteen — along with learning how to
cover the phone. He would push his arithmetic problems
against the chapel schedule board, keeping the phone where his
left hand could raise the earpiece on the first ring. Then he
spoke immediately and courteously into the flared mouth. By
the time he was a senior in high school he was used to nearly all
the work of the chapel: he knew how to lift heavy weight without
grunting, while wearing a white shirt, tie, and suit jacket. He
learnt to keep longing or anxiety from showing on his face. One
October day, in 1936, he was sitting on the football bench at St.
Aidan High School. The big St. Aidan halfback sat down next
to him, for just a minute. Jack had been sitting there, knees
together, chilled, for an hour. The halfback, a great tall boy
named Marlyn Huutula, dropped down beside him when he
was taken out to rest a minute, and his body gave off heat and

the glow of recently spent energy. It was nearly visible like a halo — that great hot energy field around the boy. Jack knew enough not to look at Marlyn for more than a second; he must not let himself be mesmerized into staring like a rabbit at a successful boy, the way he had seen others do. So Jack had given Marlyn a casual grin and both of them turned to watch the field. Then the coach snapped his fingers at Marlyn, who jumped up right in front of Jack. The coach's arm went around the leather-misshaped shoulders; Jack overheard the friendly growl of instructions. The coach pointed into the field with one hand, slapped Marlyn's buttocks with the other, and the halfback swung away towards the players, his socks sunk below his calves, jiggling in folds around the strong ankles. For the thousandth time that autumn, Jack expressed manhood by not letting his face look sad.

But the next Thursday afternoon, just as he was helping his father transfer a casket from the nervous pallbearers into the hearse, Jack recalled the bad moment on the football field. His face jerked upward in embarrassment at the memory. When his father had closed the hearse doors, he pulled Jack aside. St. Aidan's Lutheran's two bells kept tolling so the sound rang down nearly on top of them: the sidewalk was white and cold with afternoon sunlight. "I'm going to tell you this just once, but it is very important," Jack's dad said. "Do not put on a fake sad look — the way you did just now when we were taking the casket. Get this straight: they don't expect you to look sad — just professional. Just keep your face serious and considerate."

Jack became more and more carefully gauged in his appearance: he controlled his face, he maintained his grooming. But Svea Istava, whose body now lay in his operating room, had turned dirty as she aged. When Jack first knew her in 1943, she was a handsome woman of thirty-nine or so. She told him she had to give up the St. Paul house that her husband's officer's pay had been financing. She asked Jack if the World War II dead were going to be returned to the United States. Next month, she bought an old, very small farmhouse on an acre of scrubland, about a mile past St. Aidan.

The first time Jack went out there to visit, his eye passed over the turquoise-painted, fake-tile siding. He saw the string of

CAROL BLY 31

barbed wire that someone had hitched to one corner of the outhouse and then stretched over to the cornerpost of the house itself. He supposed that Mrs. Istava would gradually have trash removed from the farmyard. He hoped she would find enough money to put in plumbing. He imagined the huge shade of the oaks darkening; not these piles of rejected auto batteries and other trash, but new lawn. There was a distant view of both church spires, and to the north lay the pleasant, spooky pine forest.

To his surprise, Svea didn't remove the barbed wire; she took to leaning things against it — first a screen door that warped and she couldn't repair, next a refrigerator that stopped working. Its rounded ivory corners and its rusted base grate seemed natural after a while; Svea tied a clothesline length about it so that Momo Friesman would not climb inside and be killed. Sometimes she stood the way poor rural people stand, elbow bent, one hand planted on one irregular hip, and the face gazing vaguely past the immediate farmyard, as if to say, "There is life beyond this paltry place — I have my eyes on it."

In those days, Jack sometimes thought he would save Svea from all that. He imagined himself, in a square-shouldered way, driving out one miserable winter night, when the sky would be black and the ground-storming of down snow nearly blinding. "Oh, how did you ever make it on such a night?" she would cry, and he would say briefly, a little sharply, "Come on — we're going to town! We're going to be married!" He imagined the reliable Willys pushing through all that darkness and whiteness.

It never happened. Svea never called a junk man to pick up anything in her yard. Instead, more junk arrived. Jack had to pick his way to the doorstep over corrugated-tread wheels of broken lawnmowers. Often, Momo stared at him from a pile of rubbish near the tipped refrigerator. He knew the child trapped mice and then buried them in a distracted, faithful way, among Svea's onion sets and carrots.

As the years passed, a rumor grew up that all this while Svea Istava had been and was still worth $500,000. The more unlikely her person and possessions, the more entrenched the myth.

Meanwhile, gradually, Jack began to lose confidence. He began buying more and more expensive clothing. By the 1960s,

even his garden gloves were from L. L. Bean. He was the first
man in St. Aidan to have a wool suit after a decade of Dacrons
and polyester. By accident, he found out what was wrong with
him. One evening, he sat with the sheriff down at the station. It
had been a bitter February day, as it was now, and the sheriff
was saying that the bad news in St. Aidan County was the rising
crime rate but the good news was that more and more uranium
leases were being let out around the area. Jack listened idly,
leaning comfortably against the iron radiator, watching the heat
move the window shades a little. The sheriff held several puppies on a pillow in his lap; his hands kept passing over the little
dogs and the dogs kept rearranging themselves in a whining,
growling, moving pile of one another. As Jack looked on, he felt
that he was losing confidence because he wasn't touching other
live bodies enough; he watched in an agony of envy as the
puppies wandered with their fat paws into one another's eyes
and ears and stomachs — he got the idea they were gaining
confidence from one another every time they touched.

The next day he walked into the Feral Café to have lunch
with the new Haven Funeral Supply salesman, Bud Menge.
Haunted by the revelation of the puppies, he sensed that
women looked up at Bud Menge as he went by, and rearranged
their buttocks in the booths.

Bud was friendly, right from the first. After a year of their
acquaintance, Jack said, "Couldn't you ever stop and let me buy
you lunch without you trying to sell me something?"

Most dealing in St. Aidan took place at either the Men's Fellowship of St. Aidan Lutheran or at lunch in the Feral Café.
Bud's face grew grave and considerate. "Listen, Jack, how would
you like to discuss something that is absolutely new and different and will revolutionize your whole approach?"

In ten minutes, Bud sold Jack an industrial-psychology program that he had used ever since. The Casket Showing Room
Lighting Plan, like all of Bud's ideas, was disgusting from the
outset. "That's really revolting, Bud. Let's face it, Bud," he had
said, "that is just about the worst taste I have ever heard of!"
Jack had often made such remarks during Bud's first year as
representative for Haven Funeral Supply. Later he was slower
to speak. Bud never presented him an idea that was not absolutely profitable.

The first aspect of the Casket Showing Room Lighting Plan was simple. You lighted only those caskets you wanted a client to inspect. You placed small wall-bracketed lamps at six-foot intervals along the two long walls, and across one short end-wall of the Showing Room. These lamps had either rose or cream shades: you lit only those you wanted on each given occasion. Jack generally lighted the caskets that went with the $1500 service, the $2300 service, and the $4000 service. No one in St. Aidan ever bought the $4000 service, and in fact, it was not for sale.

This $4000 casket was an elaborate part of Bud's Lighting Plan. Jack saw that it was lighted, and left its cover up, but did not lead clients over to it. Bud explained the procedure: people shopping for caskets feel that they are likely to be cheated by the mortician. Even if the mortician is a fellow small-town citizen whom they have known for years, they still feel they must watch him like a hawk now that they are buying from him. They know perfectly well that their own harrowed feelings at the time of a death are the funeral director's pivot. They are on tiptoe against his solemnity. Therefore, Bud explained, clients want to wander around the Showing Room on their own: they feel they are getting around the funeral director if they look at caskets besides the ones he seems to want to show them. They want to be shrewd. Eventually, Bud explained, because it is lighted and open, the $4000 casket catches the client's eye. He goes over, and, wonder of wonders, finds this casket to be noticeably more elegant than anything the funeral director has shown him so far. Immediately, he thinks that it is probably priced the same as the caskets he has been shown, but simply is a better buy. He suspects it is being kept for some preferred customer of the funeral director, and that a comparative lemon is being pawned off on him at the same price. Bud told Jack, "You follow them over to the $4000 casket, but stay behind a little — as if you didn't really want to go over there. 'How come you never showed us *this* one?' they will ask. 'How come you never show us this one when it's just beautiful?' they will say. So then you tell them, 'You're right — it is the most beautiful one, by far. It is the best casket we have ever had at Canon Chapel.' Just tell them that much at this point. Let them hang a little. Sooner or later the client will stop staring at you and will say, 'So how come you didn't show it to us?' Now here is where you pull your act together," Bud told Jack. "You tell them, fairly fast, 'Because I don't want you to buy that casket, is why.' " Bud begged Jack to pause again, right at that point. "Stick with the pauses, Jack, I'm telling you. Pause right there. Every single client — I don't care if it is the middle-aged mother of an only son who just died — every single client will say, 'But why don't you want me to buy it? What does it cost?' Now you go right up to the client and say, 'Because it costs $4000. I know you can afford $4000, Mrs. So-and-so, I know you can easily raise that amount. Money isn't the problem. The reason I don't want you to buy it is that I'd a hundred times rather that you bought the $2300 casket and gave the other $1700 to church or charity in memory of' — and you insert the deceased's name here — 'I'd a hundred times rather you'd spent the $1700 extra that way than on a casket.' O.K., now, Jack, here is the third pause — don't make it very long — just a short one. Now you say, 'Or does that sound crazy, from where I'm supposed to be coming from?' "

Bud was right. No client ever said, "Yes, it sounds crazy." Men gave Jack a warm look and sometimes slapped his arm. Women sometimes came around the $4000 casket and hugged him. Everyone said, "Thanks, Jack, for being so square with us." And just as Bud had prophesied, not one of those clients ever bought the $1500 casket: they all bought the $2300 one. The whole point of the Lighting Plan was to switch people from the $1500 to the $2300 casket. During the whole sales procedure, Jack never had to lie. After explaining the Plan, Bud had paused briefly, then looked very straight at Jack across the strewn café booth table, with the chili bowls and paper sachets of coffee-whitening chemicals that both men had pushed away so they could lean forward on their forearms. "Some of them," Bud said, "I wouldn't bother to explain they don't have to lie — they wouldn't care. But with you, Jack, now that's a major thing."

The last point of the Casket Lighting Plan was to have one end of the Showing Room nearly dark. Jack made use of this point right now: he broke into the quarreling between Estona and Marlyn Huutula.

"Folks," Jack said loudly, "I am going to look over some odds and ends of paperwork. I'll be down at the other end of the room, so when you want me, give a call."

Clients needed the sense of quarreling privately. They needed to confer over how little they could spend without causing talk in town — talk about how cheap they were, after all that *he* or *she* had done for *them,* too. Jack always left people to have this quarrel, but he stayed within earshot so he could return at the right moment.

At a tiny writing table at the dark end of the room, just behind the county casket, Jack looked over an eight-page booklet showing full-color photographs of funeral customs all over the world. The photographs were on the right-hand pages, the "Discussion Questions" on the left-hand pages.

"What's the good of it?" Jack had said in the Feral Café, when Bud passed him the booklet across their coffee cups.

"It's the most practical thing we have come up with yet," Bud told him with his frank smile. "It solves the problem of the local necrophiliac. And every town has one."

Jack said, "I wish you wouldn't use that word in the Feral Café, Bud. In fact, I wish you wouldn't use it at all. And besides," he added in the no-nonsense tone he used when he had to, his mind picturing Momo Friesman, "we haven't got anyone like that in St. Aidan."

"Every town has one," Bud said. "If you haven't got him today you will have him tomorrow. When some funeral director tells me his town don't have one, I look at the funeral director himself. Ha, ha! Just joking, Jack."

Bud opened the booklet to a page called *Funeral Practises of the Frehiti People.* "O.K.," he said. "Here's how it works. Your man shows up at a visitation or a wake."

"And who are the Frehiti People? What do we care!" said Jack.

Bud grinned. "How should I know who they are? They don't live around here anyway. Anyway, they're somebody. Some sociologists or humanities people or somebody did all the research — we know it's O.K. That's a point I'm glad you asked about, Jack. You know, the research in this booklet didn't come from our publicity department like most of the stuff. This is the real thing — you can be confident when you use this. Anyway, your guy comes up at the wake so you go up to him and you put your arm around his shoulder, the nice, teaching way that a football coach throws his arm around you and you feel good because you know the coach is taking you into his confidence. O.K.? Didn't you say you played football for St. Aidan High? O.K. — then you know the way I mean. Now, with your free hand, Jack, you flip open this booklet. It is easy because they put this Frehiti People discussion at the center where the stapling is, so it naturally opens right there. So you keep your other hand on his shoulder, see, and you show him this picture, the one you see there, with the jungle huts in the background, and them carrying the corpse in a kind of thatch-covered chair with the feet hanging off like that, towards us. And the Discussion Questions at the left. So you don't have to tell this person, 'Look at the terrific picture of a dead body with the feet hanging off that kind of coolie chair or whatever it is.' What you get to say aloud is, 'I wonder, so-and-so' — you want to use their name as much as you can, Jack, as you know — 'Hey, so-and-so, I wonder if you'd look through this new book and read these Discussion Questions. Maybe this is something that would help families get through grief — would you look this over and then tell me what you think?' And Jack, all the time you are saying all this, his eyes are glued onto that picture and his mind is thinking, if people like that think, There are other full-color pictures in the book, too, and I want to see them all! Then he hears you offering to let him take the booklet home with him. Now all this time, you are pushing him along right out of your funeral chapel and he is halfway home before he realizes he is no longer at the visitation. And that is fine with you. The last thing you need is someone trying any sensitivity games at a visitation."

Bud gestured toward the booklet in Jack's hand. "That little item may not have a lot of class like our bronze desk accessories and all, but it is one hundred thousand percent effective."

Now Jack sat at the dark end of the Showing Room, looking at the dead Frehiti in the photograph. The man's feet, whitened in the foreground, in sharp focus, were separated from the gloomy jungle village in the background; the feet had come to meet the viewer; the straw hut roofs, the gnarled equatorial trees, the smudgy broken grass of the village street — all that receded and lowered behind, like a cloud departing.

Jack heard Estona Huutula's voice rise in fury. He was used to family differences in his Showing Room, but this one was

especially nasty. He listened, trying to decide when he should
break in.

"I don't see how you can be so uncaring," Estona was shouting. "You know that when they open up that will, there will be
a half million for you — probably for you, alone, too; you won't
even have to share it with me, since you did such a good job of
making up to Svea all those years! You know what people will
say, Marlyn! They'll say that there that nice aunt left him a cool
half million and all he would buy her was the county casket."

"I never said I wanted to bury Svea in the county casket!"
Marlyn shouted back.

The casket they referred to was a narrow, light blue coffin
that St. Aidan provided for welfare clients when the family
could afford nothing else. It was nicely made, but most funeral
directors, including Jack, made sure it was locally referred to
only as "the county casket" so that no one would contemplate
buying it for a loved one.

"All I meant was," Marlyn said, "why go to $2300 when we
can get the same service and a perfectly nice-looking casket for
$1500?"

Jack rose from his small desk.

Estona said, "That's going to look just fine, isn't it, when you
get all that money? I call it downright cheap!"

Marlyn grumbled, "We don't even know if Svea had any
money anyway."

"All the worse for you then!" cried Estona with a slashing
laugh. "All those Sunday afternoons you put in for nothing!
Sitting there in her filthy kitchen letting her tell you how Chuck
Noll should do this, Chuck Noll should do that, and how old
age comes even to football players, and how Cliff Stoudt was a
fool to hurt his arm. That one time I was there, you must have
said it twenty times if you said it once: 'You may have something
there, Svea!' I nearly puked. And 'Everything that goes up has
to come down, I guess, Svea — even Lynn Swann!' If you
weren't the sponging wise nephew of the sports-expert aunt!
And the two of you drunk as lords before three in the afternoon, too! I nearly threw up listening to you — I'd say 'puke'
except we're in a funeral chapel!"

Jack generally let relations quarrel until both of them had

turned their irritation, by mere exhaustion, from each other to him. As soon as he felt all the anger coming towards him — none left for each other — he would spend a minute deliberately hardselling a coffin he knew they didn't want. Then they would concentrate on outwitting this awful funeral director for a minute or so. He let them outwit him. Then he decided which coffin they would really like, and usually wrapped up the sale, including choice of Remembrance folders, in fifteen minutes. The clients left in harmony with each other, which was good: the moment they left Canon Chapel the elation of having stumped the mortician would die and they would notice and carry their grief again.

"And another thing!" Estona cried. "You know, if you had *really* respected Svea's dignity in life or death, you wouldn't have been out tomcatting the very night after they found her, would you? There we were, the sheriff and I, trying to figure out where you were, with all those kids having dug up poor Svea's yard and all! Do you know that the sheriff sent the deputy down the river because they thought you were checking your traps? Finally Mrs. Friesman said she seen you driving somewhere with that Mrs. Galan from the Adult Education. 'Oh,' I said, 'he wouldn't be with her. She always stays with us at the Nu-St. Aidan Motel.' Well, yes, she saw you though, she said, so what could the sheriff do; he drove back out to your house and there you were in the middle of the night, the both of you! Of course I'd made a fool of myself, telling the deputy I knew you wouldn't be running around with her because she seemed like such a nice widow lady and very intellectual."

Jack now made his way slowly from the dark end of the room, like someone a little off balance. He approached the brother and sister standing under the yellow wall lights and took Estona by the elbow. He explained that they would now go into his office and have a sip of something that he kept, which sometimes helped people in times of grief. He led them around behind the chapel, past the door leading to the operating area, and into his office. Sunlight poured in, dazzling after the draped and shadowy Showing Room. Jack seated Estona on the couch; he put Marlyn in the conference chair, and opened a bottle of Pinot Blanc. Although everyone in St. Aidan knew that

Estona Huutula turned on the NO part of the NO VACANCY sign at the motel each night around ten, and settled down with a whiskey, Estona said, "I don't use much alcohol, Jack, but a little wine *would* help me, I think."

Estona then allowed they ought to get the $2300 white-lined casket instead of the $1500 tan-lined one because it would be more cheerful for Svea to look out of. Both men looked out through the faint window curtains when she said that. She added, "Or maybe that's just me."

In the normal course of things, Jack would have let Estona sell Marlyn on the more expensive of the two caskets, but now he wanted this old high school classmate and his sister out of the office so badly he would have sold him a co-op burial-club service with a pine box for $34.50 if they would just get out. So he took it into his own hands. Ignoring Estona, who was tapping her glass for a refill, he spoke to Marlyn in a man-to-man tone, making fast explanations. He filled the man in on some of the side services provided in a funeral, such as getting police cooperation in case there was further trouble, or unwanted crowds to see the body of a simple old woman worth $500,000. He explained that his own man, LeVern Holpe, would park cars, assisted by the chapel man from Marrow Lake.

Marlyn responded exactly as Jack wanted: he tried to be snappy and intelligent too. Marlyn never mentioned the $1500 casket again. Then, just when Estona was beginning to look as if she felt neglected, Jack passed her the new Remembrance format that Bud Menge had brought over only the week before. Gone was the Twenty-third Psalm in Old English eleven point on the left-hand side: instead, there was a passage from *The Velveteen Rabbit* in a modern face without serif. Jack said to Estona, cutting Marlyn out of it: "Estona, I want your honest opinion of these. If you don't care for these new-style Remembrances, say so, and we will have the others printed up for Svea."

At last brother and sister were gone. Jack telephoned LeVern to say that he could come over and work any time now. He himself would have a catnap. He lay down on the small office sofa.

The winter sun, very bright and low at this time of year, sent

its long webby light through the glass curtains. Jack fell gratefully asleep, still wearing his suit jacket. Sunlight fell onto his
desk with all the accessories Bud had provided him — the
bronze-tone plastic paperweight imprinted CANON CHAPEL: CARE
WHEN CARE MATTERS MOST. The sun fell onto his red-covered
humanities notebook, too. It fell onto his own face, and made
his white hair nearly transparent and his skin luminous. Once
during the following hour and a half, his young assistant,
LeVern, looked in soundlessly, thought how sad the human face
looks asleep; he decided that Jack Canon, in his opinion anyway,
led a very crappy life. LeVern decided he could manage the job
without waking the fellow, and called Greta at the beauty parlor
when he was done to tell her she could come over and do Mrs.
Istava's head now or whenever she was ready.

In his dream, Jack went to spend the weekend in a motel
north of St. Paul. He was to meet a woman there who had
exclaimed, "My God! I think I am falling in love again! I love
you, John!" So long as Jack still believed she would show up, he
patrolled the motel room, swerving round the ocean-sized bed
and rounding the television set like an animal. Once he had
decided she was not going to show up, he took to reading all the
materials in the desk except the Bible placed there by the Gid-
eons. Everything he read swam and enlarged and darkened in
his eyes. Everything had color swimming at the edges; even the
papers he held were yellowed like church windows on Christmas cards. He read through the Room Service Menu with its
appalling prices and his eyes swam with tears. He read the Daily
Cleaning Services options with his eyes silvered with tears. He
was reminded of something that someone at a Minnesota Funeral Director's convention had once told him: the man had
said that when he became Born Again, for the first few weeks,
whenever he opened up the Bible, no matter at what place he
opened it, his eyes would fill with tears. Jack was thinking that
over, in his dream, when he waked to LeVern's tapping on the
office door.

LeVern put his head around the door. "All set now, Jack," he
said. "I'm going home now."

"Oh, then, you're ready for me," Jack said, trying not to
sound slowed with sleep.

"No, it's all done," LeVern told him. "Greta's here working now."

Jack lay vulnerable in the huge sadness of his dream. The day was nearly over. All morning he had longed for the day to be over, because it was Wednesday, the night of his class. Now the joy was gone out of it.

Eventually, he rose and bathed and shaved and put on the best sports jacket he had. He looked at his grey eyes very carefully in the mirror, but it was O.K.: none of the dream or his own feelings showed.

He locked the front door of the chapel, making sure the twin lights for visitations were both turned off; people understood by that that Svea could not be viewed until the next day. Then he went round and lighted the rear yard light, which fell upon the private entrance to his office and the garage. At nearly eight o'clock, the bell rang. Jack cried to himself, "She came after all, then!"

He swung the door open to the cold night. Outside, Momo Friesman stood on the garage cement, his bulging eyes bright from the overhead light.

"I came to pay my respects to Mrs. Istava," Momo said quickly, "and don't you turn me away, Jack. I got a right. She was neighbor to me, and my mother and I was friends. She had me come keep her company once a week and I got a right to mourn her as good as anyone else."

"Visitation isn't until tomorrow, Momo," Jack said.

Then he recalled Bud Menge's little book of photographs and discussions. "There *is* something you could help me with, though, Momo. Do you have time to come in a minute?"

Momo's eyes shone. "I can help you in the lab, Jack!"

"No," Jack said firmly, "not in the operating room — but wait." He started to go to the Casket Showing Room for the booklet, but then remembered he couldn't leave Momo alone or the man might leap through the office door towards the operating room. So he put his arm around Momo's shoulder and led him to the sofa. When he saw Momo was all the way seated, he left.

Momo had the face of a twelve-year-old; he was forty-three, in fact. Every morning in the summer, his mother drove him into town and Momo went to all the trash disposal cans in St. Aidan, recovered *Minneapolis Tribune*s from them, and sold them up and down the one street of the town, shouting, "Paper! Paper!" All the business people sent someone out, a receptionist or whoever was nearest the door, to give Momo a nickel and take a paper. When he had gone the whole length of the street, from the Canon Funeral Chapel at one end to the Rocky Mountains Prospectors' office at the other, he would find more papers lying on top of the trash cans, so he sold them again — this time to the other side of the street. At noon he waited among the boxes that came into the Red Owl on the truck; the owner would shout, "He's here, O.K., Mrs. Friesman!" when his mother came to pick him up. Once a week she took him over to Svea Istava's place across the road, and Svea would let him dig in her piles of orange crates and used winter tires.

When Jack dropped the booklet into Momo's lap, it opened as Bud had promised to the photograph of the dead Frehiti man in his grassy chair. Jack thought to himself, "It is eight-oh-five now. She hasn't shown up. She is not going to come. Well," he went on to himself, "everyone has to have some kind of memorial made in their honor. We shouldn't any of us die without someone's doing at least *something* in our honor." Jack looked down at Momo, who was bent over the photograph. "Well, Momo," Jack thought, "you're it. Svea let you into her place all those years. Tonight, then, I will let you into mine. You can sit there and gloat over that book for two hours if you want." Jack went and sat down at his desk. He said in his thoughts, "I don't suppose you'd understand, Momo, if I tried to explain to you that Molly Galan was supposed to be sitting here where you are sitting, not you. Well, anyway — it isn't her: it's you." Jack remembered how Svea remained kind to Momo even when, two weeks after her dog Biscuit died, Momo found the grave, despite the rusty refrigerator grille Svea had laid on top of it in hopes he wouldn't notice. Momo dug up Biscuit and brought the body into the house and laid it on Svea's oilcloth-covered table. Biscuit looked bad after two weeks in the earth. Even then, Svea did not lift a hand to Momo. She only telephoned Jack to ask if he ever had had any difficulty with Momo around the chapel. Jack confessed that he had to deal with Momo on various occasions.

Now he went through the little speech Bud had taught him, suggesting Momo take the booklet home. He need not have bothered. Just as Bud predicted, Momo was entranced by the pictures.

The doorbell rang again.

Jack went over to it, nearly faint with hope but still unbelieving.

"I didn't know if I ought to come," Molly Galan said. "I know you had a death."

"Oh, but visiting isn't until tomorrow!" Jack cried. He held the door wide, but didn't offer his arm. Molly Galan explained that she was a little breathless from having walked over from the motel. Then Jack remembered Momo. "This is Momo Friesman," Jack said. He went over and stood near Momo's knees. "Momo is going to zip up his jacket now and take his book home, before it gets even later and colder."

"I want to stay here," Momo said.

"Let's see your book," Molly said.

"You give that back," he told her.

"I promise," she said. She sat down beside him, turning the pages.

"And now you can take it home with you, Momo," Jack said. "But first you must zip up your jacket because it is much colder again now."

Jack realized that in one minute Momo would be out of there, and the thought made him so joyous he nearly danced the man into his zipper.

"I don't want to go," Momo said.

Jack thought, "I could just strangle him until those eyes jumped clear out of his head like twin pale spheres careening out into space and then I could pick him up and throw the whole mess of a man out the door." As soon as Jack noticed what he was thinking he backed further from the sofa. Anyway, he thought, retreating to the desk, what did he care if Momo chose to stay the evening? What good would it do *now* to have an evening with Molly Galan?

"Oh yes!" he cried, nearly aloud. "Look at that flushed face of hers! And that lively look in her eyes: that isn't from hiking over here in the cold! And her wonderful smile!" That smile was turned towards Momo, but how could such a smile be for

Momo? Women of fifty did not look like that except when love was so recent the body itself still remembered it. Jack's anger narrowed and cooled and felt permanent. "And anyway," he added to himself, "all this is just a job of work for a woman like her." She was hired to tutor adult extension students in the humanities, so she tutored adult extension students in the humanities. She had agreed to meet in his office simply because that arrangement was simpler than anything else.

Now he said aloud, "Well, if Momo wants to stay, that would be all right, wouldn't it?"

She looked at Momo and said, "Of course. Momo, you can read your book and we will work on ours."

"And afterwards I will pay my respects to Svea," Momo told her.

"Not tonight," she said. "When I say it's time you will zipper up your jacket and you can walk home with me."

In the meantime, Jack walked rapidly back and forth between his lighted desk and the sofa. Perhaps Molly Galan was going to open her copy of the red humanities workbook over there, on the sofa beside Momo. She might do that, he supposed.

But she didn't. She came to his desk and sat down in the conference chair. She picked up a bronze marker stamped CANON CHAPEL and laid it back quickly. She said, "The Extension people would like to know which subject we're going to work on. And they want us to write an evaluation as we go along. This is a kind of pilot program, you see." She smiled at him. "They want to know what your expectations are."

How could Jack tell her his expectations? All week he had planned how she was coming and he meant to tell her part of his life story. Shamelessly, he had meant to. Jack had meant to tell her how all his life he had wished to be serious, not just solemn as he must be at his work, but serious. He wanted to tell her how here in St. Aidan, where he practiced a trade he had never wanted to practice, somehow he could not rise over the chaff and small cries of daily life into some upper ring of seriousness. He imagined this ring of seriousness, like Saturn's rings, almost physically circling the planet — but he couldn't reach it because he was caught down here, blinded in the ground-storming of old jokes, old ideas, old conventions, which

no sooner were dropped than they were picked up again like
snow lifted and lifted and dropped and lifted again by blizzard
wind, blowing into everyone's face over and over.

Now Molly Galan smiled at him. She had placed the four
fingers of her right hand between five pages of the humanities
notebook, and she held these pages apart as if for ready reference; he saw the lamplight through the spread pages like a
nearly translucent Eastern fan, collapsible, of course, but taking
up its space as elegantly as sculpture does.

Jack thought, How can it be that anyone with such hands
spent last night with Marlyn Huutula? How can that be, when
Marlyn Huutula all his life had never done anything admirable
except play halfback for St. Aidan in 1936? — and Jack saw, as
sharply in his mind's eye as he had ever seen it, Marlyn's sweaty
hair as he removed his leather helmet.

Now Jack bent towards Molly under the beautiful lamplight
and shouted at her, "What I want to know is, why did you ever
do it? How could someone like you go and, go and, oh how
could someone like you for the love of God go and spend the
night with Marlyn Huutula? How could you do it?"

"I know I did not just say that aloud," Jack told himself; "I
know I did not. Nonetheless, that is what I just did. However, I
must not have really said that aloud because men in their sixties
do not ask humanities consultants why they spend the night
with whomever they spend the night with. Yet it was my voice
that said that."

Then he thought: "In one minute she will simply rise and
leave without another word. She will go over to the couch and
pick up her coat where she left it near Momo and she will leave.
I shall offer her a ride home because it is so cold again and, oh,
Christ, she will refuse even that!"

However, the ladylike fingers did not fold up the fan. Molly
Galan shouted at him, "I don't know! I don't know why I did it!
And what do you care, anyway?"

"I don't care! I don't care what you do," Jack said.

"Well," Molly shouted, "you just don't know how dumb it all
is!"

She burst into tears.

Very far inside himself, in a place really too dank to nourish a spark of happiness, Jack felt a tiny warmth: "What do you mean, 'dumb'?" he asked. But then the snarl came back into his voice. "So what's that supposed to mean, *dumb!* What is that supposed to mean, 'How dumb it all is!' Anyone can go around shouting things like that!"

"You don't know what it is to be lost in the dumbness of it!" she shouted, still crying.

"You chose it! You chose it!" he said. "You chose Marlyn Huutula!"

Suddenly then her hands fell simply, faintingly, like snow onto the booklet in her lap. Her face and voice suddenly were completely serene. "Yes," she said, pausing. "That's right," she said in an agreeable, logical tone. "Marlyn Huutula. Now he really *is* dumb." She added in an even more peaceful tone, "That is a fact, you know. He is really *very* dumb."

"The dumbest person I ever knew!" Jack said. But then he leaned forward and said, "What do you mean exactly?"

He felt a hope taking fire in him too quickly. He did not want to lose his proper anger in this hope. Already, he noticed that Molly was sitting with her head tipped to one side, nearly day-dreaming at him, and he, too, on his side of the lamplight, was tipping his head at the same angle. They regarded each other like two birds, with that great concentration and that great natural stupidity of birds.

Hope kept rising rather weakly in Jack, like a hand rising from a lap, with the fingers still fallen from the rising wrist, the fingers flowing downward like an umbrella.

Momo meanwhile had approached them, and now wavered, his face turning from one to the other of them.

Jack whispered, "Well, will we go on with the course, do you think?"

Molly said, "Of course we will."

Jack said briskly, "It is too cold for you and Momo to walk home. I will drive you both. Momo, it is time for you to zip up your jacket now."

The telephone rang. It was the sheriff. "Jack, I thought you would like to know. The Huutula family read Svea Istava's will early, and you know what? She didn't have two cents to her name! After all that fuss! So what we'll do, Jack — the Marrow

Lake patrolman and I will kind of keep an eye out the next couple of days, and we'll make sure the news gets around, so you shouldn't have any crowd-draw to the visitation hours. I expect you'll just get the usual for an old woman like that." In the background, Jack could hear the sheriff's puppies barking.

Jack and Momo and Molly all sat in the front seat of his car. The night had dropped below zero, so their breathing frosted the windshield and the side windows as well. The defroster opened up only a small space in the windshield directly in front of Jack; he had to hunch down to see through it. He guided the car gingerly through the cold town out on the north road towards the Friesmans'. The black woods were not wrecked, but they were nearly wrecked. The greater trees had been cut over. The earth under the forest was not wrecked, either — but it was staked out. Here and there, invisible to ordinary people, were concrete-stoppered holes where the uranium prospectors had pulled out their pipes and left only magnets so they could find the places again. As the car crawled along the iced highway, Jack thought of the whole countryside, nearly with tears in his eyes. He kept peering through the dark, clear part of the glass, with his whole body shivering and his skin cold in his gloves and the whole of him beginning to flood with happiness. His own life, Jack thought — it wasn't wrecked completely after all! It felt to him, since he was sixty-three and much was over for him — or rather, had gone untravelled — that his life was nearly wrecked. But not completely. He began to smile behind his cold skin. He started driving faster, feeling more jaunty and more terrific every second.

The patrolman from Marrow Lake, who had just left the St. Aidan station, happened to see the car tearing along Old 61 where it crossed the north road. He thought, "Oh, boy! Travellers' advisory or no travellers' advisory! Nothing stops some people! Car all frosted blind like that, tearing right along anyway!" Behind the car's pure white windows he did not make out the local undertaker and a comely woman and a middle-aged retarded man.

JAMES BOND

A Change of Season

(FROM EPOCH)

WHERE ARE THERE GIANTS to match these mountains? From the valley floor it looks easy enough, a river, flat farmland, gentle foothills for grazing cattle, walls of timbered mountains rising up on all sides. A country a man could make his name proud in you'd say. In the past fifty years I've seen hundreds of strong men leave here as puny as goats, packing nothing out but their names. It takes strength, be guaranteed of that, that peculiar strength of a few strong men. I taught losers' kids here for more than a year before I discovered that to whip this country it takes strength of mind as well as back. Much strength of mind, of which there can't be enough said.

It's strength of mind what prods a man into the mountains every morning before dawn and keeps him there until dark. Strength of mind as well as back that roots him to the mountain and saves him from falling off. A man with strength of mind isn't crushed under a felled tree or rolled over by loose logs. Such a man won't lose his fingers to the choker cables. And because he has mental strength he can fight breath-freezing cold one season and scorching heat the next. It saves him from drowning in rain one minute and mountains of mud the next. And there's snow. God, if a man can last the winter here he's got a chance; if he can beat the winter here, he's somebody.

You ask anybody and they know me, my sons, even my ragtag nephews. They'll tell you the ones to watch are Buck Davaz and his boys. Only this fall some city hunters stumbled onto us after my oldest son, Jim, broke through the frost and buried our Cat up to its belly pan in mud. Those hunters told him he'd never get it out. And Jim, who's as big as two of them, told them we'd dig it out. The boys and I grabbed shovels and dug trenches four feet deep underneath the Cat's tracks. We chucked the trenches full of wood and drove that Cat out, nearly ran those puny hunters down. After that two hours of shoveling we were too tired to crawl, but Jim wiped the mud off his face and said, "Hell, let's get back to work here old man." Hauled out two more loads that day. That's being alive, and those who count on luck don't know it, those who have no sense won't whip this land. Damn Yanceys.

There were Yanceys here when I first came, the luckiest wagonload of fools and weaklings it's ever been my misfortune to run onto. Whether their luck stems from being mindless or they're mindless because they're drowning in luck, I don't know. I know a man can't stop to take a leak behind a tree without finding a Yancey up in it, swinging by his knees from a limb. That's true. Only last winter I hiked two or more miles through knee-deep snow up into the government timber, looking for five of our cows. I stopped under this giant spread of a hemlock and was about settled to doing my business when I spotted snowshoes propped against the other side of its trunk. I backed out from under that tree to have a look and sure enough, up there seventy feet in the air was a Yancey grinning down at me. Randall Yancey, Bill and Helen's fourth kid.

"What the hell you doing?" I yelled up at him.

"Trying to see what's out there!" came his shout back. He started climbing higher, laughed, a couple limbs broke. I thought it certain I'd be stuck with a dead kid to pack home.

"What in Christ . . . what do you see?"

"Not a thing," he shouted.

That's a Yancey. They'll climb a tree to see nothing, only more snow, more trees, and more cold land.

Not only weak minded, they're scared of snow. The first hint of snow, down they charge off their mountain. They grab up everything and run, axes, tractors, trucks, saws, and what they can't carry they throw ahead of them. Now snow on the ground is no reason to quit and die. Three winters ago my boys and I were the only ones not to beat it out of the woods. We stuck, we fought snow, five and six feet of it, but we hauled logs. Come spring, money spilled out of our pockets. Damn any weaklings. It stands to reason if you let the weather dictate your life there's no sense to this living. Nothing to fight but your wife and kids, yourself.

These last two years we've logged the Peak, though we knew the snow would stop us eventually. In the middle of winter there'll be sixteen to twenty feet at the top of the Peak, half that further down where the timber is best. Knowing when to stop fighting, that's a side of strength most never learn. I can't afford someone on the Cat all day clearing road, so when our log-jammer went to pieces this morning I took that to be the sign. I told Jim to take our diesel truck and go cut firewood for his ma, I'd get our Cat hauled down. The hell of it, the whole year came down to getting that Cat out. Not a stick of firewood at home to the jammer turned on its side, and snow just when we were making the money.

I drove my new pickup to Yanceys' so they could see first hand the rewards of great strength.

Randall

Not knowing how I know, I do, and not just me: Dad, Mom, my brothers and sisters, all the Yanceys know when winter's coming. Nothing complicated in that — if you don't know you ask.

I could ask Dad the how of it.

But not right now. Here at this window, outside, it's snowing, and the snow and dark hide I don't know what. We know winter without searching out signs. Last year ten thousand geese swooped into the valley, flew over the house all day and night until we grabbed up shotguns and blasted a dozen holes in the sky just to escape their noise for an hour. With so many geese and all at once, most everyone expected a blizzard to come busting down from Canada, but no snow fell for three weeks and a full month passed before real winter began — without a blizzard. I remember the tamaracks holding onto their needles through December and geese dragging their tails along even later.

Signs don't mean.

Not like one morning you step out the door and the first thing you see are those snowshoes hanging inside the porch. The very same pair you've walked by every day since April without noticing once. So you strap them to your boots to get their feel and adjust the straps. It's just such a morning too that Dad announces we're pulling out of the woods, bringing down the Cat, the loader, and any pine that's fell. Mom finds the extra wool socks, the stocking caps, the sweaters, acting as though it's been planned right along, like the exact date was marked right on the calendar alongside Thanksgiving. Winter.

We stopped logging three days ago.

The first flakes fell as Dad hauled out the last of the white pine and I followed, driving the tractor-loader. They were good-sized flakes, too, big as poker chips and slow to fall. By night the snow stretched blanket-like across the fields into the woods.

Then fell four inches.

A foot.

And this morning I stepped into knee-deep snow on my way to feed the cows. Winter. Tonight maybe Buck Davaz will realize that's so.

This morning was a usual winter morning too. Dad went back to the house after we fed. He played solitaire, he read, and Mom knitted a sock. Then it was ten o'clock and half the morning gone when Buck Davaz came roaring up in a brand-new pickup, light green, the sales sheet still glued to the window. On with our boots and outside we went. The first thing Buck asked Dad was if the snow would last. Dad nodded and looked over the new pickup and asked a good dozen questions, and after Buck had told him all the answers, Dad said winter was here and we'd pulled out.

"The hell you say," Buck said. He and Dad leaned against the pickup. I paced around by the garden fence, swept snow off the rails with my arm. "I'm wondering myself," Buck said. "Can't decide whether this here is winter snow or whether it will be gone tomorrow." Buck kicked loose a ball of snow that had packed under his heel.

Right in front of his nose, everywhere, poker-chip-size flakes falling down an inch an hour.

"This will be here after tomorrow," Dad told Buck.

"The hell, I don't mind telling you I've been banking on this storm letting up. Thought maybe the boys and I could get in a week's more woods work." Buck Davaz reached inside his coat and brought out a match. "In two weeks I'd pay this rig off."

"The timber will be there yet in the spring. How much have you down?"

"Forty thousand, maybe sixty thousand feet. Fir mostly, no pine to spoil."

"We left a fir log or two."

Buck clamped his teeth on the match, folded his arms, and with the match dangling from the corner of his mouth, he talked. "Even should this weather back off, we can't load a stick. Jim ditched the jammer on the way down to the lower end of the show."

"Didn't hurt himself did he?"

"No, might as well've broke a leg. We can't move the jammer, it's tipped on its side. I figure we'll chance leaving it."

Dad nodded. "As long as there are trees to anchor it to, no problem."

"There're trees enough. The way it's setting, the spring run-off will wash the road out from under it as sure as I'm standing here. We've tied it off to every damn tree within shouting distance on that hill."

"It's a worry, I don't care to leave machinery in the mountains either," Dad said.

Now a log-jammer, that's something. It's no more than a flag-pole on wheels, only the idea is different. The idea is to pull logs from out of the woods and load them onto a truck. So you pack a pulley a hundred yards off and anchor it to a stump; and since no little rope is going to skid logs, you thread your pulley and pole with three-quarter-inch cable; and since you won't be pulling any logs by hand, you steal an engine from an old truck and gear it to two cable drums; then you set the engine up under the pole and wrap each of the cable ends around a drum. With a pair of levers and brakes apiece and a metal roof over your head to shed rain, you've got a jammer.

"But damnit, I've got my Cat to bring down yet."

"I'd hurry," Dad laughed.

"I figure so. It'd be worth a lot to us to have it hauled down.

Yeh, we'd pay a pretty penny for help hauling it." So that's what had ordered the visit, I thought, and offering to pay? Buck Davaz had offered to pay before. When Dad didn't say anything, Buck explained more. "It's like this, Bill, our Diesel Mac is broke down. I don't need a jammer to sit on this winter, but we can't make do without our Cat."

"I don't suppose."

"Your gas Jimmy running?"

"It was the other day."

"It's a good little truck. I've seen you hike all over the hills in snow deeper than this."

When? I asked myself. When?

"We make do with it."

"You'd be up the Peak and back in no time at all."

"I couldn't climb to where you are. What do you have at that height, five — six feet?"

"No, no, about four, and we've plowed down three miles past the lower face. Down in the woods there, there's no more snow than what a dog could piss in. You'll roll right up there."

So you have a jammer and you're the operator, then you need a choker setter and he'll wrap cable chokers around logs near your pulley. He'll snap a choker to the bell hook of the cable traveling near the ground and give you a wave. You'll throw your drums in gear — one will reel in the cable while the other pays slack up the pole and out — and if you don't throw your drums in gear, if you're sleeping or thinking about last night's big deal, the choker setter will run up close and pitch rocks at your head. So you drag that log up to the jammer, jump out of the shack, unhook the choker, climb back in, and send that choker flying back by reversing the direction of the drums. And the choker setter will have a choker around another log or two or three and be ready to hook you to more logs, and back you reel them. Now you're logging.

"If your Cat is down low I suppose somebody could drive to it."

"I know you can, of course the Cat isn't down there. It's up with the jammer."

"Just when did you plow?" Dad ceased leaning on the pickup and looked hard at Buck.

"Yesterday morning."

"And what would you say, two feet has fallen up there since then?"

"No more than a foot. You'll fly up there easily, Bill."

"I may have to."

You're almost logging, it's a good idea but not yet working for a number of reasons. To start with, the first log you try to skid is going to stay in the same spot while your jammer kindly pulls itself over onto its side. That's easy to prevent. You take four cables and anchor your pole off into the woods in four different directions, then you can skid logs all day — which is the second problem. You can pile logs all around the jammer but that's not loading them onto the truck. You need a loading arm. So you stick a twelve- or fifteen-foot pole out at a half-raised angle, thread it with cable. That way, with a pair of log tongs attached to the end of the dangling cable, you'll be able to pick your logs straight up in the air and, with the help of an iron mast erected at the front, swing the raised log onto the truck. And if the truck driver is a friend of yours, he'll unhook the chokers and set the log tongs, and you'll just dance around inside the jammer throwing levers and doing two things at once.

Dad rubbed his forehead, pushed back his cap. "I'll have to talk it over with the wife," Dad said. "In the winter we tend to keep ourselves to home."

"I'll pay you well for your trouble, tell Helen that." Buck stuck a second match between his teeth.

"Now there wouldn't be any complaint if I helped you get your truck to running."

"That would take some tinkering, to tell you the truth I'd hate to lose what time we have."

But then there's moving the jammer, that's why it's on wheels and built on a truck frame. You'll only be in the same place for a day or two, and as long as you move only a short distance, you can do so slowly with the jammer pole sticking straight up. But say you must move five miles or you come to an electric power line, you need to drop that pole. So you erect another iron mast, rig a hinge onto the bottom of the jammer pole, and using the loading arm and the iron masts you lay that pole down flat so it juts out the back. There's your jammer, the biggest tangle of cables, arms and poles, and drums you'll ever see.

"I'll talk to the wife."

"I have to get. I'll drive up ahead of you."

"Wasn't your truck running yesterday?" I asked.

Guessing my meaning, Buck laughed. "We were logging." Then to Dad he said, "I don't know who else I'd get. There's not many men around who can be depended on and not be more trouble than they're worth. See you, Bill, you too Randall P. Jones."

I nodded.

"Later," Dad said, and Buck Davaz was in his pickup and gone.

"Quite the pickup he has there," Dad said to me as we walked towards the house.

"We going to do it?"

"I'll see what your mother thinks first."

Mom didn't think much of the whole idea. "What did he have to boast and brag about this time?" was her first question. But Dad had said as much as yes to Buck by not saying no, that's the way he does. He's said no to us kids often enough, but when it comes to helping a neighbor, even when it's a losing proposition, he can't say it.

We readied for the trip, shoveled off the truckbed while the truck idled. Dad and I were pitching off the last shovelfuls of snow when out of the house walked Jay, all bundled up. He'd been sick for a week, right through his birthday, and Mom told him if he didn't stay inside he'd never see his tenth. But there he was standing before us, eyes level with the bed, looking up at us from out of that upturned coat collar and two stocking caps.

"Can I go up on the Peak?"

That serious face of his, too.

"I thought you were sick?"

Jay shrugged. "I don't think so, not much."

"It'll be colder up there," Dad said. "Your mother know you're out here?"

"She said I could go if you need some more help."

Dad climbed down off the truck. "There won't be anything for you to do."

Jay stood frozen in the same spot. "I'll get to see what's up there."

I felt like whacking him over the head with my shovel — what was with him wanting to make himself sicker? I'd have told that sick kid where he could go. Dad circled around the truck, he checked the front tires. I jumped to the ground. As Dad opened the door to climb in he shouted across to Jay, "Hop in the cab or go back to the house but don't stand there waiting to be run over."

I opened the door and Jay scrambled in to sit between us. I couldn't blame Jay for wanting to go. So maybe we make it up onto the Peak four or five times a summer, this was a chance in winter. By one o'clock we were climbing the Peak, up through the trees and snow and more snow and fog and up and up and the road was without end. Usually you can count on seeing a deer or a coyote or maybe a bobcat and for sure a dozen or so squirrels. But in that white world there was not a thing moving and the only tracks were those of Mr. Davaz's pickup. It's a wonder, up there as everywhere in the woods in winter, it's as still as death. And the snow kept coming down, piled high on the tree branches and sagged them down, piled deep in the road and slowed us down, and the truck's wiper blades kept swishing flakes to the side and it even piled up there in the corners of the windshield.

We passed the place the Davazes had stopped plowing snow, further on we squeezed around a yellow pickup that was half in the ditch and half out, snow piled on its hood and roof. "They had better yank that out," Dad said, "or they'll find it somewhere else in the spring."

Jay sat hunched forward, his nose an inch from the glass. Me too, when we broke out onto the lower face. We had to look past Dad to see out over the edge, four hundred feet down to a blurred end in mist and snow. It's some white world. Both Jay and I were fully amazed by what wasn't out there — then it struck me. Buck Davaz didn't know winter. And if he didn't know winter how was he to know that after feeding cows you can go sit by the stove?

When did he hunt up his snow shovels? When did he fan his seed oats?

When did he think to check the braces in the barn?

And if he didn't know winter, how did he know spring? Summer? How did he know what to do and when if he didn't even know the season he stood in?

To turn the truck around, we drove past the Cat. Mr. Davaz had worked it up onto the roadbank ready to load. The road into Davaz's logging show was blocked by a pair of felled trees, so we couldn't turn around there. In fact there were a good hundred ripples made by felled trees covered over by snow — a wide path of white waves leading off through the woods. We turned the truck around just short of Davaz's wrecked jammer. "The hell," Dad said when he saw it.

Jay and I simply stared.

The jammer rested on its side in a five-foot ditch. The operator's shack was crushed, the left mast busted clean away and the right one bent double, barely hanging on. A cable drum was against a tree off in the brush, another had been rolled off the road into the ditch. Cable lay everywhere — across the road, strung through the bushes, wrapped around trees. I've seen alarm clocks gutted by a five-year-old looking more recognizable than Davaz's jammer. They'd even shattered the jammer pole itself.

"Whose pile of junk?" Jay asked Dad. Dad laughed and backed the truck around.

Buck

I second-guessed those Yanceys and found the perfectly easiest spot to load a Cat. I knew if I didn't there'd be an afternoon of bitching and moaning until I did. Even so, before Bill Yancey backed to it, he had to climb out of his truck, look it all over, stomp around in the snow searching for a ditch where I knew there wasn't one. Anybody else would've backed up to any deck of logs and loaded that Cat in a minute. But a Yancey needed a roadbank the height of the truckbed, and not any roadbank but that of a curve so their truck would be pointed downhill, straight down the road. That sort of fussiness I could stomach if they weren't mindless besides. It was not enough that we were up there freezing our hands and toes off, they'd dragged a sick kid along, little Jay, only to see if he'd die of frostbite.

We loaded the Cat, chained it on, and began the slow crawl down. Too slow, not only because we wasted time we needed later, but also by poking along Yancey slid into trouble, making trouble for me. A man can't crawl because he's afraid of falling down. Just the same I wasn't asking that he throw his truck out of gear and sail. But if he'd rolled along in second, then his back end wouldn't have slid in every curve, and I following him wouldn't have had to fight my pickup to keep its back end from passing the front.

Not speed but bad luck had wrecked the log-jammer. Jim was towing it down the upper grade with the Cat. When the jammer began drifting sideways, Jim turned the Cat to straighten it out, both went to sliding. The Cat was whipped around beside the jammer, and, mated as they were, the pair of machines shot down the hill. The thirty-foot jammer pole stuck out into the woods like a sore finger, slicing down small trees until it met with a tree too stout to bend or break. The pole shattered, the Cat broke free, and the jammer rolled into the ditch, burying itself in the snow.

Simply to spite a man these mountains breed bad luck. It's their natural response after being lashed for a thousand centuries by snow, wind, and ice, to take the strong and weak alike, dash out their brains on the rocks and bury them in snow. The test is to have strength of mind enough to endure, be able to weather the bad luck and not quit. Giving up a couple months isn't quitting, certainly not when we charge back early in the spring twice as strong and ready to fight. And not all bad luck is the mountain's doing, it can come from the company a man keeps.

Down we crawled, and at the switchback into the lower face Bill's truck pulled a trick I was afraid our Diesel would've done. It's a steep grade there, part of the old road built for wagon teams. Out on the face the edge of the road dumps over into an eight hundred maybe a thousand-foot drop, land so steep that not even a bush grows on it. It took men with horse teams two years to carve a road across that face. The roadbank on the uphill side is ninety feet high. That's strength. They moved all that rock and dirt for a wagon path to bring out timber.

Right in the middle of the damned switchback Bill's truck

went to sliding sideways. I bet good money that my Cat was going for its last ride and ended up a worse wreck than the jammer. Yancey's truck slid down through the curve of the switchback and out towards the face. Maybe I closed my eyes when I saw that truck skating sideways down the road. Maybe I suffered a moment of their weakness. I know I cussed, swore as best I could. Cussed Yancey. And I thought of that sick kid in the cab, the three of them trapped in a sliding truck.

Randall

Though coming up the mountain through two feet of snow hadn't proved bothersome, the going down froze me in the truck seat. Dad never shifted up out of first and we eased down the grades, slid some in making those doubling-back turns in the switchbacks. Down without a scare into the lower face, there we entered the turn sliding. Dad steered into the skid, didn't overcramp the wheel, didn't brake, didn't lift his foot off the gas, but did as he should. We skidded sideways down through the curve onto the grade, the truck a ten-o'clock hour hand to the road. The rear wheels struck the ridge of frozen dirt on the road's edge, jostled us about. I saw down over the face to where snow and cloud melted into one with nothing in between for hundreds of yards to stop us. The rear wheels struck the edge again as we gained speed in our sliding. "Better jump!" I yelled. But where to go? I'd have had to climb over Jay, past the gear-shift, past Dad and the steering wheel. Only Dad could've gotten out, but he shoved Jay back in the seat with one hand and held him there. I practically climbed up over Jay's back.

The wheels struck the frozen edge again and this is it, I thought. Only we were jarred again and again and again and as suddenly as our skidding had started, it ended. The truck slowly straightened out and Dad eased it over to the center of the road. I let loose of Jay's head.

"Damn," Dad cussed, then, touching his foot lightly to the brake, "damn, damn, damn." He pumped the brakes a little harder each time while watching his mirror. I leaned back to look in the side mirror and saw a twenty-foot cloud of snow glide down the face and disappear. Behind that, Buck Davaz's pickup hung by a front wheel to the road's edge.

"What's going on?" Jay asked.

"Nothing," I said, "nothing now."

We were two hundred yards down the grade before Dad could safely stop the truck. The three of us walked back to help Buck, who was out of his pickup and down on his knees on the road, trying to peer underneath.

"Not a chance of rocking it out is there?" Dad asked.

Buck rose to his feet, brushing snow off his knees. "A piss-ant's chance, the front axle's bottomed out on the lip of the bank. I don't think the rear wheels are even touching ground."

"We'll give you a pull."

"Kick the damn thing over the bank, piss-ant's luck."

"We can use the chains from around the Cat to hook to your axle."

"It's like landing straddle of a rail fence. I got so knotted up watching you and we were moving so damned slow . . . piss-ant."

I walked to the other side to see just what did hold it.

"Kick it over the bank, Randall P. Go ahead."

"Twenty-six feet of chain altogether, the truck should pull you. We can even put on the tire chains."

"Yeh, yeh, I have two chokers. Piss-ant astraddle of a rail fence."

"I'll back up the truck."

Buck kicked snow at the pickup with the side of his boot. "Sonofabitching rig. I'll guide you back. Drag the chokers out of the back, you two," Buck said to Jay and me.

"Be careful," Dad advised.

I should have said the same to him. That was one ride I didn't want to take, coming backwards up a grade we'd almost slid off of. Dad and Buck walked to the truck; I climbed in the pickup box, untangled the chokers and tossed them out to Jay. He snapped them together and strung them out in front. I crawled under the front bumper and wrapped the choker around the axle.

"Glad it isn't us," Jay said as I fought with the choker beneath the pickup. I caught a cable sliver, it poked clear through my glove and into my palm.

"We're still up here aren't we?"

"Not because we're dumb. Want me to hook it for you?"

Smart-mouthed kid. "I've got it," I said and crawled out. Jay stood in the center of the road, whaling himself with his arms to keep warm. He was as white as the snow he was standing in, as white as that which dropped down to pile up on his shoulders and cap.

"You're sick," I said to him, and he didn't answer, only kept whaling himself and looking serious.

"I wish I was Dad's age," Jay said. "I'd tell Mr. Davaz to take a walk."

"And when you're fifty are you going to wish you were nine and playing third-grade basketball?"

Jay thought a moment. "Who'd want to be nine?"

Smart-mouthed kid. But then I thought it over too, and who'd want to be fourteen?

Dad started the truck but it would not back. Dad coasted further down the grade and tried from there, the rear wheels spun. Dad jumped out of the truck, went to talking with Mr. Davaz while pulling the tire chains from off the back. Then he threw the chains back on and waved for us to come down.

"What the hell for?" I asked out loud, but not loud enough for Dad to hear. My hands were freezing from handling the choker cables.

"What the hell for?" echoed Jay. The kid's all mouth, we started walking.

"Hurry up," Dad shouted, and we ran.

"We're going to unload the Cat and use it," Dad told us when we joined them. So we jumped in the cab and down the mountain the four of us went. A quarter-mile getting off the face and another three-quarters getting down among timber where the road leveled out to run the length of a ridge, there we found a curve with a bank to dump the Cat onto.

Dad and Buck stomped around and found the ditch, looked the bank over. The next thing I knew I was walking back up the road to fetch a chainsaw out of Buck's pickup. They needed to clear some small trees and brush out of the way. I hurried, I was thirty minutes getting the saw. Slipped and slid on my way up, slipped and fell on my way down.

"You didn't drag it down here without any gas in it did you?" Buck asked when I handed it to him.

"Of course not."

Buck gave a couple of pulls on the starter rope and nothing happened. He yanked on it some more, the saw popped and belched smoke. "Sonofabitching saw." He yanked away at it. "This is Orville's damn saw, he must've taken mine." Jay turned his back so Mr. Davaz couldn't see him grinning. Yank, yank. I once saw Jim Davaz heave a chainsaw a hundred feet into the brush. Buck slammed the saw down in the snow, held it down with his knee and yanked on it some more. It wasn't Jim's saw either. "Sonofabitching saw, damned Orville."

Dad paced the road behind Buck.

Buck jumped to his feet and yelled for an axe. I brought our axe down off the truck and Buck was right behind me, grabbed it and scrambled up the bank. He set to whacking away at an arm's-size tamarack that bounced with every stroke.

You can't chop little frozen trees like that, or ironwood either.

Dad tipped the saw on its side, shook it, and a tablespoon of gas drained out of the exhaust, making a black spot in the snow. He pulled out his knife and tinkered with the adjusting screws on the carburetor. He tried and the saw sputtered. He used his knife on the carburetor some more, gave the saw another try and it started but soon died. Out came his knife again, yank, the saw roared. He revved the engine, adjusted some more with his knife, then climbed the bank. Dad laid into those trees, falling that one to the left, another to the right, another left, another right, wading right through to slice out a ten-foot-wide path as easy as cake. Buck came sliding down off the bank and handed me the axe. He was all grin, acting as though he'd pulled off the biggest trick. "Your Dad got it started, huh?" Dad with a chain-saw made it look easy, he didn't even work up a sweat, in two minutes he was done.

"What you looking moon-faced about?" Buck asked me.

I was staring straight up at the snow coming down. I shrugged. Without a wind the flakes dove straight down out of the sky like pilots with tiny collapsed parachutes. "Snow," I said.

"You're standing in it."

Jay and I stood in the middle of the road while they ran the Cat off the truck. Jay, hunched up with his hands inside his coat, let his soaked gloves fall out of his pocket and didn't even stoop to pick them up. I stuffed them in his pocket and said to him, "Better jump around or you'll freeze."

"I know."

We leaped up and down in the road, I, with my hands tucked up under my armpits to warm fast, Jay, his teeth chattering.

Buck pointed the Cat up the road, ground it into high gear. The three of us followed, Dad and I packing the log chains. Dad turned to Jay. "You'd better stay here, crawl in the cab and keep warm." Jay turned back without complaint and we trudged up the hill. I'd have done anything so as not to carry that hand-freezing chain. We were half an hour reaching the pickup, left with no time to waste in pulling it out.

"Your winch doesn't work?" Dad yelled, hoping he'd misunderstood.

"Nope, sheared a pin in it," Buck yelled back. "Hook the chain, I'll drag it out."

Dad hooked him and stepped clear. "No damn winch, I don't believe it."

Buck worked the Cat ahead, taking up the slack in the chains and chokers.

"He'll pull it right out, won't he?" I asked.

"He might if he had anything but a frozen road for his tracks to gain a purchase on." Buck gave the Cat full throttle forward, the pickup leaped two feet along the road's edge, and just as quickly the Cat lost traction, remained in one spot, bouncing up and down in the road. "Hit it again," Dad yelled, motioning with his arm.

Buck backed the Cat up, then rammed forward again, and again the pickup did a leap along the road's edge, the front end remaining straddle of it. Two, three, four more pulls, the same result, and we unhooked the chains and chokers and rehooked them so he could pull from the uphill side. It made no difference. The Cat yanked the pickup back along the edge, back to where it had been. No matter how cornerwise we got the hookup, the results were the same. Buck, made angry, kept ramming the cable even while Dad waved his arms and yelled for him to stop.

"Sonofabitching rig, hope I've torn the bottom out of it."

"We'll hook a chain to the center of the axle again," Dad was saying, "but this time we'll do a couple wraps around the blade. See if you can lift the front end onto the road."

"I'll give her hell from the other side," Buck yelled, and we jumped out of his way as he whirled the Cat around. We unhooked the chains and chokers, my hands were numb, I dropped a chain in the snow and we couldn't find it. We kicked around until Dad kicked into it. It was past four and we were running out of light.

Buck had backed his Cat up to the front of the pickup. Dad tried to convince him to turn the Cat around so we could hook to the blade. "What, Bill? What? Get back and hook her, I'll yank her to hell out." So we hooked the old man's Cat to his pickup. Buck revved the engine, popped the clutch, and the Cat leaped forward. Wham, the cables and chains snapped tight, but that didn't jerk his pickup onto the road. He backed the Cat up, revved the engine, and wham. "The damn fool," Dad muttered. Backup, roar, wham, backup, it was time to stop and think, figure out a new plan. He jockeyed the Cat up the road more. Roar, wham, the other front wheel popped onto the road but at the same time the rear end slipped down the face. "It's going to tip," Dad yelled. Wham, the pickup eased over onto its side as the back end slipped further down. "There it goes!" I yelled. Dad sprang forward, jerked the door wide open, grabbed its upper corner and pulled down. Wham. One front wheel lifted out of the snow as the pickup tipped more. Dad lost his footing and his hold on the door and sat down on the road's edge. Buck would not quit. The pickup stopped moving and never moved again. Buck Davaz made his Cat roar, made it belch black smoke, wham, a dozen more times. It was past the time for seeing, he was past seeing.

"Damnit to hell, stop," Dad yelled, back on his feet again. We were froze, Dad had lost his gloves which were so wet they were no good anyway. Buck needed to try Dad's idea or we'd be all night not returning that pickup to the road. Wham, Buck backed up and turned off the Cat. He came off the Cat on the run, shouting so, Dad couldn't say a word.

"To hell with it, it's only a pickup. To hell with it."

"We'll try a hookup to the blade."

"No we won't, to hell with it, Bill. I'm froze, so are you and the kid. What shape do you suppose that one down at the truck is in?"

"He'll be all right."

"To hell with it for today. I can't see, I want this Cat off this mountain. I want that out of this damn day."

Without the Cat's four-cylinder engine popping and roaring, it was quiet enough to hear snow striking snow, a cold cereal-in-milk sound. We could've decided on a new plan, a dozen new plans, Dad knows.

"Whatever, we're not hurting."

"We're finished here. I'll drag the chains and chokers behind the Cat. I want everything out of the pickup."

So that's what we did, unloaded the pickup of hardhats, tools, peevies, gas cans, and tied what we could onto Buck's Cat. As Dad tied on a gas can and I packed away a toolbox, Buck was to pick up the last things. *Crash!* Glass flew past my head and I whirled around just in time to see Buck swing that twelve-pound maul a second time and connect with his pickup's front windshield.

Shouldering the maul and an axe, Buck Davaz walked towards us. "Sonofabitching rig," he cussed as he strode by me.

Buck

It was after all a piss-ant's luck creeping in to spoil the day. Had I freewheeled it down through the switchback and down the grade, we'd have been off the mountain by dark. Those damned Yanceys. First Bill wanted to pull with the truck, then he wanted a winch, and all the time a perfectly good Cat sat close enough to run him down. A Cat that could make puny a man's back strength. But no human strength, not even human-made strength, was to save that rig. After pulling it down the hill, up the hill, across the hill, all over the hellish hill and everywhere but onto the road, I realized true that it wasn't the snow I was fighting nor the Yanceys' mindlessness but the mountain itself.

As I worked the Cat the mountain's spite froze me. I held enough strength of mind, even in that bitter cold, to give it up.

A man alone can't whip the biggest peak around, not at night, not when he's up to his armpits in snow. We would've froze to death up there. I thought it likely that the little kid down at the truck was near if not dead. All the cussing and freezing and fighting chokers and chains over a damned machine, it wasn't worth it any longer. A strong man when he's knocked down by a stronger force picks himself up and plods on. A stupid man walks into the same fist.

It cost me a pickup but I don't regret calling it quits, even though little Jay had built himself a fire and not died. The Cat's home. All the way down the mountain I thought nothing else. I went for a Cat with a pack of senseless weaklings and that's what I brought back. I'll tell Jim the same when I step in the door. When he asks where the pickup is, I'll tell him where it can stay. No pickup is going to skid logs for us or make road, and with an early spring we'll earn enough to buy a half-dozen pickups. And should Jim still complain and think he's so strong, he can walk up that peak by his lonesome and pack it down. Likely he can find a Yancey up a tree who'll be happy as hell to carry a bumper.

Damn Yancey, damn these mountains. I've fought my fight for this year and I feel good about it.

Randall

We dumped the Cat and Mr. Davaz off at his place. Once we were out of the driveway, Jay asked, "When's he bringing his pickup down?"

Dad turned on us and said, "If I ever catch either of you carrying on like he did, I'll break your necks." Once we reached the house there was considerable carrying on. Jayne, my sister just older than me, yelled about having to feed the cows alone. She stomped off to her room and slammed the door, Mom had words with Dad, and my baby sister screamed the whole time. Really, it was a mess of undeserved racket. We know winter.

Nine-thirty, that gives me an hour and a half. "I'm going out to check the cows," I yell into the kitchen. Pull on my hat, my coat, dry gloves, grab up the snowshoes as I dash by. Outside. The only sound is snow striking snow and beyond the buildings it's a wall of dark. Toss one shoe in the snow, strap it to my boot — strap on the other. Take a couple of steps, beat a hasty circle around the yard. All set.

Time to see what's out there.

RAYMOND CARVER

Where I'm Calling From

(FROM THE NEW YORKER)

WE ARE ON THE FRONT PORCH at Frank Martin's drying-out facility. Like the rest of us at Frank Martin's, J.P. is first and foremost a drunk. But he's also a chimney sweep. It's his first time here, and he's scared. I've been here once before. What's to say? I'm back. J.P.'s real name is Joe Penny, but he says I should call him J.P. He's about thirty years old. Younger than I am. Not much younger, but a little. He's telling me how he decided to go into his line of work, and he wants to use his hands when he talks. But his hands tremble. I mean, they won't keep still. "This has never happened to me before," he says. He means the trembling. I tell him I sympathize. I tell him the shakes will idle down. And they will. But it takes time.

We've only been in here a couple of days. We're not out of the woods yet. J.P. has these shakes, and every so often a nerve — maybe it isn't a nerve, but it's something — begins to jerk in my shoulder. Sometimes it's at the side of my neck. When this happens my mouth dries up. It's an effort just to swallow then. I know something's about to happen and I want to head it off. I want to hide from it, that's what I want to do. Just close my eyes and let it pass by, let it take the next man. J.P. can wait a minute.

I saw a seizure yesterday morning. A guy they call Tiny. A big fat guy, an electrician from Santa Rosa. They said he'd been in here for nearly two weeks and that he was over the hump. He was going home in a day or two and would spend New Year's Eve with his wife in front of the TV. On New Year's Eve, Tiny planned to drink hot chocolate and eat cookies. Yesterday morning he seemed just fine when he came down for breakfast. He was letting out with quacking noises, showing some guy how he called ducks right down onto his head. "Blam. Blam," said Tiny, picking off a couple. Tiny's hair was damp and was slicked back along the sides of his head. He'd just come out of the shower. He'd also nicked himself on the chin with his razor. But so what? Just about everybody at Frank Martin's has nicks on his face. It's something that happens. Tiny edged in at the head of the table and began telling about something that had happened on one of his drinking bouts. People at the table laughed and shook their heads as they shovelled up their eggs. Tiny would say something, grin, then look around the table for a sign of recognition. We'd all done things just as bad and crazy, so, sure, that's why we laughed. Tiny had scrambled eggs on his plate, and some biscuits and honey. I was at the table but I wasn't hungry. I had some coffee in front of me. Suddenly Tiny wasn't there anymore. He'd gone over in his chair with a big clatter. He was on his back on the floor with his eyes closed, his heels drumming the linoleum. People hollered for Frank Martin. But he was right there. A couple of guys got down on the floor beside Tiny. One of the guys put his fingers inside Tiny's mouth and tried to hold his tongue. Frank Martin yelled, "Everybody stand back!" Then I noticed that the bunch of us were leaning over Tiny, just looking at him, not able to take our eyes off him. "Give him air!" Frank Martin said. Then he ran into the office and called the ambulance.

Tiny is on board again today. Talk about bouncing back. This morning Frank Martin drove the station wagon to the hospital to get him. Tiny got back too late for his eggs, but he took some coffee into the dining room and sat down at the table anyway. Somebody in the kitchen made toast for him, but Tiny didn't eat it. He just sat with his coffee and looked into his cup. Every now and then he moved his cup back and forth in front of him.

I'd like to ask him if he had any signal just before it happened. I'd like to know if he felt his ticker skip a beat, or else begin to race. Did his eyelid twitch? But I'm not about to say anything. He doesn't look like he's hot to talk about it anyway. But what happened to Tiny is something I won't ever forget. Old Tiny

flat on the floor, kicking his heels. So every time this little flitter
starts up anywhere, I draw some breath and wait to find myself
on my back, looking up, somebody's fingers in my mouth.

In his chair on the front porch, J.P. keeps his hands in his lap.
I smoke cigarettes and use an old coal bucket for an ashtray. I
listen to J.P. ramble on. It's eleven o'clock in the morning — an
hour and a half until lunch. Neither one of us is hungry. But
just the same we look forward to going inside and sitting down
at the table. Maybe we'll get hungry.
    What's J.P. talking about, anyway? He's saying how when he
was twelve years old he fell into a well in the vicinity of the farm
he grew up on. It was a dry well, lucky for him. "Or unlucky,"
he says, looking around him and shaking his head. He says how
late that afternoon, after he'd been located, his dad hauled him
out with a rope. J.P. had wet his pants down there. He'd suffered all kinds of terror in that well, hollering for help, waiting,
and then hollering some more. He hollered himself hoarse before it was over. But he told me that being at the bottom of that
well had made a lasting impression. He'd sat there and looked
up at the well mouth. Way up at the top he could see a circle of
blue sky. Every once in a while a white cloud passed over. A
flock of birds flew across, and it seemed to J.P. their wingbeats
set up this odd commotion. He heard other things. He heard
tiny rustlings above him in the well, which made him wonder if
things might fall down into his hair. He was thinking of insects.
He heard wind blow over the well mouth, and that sound made
an impression on him, too. In short, everything about his life
was different for him at the bottom of that well. But nothing
fell on him and nothing closed off that little circle of blue. Then
his dad came along with the rope, and it wasn't long before J.P.
was back in the world he'd always lived in.
    "Keep talking, J.P. Then what?" I say.
    When he was eighteen or nineteen years old and out of high
school and had nothing whatsoever he wanted to do with his
life, he went across town one afternoon to visit a friend. This
friend lived in a house with a fireplace. J.P. and his friend sat
around drinking beer and batting the breeze. They played some
records. Then the doorbell rings. The friend goes to the door.

This young woman chimney sweep is there with her cleaning
things. She's wearing a top hat, the sight of which knocked J.P.
for a loop. She tells J. P.'s friend that she has an appointment to
clean the fireplace. The friend lets her in and bows. The young
woman doesn't pay him any mind. She spreads a blanket on the
hearth and lays out her gear. She's wearing these black pants,
black shirt, black shoes and socks. Of course by now she's taken
her hat off. J.P. says it nearly drove him nuts to look at her. She
does the work, she cleans the chimney, while J.P. and his friend
play records and drink beer. But they watch her and they watch
what she does. Now and then J.P. and his friend look at each
other and grin, or else they wink. They raise their eyebrows
when the upper half of the young woman disappears into the
chimney. She was all-right-looking, too, J.P. said. She was about
his age.

When she'd finished her work, she rolled her things up in the
blanket. From J.P.'s friend she took a check that had been made
out to her by his parents. And then she asks the friend if he
wants to kiss her. "It's supposed to bring good luck," she says.
That does it for J.P. The friend rolls his eyes. He clowns some
more. Then, probably blushing, he kisses her on the cheek. At
this minute J.P. made his mind up about something. He put his
beer down. He got up from the sofa. He went over to the young
woman as she was starting to go out the door.

"Me, too?" J.P. said to her. She swept her eyes over him. J.P.
says he could feel his heart knocking. The young woman's
name, it turns out, was Roxy.

"Sure," Roxy says. "Why not? I've got some extra kisses." And
she kissed him a good one right on the lips and then turned to
go.

Like that, quick as a wink, J.P. followed her onto the porch.
He held the porch screen door for her. He went down the steps
with her and out to the drive, where she'd parked her panel
truck. It was something that was out of his hands. Nothing else
in the world counted for anything. He knew he'd met somebody
who could set his legs atremble. He could feel her kiss still
burning on his lips, etc. At that minute J.P. couldn't begin to
sort anything out. He was filled with sensations that were carrying him every which way.

He opened the rear door of the panel truck for her. He helped her store her things inside. "Thanks," she told him. Then he blurted it out — that he'd like to see her again. Would she go to a movie with him sometime? He'd realized, too, what he wanted to do with his life. He wanted to do what she did. He wanted to be a chimney sweep. But he didn't tell her that then.

J.P. says she put her hands on her hips and looked him over. Then she found a business card in the front seat of her truck. She gave it to him. She said, "Call this number after ten o'clock tonight. The answering machine will be turned off then. We can talk. I have to go now." She put the top hat on and then took it off. She looked at J.P. once more. She must have liked what she saw, because this time she grinned. He told her there was a smudge near her mouth. Then she got into her truck, tooted the horn, and drove away.

"Then what?" I say. "Don't stop now, J.P." I was interested. But I would have listened if he'd been going on about how one day he'd decided to start pitching horseshoes.

It rained last night. The clouds are banked up against the hills across the valley. J.P. clears his throat and looks at the hills and the clouds. He pulls his chin. Then he goes on with what he was saying.

Roxy starts going out with him on dates. And little by little he talks her into letting him go along on jobs with her. But Roxy's in business with her father and brother and they've got just the right amount of work. They don't need anybody else. Besides, who was this guy J.P.? J.P. what? Watch out, they warned her.

So she and J.P. saw some movies together. They went to a few dances. But mainly the courtship revolved around their cleaning chimneys together. Before you know it, J.P. says, they're talking about tying the knot. And after a while they do it, they get married. J.P.'s new father-in-law takes him in as a full partner. In a year or so, Roxy has a kid. She's quit being a chimney sweep. At any rate, she's quit doing the work. Pretty soon she has another kid. J.P.'s in his mid-twenties by now. He's buying a house. He says he was happy with his life. "I was happy with the way things were going," he says. "I had everything I wanted. I had a wife and kids I loved, and I was doing what I wanted to do with my life." But for some reason — who knows why we do

what we do? — his drinking picks up. For a long time he drinks
beer and beer only. Any kind of beer — it didn't matter. He
says he could drink beer twenty-four hours a day. He'd drink
beer at night while he watched TV. Sure, once in a while he
drank hard stuff. But that was only if they went out on the
town, which was not often, or else when they had company over.
Then a time comes, he doesn't know why, when he makes the
switch from beer to gin and tonic. And he'd have more gin and
tonic after dinner, sitting in front of the TV. There was always
a glass of gin and tonic in his hand. He says he actually liked the
taste of it. He began stopping off after work for drinks before
he went home to have more drinks. Then he began missing
some dinners. He just wouldn't show up. Or else he'd show up
but he wouldn't want anything to eat. He'd filled up on snacks
at the bar. Sometimes he'd walk in the door and for no good
reason throw his lunch pail across the living room. When Roxy
yelled at him, he'd turn around and go out again. He moved his
drinking time up to early afternoon, while he was still supposed
to be working. He tells me that he was starting off the morning
with a couple of drinks. He'd have a belt of the stuff before he
brushed his teeth. Then he'd have his coffee. He'd go to work
with a thermos bottle of vodka in his lunch pail.

  J.P. quits talking. He just clams up. What's going on? I'm
listening. It's helping me relax, for one thing. It's taking me
away from my own situation. After a minute, I say, "What the
hell? Go on, J.P." He's pulling his chin. But pretty soon he starts
talking again.

  J.P. and Roxy are having some real fights now. I mean *fights*.
J.P. says that one time she hit him in the face with her fist and
broke his nose. "Look at this," he says. "Right here." He shows
me a line across the bridge of his nose. "That's a broken nose."
He returned the favor. He dislocated her shoulder for her on
that occasion. Another time he split her lip. They beat on each
other in front of the kids. Things got out of hand. But he kept
on drinking. He couldn't stop. And nothing could make him
stop. Not even with Roxy's dad and her brother threatening to
beat hell out of him. They told Roxy she should take the kids
and clear out. But Roxy said it was her problem. She got herself
into it, and she'd solve it.

Now J.P. gets real quiet again. He hunches his shoulders and
pulls down in his chair. He watches a car driving down the road
between this place and the hills.

I say, "I want to hear the rest of this, J.P. You better keep
talking."

"I just don't know," he says. He shrugs.

"It's all right," I say. And I mean it's O.K. for him to tell it.
"Go on, J.P."

One way she tried to solve things, J.P. says, was by finding a
boyfriend. J.P. would like to know how she found the time with
the house and kids.

I looked at him and I'm surprised. He's a grown man. "If you
want to do that," I say, "you find the time. You make the time."

J.P. shakes his head. "I guess so," he says.

Anyway, he found out about it — about Roxy's boyfriend —
and he went wild. He manages to get Roxy's wedding ring off
her finger. And when he does he cuts it into several pieces with
a pair of wire cutters. Good solid fun. They'd already gone a
couple of rounds on this occasion. On his way to work the next
morning he gets arrested on a drunk-driving charge. He loses
his driver's license. He can't drive the truck to work anymore.
Just as well, he says. He'd already fallen off a roof the week
before and broken his thumb. It was just a matter of time until
he broke his God-damned neck, he says.

He was here at Frank Martin's to dry out and to figure how
to get his life back on track. But he wasn't here against his will,
any more than I was. We weren't locked up. We could leave
anytime we wanted. But a minimum stay of a week was recommended, and two weeks or a month was, as they put it, "strongly
advised."

As I said, this is my second time at Frank Martin's. When I
was trying to sign a check to pay in advance for a week's stay,
Frank Martin said, "The holidays are always a bad time. Maybe
you should think of sticking around a little longer this time?
Think in terms of a couple of weeks. Can you do a couple of
weeks? Think about it, anyway. You don't have to decide anything right now," he said. He held his thumb on the check and
I signed my name. Then I walked my girlfriend to the front
door and said goodbye. "Goodbye," she said, and she lurched

into the doorjamb and then onto the porch. It's late afternoon. It's raining. I go from the door to the window. I move the curtain and watch her drive away. She's in my car. She's drunk. But I'm drunk, too, and there's nothing I can do. I make it to a big old chair that's close to the radiator, and I sit down. Some guys look up from their TV. Then slowly they shift back to what they were watching. I just sit there. Now and then I look up at something that's happening on the screen.

Later that afternoon the front door banged open and J.P. was brought in between these two big guys — his father-in-law and brother-in-law, I find out afterward. They steered J.P. across the room. The old guy signed him in and gave Frank Martin a check. Then these two guys helped J.P. upstairs. I guess they put him to bed. Pretty soon the old guy and the other guy came downstairs and headed for the front door. They couldn't seem to get out of this place fast enough. It was as if they couldn't wait to wash their hands of all this. I didn't blame them. Hell, no. I don't know how I'd act if I was in their shoes.

A day and a half later J.P. and I meet up on the front porch. We shake hands and comment on the weather. J.P. has a case of the shakes. We sit down and prop our feet on the railing. We lean back in our chairs as if we're just out there taking our ease, as if we might be getting ready to talk about our bird dogs. That's when J.P. gets going with his story.

It's cold out, but not too cold. It's a little overcast. At one point Frank Martin comes outside to finish his cigar. He has on a sweater buttoned up to his Adam's apple. Frank Martin is short and heavyset. He has curly gray hair and a small head. His head is out of proportion with the rest of his body. Frank Martin puts the cigar in his mouth and stands with his arms crossed over his chest. He works that cigar in his mouth and looks across the valley. He stands there like a prizefighter, like somebody who knows the score.

J.P. gets real quiet again. I mean, he's hardly breathing. I toss my cigarette into the coal bucket and look hard at J.P., who scoots farther down in his chair. J.P. pulls up his collar. What the hell's going on, I wonder. Frank Martin uncrosses his arms and takes a puff on the cigar. He lets the smoke carry out of his mouth. Then he raises his chin toward the hills and says, "Jack London used to have a big place on the other side of this valley. Right over there behind that green hill you're looking at. But alcohol killed him. Let that be a lesson. He was a better man than any of us. But he couldn't handle the stuff, either." He looks at what's left of his cigar. It's gone out. He tosses it into the bucket. "You guys want to read something while you're here, read that book of his *The Call of the Wild*. You know the one I'm talking about? We have it inside, if you want to read something. It's about this animal that's half dog and half wolf. They don't write books like that anymore. But we could have helped Jack London, if we'd been here in those days. And if he'd let us. If he'd asked for our help. Hear me? Like we can help you. *If. If* you ask for it and *if* you listen. End of sermon. But don't forget. If," he says again. Then he hitches his pants and tugs his sweater down. "I'm going inside," he says. "See you at lunch."

"I feel like a bug when he's around," J.P. says. "He makes me feel like a bug. Something you could step on." J.P. shakes his head. Then he says, "Jack London. What a name! I wish I had me a name like that. Instead of the name I got."

Frank Martin talked about that "if" the first time I was here. My wife brought me up here that time. That's when we were still living together, trying to make things work out. She brought me here and she stayed around for an hour or two, talking to Frank Martin in private. Then she left. The next morning Frank Martin got me aside and said, "We can help you. If you want help and want to listen to what we say." But I didn't know if they could help me or not. Part of me wanted help. But there was another part. All said, it was a very big if.

This time around, six months after my first stay, it was my girlfriend who drove me here. She was driving my car. She drove us through a rainstorm. We drank champagne all the way. We were both drunk when she pulled up in the drive. She intended to drop me off, turn around, and drive home again. She had things to do. One thing she had to do was to go to work the next day. She was a secretary. She had an O.K. job with this electronic-parts firm. She also had this mouthy teen-age son. I wanted her to get a motel room in town, spend the night, and

then drive home. I don't know if she got the room or not. I
haven't heard from her since she led me up the front steps the
other day and walked me into Frank Martin's office and said,
"Guess who's here."

But I wasn't mad at her. In the first place she didn't have any
idea what she was letting herself in for when she said I could
stay with her after my wife asked me to leave. I felt sorry for
her. The reason I felt sorry for her was on the day before
Christmas her Pap smear came back from the lab, and the news
was not cheery. She'd have to go back to the doctor, and real
soon. That kind of news was reason enough for both of us to
start drinking. So what we did was get ourselves good and
drunk. And on Christmas Day we were still drunk. We had to
go out to a restaurant to eat, because she didn't feel anything
like cooking. The two of us and her mouthy teen-age son
opened some presents, and then we went to this steak house
near her apartment. I wasn't hungry. I had some soup and a
hot roll. I drank a bottle of wine with the soup. She drank some
wine, too. Then we started in on Bloody Marys. For the next
couple of days I didn't eat anything except cashew nuts. But I
drank a lot of bourbon. On the morning of the twenty-eighth I
said to her, "Sugar, I think I'd better pack up. I better go back
to Frank Martin's. I need to try that place on again. Hey, how
about you driving me?"

She tried to explain to her son that she was going to be gone
that afternoon and evening, and he'd have to get his own dinner. But right as we were going out the door this God-damned
kid screamed at us. He screamed, "You call this love? The hell
with you both! I hope you never come back. I hope you kill
yourselves!" Imagine this kid!

Before we left town I had her stop at the liquor store, where
I bought us three bottles of champagne. Quality stuff — Piper.
We stopped someplace else for plastic glasses. Then we picked
up a bucket of fried chicken. We set out for Frank Martin's in
this rainstorm, drinking champagne and listening to music on
the radio. She drove. I looked after the radio and poured champagne. We tried to make a little party out of it. But we were sad,
too. There was that fried chicken, but we didn't eat any of it.

I guess she got home O.K. I think I would have heard something if she hadn't made it back. But she hasn't called me, and I

haven't called her. Maybe she's had some news about herself by now. Then again, maybe she hasn't heard anything. Maybe it was all a mistake. Maybe it was somebody else's test. But she has my car, and I have things at her house. I know we'll be seeing each other again.

They clang an old farm bell here to signal mealtime. J.P. and I get out of our chairs slowly, like old geezers, and we go inside. It's starting to get too cold on the porch anyway. We can see our breath drifting out from us as we talk.

New Year's Eve morning I try to call my wife. There's no answer. It's O.K. But even if it wasn't O.K., what am I supposed to do? The last time we talked on the phone, a couple of weeks ago, we screamed at each other. I hung a few names on her. "Wet brain!" she said, and put the phone back where it belonged.

But I wanted to talk to her now. Something had to be done about my stuff. I still had things at her house, too.

One of the guys here is a guy who travels. He goes to Europe and the Middle East. That's what he says, anyway. Business, he says. He also says he has his drinking under control and doesn't have any idea why he's here at Frank Martin's. But he doesn't remember getting here. He laughs about it, about his not remembering. "Anyone can have a blackout," he says. "That doesn't prove a thing." He's not a drunk — he tells us this and we listen. "That's a serious charge to make," he says. "That kind of talk can ruin a good man's prospects." He further says that if he'd only stick to whiskey and water, no ice, he'd never get "intoxicated" — his word — and have these blackouts. It's the ice they put into your drink that does it. "Who do you know in Egypt?" he asks me. "I can use a few names over there."

For New Year's Eve dinner Frank Martin serves steak and baked potato. A green salad. My appetite's coming back. I eat the salad. I clean up everything on my plate and I could eat more. I look over at Tiny's plate. Hell, he's hardly touched anything. His steak is just sitting there getting cold. Tiny is not the same old Tiny. The poor bastard had planned to be at home tonight. He'd planned to be in his robe and slippers in front of the TV, holding hands with his wife. Now he's afraid to leave. I can understand. One seizure means you're a candidate for an-

other. Tiny hasn't told any more nutty stories on himself since
it happened. He's stayed quiet and kept to himself. Pretty soon
I ask him if I can have his steak, and he pushes his plate over to
me.

They let us keep the TV on until the New Year has been rung
in at Times Square. Some of us are still up, sitting around the
TV, watching the crowds on the screen, when Frank Martin
comes in to show us his cake. He brings it around and shows it
to each of us. I know he didn't make it. It's a God-damned
bakery cake. But still it's a cake. It's a big white cake. Across the
top of the cake there's writing in pink letters. The writing says
"Happy New Year — 1 Day At A Time."

"I don't want any stupid cake," says the guy who goes to
Europe and the Middle East. "Where's the champagne?" he
says, and laughs.

We all go into the dining room. Frank Martin cuts the cake. I
sit next to J.P. J.P. eats two pieces and drinks a Coke. I eat a
piece and wrap another piece in a napkin, thinking of later.

J.P. lights a cigarette — his hands are steady now — and he
tells me his wife is coming to visit him in the morning. The first
day of the New Year.

"That's great," I say. I nod. I lick the frosting off my finger.
"That's good news, J.P."

"I'll introduce you," he says.

"I look forward to it," I say.

We say good night. We say Happy New Year. Sleep well. I
use a napkin on my fingers. We shake hands.

I go to the pay phone once more, put in a dime, and call my
wife collect. But nobody answers this time, either. I think about
calling my girlfriend, and I'm dialing her number when I realize
I don't want to talk to her. She's probably at home watching the
same thing on TV that I've been watching. But maybe she isn't.
Maybe she's out. Why shouldn't she be? Anyway, I don't want
to talk to her. I hope she's O.K. But if she has something wrong
with her I don't want to know about it. Not now. In any case, I
won't talk to her tonight.

After breakfast J.P. and I take coffee out to the porch, where
we plan to wait for his wife. The sky is clear, but it's cold enough
so we're wearing our sweaters and jackets.

"She asked me if she should bring the kids," J.P. says. "I told her she should keep the kids at home. Can you imagine? My God, I don't want my kids up here."

We use the coal bucket for an ashtray. We look across the valley where Jack London used to live. We're drinking more coffee, when this car turns off the road and comes down the drive.

"That's her!" J.P. says. He puts his cup next to his chair. He gets up and goes down the steps to the drive.

I see this woman stop the car and set the brake. I see J.P. open the car door. I watch her get out, and I see them embrace. They hug each other. I look away. Then I look back. J.P. takes the woman's arm and they come up the stairs. This woman has crawled into chimneys. This woman broke a man's nose once. She has had two kids, and much trouble, but she loves this man who has her by the arm. I get up from the chair.

"This is my friend," J.P. says to his wife. "Hey, this is Roxy."

Roxy takes my hand. She's a tall, good-looking woman in a blue knit cap. She has on a coat, a heavy white sweater, and dark slacks. I recall what J.P. told me about the boyfriend and the wire cutters — all that — and I glance at her hands. Right. I don't see any wedding ring. That's in pieces somewhere. Her hands are broad and the fingers have these big knuckles. This is a woman who can make fists if she has to.

"I've heard about you," I say. "J.P. told me how you got acquainted. Something about a chimney, J.P. said."

"Yes, a chimney," she says. Her eyes move away from my face, then return. She nods. She's anxious to be alone with J.P., which I can understand. "There's probably a lot else he didn't tell you," she says. "I bet he didn't tell you everything," she says, and laughs. Then — she can't wait any longer — she slips her arm around J.P.'s waist and kisses him on the cheek. They start to move toward the door. "Nice meeting you," she says over her shoulder. "Hey, did he tell you he's the best sweep in the business?" She lets her hand slide down from J.P.'s waist onto his hip.

"Come on now, Roxy," J.P. says. He has his hand on the doorknob.

"He told me he learned everything he knew from you," I say.

"Well, that much is sure true," she says. She laughs again. But it's as if she's thinking about something else. J.P. turns the doorknob. Roxy lays her hand over his hand. "Joe, can't we go into town for lunch? Can't I take you someplace for lunch?"

J.P. clears his throat. He says, "It hasn't been a week yet." He takes his hand off the doorknob and brings his fingers to his chin. "I think they'd like it, you know, if I didn't leave the place for a little while yet. We can have some coffee inside," he says.

"That's fine," she says. Her eyes light on me once more. "I'm glad Joe's made a friend here. Nice to meet you," she says again.

They start to go inside. I know it's a foolish thing to do, but I do it anyway. "Roxy," I say. And they stop in the doorway and look at me. "I need some luck," I say. "No kidding. I could do with a kiss myself."

J.P. looks down. He's still holding the doorknob, even though the door is open. He turns the doorknob back and forth. He's embarrassed. I'm embarrassed, too. But I keep looking at her. Roxy doesn't know what to make of it. She grins. "I'm not a sweep anymore," she says. "Not for years. Didn't Joe tell you? What the hell. Sure, I'll kiss you. Sure. For luck."

She moves over, she takes me by the shoulders — I'm a big man — and she plants this kiss on my lips. "How's that?" she says.

"That's fine," I say.

"Nothing to it," she says. She's still holding me by the shoulders. She's looking me right in the eyes. "Good luck," she says, and then she lets go of me.

"See you later, pal," J.P. says. He opens the door all the way, and they go inside.

I sit down on the front steps and light a cigarette. I watch what my hand does, then I blow out the match. I've got a case of the shakes. I started out with them this morning. This morning I wanted something to drink. It's depressing, and I didn't say anything about it to J.P. I try to put my mind on something else and for once it works.

I'm thinking about chimney sweeps — all that stuff I heard from J.P. — when for some reason I start to think about the house my wife and I lived in just after we were married. That house didn't have a chimney — hell, no — so I don't know what

makes me remember it now. But I remember the house and
how we'd only been in there a few weeks when I heard a noise
outside one morning and woke up. It was Sunday morning and
so early it was still dark in the bedroom. But there was this pale
light coming in from the bedroom window. I listened. I could
hear something scrape against the side of the house. I jumped
out of bed and went to the window.

"My God!" my wife says, sitting up in bed and shaking the
hair away from her face. Then she starts to laugh. "It's Mr.
Venturini," she says. "The landlord. I forgot to tell you. He said
he was coming to paint the house today. Early. Before it gets
too hot. I forgot all about it," she says, and laughs some more.
"Come on back to bed, honey. It's just the landlord."

"In a minute," I say.

I push the curtain away from the window. Outside, this old
guy in white coveralls is standing next to his ladder. The sun is
just starting to break above the mountains. The old guy and I
look each other over. It's the landlord, all right — this old guy
in coveralls. But his coveralls are too big for him. He needs a
shave, too. And he's wearing this baseball cap to cover his bald
head. God damn it, I think, if he isn't a weird old hombre, then
I've never seen one. And at that minute a wave of happiness
comes over me that I'm not him — that I'm me and that I'm
inside this bedroom with my wife. He jerks his thumb toward
the sun. He pretends to wipe his forehead. He's letting me know
he doesn't have all that much time. The old duffer breaks into
a grin. It's then I realize I'm naked. I look down at myself. I
look at him again and shrug. I'm smiling. What'd he expect?

My wife laughs. "Come *on*," she says. "Get back in this bed.
Right now. This minute. Come on back to bed."

I let go of the curtain. But I keep standing there at the window. I can see the landlord nod to himself as if to say, "Go on,
sonny, go back to bed. I understand," as if he'd heard my wife
calling me. He tugs the bill of his cap. Then he sets about his
business. He picks up his bucket. He starts climbing the ladder.

I lean back into the step behind me now and cross one leg
over the other. Maybe later this afternoon I'll try calling my wife
again. And then I'll call to see what's happening with my girlfriend. But I don't want to get her mouthy son on the line. If I

do call, I hope he'll be out somewhere doing whatever he does when he's not hanging around the house. I try to remember if I ever read any Jack London books. I can't remember. But there was a story of his I read in high school. "To Build a Fire" it was called. This guy in the Yukon is freezing. Imagine it — he's actually going to freeze to death if he can't get a fire going. With a fire he can dry his socks and clothing and warm himself. He gets his fire going, but then something happens to it. A branchful of snow drops on it. It goes out. Meanwhile, the temperature is falling. Night is coming on.

I bring some change out of my pocket. I'll try my wife first. If she answers, I'll wish her a Happy New Year. But that's it. I won't bring up business. I won't raise my voice. Not even if she starts something. She'll ask me where I'm calling from, and I'll have to tell her. I won't say anything about New Year's resolutions. There's no way to make a joke out of this. After I talk to her, I'll call my girlfriend. Maybe I'll call her first. I'll just have to hope I don't get her son on the line. "Hello, sugar," I'll say when she answers. "It's me."

CAROLYN CHUTE

"Ollie, oh . . ."

(FROM PLOUGHSHARES)

ERROLL, THE DEPUTY WHO WAS known to litter, did not toss any Fresca cans or Old King Cole bags out this night. Erroll brought his Jeep to a stop in the yard right behind Lenny Cobb's brand-new Dodge pickup. The brakes of Erroll, the deputy's, Jeep made a spiritless dusky squeak. Erroll was kind of humble this night. The greenish light of his police radio shone on his face and yes, the froggishly round eyes, mostly pupil because it was dark, were humble. His lips were shut down over his teeth that were usually laughing and clicking. Humbleness had gone so far as to make that mouth look almost *healed* over like the holes in women's ears when they stop putting earrings through. He took off his knit cap and lay it on the seat beside the empty Fresca can, potato chip bag, and cigar cellophanes. He put his gloved hand on the door opener to get out. But he paused. He was scared of Ollie Cobb. He wasn't sure how she would take the news. But she wasn't going to take it like other women did. Erroll tried to swallow but there was no saliva there to work around in his throat.

He looked at Lenny Cobb's brand-new Dodge in the lights of his Jeep. It was so cold out there that night that the root-beer-color paint was sealed over every inch in a delicate film like an apple still attached, still ripening, never been handled. Wasn't Lenny Cobb's truck the prince of trucks? Even the windshield and little vent windows looked heavy-duty . . . as though congealed inside their rubber strips thick and deep as the frozen Sebago. And the chrome was heavy as pots. And the plow! It was constricted into travel gear, not yet homely from running into stone walls and frost heaves. And on the cab roof an amber light, the swivel kind, big as a man's head. Of course it had four-wheel drive. It had shoulders! Thighs. Spine. It might be still growing.

The Jeep door opened. The minute he stood up out in the crunchy driveway he wished he had left his cap on. The air was like paper, could have been thirty below. His breath leaving his nose turned to paper. It was all so still and silent. With no lights on in Lenny Cobb's place, a feeling came over Erroll of being alone at the North Pole. Come to his ears a lettucelike crispness, a keenness . . . so that to the top arch of each ear his spinal cord plugged in. A cow murred in the barn. One murr. A single note. And yet the yard was so thirsty for sound . . . all planes gave off the echo: a stake to mark a rosebush under snow . . . an apple basket full of snow on the top step. He gave the door ten or twelve thonks with his gloved knuckles. It *hurt*.

Ollie Cobb did not turn on a light inside or out. She just spread open the door and stood looking down at him through the small round frames of her glasses. She wore a long rust-colored robe with pockets. The doorway was outside the apron of light the Jeep headlights made. Erroll had to squint to make her out, the thin hair. It was black, parted in the middle of her scalp, yanked back with such efficiency that the small fruit-shape of her head was clear: a lemon or a lime. And just as taut and businesslike, pencil-hard, pencil-sized, a braid was drawn nearly to her heels . . . the toes, long as thumbs, clasped the sill. "Deputy Anderson," she said. She had many teeth. Like shingles. They seemed to start out of her mouth when she opened it.

He said: "Ah . . ."

Erroll couldn't know when the Cobb house had rotted past saving, yet more certain than the applewood banked in the stove, the smell of dying timbers came to him warmly . . . almost rooty, like carrots . . .

"What *is* it?" she said.

He thought of the great sills of that old house being soft as carrots. "Lenny has passed away," he said.

She stepped back. He was hugged up close to the openness of

the door, trying to get warm, so when the door whapped shut, his foot was in it. *"Arrrrr!"* So he got his foot out. She slammed the door again. When he got back in his Jeep, his coffee fell off the dash and burned his leg.

II

The kitchen light came on. All Ollie's white-haired children came into the living room when she started to growl and rub her shoulder on the refrigerator. This was how Ollie grieved. She rolled her shoulders over the refrigerator door so some of the magnetic fruits fell on the floor. A math paper with a 98 on top seesawed downward and landed on the linoleum. The kids were happy for a chance to be up. "Oh, boy!" they said. All but Aspen who was twelve and could understand. She remained at the bottom of the stairs afraid to ask Ollie what the trouble was. Aspen was in a lilac-color flannel gown and gray wool socks. She sucked the thumb of her right hand and hugged the post of the banister with her left. It was three-fifteen in the morning. Applewood coals never die. All 'round the woodstove was an aura of summer. The socks and undershirts and mittens pinned in scores to a rope across the room had a summer stillness. They heard Ollie growl and pant. They giggled. Sometimes they stopped and looked up when she got loud. They figured she was not getting her way about something. They had seen the deputy, Erroll, leave from the upstairs windows. They associated Erroll with crime. Crime was that vague business of speeding tickets and expired inspection stickers. This was not a new thing. Erroll had come up in his Jeep behind Ollie a time or two in the village. He said "Red light" and she bared her teeth at him like a dog. She was baring her teeth now.

There was an almost Christmas spirit among the children to be wakened in the night like that. There was wrestling. There was wriggling. Tim rode the dog, Dick Lab. He, Dick Lab, would try to get away, but hands on his hocks would keep him back. Judy turned on the TV. Nothing was on the screen but bright fuzz. The hair of them all flying through the night was the torches of after-dark skiers: crackling white from chair to couch to chair to stairway, rolling Dick Lab on his side, carouseling twelve-year-old Aspen who sucked her thumb. Eddie and Arnie, Tim and Judy.

The herdsman's name was Jarrell Bean. He was like all Beans, silent and touchy, and had across his broad coffee-color face a look that made you suspect he was related somehow, perhaps on his mother's side, to some cows. The eyes were slate color and were of themselves lukewarm-looking, almost steamy, very huge, browless, while like hands they reached out and patted things that interested him. He inherited from his father, Bingo Bean, a short haircut . . . a voluntary baldness: the father's real name was also Jarrell, killed chickens for work and had the kind of red finely lined fingers you'd expect from so much murder. But Bingo's eyes everybody knows were yellow and utility. It was from his mother's side that Jarrell the herdsman managed to know what tact was. He came to the Cobbs' door from his apartment over the barn. He had seen the deputy Erroll's Jeep and figured Lenny's time had come. He was wearing a black-and red-checked coat and the spikes of a three-day beard, auburn. It was the kind of beard men adrift in lifeboats have. Unkind weather had spread each of the hairs its own way.

He had travelled several yards through that frigid night with *no hat*. This was nudity for a man so bald.

In his mouth was quite a charge of gum. He didn't knock. The kitchen started to smell of spearmint as soon as he closed the door behind him. Ollie was rolled into a ball on the floor, grunting, one bare foot, bare calf and knee extended. He stepped over the leg. He made Ollie's children go up the stairs. He dragged one by the arm. It howled. Its flare of pale hair spurted here and there at the herdsman's elbow. The entire length of the child was twisting. It was Randy who was eight and strong. Dick Lab sat down on the twelve-year-old Aspen's ankles and feet, against the good wool. Jarrell came down the stairs hard. His boots made a booming through the whole big house. He took Dane and Linda and Hannah all at once. Aspen kept sucking her thumb. She looked up at him as he came down toward her, seeing him over her fingers. She was big as a woman. Her thumb in her mouth was longer and lighter than the other fingers from twelve years of sucking. He fetched her by the blousey part of her lilac gown. She came away from the banister with a snap: like a Band-Aid from a hairy arm . . . "Cut it out!" she cried. His hands were used only to cattle. He thought of himself as *good* with cattle, not at all cruel. And yet with cattle what is to be done is always the will of the herdsman.

III

When Jarrell came downstairs, Ollie was gone. She had been thinking of Lenny's face, how it had been evaporating for months into the air, how the lip had gotten short, how the cheeks fell into the bone. While Jarrell stood in the kitchen, he picked up the magnetic fruits and stuck them in a row on the top door of the refrigerator. He figured Ollie had slipped into her room to be alone.

He walked out into the yard past Lenny's new root-beer-color truck. He remembered how it roared when Leo at the Mobil had fiddled with the accelerator and everyone — Merritt and Poochie and Poochie's brother and Kenny, even Quinlan — stood around looking in at the big 440 and Lenny was resting on the running board. Lenny's neck was getting much too small for his collar even then.

Jarrell went up to his apartment over the barn, his head stinging from the deep-freeze night, then his lamp went out and the yard was noiseless.

Under the root beer truck Ollie was curled with her braid in the snow. She had big bare feet. Under the rust-color robe the goosebumps crowned up. Her eyes were squeezed shut like children do when they pretend to be sleeping. Her lip was drawn back from the elegantly twisted teeth, twisted like the stiff feathers of a goose are overlaid. And filling one eyeglass lens a dainty ice fern.

IV

It was Ollie whose scheduled days and evenings were on a tablet taped to the bathroom door. Every day Ollie got up at 4:30 A.M. Every evening supper was at 5:45. If visitors showed up late by fifteen minutes, she would whine at them and punish them with remarks about their character. If she was on her way to the feed store in the pickup and there was a two-car accident blocking the road up ahead, Ollie would roll down the window and yell: *"Move!"*

Once Aspen's poor body nearly smoked, 102 temperature, and blew a yellow mass from her little nose holes . . . a morning when Ollie had plans for the lake . . . Lenny was standing in the yard with his railroad cap on and his ringless hands in the pockets of his cardigan, leaning on the new root beer truck . . . Ollie came out on the porch where many wasps were circling between her face and his eyes looking up: "She's going to spoil our time," Ollie said. "We've got to go down to the store and call for an appointment now. She couldn't have screwed up the day any better." Then she went back inside and made her hand like a clamp on the girl's bicep, bore down on it with the might of a punch or a kick, only more slow, more deep. Tears came to Aspen's eyes. Outside Lenny heard nothing. Only the sirens of wasps. And stared into the very middle of their churning.

Oh, that Ollie. Indeed, Lenny months before must have planned his cancer to ruin her birthday. That was the day of the doctor's report. All the day Lenny cried. Right in the lobby of the hospital . . . a scene . . . Lenny holding his eyes with the palms of his hands: "Help me! Help me!" he wailed . . . she steered him to a plastic chair. She hurried down the hall to be alone with the snack machine . . . HEALTHY SNACKS: apples and pears, peanuts. She despised *him* this way. *This* was her birthday.

V

In the thirty below *zero* morning jays' voices cracked from the roof. Figures in orange nylon jackets hustled over the snow. They covered Ollie with a white wool blanket. The children were steady with their eyes and statuesque as they arranged themselves around the herdsman. Aspen held the elbow of his black and red coat. Everyone's breath flattened out like paper, like those clouds cartoon personalities' words are printed on. It may have warmed up some. Twenty below or fifteen below. The cattle had not been milked, shuffling and ramming and murring, cramped near the open door of the barn . . . in pain . . . their udders as vulgar and hard as the herdsman's velvet head.

VI

At the hospital surgeons removed the ends of Ollie's fingers, most of her toes and her ears. She drank Carnation Instant Breakfast, grew sturdy again, and learned to keep her balance.

She came home with her thin hair combed to cover her earholes. In the back her hair veiled her ruby coat.

She got up every morning at 4:30 and hurtled herself out to the barn to set up for milking. Jarrell feared every minute that her hair might fall away from her missing ears. He would squint at her. Together they sold some of the milk to the neighborhood, those who came in cars and pulling sleds, unloading plastic jugs and glass jars to be filled at the sink, and the children of these neighbors would stare at Ollie's short fingers, the parents would look all around everyplace *but* the short fingers. Jarrell: "Whatcha got today, only two . . . is ya company gone?" or "How's Ralph's team doin now? . . . that's good ta hear," or "Fishin any good now? I ain't heard." He talked a lot these days. When they came around he brightened up. He opened doors for them and listened to gossip and passed it on. They teased him a lot about his lengthening beard. Sometimes Tim would stand between Jarrell and Ollie and somehow managed to have his hand on the backs of Jarrell's knees most of the time. As Ollie hosed out the stainless-steel sink there in the wood and glass white white room, Tim's eyes came over the sink edge and watched the water whirl.

At night Jarrell would open Mason jars and slice carrots or cut the tops off beets. Ollie would lift things slowly with her purply stubs. She set the table. She would look at Jarrell to see if he saw how slick she did this. But he was not looking. The children, all those towheads, would be throwing things and running in the hall. There had come puppies of Dick Lab. Tim and a buff puppy pulled on a sock. Tim dragged the puppy by the sock across the rug. Ollie would stand by the sink and look straight ahead. She had a spidery control over her short fingers. She once hooked small Marsha up by the hair and pressed her to the woodbox with her knee. But Ollie was wordless. Things would usually go well. By 5:45 forks of beets and squash were lifted to mouths and glasses of milk were draining.

After supper Jarrell would go back to his apartment and watch *Real People* and *That's Incredible* or *60 Minutes* and fall asleep with his clothes on. He had a pile of root beer cans by the bed. Sometimes mice would knock them over and the cans would roll out of the room, but it never woke him.

Jarrell could not go to the barn in the morning without thinking of Lenny. He would go along and pull the rows of chains to all the glaring gray lights. He and Lenny used to stand by the open door together. The black and white polka-dot *sea* of cows would clatter between them. And over and between the blowing mouths and oily eyes, Lenny's dollar-ninety-eight-cent gloves waved them on, and he'd say: "Oh, girl . . . oh, girl . . ." Their thundering never ever flicked Lenny's watered-down auburn hair that was thin on top. And there were the hairless temples where the chemotherapy had seared from the inside out.

Jarrell could recall Lenny's posture, a peculiar tired slouch in his pea coat. Lenny wore a watch cap in midwinter and a railroad cap in sweaty weather and the oils of his forehead were on the brims of both.

Jarrell remembered summer when there was a big corn-on-the-cob feast and afterward Lenny lay on the couch with just his dungarees on and his veiny bare feet kicking. His hairless chest was stamped with three black tattoos; two sailing ships and a lizard. Tim was jumping on his stomach. A naked baby lay on its back, covering the two ships. Lenny put his arm around the baby and it seemed to melt into him. Lenny's long face had that sleepy look of someone whose world is interior, immediate to the skin, never reaching outside his 120 acres. That very night that Lenny played on the couch with his children, Jarrell left early and stayed awake late in his apartment watching Tim Conway dictating in a German accent to his nitwit secretary.

Jarrell heard Ollie yelling. He leaned out his window and heard more clearly Ollie rasping out her husband's name. Once she leaped across the gold square of light of their bedroom window. Jarrell knew that Lenny was sitting on the edge of the bed, perhaps with his pipe in his mouth, untying his gray peeling workboots. Lenny would not argue, nor cry, nor turn red, but say: ". . . oh, girl . . . oh, Ollie, oh . . ." And he would look up at her with his narrow face, his eyes turning here and there on his favorite places of her face. She would be enraged the more. She picked up the workboot he had just pulled off his foot and turned it in her hand . . . then spun it through the air . . . the lamp went out and crashed.

Lenny began to lose weight in the fall. In his veins white blood cells roared. The cancer was starting to make Lenny irritable. He stopped eating supper. Ollie called it fussy. Soon Ollie and Jarrell were doing the milking alone. Sometimes Aspen would help. Lenny lay on the couch and slept. He slept all day.

VII

One yellowy morning Ollie made some marks on the list on the bathroom door and put a barrette on the end of her braid. She took the truck to Leo's and had the tank filled. She drove all day with Lenny's face against her belly. Then with her hard spine and convexed shoulders she balanced Lenny against herself and steered him up the stairs of the Veterans' hospital. She came out alone and her eyes were wide behind the round glasses.

VIII

Jarrell had driven Lenny's root beer Utiline Dodge for the first time when he drove to the funeral alone. Lenny had a closed casket. The casket was in an alcove with pink lights and stoop-shouldered mumbly Cobbs. They all smelled like old Christmas cologne. There must have been a hundred Cobbs. Most of the flowers around the coffin were white. Jarrell stood. The rest were sitting. The herdsman's head was pink in the funny light and he tilted his head as he considered how Lenny looked inside the coffin, under the lid. Cotton was in Lenny's eyes. He probably had skin like those plaster-of-Paris ducks that hike over people's lawns single file. He was most likely in there in some kind of suit, no pea coat, no watch cap, no pipe, no babies, no grit of Flash in his nails. Someone had undoubtedly scrubbed all the cow smell off him and he probably smelled like a new doll now. Jarrell drove to the interment at about eighty to eighty-five miles per hour and was waiting when the head-lighted caravan dribbled into the cemetery and the stooped Cobbs ambled out of about fifty old cars.

IX

Much later, after Lenny was dead awhile and Ollie's fingers were healed, Ollie came into the barn about 6:10. They were running late. The dairy truck from Portland was due to arrive in the yard. Ollie was wearing Lenny's old pea coat and khaki

shirt with her new knit pants. Tim was with her. Tim had a brief
little mouth and freakish coarse hair, like white weeds. His coat
was fastened with safety pins. Ollie started hooking up the machines with her quick half-fingers. They rolled like sausages
over the stainless-steel surfaces. Jarrell, hurrying to catch up,
was impatient with the cows when they wanted to shift around.
Ollie was soundless but Jarrell could locate her even if he didn't
see her, even as she progressed down the length of the barn.
He had radar in his chest (the heart, the lungs, even the bladder) for her position when things were running late. God! It
was like trying to walk through a wall of sand. Tim came over
and stood behind him. Tim was digging in his nose. He was
dragging out long strings of discolored matter and wiping it on
his coat that was fastened with pins. One cow pulled far to the
right in the stanchion, almost buckling to her knees as a hind
foot slipped off the edge of the concrete platform. The milking
machine thunked to the floor out of Jarrell's hands. Ollie heard.
Her face came as if from out of the loft, sort of downward. *Her
hair was pulled back* caught up by her glasses when she had hur-
riedly shoved them on. *She did not have ears. He saw for the first
time they had taken her ears.* His whole shape under his winter
clothes went hot as though common pins were inserted over
every square inch. He squinted, turned away . . . ran out of the
milking room into the snow. The dairy truck from the city was
purring up the hill. The fellow inside flopped his arm out for
his routine wave. Jarrell didn't wave back, but used both hands
to pull himself up into the root beer truck, slid across the cold
seat, made the engine roar. He remembered Lenny saying once
while they broke up bales of hay: "I just ordered a Dodge last
week, me and my wife . . . be a few weeks, they said. Prob'ly
for the President they'd have it to him the next day. Don't it *hurt*
to wait for somethin like that. Last night I dreamed I was in it,
and was revvin it up out here in the yard when all of a sudden
it took off . . . right up in the sky . . . and all the cows down in
the yard looked like dominoes."

X

That afternoon Jarrell Bean returned. He came up the old Nathan Lord Road slow. Had his arm out the window. When he

got near the Cobb place he ascended the hill in a second-gear roar. As he turned in the drive he saw Ollie in Lenny's pea coat standing by the doorless Buick sedan in which the hens slept at night. She lined the sights of Lenny's rifle with the right lens of her glasses. One of her sausage fingers was on the trigger. She put out two shots. They turned the right front tire to rags. The Dodge screamed and plowed sideways into the culvert. Jarrell felt it about to tip over. But it only listed. He lay flat on the seat for a quarter of an hour even after he was certain Ollie had gone into the house.

Aspen and Judy came out for him. He was crying, lying on his stomach. When they saw him crying, their faces went white. Aspen put her hard gray fingers on his back, between his shoulders. She turned to Judy . . . Judy, fat and clear-skinned with the whitest hair of all . . . and said: "I think he's sorry."

XI

Ollie lay under the mint-green bedspread. The window was open. All the yard, the field, the irrigation ditches, the dead birds were thawing, and under the window she heard a cat digging in the jonquils and dried leaves. She raised her hand of partial fingers to her mouth to wipe the corners. She had slept late again and now her blood pressure pushed at the walls of her head. She flipped out of the bed and thunked across the floor to the window. She was in a yellow print gown. The sunrise striking off the vanity mirror gave Ollie's face and arms a yellowness, too. She seized her glasses under the lamp. She peered through them, downward . . . *startled*. Jarrell was a few yards from his apartment doorway, taking a pair of dungarees from the clothesline. There were sheets hanging there, too, so it was hard to be sure at first . . . then as he strode back toward his doorway, she realized he had nothing on. He was corded and pale and straight-backed and down front of his chest dripped wet his now-full auburn beard. The rounded walls of his genitals gave little flaccid jogglings at each stride and on all of him his flesh like unbroken yellow water paused satisfyingly and seldomly at a few auburn hairs. On top, the balded head, a seamless hood, trussed up with temples all the way in that same seamless fashion to his eyes that were merry in the most irritat-

ing way. Ollie mashed her mouth and shingled teeth to the
screen and moaned full and cowlike. And when he stopped and
looked up, she screeched: *"I hate you! Get out of here! Get out of
here!"*

She scuttled to the bed and plunked to the edge. Underneath,
the shoes that Lenny wore to bean suppers and town council
meetings were still crisscrossed against the wall.

XII

That summer Jarrell and the kids played catch in the middle of
the Nathan Lord Road. Jarrell waded among them at the green
bridge in knee-deep water, slapped Tim a time or two for per-
sisting near the drop-off. They laughed at the herdsman in his
secondhand tangerine trunks and rubber sandals. He took them
to the drive-in movies in that root beer truck. They saw *Benji*
and *Last Tango in Paris*. They got popcorn and Good and Plentys
all over the seat and floor and empty paper cups were mashed
in the truck bed, blew out one by one onto different people's
lawns. He splurged on them at Old Orchard Beach, rides and
games, and coordinated Aspen won stuff with darts: a psyche-
delic poster, a stretched-out Pepsi bottle and four paper leis.
Then under the pier they were running with huge ribbons of
seaweed and he cut his foot on a busted Miller High Life bottle
. . . slumped in the sand to fuss over himself. It didn't bleed.
You could see into his arch, the meat, but no blood. Aspen's
white hair waved 'round her head as she stooped in her sunsuit
of cotton dots, blue like babies' clothes are blue. She cradled his
poor foot in her fingers and looked him in the eye.

Ollie *never* went with them. No one knew what she did alone
at home.

One afternoon Ollie stared through the heat to find Jarrell
on the front porch, there in a rocking chair with the sleeping
baby's open mouth spread on his bare arm. Nearly grown puppies were at his feet. He was almost asleep himself and mosqui-
toes were industriously draining his throat and shirtless chest.
On the couch after supper the little girls nestled in his auburn
beard and rolled in their fingers wads of the coarse stuff. The
coon cat with the abscesses all over his head swallowed whole
the red tuna Jarrell bought for him and set out at night on an

aluminum pie plate. Jarrell whenever he was close smelled like
cows.

XIII

Ollie drove to the drugstore for pills that were for blood pressure. Aspen went along. The root beer truck rattled because
Jarrell had left a yarding sled and chains in the back. Ollie
turned her slow rust-color eyes onto Aspen's face and Aspen
felt suddenly panicked. It seemed as though there was something changing about her mother's eyes: one studied your skin,
one bored dead-center in your soul. Aspen was wearing her
EXTINCT IS FOREVER T-shirt. It was apricot colored and there was
a leopard's face in the middle of her chest.

"Do you want one of those?" Ollie asked Aspen, who was
poking at the flavored Chap Sticks by the cash register.

"Could I?"

"Sure." Ollie pointed somewhere. "And I was thinking you
might like some colored pencils or a . . . you know . . . movie
magazine."

Aspen squinted. "I would, yes, I would."

A trio of high-school-aged Crocker boys in stretched-out
T-shirts trudged through the open door in a bowlegged way
that made them seem to be carrying much more weight than
just their smooth long bones and little gummy muscles. One
wore a baseball hat and had sweat in his hair and carried his
sneakers. He turned his flawless neck, and his pink hair cropped
there in a straight line was fuzzy and friendly like ruffles on a
puppy's shoulders where you pat. He looked right at Aspen's
leopard . . . right in the middle and read: "Extinct is forever."

His teeth lifted in a perfect cream-color line over the words
and his voice was low and rolled, one octave above adulthood.
Both the other boys laughed. One made noises like he was
dying. Then all of them pointed their fingers at her and said:
"Bang! Bang! Bang!" There are the insightful ones who realize
a teenager's way of flirting, and then there was Aspen who could
not. To see all the boys' faces from her plastic desk in school
was to Aspen like having a small easily destructible boat with
sharks in all directions. Suddenly self-conscious, suddenly
stoop-shouldered as it was for all Cobbs in moments of hell,

Aspen stood one shoe on top of the other and stuck her thumb in her mouth. There is something about drugstore light with its smells of sample colognes passing up like moths through a brightness bigger and pinker than sun that made Aspen Cobb look large and old, and the long thumb there was nasty looking. The pink-haired Crockers had never seen a big girl do this. They looked at each other gravely.

She walked over to where her mother was holding a jar of vitamin C. Her mother was arched over it, the veils of her thin black hair covering her earholes, falling forward, and her stance was gathering, coordinated like a spider, the bathtub spider, the horriblest kind. She lifted her eyes. Aspen pulled her thumb out of her mouth and wiped it on her shirt. Ollie put her arm around Aspen. She never did this as a rule. Aspen looked at her mother's face disbelievingly. Ollie pointed with one stub to the vitamin C bottle. It said: "200% of the adult minimum daily requirement." Aspen pulled away. The Crocker boys at the counter looked from Ollie's fingers to Aspen's thumb. But not till they were outside did they shriek and hoot.

On the way home in the truck Aspen wished her mother would hug her again now that they were alone. But Ollie's fingers were sealed to the wheel and her eyes blurred by the glasses were looking out from a place where no hugging ever happened. There was a real slow Volkswagen up ahead driven by a white-haired man. Ollie gave him the horn.

XIV

The list of activities on the bathroom door became more rigidly ordered . . . with even trips to the flush, snacks and rests, and conversations with the kids prescheduled . . . peanut butter and saltines: 3:15 . . . clear table: 6:30 . . . brush hair: 9:00 . . . and Ollie moved faster and faster and her cement-color hands and face were always across the yard somewhere or in the other room . . . singular of other people. And Jarrell looked in at her open bedroom door as he scooted Dane toward the bathroom for a wash . . . Ollie was *cleaning out the bureau again; the third time that week* . . . and she was doing it very fast.

In September there was a purple night and the children all loaded into the back of the truck. Randy strapped the baby into her seat in the cab. The air had a dry grasshopper smell and the truck bed was still hot from the day. Jarrell turned the key to the root-beer-color truck. "I'm getting a Needham!" he heard Timmy blat from the truck bed. He pulled on the headlights knob. He shifted into reverse. The truck creaked into motion. The rear wheel went up, then down. Then the front went up and down. Sliding into the truck lights was the yellow gown, the mashed gray arm, the black hair unbraided, the face unshowing but with a purple liquid going everywhere from out of that hair, the half-fingers wriggling just a little. She had been under the truck again.

From the deepest part of Jarrell Bean the scream would not stop even as he hobbled out of the truck. Oh, he feared to touch her, just rocked and rocked and hugged himself and howled. The children's high whines began. They covered Ollie like flies. As with blueberry jam their fingers were dipped a sticky purple. The herdsman reached for the twelve-year-old Aspen. He pulled at her. Her lids slid over icy eyes. Her breath was like carrots into his breath. He reached. And her frame folded into his hip.

LAURIE COLWIN

My Mistress

(FROM PLAYBOY)

MY WIFE IS PRECISE, elegant and well dressed, but the sloppiness of my mistress knows few bounds. Apparently, I am not the sort of man who acquires a stylish mistress like the mistresses in French movies. Those women rendezvous at the café of an expensive hotel and take their cigarette cases out of alligator handbags, or they meet their lovers on bridges in the late afternoon, wearing dashing capes. My mistress greets me in a pair of worn corduroy trousers, once green and now no color at all, a gray sweater and an old shirt of her younger brother's that has a frayed collar, and a pair of very old, broken shoes with tassels, the backs of which are held together with electrical tape. The first time I saw those shoes, I found them remarkable.

"What are those?" I said. "And why do you wear them?"

My mistress is a serious person, often glum, who likes to put as little inflection into a sentence as she can. She always answers a question.

"They used to be quite nice," she said. "I wore them out. Now I use them for slippers. These are my house shoes."

This person's name is Josephine Delielle, nicknamed Billy, called Josephine by her husband. I am Francis Clemens and no one but my mistress calls me Frank. The first time we went to bed, after months of longing and abstinence, my mistress turned to me, fixed me with an indifferent stare and said, "Well, well. In bed with Frank and Billy."

My constant image of Billy is of her pushing her hair off her forehead with an expression of exasperation. She frowns easily, often looks puzzled and is frequently irritated. In movies, men have mistresses who soothe and pet them, who are consoling, passionate and ornamental. But I have a mistress who, while she is passionate, is mostly grumpy. Traditional things mean nothing to her. She does not flirt, cajole or wear fancy underwear. She has taken to referring to me as her "little bit of fluff" and she refers to me as *her* mistress, as in the sentence "Before you became my mistress, I led a blameless life."

But in spite of this, I am secure in her affections. I know she loves me — not that she would ever come right out and tell me. She prefers the oblique line of approach. She may say something like, "Being in love with you is making me a nervous wreck." Or, "Falling in love with you is the hobby I took up instead of knitting or wood engraving."

Here is a typical encounter. It is between two and three o'clock in the afternoon. I arrive and ring the doorbell. The Delielles, who have a lot of money, live in the duplex apartment of an old town house. Billy opens the door. There I am, an older man in my tweed coat. My hands are cold. I'd like to get them underneath her ratty sweater. She looks me up and down. "Gosh, you look sweet," she might say, or, "My, what an adorable pair of trousers."

Sometimes she gets her coat and we go for a bracing walk. Sometimes we go upstairs to her study. Billy is an economist and teaches two classes at the business school. She writes for a couple of highbrow journals. Her husband, Grey, whom she met when she worked as a securities analyst, is a Wall Street wonder boy. They are one of those dashing couples, or at least they sound like one. I am no slouch, either. For years, I was an investment banker, and now I consult from my own home. I own a rare-book store — modern English and American first editions — which is excellently run for me so that I can visit and oversee it. I, too, write for a couple of highbrow journals. We have much in common, my mistress and I, or so it looks.

Billy's study is untidy. She likes to spread her papers out. Since her surroundings mean nothing to her, her study is bare of ornament and actually cheerless.

"What have you been doing all day?" she says.

I tell her. Breakfast with my wife, Vera; newspaper reading after Vera has gone to work; an hour or so on the telephone with clients; a walk over to my shop; more telephoning; a quick sandwich; her.

"You and I ought to go out for lunch someday," she says. "One should always take one's mistress out for lunch. We could go Dutch, thereby taking both mistresses at once."

"I try to take you for lunch," I say, "but you don't like to be taken out for lunch."

"Huh," utters Billy. She stares at her bookcase as if looking for a misplaced volume, and then she may say something like, "If I gave you a couple of dollars, would you take your clothes off?"

Instead, I take her into my arms. Her words are my signal that Grey is out of town. Often he is not, and then I merely get to kiss my mistress, which makes us both dizzy. To kiss her and know that we can go forward to what Billy tonelessly refers to as "the rapturous consummation" reminds me that in relief is joy.

After kissing for a few minutes, Billy closes the study door and we practically throw ourselves at each other. After the rapturous consummation has been achieved, during which I can look upon a mistress recognizable as such to me, my mistress will turn to me and, in a voice full of the attempt to stifle emotion, say something like, "Sometimes I don't understand how I got so fond of a beat-up old person such as you."

These are the joys adulterous love brings to me.

Billy is indifferent to a great many things: clothes, food, home decor. She wears neither perfume nor cologne. She uses what is used on infants: talcum powder and Ivory soap. She hates to cook and will never present me with an interesting postcoital snack. Her snacking habits are those, I have often remarked, of a late-nineteenth-century English clubman. Billy will get up all naked and disarrayed and present me with a mug of cold tea, a plate of hard wheat biscuits or a squirt of tepid soda from the siphon on her desk. As she sits under her quilt nibbling those resistant biscuits, she reminds me of a creature from another universe — the solar system that contains the alien features of her real life: her past, her marriage, why I am in her life and what she thinks of me.

I drink my soda, put on my clothes and, unless Vera is out of town, I go home to dinner. If Vera and Grey are out of town at the same time, Billy and I go out to dinner, during the course of which she either falls asleep or looks as if she is about to. Then I take her home, go home and have a large, steadying drink.

I was not entirely a stranger to adulterous love when I met Billy. I have explained this to her. In all long marriages, I expound, there are certain lapses. The look on Billy's face as I lecture is one of either amusement or contempt or both. The dinner party you are invited to as an extra man when your wife is away, I tell her. You are asked to take the extra woman, whose husband is away, home in a taxi. The divorced friend of yours and your wife's who invites you for a drink one night, and so on. These fallings into bed are the friendliest things in the world, I add. I look at my mistress.

"I see," she says. "Just like patting a dog."

My affair with Billy, as she well knows, is nothing of the sort. I call her every morning. I see her almost every afternoon. On the days she teaches, she calls me. We are as faithful as the Canada goose, more or less. She is an absolute fact of my life. When not at work, and when not with her, my thoughts rest upon the subject of her as easily as you might lay a hand on a child's head. I conduct a mental life with her when we are apart. Thinking about her is like entering a study or office, a room to which only I have access.

I, too, am part of a dashing couple. My wife is an industrial designer who has dozens of commissions and consults to everyone. Our two sons are grown up. One is a lawyer and one is a journalist. The lawyer is married to a lawyer and the journalist keeps company with a dancer. Our social life is a mixture of our friends, our children and their friends. What a lively table we must be, all of us together. So I tell my mistress. She gives me a baleful look.

"We get plenty of swell types in for meals," she says. I know this is true and I know that Billy, unlike my gregarious and party-giving wife, thinks that there is no hell more hellish than the hell of social life. She has made up a tuneless little chant, like a football cheer, to describe it. It goes:

> They invited us
> We invited them
> They invited us
> We invited them
> They invited us
> We invited them.

Billy and I met at a reception to celebrate the twenty-fifth anniversary of one of the journals to which we are both occasional contributors. We fell into a spirited conversation during which Billy asked me if that reception weren't the most boring thing I had ever been to. I said it wasn't, by a long shot. Billy said, "I can't stand these things where you have to stand up and be civilized. They make me itch. People either yawn, itch or drool when they get bored. Which do you do?"

I said I yawned.

"Huh," said Billy. "You don't look much like a drooler. Let's get out of here.

This particular interchange is always brought up when intentionality is discussed. Did she mean to pick me up? Did I look available? And so on. Out on the street, we revealed that while we were both married, both of our spouses were out of town on business. Having made that clear, we went out to dinner and talked shop.

After dinner, Billy said why didn't I come have a drink or a cup of tea? I did not know what to make of this invitation. I remembered that young people are more casual about these things and that a cup of tea probably meant a cup of tea. My reactions to this offer are also discussed when cause is under discussion. Did I want her to seduce me? Did I mean to seduce her? Did this mean that I, having just met her, lusted for her?

Of her house, Billy said, "We don't have good taste or bad taste. We have no taste." Her living room had no style whatsoever, but it was comfortable enough. There was a portrait of what looked like an ancestor over the fireplace. It was not a room that revealed a thing about its occupants except solidity and a lack of decorative inspiration. Billy made herself a cup of tea and gave me a drink. We continued our conversation, and when Billy began to look sleepy, I left.

After that, we made a pass at social life. We invited them for dinner, along with some financial types, a painter and our lawyer son. At this gathering, Billy was mute, and Grey, a very clever fellow, chatted interestingly. Billy did not seem at all comfortable, but the rest of us had a fairly good time. Then they invited us, along with some financial types they knew and a music critic and his book-designer wife. At this dinner, Billy looked tired. It was clear that cooking was a strain on her. She told me later that she was the type who, when forced to cook, did every little thing, like making and straining the veal stock. From the moment she entered the kitchen, she looked longingly forward to the time when all the dishes would be clean and put away and the guests would all have gone home.

Then we invited them, but Grey had a bad cold and they had to cancel. After that, Billy and I ran into each other one day when we were both dropping off articles at the same journal, and we had lunch. She said she was looking for an article of mine and two days later, after rummaging in my files, I found it. Since I was going to be in her neighborhood, I dropped it off. She wrote me a note about this article, and then I called her to discuss it further. This necessitated a lunch meeting. Then she said she was sending me a book I had said I wanted to read, and then I sent her a book, and so it went.

One evening, I stopped by to have a chat with Billy and Grey. Vera was in California and I had been out to dinner in Billy's part of town. I called her from a pay phone, and when I got there, it turned out that Grey was out of town, too. Had I been secretly hoping that this would be the case? Billy had been working in her study and without thinking about it, she led me up the stairs. I followed her, and at the door of her study, I kissed her. She kissed me right back and looked awful about it, too.

"Nothing but a kiss!" I said, rather frantically. My mistress was silent.

"A friendly kiss," I said.

My mistress gave me the sort of look that is supposed to make your blood freeze, and said, "Your friends must be very advanced. Do you kiss them all this way?"

"It won't happen again," I said. "It was all a mistake."

Billy gave me a stare so bleak and hard that I had no choice but to kiss her, and that, except for the fact that it took us a couple of months to get into bed, was the beginning of that.

That was a year ago, and it is impossible for me to figure out what is going on in Billy's life that has me into it. She once remarked that in her opinion, there is frequently too little kissing in marriage, through which frail pinprick was a microscopic dot of light thrown on the subject of her marriage, or was it? She is like a red Indian and says nothing at all, nor does she ever slip.

I, however, do slip, and I am made aware of this by the grim, sidelong glance I am given. I once told Billy that until I met her, I had never given kissing much thought — she is an insatiable kisser for an unsentimental person — and I was rewarded for this utterance by a well-raised eyebrow and a rather frightening look of registration.

From time to time, I feel it is wise to tell Billy how well Vera and I get along.

"Swell," says Billy. "I'm thrilled for you."

"Well, it's true," I say.

"I'm sure it's true," says Billy. "I'm sure there's no reason in the world why you come and see me almost every day. It's probably just an involuntary action, like sneezing."

"But you don't understand," I say. "Vera has men friends. I have women friends. The first principle of a good marriage is freedom."

"Oh, I see," says Billy. "You sleep with your other women friends in the morning and come over here in the afternoon. What a lot of stamina you have for an older person."

One day this conversation had unexpected results. I said how well Vera and I got along, and Billy looked unadornedly hurt.

"God hates a mingy lover," she said. "Why don't you just say that you're in love with me and that it frightens you and have done with it?"

An unexpected lump rose in my throat.

"Maybe you're not in love with me," said Billy in her flattest voice. "It's nothing to me."

I said, "I am in love with you."

"Well, there you are," said Billy.

My curiosity about Grey is a huge, violent dog on a very tight leash. He is four years older than Billy, a somewhat sweet-looking boy with rumpled hair who looks as if he is working out problems in higher math as you talk to him. He wears wire-rimmed glasses and his shirttail hangs out. He has the body of a young boy and the air of a genius or someone constantly preoccupied by the intense pressure of a rarefied mental life. Together he and Billy look not so much like husband and wife as like coconspirators. How often does she sleep with him? What are her feelings about him?

I begin preliminary queries by hemming and hawing. "Umm," I say, "it's, umm, it's a little hard for me to picture your life with Grey. I mean, it's hard to picture your everyday life."

"What you want to know is how often we sleep together and how much I like it," says Billy.

Well, she has me there, because that is exactly what I want to know.

"Tell you what," says my mistress. "Since you're so forthcoming about *your* life. We'll write down all about our home fronts on little slips of paper and then we'll exchange them. How's that?"

Well, she has me there, too. What we are doing in each other's lives is an unopened book.

I know how she contrasts to my wife: My wife is affable, full of conversation, loves a dinner party and is interested in clothes, food, home decor and the issues of the day. She loves to entertain, is sought out in times of crisis by her numerous friends and has a kind or original word for everyone. She is methodical, hard-working and does not fall asleep in restaurants. How I contrast to Grey is another matter, a matter about which I know nothing. I am considerably older and perhaps I appeal to some father longing in my mistress. Billy says Grey is a genius — a thrilling quality but not one that has any real relevance to life with another person. He wishes, according to his wife, that he were the conductor of a symphony orchestra, and for this reason, he is given scores, tickets and batons for his birthday. He has studied Russian and can sing Russian songs.

"He sounds so charming," I say, "that I can't imagine why you would want to know someone like me." Billy's response to this is pure silence.

Once in a while, she quotes him on the subject of the stock market. If life were not so complicated, I might very well be calling him up for tips. I hunt for signs of him on Billy — jewelry, marks, phrases. I know that he reads astronomy books for pleasure, enjoys cross-country skiing and likes to travel. Billy says she loves him, but she also says she loves several paintings in the Museum of Modern Art.

"If you love him so much," I say, taking a page from her book, "why are you hanging around with me?"

" 'Hanging around,' " Billy says in a bored monotone.

"Well?"

" 'I am large and contain multitudes,' " she says, misquoting a line from Walt Whitman.

This particular conversation took place en route to a cottage in Vermont that I had rented for a week when both Grey and Vera were going to be away for ten days.

I remember clearly with what happy anticipation I presented the idea of this cottage to her.

"Guess what," I said.

"You're pregnant," said Billy.

"I have rented a little cottage for us, in Vermont. For a week, when Grey and Vera are away on their long trips. We can go there and watch the leaves turn."

"Great," said Billy faintly. She looked away and didn't speak for some time.

"We don't have to go, Billy," I said. "I only sent the check yesterday. I can cancel it."

There appeared to be tears in my mistress' eyes.

"No," she said. "Don't do that. I'll split it with you."

"You don't seem pleased," I said.

"Pleased," said Billy. "Being pleased doesn't strike me as the appropriate response to the idea of going off to a love nest with your lover."

"What *is* the appropriate response?" I said.

"Oh," said Billy, her voice now blithe, "sorrow, guilt, craving, glee, horror, anticipation."

Well, she can run, but she can't hide. My mistress is given away from time to time by her own expressions. No matter how hard she tries to suppress the visible evidence of what she feels, she is not always successful. Her eyes turn color, becoming dark and rather smoky. This is as good as a plain declaration of love. Billy's mental life, her grumpiness, her irritability, her crotchets are like static that from time to time gives way to a clear signal, just as you often hit a pure band of music on a car radio after turning the dial through a lot of chaotic squawk.

In French movies of a certain period, the lovers are seen leaving the woman's apartment or house. His car is parked on an attractive side street. She is carrying a leather valise and is wearing a silk scarf around her neck. He is carrying the wicker basket she has packed with their picnic lunch. They will have the sort of food lovers have for lunch in these movies: a roast chicken, a bottle of champagne and a cheese wrapped up in leaves. Needless to say, when Billy and I finally left to go to our love nest, no such sight presented itself to me. First of all, she met me around the corner from my garage after a number of squabbles about whose car to take. My car is bigger, so I won. I found her on an unattractive side street, which featured a rent-a-car place and an animal hospital. Second of all, she was wearing an old skirt, her old jacket and was carrying a canvas overnight bag. No lacy underwear would be withdrawn from it, I knew. My mistress buys her white-cotton undergarments at the five-and-ten-cent store. She wears an old T-shirt of Grey's to sleep in, she tells me.

For lunch we had hamburgers — no romantic rural inn or picnic spot for us — at Hud's Burger Hut on Route 22.

"We go to some swell places," Billy said.

As we drew closer to our destination, Billy began to fidget, reminding me that having her along was sometimes not unlike traveling with a small child.

In the nearest town to our love nest, we stopped and bought coffee, milk, sugar and corn flakes. Because I am a domestic animal and not a mere savage, I remembered to buy bread, butter, cheese, salami, eggs and a number of cans of tomato soup.

Billy surveyed these items with a raised eyebrow.

"This is the sort of stuff you buy when you intend to stay indoors and kick up a storm of passion," she said.

It was an off-year Election Day — Congressional and Senate races were being run. We had both voted, in fact, before taking off. Our love nest had a radio I instantly switched on to hear if there were any early returns while we gave the place a cursory glance and put the groceries away. Then we flung ourselves onto the unmade bed for which I had thoughtfully remembered to pack sheets.

When our storm of passion had subsided, my mistress stared impassively at the ceiling.

"In bed with Frank and Billy," she intoned. "It was Election Day, and Frank and Billy were once again in bed. Election returns meant nothing to them. The future of their great nation was inconsequential; so busy were they flinging themselves at each other, they could barely be expected to think for one second of any larger issue. The subjects to which these trained economists could have spoken, such as inflationary spirals or deficit budgeting, were as mere dust."

"Shut up, Billy," I said.

She did shut up. She put on my shirt and went off to the kitchen. When she returned, she had two cups of coffee and a plate of toasted-cheese sandwiches on a tray. With the exception of her dinner party, this was the first meal I had ever had at her hands.

"I'm starving," she said, getting under the covers. We polished off our snack, propped up with pillows. I asked Billy if she might like a second cup of coffee and she gave me a look of remorse and desire that made my head spin.

"Maybe you wanted to go out for dinner," she said. "You like a proper dinner." Then she burst into tears. "I'm sorry," she said. These were words I had never heard her speak before.

"Sorry?" I said. "Sorry for what?"

"I didn't ask you what you wanted to do," my mistress said. "You might have wanted to take a walk, or go for a drive, or look around the house, or make the bed."

I stared at her.

"I don't want a second cup of coffee," Billy said. "Do you?"

I got her drift and did not get out of bed. I tried to do an imitation of a man giving in to a woman, because, in fact, my thirst for her embarrassed me and I did not mind imagining that it was her thirst I was being kind enough to quench, but the forthrightness of her desire for me melted my heart.

During that week, none of my expectations came to pass. We did not, for example, have long talks about our respective marriages or our future together or apart. We did not discover what our domestic life might be like. We lived like graduate students, or mice, and not like normal people at all, but like lovers. We kept odd hours and lived off sandwiches. We stayed in bed and both were glad that it rained four days out of five. When the sun came out, we went for a walk and watched the leaves turn. From time to time, I would switch on the radio to find out what the news commentators were saying about the election results.

"Because of this historic time," Billy said, "you will never be able to forget me. It is a rule of life that care must be taken in choosing whom one will be in bed with during Great Moments in History. You are now stuck with me and this week of important Congressional elections twined in your mind forever."

It was in the car on the way home that the subject of what we were doing together came up. It was twilight and we had both been rather silent.

"This is the end of the line," said Billy.

"What do you mean?" I said. "Do you mean you want to break this up?"

"No," said Billy. "It would be nice, though, wouldn't it?"

"No, it would not be nice," I said.

"I think it would," said Billy. "Then I wouldn't spend all my time wondering what we are doing together when I could be thinking about other things, like the future of the dollar."

"What do you think we are doing together?" I said.

"It's simple," said Billy. "Some people have dogs or kitty cats. You're my pet."

"Come on."

"O.K., you're right. Those are only child substitutes. You're my child substitute until I can make up my mind about having a child."

At this, my blood does freeze. Whose child does she want to have?

Every now and then, when overcome with tenderness — on these occasions naked, carried away and looking at each other with sweetness in our eyes — my mistress and I smile dreamily and realize that if we dwelled together for more than a week, in the real world and not in some love nest, we would soon learn to hate each other. It would never work. We both know it. She is too relentlessly dour and too fond of silence. I prefer false cheer to no cheer and I like conversation over dinner no matter what. Furthermore, we would never have proper meals, and although I cannot cook, I like to dine. I would soon resent her lack of interest in domestic arrangements and she would resent me for resenting her. Furthermore, Billy is a slob. She does not leave the towels lying on the bathroom floor, but she throws them over the shower curtain any old way, instead of folding them or hanging them properly so they can dry. It is things like this — it is actually the symbolic content of things like this — that squash out romance over a period of time.

As for Billy, she often sneers at me. She finds many of my opinions quaint. She laughs up her sleeve at me, often actually unbuttoning her cuff button (when the button is actually on the cuff) to demonstrate laughing up her sleeve. She thinks I am an old-time domestic fascist. She refers to me as "an old-style heterosexual throwback" or "old hetero" because I like to pay for dinner, open car doors and often call her at night when Grey is out of town to make sure she is safe. The day the plumber came to fix a leak in the sink, I called several times.

"He's gone," Billy said, "and he left big, greasy paw prints all over me." She found this funny, but I did not.

After a while, I believe I would be driven nuts and she would come to loathe me. My household is well run and well regulated. I like routine and I like things to go along smoothly. We employ a flawless person by the name of Mrs. Ivy Castle, who has been flawlessly running our house for some time. She is an excellent housekeeper and a marvelous cook. Our relations with her are formal.

The Delielles employ a feckless person called Mimi-Ann Browning, who comes in once a week to push the dust around. Mimi-Ann hates routine and schedules and is constantly changing the days of the people she works for. It is quite something to hear Billy on the telephone with her.

"Oh, Mimi-Ann," she will say, "please don't switch me, I beg you. I have to feed some friends of Grey's and the house is really disgusting. Please, Mimi. I'll do anything. I'll do your mother-in-law's tax return. I'll be your eternal slave. *Please.* Oh, thank you, Mimi. Thank you a million times."

Now, why, I ask myself, does my mistress never speak to me like that?

In that sad twilight on the way home from our week together, I asked myself, as I am always asking myself: Could I exist in some ugly flat with my cheerless mistress? I could not, as my mistress was the first to point out.

She said that the expression on my face at the sight of the towels thrown over the shower-curtain rod was similar to what you might find on the face of a vegetarian walking through an abattoir. She said that the small doses we got of each other made it possible for us to have a love affair but that a taste of ordinary life would do us both in. She correctly pointed out that our only real common interest was each other, since we had such vast differences of opinion on the subject of economic theory. Furthermore, we were not simply lovers, nor were we mere friends, and since we were not going to end up together, there was nothing for it.

I was silent.

"Face it," said my tireless mistress, "we have no *raison d'être.*"

There was no disputing this.

I said, "If we have no *raison d'être*, Billy, then what are we to do?"

These conversations flare up like tropical storms. The climate is always right for them. It is simply a question of when they will occur.

"Well?" I said.

"I don't know," said my mistress, who generally has a snappy answer for everything.

A wave of fatherly affection and worry came over me. I said, in a voice so drenched with concern it caused my mistress to scowl like a child about to receive an injection, "Perhaps you should think about this more seriously, Billy. You and Grey are really just starting out. Vera and I have been married a long, long time. I think I am more a disruption in your life than you are in mine."

"Wanna bet?" said Billy.

"Perhaps we should see each other less," I said. "Perhaps we should part."

"O.K., let's part," said Billy. "You go first." Her face was set and I entertained myself with the notion that she was trying not to burst into tears. Then she said, "What are you going to do all day after we part?"

This is not a subject to which I wanted to give much thought.

"Isn't our *raison d'être* that we're fond of each other?" I said. "I'm awfully fond of you."

"Gee, that's interesting," Billy said. "You're fond of me. I *love* you." Of course, she would not look me in the eye and say it.

"Well, I love you," I said. "I just don't quite know what to do about it."

"Whatever our status quos are," Billy said, "they are being maintained like mad."

This silenced me. Billy and I have the world right in place. Nothing flutters, changes or moves. Whatever is being preserved in our lives is safely preserved. It is quite true, as Billy, who believes in function, points out, that we are in each other's life for a reason, but neither of us will state the reason. Nevertheless, although there are some cases in which love is not a good or sufficient excuse for anything, the fact is, love is undeniable.

Yes, love is undeniable and that is the tricky point. It is one of the sobering realizations of adult life that love is often not a propellent. Thus, in those romantic movies, the tender mistress stays married to her stuffy husband — the one with the mustache and the stiff tweeds — while the lover is seen walking through the countryside with his long-suffering wife and faithful dog. It often seems that the function of romance is to give people something romantic to think about.

The question is: If it is true, as my mistress says, that she is going to stay with Grey and I am going to stay with Vera, why is it that we are together every chance we get?

There was, of course, an explanation for this and my indefat-
igable mistress came up with it, God bless her.

"It's an artistic impulse," she said. "It takes us out of reality
and gives us a secret context all our own."

"Oh, I see," I said. "It's only art."

"Don't get in a huff," Billy said. "We're in a very unusual
situation. It has to do with limited doting, restricted thrall and
situational adoration."

"Oh, how interesting," I said. "Are doting, thrall and adoration things you actually feel for me?"

"Could be," said Billy. "But, actually, I was speaking for you."

Every adult knows that facts must be faced. In adult life, it often
seems that's all there is. Prior to our week together, the un-
guarded moments between us had been kept to a minimum.
Now they came rather more frequently. That week together
haunted us. It dogged our heels. It made us long for and dread
— what an unfortunate combination! — each other.

One evening, I revealed to her how I sometimes feel as I
watch her walk up the stairs to the door of her house. I feel she
is walking into her real and still fairly young life. She will leave
me in the dust, I think. I think of all the things that have not
yet happened to her, that have not yet gone wrong, and I think
of her life with Grey, which is still mostly unlived.

One afternoon, she told me how it makes her feel when she
thinks of my family table — with Vera and our sons and our
daughter-in-law and our daughter-in-law-to-be, of our years of
shared meals, of all that lived life. Billy described this feeling as
a band around her head and a hot pressure in the area of her
heart. I, of course, merely get a lump in my throat. Why do
these admittings take place at twilight or at dusk, in the gloom-
iest light, when everything looks dirty, eerie, faded or inevitable?

Our conversation comes to a dead halt, like a horse balking
before a hurdle, on the issue of what we want. I have tried my
best to formulate what it is I want from Billy, but I have not
gotten very far. Painful consideration has brought forth this
revelation: I want her not ever to stop being. This is as close as
grammar or reflection will allow.

One day, the horse will jump over the hurdle and the end will come. The door will close. Perhaps Billy will do the closing. She will decide she wants a baby, or Grey will be offered a job in London, or Billy will get a job in Boston and the Delielles will move. Or perhaps Vera will come home one evening and say that she longs to live in Paris or San Francisco and the Clemenses will move. What will happen then?

Perhaps my mistress is right. A love affair is like a work of art. The large store of references, and jokes, the history of our friendship, our week together in Vermont, our numberless telephone calls, this edifice, this monument, this civilization known only to and constructed by us will be — what will it be? Billy once read to me an article in an anthropological journal about the last Coast Salish Indian to speak Wintun. All the others of his tribe were dead. That is how I would feel, deprived of Billy.

The awful day will doubtless come. It is like thinking about the inevitability of nuclear war. But as for now, I continue to ring her doorbell. Her greeting is delivered in her bored monotone. "Oh, it's you," she will say. "How sweet you look."

I will follow her up the stairs to her study and there we will hurl ourselves at each other. I will reflect, as I always do, how very bare the setting for these encounters is. Not a picture on the wall. Not an ornament. Even the quilt that keeps the chill off us on the couch is faded.

In one of her snootier moments, my mistress said to me, "My furnishings are interior. I care about what I think about."

As I gather her into my arms, I cannot help imagining all that interior furniture, those hard-edged things she thinks about, whatever is behind her silence, whatever, in fact, her real story is.

She may turn to me and in a moment of tenderness say, "What a cute boy." This remark always sounds exotic to me — no one has ever addressed me this way, especially not at my age and station.

I imagine that someday she will turn to me and, with some tone in her voice I have never heard before, say, "We can't see each other anymore." We will both know the end has come. But, meanwhile, she is right close by. After a fashion, she is mine. I watch her closely to catch the look of true love that every once in a while overtakes her. She knows I am watching, and she knows the effect her look has. "A baby could take candy from you," she says.

Our feelings have edges and spines and prickles like cactus, or a porcupine. Our parting when it comes will not be simple, either. Depicted, it would look like one of those medieval beasts that has fins, fur, scales, feathers, claws, wings and horns. In a world apart from anyone else, we are Frank and Billy, with no significance to anyone but the other. Oh, the terrible privacy and loneliness of love affairs.

Under the quilt with our arms interlocked, I look into my mistress' eyes. They are dark and full of concealed feeling. If we hold each other close enough, that darkness is held at bay. The mission of the lover is, after all, to love. I can look at Billy and see clear back to the first time we met, to our hundreds of days together, to her throwing the towels over the shower-curtain rod, to each of her gestures and intonations. She is the road I have traveled to her, and I am hers.

Oh, Billy! Oh, art! Oh, memory!

JOSEPH EPSTEIN

The Count and the Princess

(FROM THE HUDSON REVIEW)

COUNT PETER KINSKI had of course dropped the title from his name when he came to live in the United States at the age of twenty-two. But he had never quite succeeded in dropping the idea of himself as an aristocrat; and while his own stay in America was now more than three decades long, and he had become an American citizen, he continued to think himself a visitor. Perhaps visitor-observer would be more precise, for Count Kinski fancied himself rather in the tradition of those other aristocratic observers of America, Tocqueville and Lord Bryce. (Although he had not yet actually written a line of it, for the past eight years he had been gathering material for a work he had tentatively entitled "America in Her Decline.") Yet unlike either Tocqueville or Bryce, Count Kinski was tossed by circumstances into the chirring of local life — in the City of Chicago, of all places — riding buses and subways, shopping for and preparing his own meals, paying bills and earning money to pay them by teaching political theory at a city college on the northwest side. The Count alternated in his feelings about all this: sometimes he felt an almost unbearable bitterness because he had to undergo such indignities; but sometimes he felt proud because he had been able to survive them.

Certainly he had not been born for such a life. His childhood had been spent on the family estate, seventy kilometers to the south of Lodz, where he was brought up by various French governesses and educated by his tutor, a German Tolstoyan, Herr Kügler, in foreign languages, rudimentary science, and

history. Before the Nazis swept through Poland, he had been
sent off to school in Switzerland. He returned briefly — oh, so
briefly — at the end of the war to the world he had known of
large hunting parties, a household staff of more than twenty
servants, and his father's, the old Count's, life of leisurely ele-
gance. But no sooner had he begun to settle into the life for
which he was intended than the Communists had taken over
Poland. Although an aristocrat, the old Count was a liberal in
politics and a Westerner in culture — exactly the sort of man
the new regime wished to remove. Peter and his mother were
packed off to Paris, where they installed themselves in the Ritz,
there later to be joined by his father. But before he could join
them, his father, under the strain of this, his second reversal of
fortune, died of a heart attack. Peter (now Count) Kinski and
his mother were left stranded at the Ritz, with very little money
and only the jewelry she had managed to smuggle out of Poland
at their departure.

Between them Peter and his mother decided upon an aca-
demic career for him. He enrolled as a doctoral candidate in
political philosophy at the University of Chicago. The plan was
for him to go off to America first. His mother would remain in
Europe, in the hope of salvaging something from the family's
latest disaster. But it came to nothing, and before she could join
her son Countess Kinski suffered a stroke, and died less than
two weeks later. One of the Kinski family's agents sent on the
money her jewelry had fetched to Peter — some $16,000 in
American currency. She was buried in Père Lachaise Cemetery.
Peter never knew where his father was buried, or if he was
buried at all. An only child, he was the last of his line, the final
Count Kinski of a family that traced its descent back to the
thirteenth century.

Even at the University of Chicago, that most cosmopolitan of
American universities, he was an oddity. In an otherwise bohe-
mian graduate student setting, he wore suits of an English cut,
carried a walking stick, read Proust. He lived alone at International House, among students from India and Nigeria and veterans from World War II on the GI Bill. He studied under Leo
Straus, and chose an ambitious dissertation on Thucydides and
the origins of totalitarianism in Sparta. It was a dissertation he

was never to finish, for before it was really under way his money had all but run out, and he was forced to take a teaching job at the school at which he had now been teaching for more than twenty years.

After leaving the University of Chicago the Count moved to the somewhat rundown Chicago neighborhood called Rogers Park. He rented a one-bedroom apartment in an older building on Pratt Avenue less than a block from Lake Michigan. Slowly he acquired furniture, bought many books, a few good rugs. When his English clothes wore out, he bought American ones that roughly — rather too roughly for his taste — approximated them. His only palpable evidence of his old life was four undershirts, with the Kinski family crest sewn into them by Panushka, an elderly family maid who had helped to raise him as a child; these he kept in a bottom drawer of a mahogany chiffonier he had purchased at a Salvation Army store.

Living among his books and pipes, taking the El and then a bus to the college three days each week, cooking his meals, the ingredients for which he bought at a locally famous German delicatessen called Kuhn's, he somehow reached his fiftieth year. He had grown heavier and lost much of his hair. He still carried his walking stick. He read, attended the Chicago Symphony downtown, went occasionally to the movies, kept no television set nor ever learned to drive a car. By carefully husbanding his salary — he taught most summers; what else was there for him to do? — he was able to afford himself a holiday in Europe once every four or five years, where he could speak the French and German that had never left him. Christmas Eves he took himself, with the aid of the El and two buses, to a Polish restaurant in the suburb of Berwyn, where he ate a traditional meal of duck and dumplings and spoke Polish with the owners.

At the college he made no real friends. When he first arrived there an attempt had been made to throw him together with a teacher of Russian, also an émigré, named Dimitri Suslovich, who spoke Russian with an atrocious Ukrainian accent. To Americans a Slav was a Slav, and how could they know the age-old enmity between Poles and Russians? Suslovich, though rough-cut, doubtless of peasant origins, was a decent enough

fellow in his boorish way, but the Count, an admirer of Santayana and Henry Adams, a reader of Schopenhauer and the Duc
de Saint-Simon, could not hope to find any common ground
with him. To himself he laughed to think of this Suslovich
teaching young students to speak Russian with a heavy Ukrainian accent, which was tantamount to teaching English with a
heavy Yiddish accent. But no one else at the college could know
this, of course, and he was not about to remark upon it.

In his way Count Kinski loved America. He would always be
grateful to the country for providing him a safe port after the
storms of his last years in Europe. But grateful though he was
to this country, there were things about it, small things, to which
he could never reconcile himself. Above all, the familiarity of
Americans he could not, after all these years, quite manage. The
waitresses, for example, who would set a cup of tea before him,
then ask, "Anything else, honey?" Or the occasional Negro student who would address him as "man," as in "You gonna want
that term paper typed, man?" The man with whom he shared
his office at the college seemed to specialize in such familiarities.
Six years ago, when he moved into the Count's office, upon
introduction he said, "Nice to know you, Pete." The Count continued to address him as Professor Ginsberg, and only after
three years of sharing an office could he bring himself, after
insistent pleas, to call him by his first name, Barney. Meanwhile,
Barney Ginsberg had advanced to calling him, the Count,
"babes." "How're you making it, babes?" he would say when
Count Kinski arrived at the office in the morning.

Ginsberg was a puzzle to the Count. He was a man of the
Count's own age; in fact, he was fifty-three, a year older. Yet he
seemed to dress like a boy. He taught in blue jeans; he wore a
variety of caps, sometimes a baseball cap, sometimes a Greek
fisherman's cap, sometimes a tennis visor. He had long grey
sideburns and a drooping mustache in the style of the cossacks.
He seemed not so much to wear clothes as to sport a number of
costumes, disguises. He was a sociologist by training, with a
Ph.D. from New York University, but he taught courses with
titles that sounded like magazine articles: Blacks and Jews, The
Holocaust and the Suburbs, Sex and the Changing Middle
Class. His students called him by his first name. Once, when the

Count was in the office, a young girl came to see Ginsberg with tears in her eyes; as the Count was leaving the room, to give his office-mate privacy, he heard the girl mention that she was pregnant and ask what he intended to do about it.

Barney Ginsberg was a popular teacher; Count Kinski, as he himself knew, was not. If many of the courses he taught had not been required for a degree in political science, the numbers of students who enrolled for his courses would have been even smaller than they were. And there were sometimes as few as seven or nine students in his courses. He taught the only way he knew how — from on high. He lectured for the full fifty minutes: on Locke, Rousseau, Montesquieu, Marx, his beloved Tocqueville. Sometimes he would close his eyes and imagine himself delivering these lectures at Oxford or the Sorbonne. Then he would open them to note that a few of his students had closed theirs, to dream surely of places far distant from these citadels of learning. He had a reputation as a hard grader. He filled the margins of his students' papers, questioning their inchoate ideas, correcting their English. They must have thought him a little mad.

They, his students, were themselves a strange lot. Most of them worked, and were not students full-time. They wanted, for their various reasons, a degree, perhaps to get a better job. Many were Negroes; a few were Mexican. A number of them were housewives whose children were grown, or at least old enough for them to return to school. Count Kinski of course encouraged no intimacy between them and himself. When they came into his office, as one or another occasionally did, to question him about a term paper, he always addressed them as Miss or Mister; they called him Professor. Over the years he had had a few bright students: a Japanese boy named Bob Anoba, who went on to law school; a Swedish girl named Karen Lingren, who went on to graduate studies at the University of Chicago. But he, the Count, had lost touch with them.

Was Mrs. Sheila Skolnik to be another of his memorable students? It was difficult to say, though it seemed unlikely. This was the second of his courses she had taken; autumn term she had written a quite respectable paper for his course in Political

Theory. No power of thought, you understand, but well organized, neatly typed, largely grammatical. Under the current dispensation, such small blessings loomed large. She had made an appointment to discuss her paper for the current semester's course in Continental Political Thinkers. She had told him she wished to write on the subject of Tocqueville and the Ancien Régime. It was late afternoon. She was due for her appointment twenty minutes ago. The Count had given up on her, and had begun to pack his briefcase. Across the room, Barney Ginsberg, feet on his desk, was reading a paperback, a detective story with rather a lurid cover.

A knock on the door. "Enter," said the Count.

"Excuse my being so late," said Mrs. Skolnik. A Jewess, in her early thirties, she was tall, had thick dark hair but blue eyes, was slender but of ample bosom. Ginsberg dropped his feet from the top of his desk at her entrance, set down his detective story, and stared.

"I am very sorry, Professor Kinski," she said. "Is there still time for our meeting?"

"I fear not," said the Count. "My bus leaves in ten minutes. Perhaps on Friday we can meet."

"Can I drive you home, Professor? Maybe we could talk about my paper on the way."

"Very well, Mrs. Skolnik," said the Count, feeling there was perhaps something slightly irregular about this. "My apartment is on Pratt Avenue, near the lake. Are you certain I shall not be taking you out of your regular way?"

She said not at all. The Count put on his overcoat. As he held the door open for his student, he bade Professor Ginsberg good evening.

"Right on, Pete," said Ginsberg, and, though he could not be certain, the Count thought he saw him wink.

Mrs. Skolnik had a red sports car, a Japanese model, and getting into it, his legs stretched straight out, his briefcase on his lap, the Count felt as if he were sitting on the ground. They talked about Mrs. Skolnik's paper. The Count suggested books she might consult; she asked questions about the paper's length, its deadline, what he expected it to accomplish. The subject was quickly exhausted, and a long ride still lay ahead. The Count would have been perfectly happy to remain silent the remainder of the way, but felt that it would not perhaps be courteous to do so.

"What does your husband do, Mrs. Skolnik, if I may ask?"

"Oh," she said, "Larry was a dentist."

"I am sorry," said the Count, "I did not know you were a widow."

"I'm not," she said.

"But you spoke of your husband in the past tense?"

"I guess I did. I didn't notice. No, Larry and I were divorced four years ago."

"Have you children?" the Count asked.

"Yes, two. A boy and a girl, Ronnie and Melissa. They're both in school now, which makes it possible for me to go back to school. I'd like eventually to go to law school. That's why I'm majoring in political science."

"I see," said the Count.

"I live with my parents now. My mother's being able to watch the kids is a great help. Larry still sees them every Sunday. But it was tough on them for a while, not having their father with them."

"I see," said the Count, who felt the conversation getting rather more intimate than he liked. He asked her where her parents lived, and they fell into a general discussion of neighborhoods in Chicago and its suburbs. Her parents lived in the suburb called Northbrook, a relatively new and rather wealthy one. When she pulled up in front of his apartment building, she remarked on how nice it must be to live so close to the lake. The Count agreed that it was, especially in summer, then crept out of the sports car, thanked her, and waved good-by from a crouching position as she drove off.

The day's mail brought a copy of the Zurich monthly *Schweizer Monatshefte,* which he read with his evening meal: herring in aspic, a Hungarian sausage and green beans, with a torte and tea for dessert. After clearing and washing his evening's dishes, he poured himself a digestif, put some Mozart quartets on his phonograph, and read in Santayana's *Dominations and Powers.* Towards eleven o'clock, as was his custom, he retired to bed, there, as was distinctly not his custom, to dream of making unspeakably passionate love to Sheila Skolnik.

•

When he arrived at his office on Friday morning, Barney Ginsberg was already there. He seemed to be dressed in the outfit of
a stevedore. He wore blue jeans, a thick sweater with a high
neck, the sleeves pushed up on his hairy forearms, and a blue
wool cap that he had on indoors.

"So?" Ginsberg said.

"Pardon?" said the Count.

"So — did you boff her?"

"Sir?" asked the Count.

"Forget it, babes. I already know the answer. No chance. I
already know the type, all too well. She's a princess, if ever there
was one."

"A princess?" The Count's interest was piqued.

"A Jewish Princess, babes, for Christ's sake."

"I see," said the Count, not really seeing at all, but not wishing
to carry on the conversation any further.

Sheila Skolnik was not in class that day; nor was she in class
again on Monday. Wednesday, when the papers were due, she
called the Count on his office phone.

"I'm sorry to have missed class," she said. "I've had the flu.
But I've finished my paper. Can I deliver it to you tonight at
your apartment?"

"That is not truly necessary, Mrs. Skolnik. If you have it to
me in class on Friday, that will be sufficient."

"But I don't really want to be late. Will you be at home tonight?"

"Yes, but . . ."

"Good. I'll be there around eight."

"Yes, but . . ." She had already hung up.

"Most irregular," Count Kinski muttered, "most irregular." He
cleared his dishes, poured the remains of the consommé from
the small pot into a jar, wrapped the remaining slice of West-
phalian ham for the refrigerator, returned the heavy textured
Lithuanian bread to his bread box. "Most irregular."

The Count decided to take his tea this evening in his wing
chair, the chair in which he sat most evenings to do his reading.
It was 7:40; Mrs. Skolnik was to arrive at 8:00. A heavy rain

pattered against the metal portion of the air conditioner that
rested on the sill outside his living room window. He thought,
as he perhaps did too often, of his boyhood at his family's estate.
Of his life there among the servants. Of Herr Kügler's accounts
of Yasnaya Polyana. Of his mother, a fragile woman of artistic
temperament, playing Chopin on the grand piano in the drawing room. Of a trip his father took him on to Warsaw, and of
their going together, just he and his father, to a puppet opera
with a full puppet orchestra. He must have been eight years old
at the time.

The Count no longer asked why history had done to him what
it had — why it had allowed him to glimpse the old life, to live
it long enough to develop a taste for it, and then, like a rug
from under a clown, had pulled it roughly away. Still, he often
thought, had history not intervened, first in the form of the
Nazis and then in that of the Communists, one barbarian horde
replacing another, what might his own life have been like?
Much, he supposed, like his father's: seeing after the family
business, sitting in the Provincial Assembly, organizing the
rounds of hunts, buying horses, travelling to European capitals
for business and pleasure. (His father was an ardent Anglo-
phile, and loved London above all other world cities.) Although
his own habits were more bookish than his father's, his responsibilities, and hence his life, would not have been much different. Where his father had improved the family stables, he
perhaps, given the chance, would have enriched the family library. Doubtless by now he would have long been married, have
had children, a son of his own to take to the famous puppet
opera in Warsaw.

Twenty minutes after eight and still Mrs. Skolnik had not
arrived. Outside the rain continued, undiminished in force. It
was a grave mistake allowing her to deliver her paper to him at
home. Most irregular, and now to irregularity was added tardi-
ness. By this hour the Count had generally settled into his work
—grading student papers, going over lecture notes — or his
reading for the book on America he hoped to write one day. He
did not appreciate his customary schedule being interrupted in
this way. He would not permit it to happen again.

At 8:45 the doorbell rang. Having rung the bell to let his

visitor in, the Count walked to his front door. He lived on the third floor of a walk-up building. Coming out to the hallway he watched Mrs. Skolnik climb the last half flight of steps. She was utterly drenched by the rain.

"Sorry to be so late," she said. "I couldn't find a parking space." She brought a large manila envelope out of an ample leather shoulder bag. "Here is my paper. At least it's dry, even if its author isn't." She stood out in the hall, water dripping off her. Her hair was a great dishevelment. She sneezed, said good night, turned to depart, when the Count heard himself say:

"See here, you are very wet. Please come in to dry off for a bit. Perhaps you will have a cup of tea."

"Thanks. I'd like that." She removed her boots in the hall, also her raincoat, which was soaked through. Underneath the coat her skirt and blouse were greatly blotched with rain.

"Allow me to get you a towel," said the Count, leading the way toward his bathroom. "Will Earl Grey be acceptable? Or is there another sort of tea you prefer?"

"Whatever you have will be fine," she said, the towel under her arm, slowly closing the bathroom door.

The Count put on the water, got out a fresh set of tea things, set out some biscuits and chocolates on a small teak platter. He had inserted two linen tea napkins in small pewter rings, when he heard his bathroom door open. Setting down the tea things in the living room, he turned to see Mrs. Skolnik, barefoot, drying her hair roughly with the towel, and wearing, so far as he could make out, nothing but his yellow terry-cloth robe, which she must have discovered hanging on its place on the back of the bathroom door.

"I hope you don't mind my borrowing this for a while, Professor," she said. "My clothes are soaked through, and I put them on the bathroom radiator to dry."

"I see," said the Count. "I see."

He bent over to pour the tea, but his hands shook. The tea pot made a great clatter against the thin china cup and saucer. Mrs. Skolnik put her hand over his to steady it. He turned and her eyes were only inches from his. He stood, and so did she; her robe had come slightly open. He was about to speak, when she gently covered his mouth with her hand. They embraced and she took him by the hand into the bedroom, where they did things together that the Count hadn't even dared to dream of.

When he woke in the morning the Count found a note on the kitchen counter next to her Tocqueville essay, still in its manila envelope.

Dear Professor,
    Excuse my calling you professor but it occurs to me I don't know your first name. For complicated reasons, mostly having to do with my kids, I had to return home late last night. If I had any choice in the matter, I would have liked to stay, so that I could be with you now instead of this note. I hope you do not mind if I call you sometime later this afternoon at your office.

Truly,
Sheila S.

The Count felt himself greatly confused. What would he say when next he spoke to her? Before last night life had seemed so orderly, so simple. No longer. What was the American idiom? In the soup. Yes, he was definitely in the soup now.

In the office Barney Ginsberg was dressed in what the Count considered his mufti. Which for Barney Ginsberg meant jeans, a shirt of flowery pattern, the top three buttons undone, and three neck chains, one with a Star of David, another with an astrological sign, the third with an animal's tooth.

"You've come to the right man, Pete," said Ginsberg, when the Count had most tentatively broached the subject pressing on his mind. He, the Count, had not mentioned Mrs. Skolnik's name.

"Yep, you've come to the right doctor, kiddo," Ginsberg said. "Since my divorce nine years ago the subject of women is my great subject. If I was twenty years younger, I'd write my dissertation on it. 'Unattached and Attached Women in the Last Quarter of the Twentieth Century: A Field Study,' by B. L.

Ginsberg. Dissertation hell, we're talking about a goddamn best-seller."

"It is not disconcerting to you, Barney, seeing many different women?"

"Not in the least, babes. I ask only two prerequisites: women I go out with must have a job and they must have no sex hang-ups. With my alimony and support payments I'm too broke to help support anyone, and I'm too old to teach the basic course in human sexuality."

"But do you not find yourself in — how to put it? — emotional entanglements?"

"What kind of entanglements? Look, Pete, these ladies know what they're getting into with me up-front. We provide each other a little service. When this loses its interest, we split. No hard, no complicated, feelings. You only go around once."

"But you feel no misgivings?"

"Only when some chick I'm still interested in splits before I do."

"No responsibility accompanies these intimacies?" asked the Count.

"What am I supposed to do, babes, propose marriage because some bimbo agrees to sleep with me? Come off it. The way I look at it I'm grateful but so should she be. There's no longer any such thing as an innocent woman, if ever there was, which I frankly doubt." Ginsberg brought his feet up on his desk. He was wearing red shoes with blue stripes across them.

"I see," said the Count, who was not certain he did.

The Count was gratified that Barney Ginsberg was out of the office when Mrs. Skolnik called. He asked if she had arrived home without any difficulties. He asked after her illness. Was she feeling any better? She said she was but thought it would be better to remain home for a few days.

"Won't you call me Sheila?" she asked.

"Yes," said the Count, failing to do so.

"And what can I call you?"

"My *prenom*," said the Count, noting a slight quaver in his voice, "is Peter."

"Are you free on Sunday, Peter?"

"Yes," he said. "Yes, I suppose I am."

"That's the day Larry spends with the children. It's sometimes a lonely day for me. Can we spend it together?"

"I think that will be very nice."

"Please call me Sheila."

"Yes," said the Count, "I should like to be with you on Sunday, Sheila. I should like it very much."

"I would too, Peter."

Sunday was a bright day, and a warm one for late March in Chicago. Because the Count did not drive a car — yet another American thing he had failed to learn — she was to come to him. The day before he had bought a pheasant from a Czech butcher on the Near North Side. He planned dinner, and perhaps a walk along the lakefront into Evanston. He was tidying his apartment, putting away books and his pipes, a Bach cantata was playing over the radio, when, a little past noon, the doorbell rang.

She wore grey trousers — did Americans still call them slacks? —a white blouse with a small soft collar under a yellow sweater. The yellow of the sweater made her dark hair seem even lusher than he had remembered it; the color also did fine things for her eyes. As he took her coat, she leaned in, touching her cheek to his. His heart jumped.

"Well, Peter," she said. "Here we are."

"Exactly. Just so," he said.

"It's a beautiful day."

"It is indeed. Can I get you a cup of tea," the Count gulped slightly, "Sheila?"

"None for me. I had late breakfast with the children before their father came for them. A shame to waste a day like this. Maybe we ought to be outdoors?"

Not until they reached Evanston, nearly two miles from his apartment, did the Count note that he had forgot his walking stick. They spoke easily together — more easily than he would have thought. She told him of her girlhood in the Chicago suburbs; spoke of her marriage, which had ended after her father had revealed to her that her husband had been cheating on her with other women, many of them his patients. She told him of the effects of the divorce on the children, her love for whom, so evident, touched the Count in its simplicity and strength of feeling. He spoke of his own childhood, so different from hers, of his schooling, of his dead parents. When he talked of his life since arriving in America, he realized, hearing himself describe the routine of his days, that he hadn't much of a life, at least in any sense that she was likely to understand: he taught, he read, he shopped, he fixed his meals, one day led into another and thirty years had gone by.

Dinner was a great success. She had never eaten pheasant before, and this pheasant, although she could not have known it, was a particularly delicious one. They drank two bottles of wine. She asked him if he had read all the books in his apartment. He said not nearly but was afraid buying books was his great vice. She said her son looked as if he might be a serious reader one day; at any rate, she hoped so. When she asked him, he told her that he spoke four languages and read six. She said she took Spanish in high school but was not very good at it. The Count had bought Napoleon for dessert, but when she looked at her wristwatch she said she was afraid she hadn't time, because she liked to be home when their father brought her children back. He walked her to her car, where before getting in she kissed him lightly, telling him she had had a marvelous day.

The Count felt exhilarated. Back in his apartment he made himself a cup of tea, lit a pipe, and sat down to read dear Sheila's paper on Tocqueville. It began:

> Alexis de Tocqueville was born in 1805 and died in 1859. He was a nobleman by birth, his title being that of a Count. His ancestors were also noblemen. The Tocquevilles, like so many other families of aristocrats, did not fare well during the French Revolution of 1789.

He could bring himself to read no further. The paper, in its rudimentariness, its utter lack of intellectual sophistication, depressed him. How could he care so for a woman who wrote such sentences! Yet he did, did he not? He put the paper back in its envelope. He couldn't bear to read it, no, not this evening.

•

Sundays became their regular day together. They went for walks. Occasionally they would go downtown. She liked movies. Once he took her to the Art Institute, showing her the five or six paintings there that he loved. Less successful was an outing to a concert of Baroque music, during which he noticed her nodding off. She had no interest in serious music. Politics, too, were of no interest to her; not even the woman's liberation, which seemed to put so many other women into a state of agitation. She had never been to Europe, and showed little curiosity about it. The farthest she had been from Chicago was on a trip to Hawaii, where she had gone to a dental convention with her husband. Once, as a special treat, the Count bought caviar for their hors d'oeuvres; she complained about its saltiness. Most Sundays he prepared their dinner; when she did so the fare was usually plain, steak and fried potatoes, roast chicken and rice. When they went out the Count noted that other men stared at her, which made him proud but uneasy. Some Sundays they made love, but not every Sunday. In class they pretended scarcely to know each other, though the Count sometimes found himself lecturing to her alone, like a Spanish gentleman serenading his lady on her balcony.

The Count was made nervous by her invitation to meet her parents and children. She arrived to pick him up at 4:00 on the Sunday afternoon of their meeting. He wore an English suit with a waistcoat; something told him not to bring along his walking stick. It was possible, he considered, that Sheila's father and mother were only a few years older than he; they could indeed be his contemporaries. This was one among several things the Count hesitated then chose not to ask her about as they drove along the freeway out to her parents' home in Northbrook.

"Peter Kinski," said Sheila, once they were in the house, "I would like you to meet my parents, Mr. and Mrs. Sidney Feinberg."

"It's very nice to make your acquaintance," said Mrs. Feinberg. She struck the Count as being perhaps four or five years older than himself, slightly heavyset with a reddish tint to her hair. She wore an inordinately large diamond ring on her left hand. In the face of the mother, an old Polish proverb held, is written the future of the daughter. The prospect was not at all displeasing to the Count.

"Professor," said Mr. Feinberg, vigorously shaking the Count's hand, "my pleasure, I'm sure." He, too, could not have been more than four or five years older than the Count. He appeared to have lost none of his hair, which was thick and still quite black. He had on plaid trousers and a golf shirt with an alligator over the left breast; his upper arm muscles bulged. He wore one of the new digital watches, very large with a black face and a heavy silver band. The Count himself carried a thin pocket watch of French make.

"Sheila, dear," said Mrs. Feinberg, "maybe the Professor would like to go into the family room with Daddy, while we put the finishing touches on dinner."

"You care at all about baseball, Professor?" asked Mr. Feinberg. They were in a room whose walls were covered with knotty pine. At one end was a bar. At the other a television screen that looked to be five feet wide and four feet high, beneath which was some very complicated-looking equipment. Chairs and couches were placed about the room. A bookcase along one wall had a set of *World Book* encyclopaedias, *A History of the Jews* by Abraham Sachar, and a number of trophies with figures swinging golf clubs atop them.

"No," said the Count, "I fear athletics marks yet another gap in my knowledge of America."

"Sure," said Feinberg, "I can understand that." He picked up a small box on a lamp table, which turned on the television set, on which appeared men in pyjamalike outfits, going through movements and motions altogether mysterious to the Count. "I grew up playing the game, and I still love to watch it. Sheila tells me you teach politics."

"Yes," said the Count, vaguely distracted by the darkness of the room and the colors floating about on the large screen.

"I have to tell you that this year was the first time I voted for a Republican for President. That's something I thought I'd never live long enough to see."

"The United States has gone through great turmoil. Perhaps it is not so surprising that your own politics would change."

"Still, in the house I grew up in FDR was like a god. He could do no wrong. Sheila tells me you were born in Poland."

"This is true."

"Our family, as far as we trace it, was from Poland, too. From Galicia. Life was never very good for the Jews in Poland. There are even people who say that under Hitler the Poles were worse even than the Nazis."

"It was less than good," said the Count. "Sometimes, when I brood upon the tortured history of my country, I think it has been so tortured — so deserving of its torturers — because of its treatment of the Jews. It makes a shameful chapter in our history, Mr. Feinberg."

"Let me turn this goddamn thing off." Feinberg picked up the gadget, pressed the button, and the colors on the screen faded softly away. "I'd like it if you'd call me Sid. My guess is we're not that far apart in age."

"I should like to, but only if you will agree to call me Peter."

"So tell me, Pete, what's the story with you and my daughter?"

"The story?" asked the Count.

"You know, where's it headed?"

"Headed?" asked the Count. "I do not know. I do know that I am greatly fond of your daughter."

"Excuse my giving you the third degree. I've no real right. But I hate to see her hurt again. Did she tell you it was me who found her husband cheating on her? I'll spare you the details. But I could've killed him at the time. He made too much money too fast. Couldn't handle it. But it broke my kid's heart. Have you been married before?"

"No," said the Count, "I have not."

A door opened. "Soup's on," said Mrs. Feinberg.

The dinner was chopped liver, a chicken soup with dumplings, a beef tenderloin, broccoli, salad, coffee, and ice cream. Much of the conversation was about the Feinbergs' grandchildren. The boy, Ronnie, played hockey, which pleased Sidney Feinberg. The girl, Melissa, was said to be very shy, and soon, according to her father, she was going to need braces on her teeth, which wasn't going to help her shyness any. Mrs. Feinberg asked the Count to call her Sylvia.

"You know, Peter," she said, "we really are very fortunate

to have the children with us. We have friends whose kids have moved to California, or who themselves have moved to Florida, who get to see their grandchildren once, maybe twice a year."

At eight o'clock their father brought the children home. Sheila met them at the door. The Count saw him standing in the foyer; she did not invite him in. He was tall, suntanned, expensively dressed, his hair, blondish, combed over his ears. The Count felt awkward looking out at him from his chair in the living room. No, he decided, it was not awkwardness, it was jealousy he felt. He wished this man had never existed.

"Ronnie, Melissa," said Sheila, a hand on each child's shoulder. "I want you to meet a very good friend of your mommy's. This is Professor Kinski."

The boy shook hands manfully; the little girl looked away bashfully. The Count was pleased to see that both children resembled their mother. He thought the girl dear; he preferred children shy, as he had been when a child. Their grandparents asked them what they had done on their day with their father, and Sheila rose to say that she probably ought to take Professor Kinski home.

On the drive back the Count told Sheila about his conversation with her father. "He wanted to know what was the story between us. What, my dear girl, do you suppose the story is?"

"I don't know, Peter," she said. "What do you want it to be?"

"I shall require some time to think about it," the Count said.

"There is no one hurrying you," she said.

"Let me get this straight," said Barney Ginsberg. He was dressed today as what the Count assumed was a cowboy: boots, jeans, a leather shirt, a red bandana round his neck. "Now let me get this straight. You've dipped your wick a few times and now you're thinking of getting married?"

"Dipped my wick?" asked the Count.

"You know, slept with this chick. Let's get serious, Pete. You're in your fifties, babes, and you don't exactly have a lot of turnaround time. One big mistake now and it's ballgame for you."

"I don't think you quite understand, Barney. I am happy when I am with this woman. My life seems better with her near."

"I see, pal, I see. But tell me, what will you live on? Her annual wardrobe probably equals your salary. I know these kind of Jews. Country club *yidlach*. You're a highly educated man, Pete. Let's face it, what'll you talk to her about — designer jeans? Get serious, friend, get serious."

"But serious is precisely what I am."

"And you say there's two kids thrown into this fine bargain?"

"Yes. Two children. That is correct."

"Get serious, man, I mean, get serious."

Of his own seriousness the Count had no doubt. He had never, he thought, been more serious in his life. Marrying this woman could not but change his life, and in the most radical ways. He may not have known much happiness since arriving in America but he had succeeded in establishing order in his life, and there was a measure of happiness in that. Until Sheila, he had assumed he would end his days a bachelor, among his books, his music, his pipes, his plan for writing his great book on America in her decline. Perhaps it was time to admit that he would never write such a book — that the book, or at any rate the idea of the book, was important to him only so long as there was nothing else in his life. He was, he could tell himself, a man who was planning an important book. But if it was so important why hadn't he by now sat down to the writing of it? It was perhaps time to ask such questions.

Between this book, which was his future, and his early years in Poland, which was his past, the Count realized that until now he had spent almost no time in the present. Sheila Skolnik was the present. She represented life at the quotidian: living, breathing life in its daily aspect. The past, while he could not help but dwell on it, was never to be returned; the future, this book written for the ages, was never to be. Was his life, then, no more than two fantasies, one of the past and one of the future, while the present, life itself, was escaping him?

But did he really want to face the present? He tried to imagine his and Sheila's life together once they were marrried. An immensity of detail flooded him. Where would they live? Would he have to buy a car, to learn to drive it? What would Sheila's very American children make of his very un-American ways? Would the next Count Kinski, albeit by adoption, turn out to be a hockey player? Would Sheila, who was still young, want more children — his children? Where would the money come from to run this complicated ménage?

No less difficult was it for him to imagine their evenings together. Their Sundays were leisurely and lovely, true enough, but what about, once married, Wednesday nights? He would doubtless not be able to eat the same foods he now ate, but would have to change his diet to accommodate the children. After dinner, which would have to be eaten earlier than he now ate — again as a concession to the children — what would they all do? Would he have to buy a television set, round which they would all sit, *en famille*, jaws agape, watching God knows what inanities? Would he, as now, have his evenings free to read? Doubtless not. And Sheila? What did she do with her evenings now? He didn't know; he couldn't imagine. What, really, did he know about her?

No, it was quite impossible. The risks were simply too great. Barney Ginsberg was correct; it was too late to change his life. He had gained order. Why trade it for chaos, on the slim thread of a hope of happiness. Happiness, that essentially American ideal, what had it to do with him? History had already decreed that happiness was not to be his lot. So be it — it was time, finally, to accept the decree. He would one day die alone but at least he would live in peace. Better to allow his life to continue as it had been before. He would break with Sheila Skolnik, this woman who threatened his order, this — what had Barney Ginsberg called her? — Jewish Princess. It was all quite impossible.

The Sunday on which the Count intended to inform Sheila that things must end between them she arrived at his apartment around one o'clock with Melissa in hand. The little girl was getting over a cold, and was not feeling well enough to go off for the day with her father. The Feinbergs had made plans for the day, so Sheila brought her along to spend the day with them. She had brought crayons and a coloring book from home. The Count set out a glass of milk and a plate of Swedish cookies for her; she worked at her coloring book at his small dining room table. Sheila suggested that they take her to a movie; a nearby theatre, The 400, was showing a rerun of Walt Disney's *Bambi*. The Count had purchased two sea bass for his and Sheila's dinner, but this, as even he recognized, was not child's food, so they decided to go out for dinner after the movie.

The Count took his walking stick, which was a damnable nuisance getting into Sheila's sports car. Melissa sat on his lap. At the movie theatre she sat between him and her mother. Sheila bought her a large plastic cup of Coca-Cola and a box of popcorn; also a box of something called Black Crows. What extraordinary things American children insert into their mouths, thought the Count. The seven-year-old child snuffled at his side. The movie turned out to be quite terrifying, even though done in animation. A forest fire scene in which the little deer loses its mother brought Melissa to tears; as the scene unrolled, she, who had until now scarcely spoken a word to him, clutched at the Count's arm. Later she slipped her hand into his. He was touched by this.

After the movie they drove to a place called McDonald's for dinner, a restaurant, Sheila told him, that Melissa adored. The Count had seen these McDonald's dotting — scarring? — the cityscape, but of course had never been in one. The one they were in, on Clark Street in a working-class neighborhood, seemed to be run by children, for of the ten or twelve uniformed workers behind the long counter none seemed older than sixteen. Sheila and Melissa ordered easily enough. But the Count found himself befuddled. He was unable to decipher the menu on the wall behind the counter; the light and din in the place further disoriented him.

"A hamburger, please," he finally said, "and a cup of coffee."

"What kind of hamburger, sir?" the girl taking his order asked.

"What kind?" asked the Count.

"Have a Big Mac, Mr. Kinki," said Melissa.

"Kinski, dear," Sheila corrected her. "Kinski, not Kinki."

"Very well. A Big Mac, then," said the Count.

They found a table, and the three of them began unpacking what seemed to the Count innumerable little plastic and paper packages. Melissa seemed in a state of high delight. The Count removed his sandwich from its plastic crate, and examined it. He had been brought up on European gastronomy, and, insofar as he was able in America, kept to this diet. This was a sandwich, he concluded, that required two hands to manipulate. Thus he lifted it to his mouth, and bit into a mélange of condiments and what the Russians call grasses and a simulacrum of bread and meat. *Echt*-ersatz, he thought. As he chewed he felt a sensation akin to listening to Mozart's *Twentieth Piano Concerto* played on a wet tuba.

"How d'ya like the Big Mac, Mr. Kinki?"

"Kinski, darling, Kinski."

"I find it," said the Count, "very splendid. Most delicious." He wondered how he could dispose of the remainder, but, seeing no way to do so without hurting the child's feelings, he managed, with the aid of large draughts of tasteless coffee, to swallow down nearly half the sandwich.

Back at the Count's apartment, Melissa returned to her coloring book in the dining room, while Sheila and the Count settled in the living room.

"Thank you," Sheila said, "for putting up with that restaurant. I saw it wasn't easy for you."

"No, no," said the Count. "Not at all. I found it — how shall I say? — edifying."

"Well, you're nice to have done it."

"Sheila," said the Count, hearing a tremor in his voice, "I have some sad things I must say."

"Sad things?"

"Yes. I fear, though this is not easy for me to say, that there is little point in our continuing to see each other in this way."

"Why do you say this?" She seemed shocked; she hadn't been expecting this.

"Because I have been alone too long. I cannot change my ways. No. Perhaps it is more honest to say that I do not want to change my ways. Not now that I am more than fifty years old."

"Are you sure about this, Peter?"

"I have thought much about it."

"I see."

"I shall always be grateful to you for your friendship."

"I see."

"Do you understand?"

"Yes," she said, "I do." And then she called: "Melissa, it's time for us to go home."

The child had put her coat on. "Thank you for a very nice day, Mr. Kinski," she said, holding her mother's hand at the door. The Count touched the girl's cheek. He would never see her again.

"May I see you down to the car?" he asked.

"I don't think so, Peter. Maybe it's better to say good-by here." She appeared to the Count as if she were holding back tears. She put out her hand. A century ago the Count would have bowed and kissed it. Now he held it, not truly wishing to relinquish it. And then she and the child were gone.

The Count felt relief. He poured a cognac, put Handel's *Wassermusik* on the phonograph, took down a Pléiade volume of *Les mémoires du Duc de Saint-Simon*. He could go undisturbed back to the old life now. Order and quiet. He sipped his cognac. He read about *le roi soleil*. He closed his eyes, the better to imagine King George in his barge floating down the Thames listening to Handel's lovely music. The book dropped to his lap when he put his hands to his eyes to stop the flow of tears.

He had made a hideous error. He didn't want to live, nor to die, alone. He had turned away a woman who had loved him, whom he had loved — loved still. But was it too late? Why need it be? He would call Sheila tomorrow. No. Why wait? He would go to her tonight. He would ask forgiveness, propose marriage, give up whatever was required of him to give up of the old life, take on all that was implied in the new. Time was left to him, and he would make it matter. Let chaos come. He would buy a television set for the children; dogs and cats, if need be. Hundreds of details would have to be worked out. He welcomed them. He telephoned for a cab, and, when asked where he was going, announced his destination as Northbrook. At the closet, he put on his coat. He looked at his walking stick, which he picked up, held before him in both hands, and, in a quick motion, over his raised knee broke it in two. As he ran down the stairs to meet his cab, Count Kinski's laughter rang round his empty apartment.

LOUISE ERDRICH

Scales

(FROM THE NORTH AMERICAN REVIEW)

for I.G. & B.P.

I WAS SITTING BEFORE MY THIRD or fourth Jellybean — which is anisette, grain alcohol, a lit match, and a small, wet explosion in the brain. On my left sat Gerry Nanapush of the Chippewa Tribe. On my right sat Dot Adare of the has-been, of the never-was, of the what's-in-front-of-me people. Still in her belly and tensed in its fluids coiled the child of their union, the child we were waiting for, the child whose name we were making a strenuous and lengthy search for in a cramped and littered bar at the very edge of that Dakota town.

Gerry had been on the wagon for thirteen years. He was drinking a tall glass of tonic water in which a crescent of soiled lemon bobbed, along with a maraschino cherry or two. He was thirty-six years old and had been in prison, or out of prison and on the run, for exactly half of those years. He was not in the clear yet nor would he ever be, that is why the yellow tennis player's visor was pulled down to the rim of his eyeglass frames. The bar was dimly lit and smoky; his glasses were very dark. Poor visibility must have been the reason Officer Lovchik saw him first.

Lovchik started toward us with his hand on his hip, but Gerry was over the backside of the booth and out the door before Lovchik got close enough to make a positive identification.

"Siddown with us," said Dot to Lovchik when he neared our booth. "I'll buy you a drink. It's so dead here. No one's been through all night."

Lovchik sighed, sat, and ordered a blackberry brandy.

"Now tell me," she said, staring up at him, "honestly. What do you think of the name Ketchup Face?"

It was through Gerry that I first met Dot, and in a bar like that one, only denser with striving drinkers, construction crews in town because of the highway. I sat down by Gerry early in the evening and we struck up a conversation, during the long course of which we became friendly enough for Gerry to put his arm around me. Dot entered at exactly the wrong moment. She was quick-tempered anyway and being pregnant (Gerry had gotten her that way on a prison visit five months previous) increased her irritability. It was only natural then, I guess, that she would pull the barstool out from under me and threaten my life. Only I didn't know she was threatening my life at the time. I didn't know anyone like Dot, so I didn't know she was serious.

"I'm gonna bend you out of shape," she said, flexing her hands over me. Her hands were small, broad, capable, with pointed nails. I used to do the wrong thing sometimes when I was drinking, and that time I did the wrong thing even though I was stretched out on the floor beneath her. I started laughing at her because her hands were so small (though strong and determined looking, I should have been more conscious of that). She was about to dive on top of me, five-month belly and all, but Gerry caught her in mid-air and carried her, yelling, out the door. The next day I reported for work. It was my first day on the job, and the only other woman on the construction site besides me was Dot Adare.

The first day Dot just glared toward me from a distance. She worked in the weighshack and I was hired to press buttons on the conveyor belt. All I had to do was adjust the speeds on the belt for sand, rocks, or gravel, and make sure it was aimed toward the right pile. There was a pyramid for each type of material, which was used to make hot-mix and cement. Across the wide yard, I saw Dot emerge from the little white shack from time to time. I couldn't tell whether she recognized me and thought, by the end of the day, that she probably didn't. I found out differently the next morning when I went to the company truck for coffee.

She got me alongside of the truck somehow, away from the men. She didn't say a word, just held a buck knife out where I could see it, blade toward me. She jiggled the handle and the tip waved like the pointy head of a pit viper. Blind. Heat-seeking. I was completely astonished. I had just put the plastic cover on my coffee and it steamed between my hands.

"Well I'm sorry I laughed," I said. She stepped back. I peeled the lid off my coffee, took a sip, and then I said the wrong thing again.

"And I wasn't going after your boyfriend."

"Why not!" she said at once. "What's wrong with him!"

I saw that I was going to lose this argument no matter what I said, so, for once, I did the right thing. I threw my coffee in her face and ran. Later on that day Dot came out of the weighshack and yelled "Okay then!" I was close enough to see that she even smiled. I waved. From then on things were better between us, which was lucky, because I turned out to be such a good button presser that within two weeks I was promoted to the weighshack, to help Dot.

It wasn't that Dot needed help weighing trucks, it was just a formality for the State Highway Department. I never quite understood, but it seems Dot had been both the truck weigher and the truck weight inspector for a while, until someone caught wind of this. I was hired to actually weigh the trucks then, for the company, and Dot was hired by the state to make sure I recorded accurate weights. What she really did was sleep, knit, or eat all day. Between truckloads I did the same. I didn't even have to get off my stool to weigh the trucks, because the arm of the scale projected through a rectangular hole and the weights appeared right in front of me. The standard back dumps, belly dumps, and yellow company trucks eased onto a platform built over the arm next to the shack. I wrote their weight on a little pink slip, clipped the paper in a clothespin attached to a broom handle, and handed it up to the driver. I kept a copy of the pink slip on a yellow slip that I put in a metal file box — no one ever picked up the file box, so I never knew what the yellow slips were for. The company paid me very well.

It was early July when Dot and I started working together. At first I sat as far away from her as possible and never took my eyes off her knitting needles, although it made me a little dizzy to watch her work. It wasn't long before we came to an understanding though, and after this I felt perfectly comfortable with Dot. She was nothing but direct, you see, and told me right off that only three things made her angry. Number one was someone flirting with Gerry. Number two was a cigarette leech (someone who was always quitting but smoking yours). Number three was a piss-ant. I asked her what that was. "A piss-ant," she said, "is a man with fat buns who tries to sell you things, a Jaycee, an Elk, a Kiwanis." I always knew where I stood with Dot, so I trusted her. I knew that if I fell out of her favor she would threaten me and give me time to run before she tried anything physical.

By mid-July our shack was unbearable, for it drew heat in from the bare yard and held it. We sat outside most of the time, moving around the shack to catch what shade fell, letting the raw hot wind off the beet fields suck the sweat from our armpits and legs. But the seasons change fast in North Dakota. We spent the last day of August jumping from foot to numb foot before Hadji, the foreman, dragged a little column of bottled gas into the shack. He lit the spoked wheel on its head, it bloomed, and from then on we huddled close to the heater — eating, dozing, or sitting blankly in its small radius of dry warmth.

By that time Dot weighed over two hundred pounds, most of it peanut-butter cups and egg salad sandwiches. She was a short, broad-beamed woman with long yellow eyes and spaces between each of her strong teeth. When we began working together, her hair was cropped close. By the cold months it had grown out in thick quills — brown at the shank, orange at the tip. The orange dye job had not suited her coloring. By that time, too, Dot's belly was round and full, for she was due in October. The child rode high, and she often rested her forearms on it while she knitted. One of Dot's most peculiar feats was transforming that gentle task into something perverse. She knit viciously, jerking the yarn around her thumb until the tip whitened, pulling each stitch so tightly that the little garments she finished stood up by themselves like miniature suits of mail.

But I thought that the child would need those tight stitches when it was born. Although Dot, as expecting mother, lived a fairly calm life, it was clear that she had also moved loosely among dangerous elements. The child, for example, had been conceived in a visiting room at the state prison. Dot had straddled Gerry's lap, in a corner the closed circuit TV did not quite scan. Through a hole ripped in her pantyhose and a hole ripped in Gerry's jeans they somehow managed to join and, miraculously, to conceive. When Dot was sure she was pregnant, Gerry escaped from the prison to see her. Not long after my conversation with Gerry in the bar, he was caught. That time he went back peacefully, and didn't put up a fight. He was mainly in the penitentiary for breaking out of it, anyway, since for his crime (assault and battery when he was eighteen) he had received three years and time off for good behavior. He just never managed to serve those three years or behave well. He broke out time after time, and was caught each time he did it, regular as clockwork.

Gerry was talented at getting out, that's a fact. He boasted that no steel or concrete shitbarn could hold a Chippewa, and he had eel-like properties in spite of his enormous size. Greased with lard once, he squirmed into a six-foot-thick prison wall and vanished. Some thought he had stuck there, immured forever, and that he would bring luck like the bones of slaves sealed in the wall of China. But Gerry rubbed his own belly for luck and brought luck to no one else, for he appeared, suddenly, at Dot's door and she was hard-pressed to hide him.

She managed for nearly a month. Hiding a six-foot-plus, two hundred and fifty pound Indian in the middle of a town that doesn't like Indians in the first place isn't easy. A month was quite an accomplishment, when you know what she was up against. She spent most of her time walking to and from the grocery store, padding along on her swollen feet, astonishing the neighbors with the size of what they thought was her appetite. Stacks of pork chops, whole fryers, thick steaks disappeared overnight, and since Gerry couldn't take the garbage out by day sometimes he threw the bones out the windows, where they

collected, where dogs soon learned to wait for a handout and
fought and squabbled over whatever there was.

The neighbors finally complained, and one day, while Dot
was at work, Lovchik knocked on the door of the trailerhouse.
Gerry answered, sighed, and walked over to their car. He was
so good at getting out of the joint and so terrible at getting
caught. It was as if he couldn't stay out of their hands. Dot knew
his problem, and told him that he was crazy to think he could
walk out of prison and then live like a normal person. Dot told
him that didn't work. She told him to get lost for a while on the
reservation, any reservation, to change his name and although
he couldn't grow a beard to at least let the straggly hairs above
his lip form a kind of mustache that would slightly disguise his
face. But Gerry wouldn't do that. He simply knew he did not
belong in prison, although he admitted it had done him some
good at eighteen, when he hadn't known how to be a criminal
and so had taken lessons from professionals. Now that he knew
all there was to know, however, he couldn't see the point of
staying in a prison and taking the same lessons over and over.
"A hate factory," he called it once, and said it manufactured
black poisons in his stomach that he couldn't get rid of although
he poked a finger down his throat and retched and tried to be
a clean and normal person in spite of everything.

Gerry's problem, you see, was he believed in justice, not laws.
He felt he had paid for his crime, which was done in a drunk
heat and to settle the question with a cowboy of whether a Chippewa was also a nigger. Gerry said that the two had never settled
it between them, but that the cowboy at least knew that if a
Chippewa was a nigger he was sure also a hell of a mean and
low-down fighter. For Gerry did not believe in fighting by any
rules but reservation rules, which is to say the first thing Gerry
did to the cowboy, after they squared off, was kick his balls.

It hadn't been much of a fight after that, and since there were
both white and Indian witnesses Gerry thought it would blow
over if it ever reached court. But there is nothing more vengeful
and determined in this world than a cowboy with sore balls, and
Gerry soon found this out. He also found that white people are
good witnesses to have on your side since they have names,
addresses, social security numbers, and work phones. But they

are terrible witnesses to have against you, almost as bad as having Indians witness for you.

Not only did Gerry's friends lack all forms of identification except their band cards, not only did they disappear (out of no malice but simply because Gerry was tried during powwow time), but the few he did manage to get were not interested in looking judge or jury in the eye. They mumbled into their laps. Gerry's friends, you see, had no confidence in the United States Judicial System. They did not seem comfortable in the courtroom, and this increased their unreliability in the eyes of judge and jury. If you trust the authorities, they trust you better back, it seems. It looked that way to Gerry anyhow.

A local doctor testified on behalf of the cowboy's testicles, and said his fertility might be impaired. Gerry got a little angry at that, and said right out in court that he could hardly believe he had done that much damage since the cowboy's balls were very small targets, it had been dark, and his aim was off anyway because of three, or maybe it was only two, beers. That made matters worse, of course, and Gerry was socked with a heavy sentence for an eighteen-year-old, but not for an Indian. Some said he got off lucky.

Only one good thing came from the whole experience, said Gerry, and that was maybe the cowboy would not have any little cowboys, although, Gerry also said, he had nightmares sometimes that the cowboy did manage to have little cowboys, all born with full sets of grinning teeth, Stetson hats, and little balls hard as plum pits.

So you see, it was difficult for Gerry, as an Indian, to retain the natural good humor of his ancestors in these modern circumstances. He tried though, and since he believed in justice, not laws, Gerry knew where he belonged (out of prison, in the bosom of his new family). And in spite of the fact that he was untrained in the honest life, he wanted it. He was even interested in getting a job. It didn't matter what kind of job. "Anything for a change," Gerry said. He wanted to go right out and apply for one, in fact, the moment he was free. But of course Dot wouldn't let him. And so, because he wanted to be with Dot, he stayed hidden in her trailerhouse even though they both realized, or must have, that it wouldn't be long before the police came asking around or the neighbors wised up and Gerry Nanapush would be back at square one again. So it happened. Lovchik came for him. And Dot now believed she would have to go through the end of her pregnancy and the delivery all by herself.

Dot was angry about having to go through it alone, and besides that, she loved Gerry with a deep and true love — that was clear. She knit his absence into thick little suits for the child, suits that would have stopped a truck on a dark road with their colors — bazooka pink, bruise blue, the screaming orange flagmen wore.

The child was as restless a prisoner as his father, and grew more anxious and unruly as his time of release neared. As a place to spend a nine-month sentence in, Dot wasn't much. Her body was inhospitable. Her skin was slack, sallow, and draped like upholstery fabric over her short, boardlike bones. Like the shack we spent our days in, she seemed jerry-built, thrown into the world with loosely nailed limbs and lightly puttied joints. Some pregnant women's bellies look like they always have been there. But Dot's stomach was an odd shape, almost square, and had the tacked-on air of a new and unpainted bay window. The child was clearly ready for a break and not interested in earning his parole, for he kept her awake all night by pounding reasonlessly at her inner walls, or beating against her bladder until she swore. "He wants out, bad," poor Dot would groan. "You think he might be premature?" From the outside, anyway, the child looked big enough to stand and walk and maybe even run straight out of the maternity ward the moment he was born.

The sun, at the time, rose around seven and we got to the weighshack while the frost was still thick on the gravel. Each morning I started the gas heater, turning the nozzle and standing back, flipping the match at it the way you would feed a fanged animal. Then one morning I saw the red bud through the window, lit already. But when I opened the door the shack was empty. There was, however, evidence of an overnight visitor — cigarette stubs, a few beer cans crushed to flat disks. I swept these things out and didn't say a word about them to Dot when she arrived.

She seemed to know something was in the air, however; her face lifted from time to time all that morning. She sniffed, and even I could smell the lingering odor of sweat like sour wheat, the faint reek of slept-in clothes and gasoline. Once, that morning, Dot looked at me and narrowed her long, hooded eyes. "I got pains," she said, "every so often. Like it's going to come sometime soon. Well all I can say is he better drag ass to get here, that Gerry." She closed her eyes then, and went to sleep.

Ed Rafferty, one of the drivers, pulled in with a load. It was overweight, and when I handed him the pink slip he grinned. There were two scales, you see, on the way to the cement plant, and if a driver got past the state-run scale early, before the state officials were there, the company would pay for whatever he got away with. But it was not illicit gravel that tipped the wedge past the red mark on the balance. When I walked back inside I saw the weight had gone down to just under the red. Ed drove off, still laughing, and I assumed that he had leaned on the arm of the scale, increasing the weight.

"That Ed," I said, "got me again."

But Dot stared past me, needles poised in her fist like a picador's lances. It gave me a start, to see her frozen in such a menacing pose. It was not the sort of pose to turn your back on, but I did turn, following her gaze to the door that a man's body filled suddenly.

Gerry, of course it was Gerry. He'd tipped the weight up past the red and leapt down, cat-quick for all his mass, and silent. I hadn't heard his step. Gravel crushed, evidently, but did not roll beneath his tight, thin boots.

He was bigger than I remembered from the bar, or perhaps it was just that we'd been living in that dollhouse of a weighshack so long I saw everything else as huge. He was so big that he had to hunker one shoulder beneath the lintel and back his belly in, pushing the door frame wider with his long, soft hands. It was the hands I watched as Gerry filled the shack. His plump fingers looked so graceful and artistic against his smooth mass. He used them prettily. Revolving agile wrists, he reached across the few inches left between himself and Dot. Then his littlest fingers curled like a woman's at tea, and he disarmed his wife. He drew

the needles out of Dot's fists, and examined the little garment
that hung like a queer fruit beneath.

"'S very, very nice," he said, scrutinizing the tiny, even
stitches. "'S for the kid?"

Dot nodded solemnly and dropped her eyes to her lap. It was
an almost tender moment. The silence lasted so long that I got
embarrassed and would have left, had I not been wedged firmly
behind his hip in one corner.

Gerry stood there, smoothing black hair behind his ears.
Again, there was a queer delicacy about the way he did this. So
many things Gerry did might remind you of the way that a
beautiful woman, standing naked before a mirror, would touch
herself — lovingly, conscious of her attractions. He nodded en-
couragingly. "Let's go then," said Dot.

Suave, grand, gigantic, they moved across the parking lot and
then, by mysterious means, slipped their bodies into Dot's compact car. I expected the car to belly down, thought the muffler
would scrape the ground behind them. But instead they flew,
raising a great spume of dust that hung in the air a long time
after they were out of sight.

I went back into the weighshack when the air behind them
had settled. I was bored, dead bored. And since one thing meant
about as much to me as another, I picked up her needles and
began knitting, as well as I could anyway, jerking the yarn back
after each stitch, becoming more and more absorbed in my work
until, as it happened, I came suddenly to the end of the garment, snipped the yarn, and worked the loose ends back into
the collar of the thick little suit.

I missed Dot in the days that followed, days so alike they welded
seamlessly to one another and took your mind away. I seemed
to exist in a suspension and spent my time sitting blankly at the
window, watching nothing until the sun went down, bruising
the whole sky as it dropped, clotting my heart. I couldn't name
anything I felt anymore, although I knew it was a kind of bore-
dom. I had been living the same life too long. I did jumping
jacks and push-ups and stood on my head in the little shack to
break the tedium, but too much solitude rots the brain. I wondered how Gerry had stood it. Sometimes I grabbed drivers out

of their trucks and talked loudly and quickly and inconsequentially as a madwoman. There were other times I couldn't talk at all because my tongue had rusted to the roof of my mouth.

Sometimes I daydreamed about Dot and Gerry. I had many choice daydreams, but theirs was my favorite. I pictured them in Dot's long tan and aqua trailerhouse, both hungry. Heads swaying, clasped hands swinging between them like hooked trunks, they moved through the kitchen feeding casually from boxes and bags on the counters, like ponderous animals alone in a forest. When they had fed, they moved on to the bedroom and settled themselves upon Dot's king-size and sateen-quilted spread. They rubbed together, locked and unlocked their parts. They set the trailer rocking on its cement-block and plywood foundation and the tremors spread, causing cups to fall, plates to shatter in the china hutches of their more-established neighbors.

But what of the child there, suspended between them? Did he know how to weather such tropical storms? It was a week past the week he was due, and I expected the good news to come any moment. I was anxious to hear the outcome, but still I was surprised when Gerry rumbled to the weighshack door on a huge and ancient, rust-pocked, untrustworthy-looking machine that was like no motorcycle I'd ever seen before.

"She asst for you," he hissed. "Quick, get on!"

I hoisted myself up behind him, although there wasn't room on the seat. I clawed his smooth back for a handhold and finally perched, or so it seemed, on the rim of his heavy belt. Flylike, glued to him by suction, we rode as one person, whipping a great wind around us. Cars scattered, the lights blinked and flickered on the main street. Pedestrians swiveled to catch a glimpse of us — a mountain tearing by balanced on a toy, and clinging to the sheer northwest face, a young and scrawny girl howling something that dopplered across the bridge and faded out, finally, in the parking lot of the Saint Francis Hospital.

In the waiting room we settled on chairs molded of orange plastic. The spike legs splayed beneath Gerry's mass, but managed to support him the four hours we waited. Nurses passed, settling like field gulls among reports and prescriptions, eyeing us with reserved hostility. Gerry hardly spoke. He didn't have to. I watched his ribs and the small of his back darken with sweat, for that well-lighted tunnel, the waiting room, the tin rack of magazines, all were the props and inevitable features of institutions. From time to time Gerry paced in the time-honored manner of the prisoner or expectant father. He made lengthy trips to the bathroom. All the quickness and delicacy of his movements had disappeared, and he was only a poor weary fat man in those hours, a husband worried about his wife, menaced, tired of getting caught.

The gulls emerged finally, and drew Gerry in among them. He visited Dot for perhaps half an hour, and then came out of her room. Again he settled; the plastic chair twitched beneath him. He looked bewildered and silly and a little addled with what he had seen. The shaded lenses of his glasses kept slipping down his nose. Beside him, I felt the aftermath of the shock wave, traveling from the epicenter deep in his flesh, outward from part of him that had shifted along a crevice. The tremors moved in widening rings. When they reached the very surface of him, and when he began trembling, Gerry stood suddenly. "I'm going after cigars," he said, and walked quickly away.

His steps quickened to a near-run as he moved down the corridor. Waiting for the elevator, he flexed his nimble fingers. Dot told me she had once sent him to the store for a roll of toilet paper. It was eight months before she saw him again; for he'd met the local constabulary on the way. So I knew, when he flexed his fingers, that he was thinking of pulling the biker's gloves over his knuckles, of running. It was perhaps the very first time in his life he had something to run for.

It seemed to me, at that moment, that I should at least let Gerry know it was all right for him to leave, to run as far and fast as he had to now. Although I felt heavy, my body had gone slack, and my lungs ached with smoke, I jumped up. I signaled him from the end of the corridor. Gerry turned, unwillingly turned. He looked my way just as two of our local police — officers Lovchik and Harriss — pushed open the fire door that sealed off the staircase behind me. I didn't see them, and was shocked at first that my wave caused such an extreme reaction in Gerry.

His hair stiffened. His body lifted like a hot-air balloon filling suddenly. Behind him there was a wide, tall window. Gerry opened it and sent the screen into thin air with an elegant, chorus-girl kick. Then he followed the screen, squeezing himself unbelievably through the frame like a fat rabbit disappearing down a hole. It was three stories down to the cement and asphalt parking lot.

Officers Lovchik and Harriss gained the window. The nurses followed. I slipped through the fire exit and took the back stairs down into the parking lot, believing I would find him stunned and broken there.

But Gerry had chosen his window with exceptional luck, for the officers had parked their car directly underneath. Gerry landed just over the driver's seat, caving the roof into the steering wheel. He bounced off the hood of the car and then, limping, a bit dazed perhaps, straddled his bike. Out of duty, Lovchik released several rounds into the still trees below him. The reports were still echoing when I reached the front of the building.

I was just in time to see Gerry Nanapush, emboldened by his godlike leap and recovery, pop a wheelie and disappear between the neat shrubs that marked the entrance to the hospital.

Two weeks later Dot and her boy, who was finally named Jason like most boys born that year, came back to work at the scales. Things went on as they had before, except that Jason kept us occupied during the long hours. He was large, of course, and had a sturdy pair of lungs he used often. When he cried, Jason screwed his face into fierce baby wrinkles and would not be placated with sugar tits or pacifiers. Dot unzipped her parka halfway, pulled her blouse up, and let him nurse for what seemed like hours. We could scarcely believe his appetite. Dot was a diligent producer of milk, however. Her breasts, like overfilled inner tubes, strained at her nylon blouses. Sometimes, when she thought no one was looking, Dot rose and carried them in the crooks of her arms, for her shoulders were growing bowed beneath their weight.

The trucks came in on the hour, or half hour. I heard the rush of airbrakes, gears grinding only inches from my head. It occurred to me that although I measured many tons every day,

I would never know how heavy a ton was unless it fell on me. I wasn't lonely now that Dot had returned. The season would end soon, and we wondered what had happened to Gerry.

There were only a few weeks left of work when we heard that Gerry was caught again. He'd picked the wrong reservation to hide on — Pine Ridge. At the time it was overrun with Federal Agents and armored vehicles. Weapons were stashed everywhere and easy to acquire. Gerry got himself a weapon. Two men tried to arrest him. Gerry would not go along and when he started to run and the shooting started Gerry shot and killed a clean-shaven man with dark hair and light eyes, a Federal Agent, a man whose picture was printed in all the papers.

They sent Gerry to prison in Marion, Illinois. He was placed in the control unit. He receives his visitors in a room where no touching is allowed, where the voice is carried by phone, glances meet through sheets of Plexiglas, and no children will ever be engendered.

Dot and I continued to work the last weeks together. Once we weighed baby Jason. We unlatched his little knit suit, heavy as armor, and bundled him in a light, crocheted blanket. Dot went into the shack to adjust the weights. I stood there with Jason. He was such a solid child, he seemed heavy as lead in my arms. I placed him on the ramp between the wheel sights and held him steady for a moment, then took my hands slowly away. He stared calmly into the rough, distant sky. He did not flinch when the wind came from every direction, wrapping us tight enough to squeeze the very breath from a stone. He was so dense with life, such a powerful distillation of Dot and Gerry, it seemed he might weigh about as much as any load. But that was only a thought, of course. For as it turned out, he was too light and did not register at all.

URSULA K. LE GUIN

The Professor's Houses

(FROM THE NEW YORKER)

THE PROFESSOR HAD TWO HOUSES, one inside the other. He lived with his wife and child in the outer house, which was comfortable, clean, disorderly, not quite big enough for all his books, her papers, their daughter's bright deciduous treasures. The roof leaked after heavy rains early in the fall before the wood swelled, but a bucket in the attic sufficed. No rain fell upon the inner house, where the professor lived without his wife and child, or so he said jokingly sometimes: "Here's where I live. My house." His daughter often added, without resentment, for the visitor's information, "It started out to be for me, but it's really his." And she might reach in to bring forth an inch-high table lamp with fluted shade, or a blue bowl the size of her little fingernail, marked "Kitty" and half full of eternal milk; but she was sure to replace these, after they had been admired, pretty near exactly where they had been. The little house was very orderly, and just big enough for all it contained, though to some tastes the bric-a-brac in the parlor might seem excessive. The daughter's preference was for the store-bought gimmicks and appliances, the toasters and carpet sweepers of Lilliput, but she knew that most adult visitors would admire the perfection of the furnishings her father himself had so delicately and finely made and finished. He was inclined to be a little shy of showing off his own work, so she would point out the more ravishing elegances: the glass-fronted sideboard, the hardwood parquetry and the dadoes, the widow's walk. No visitor, child or adult, could withstand the fascination of the Venetian blinds, the infinitesimal slats that slanted and slid in perfect order on their cords of double-weight sewing thread. "Do you know how to make a Venetian blind?" the professor would inquire, setting up the visitor for his daughter, who would forestall or answer the hesitant negative with a joyful "Put his eyes out!" Her father, who was entertained by involutions and, like all teachers, willing to repeat a good thing, would then remark that after working for two weeks on those blinds he had established that a Venetian blind can also make an American blind.

"I did that awful rug in the nursery," the professor's wife, Julia, might say, evidencing her participation in the inner house, her approbation, her incompetence. "It's not up to Ian's standard, but he accepted the intent." The crocheted rug was, in fact, coarse-looking and curly-edged; the needlepoint rugs in the other rooms, miniature Orientals and a gaudy floral in the master bedroom, lay flat and flawless.

The inner house stood on a low table in an open alcove, called "the bookshelf end," of the long living room of the outer house. Friends of the family checked the progress of its construction, furnishing, and fitting out as they came to dinner or for a drink from time to time, from year to year. Occasional visitors assumed that it belonged to the daughter and was kept downstairs on display because it was a really fine doll's house, a regular work of art, and miniatures were coming into or recently had been in vogue. To certain rather difficult guests, including the dean of his college, the professor, without affirming or denying his part as architect, cabinetmaker, roofer, glazier, electrician, and *tapissier,* might quote Claude Lévi-Strauss. "It's in *La Pensée Sauvage,* I think," he would say. "His idea is that the reduced model — the miniature — allows a knowledge of the whole to precede the knowledge of the parts. A reversal of the usual process of knowing. Essentially, all the arts proceed that way, reducing a material dimension in favor of an intellectual dimension." He found that persons entirely incapable of, and averse to, the kind of concrete thought that was his chief pleasure in working on the house went rigid as bird dogs at the name of the father of structuralism, and sometimes continued to gaze at the doll's house for some minutes with the tense and earnest gaze of a pointer at a sitting duck. The professor's wife had to entertain a good many strangers when she became state coordinator of the conservation organization for which she worked, but her guests, with urgent business on their minds, admired the doll's house perfunctorily if they noticed it at all.

As the daughter, Victoria, passed through the Vickie period and, at thirteen, entered upon the Tori period, her friends no longer had to be restrained or distracted from fiddling with the fittings of the little house, wearing out the fragile mechanisms, sometimes handling the furniture carelessly in their story games with its occupants. For there was, or had been, a family living in it. Victoria at eight had requested and received for Christmas a rather expensive European mama, papa, brother, sister, and baby, all cleverly articulated so that they could sit in the armchairs, and reach up to the copper-bottom saucepans hung above the stove, and hit or clasp one another in moments of passion. Family dramas of great intensity were enacted from time to time in the then incompletely furnished house. The brother's left leg came off at the hip and was never properly mended. Papa Bendsky received a marking-pen mustache and eyebrows that gave him an evil squint, like the half-breed lascar in an Edwardian thriller. The baby got lost. Victoria no longer played with the survivors; and the professor gratefully put them into the drawer of the table on which the house stood. He had always hated them, invaders, especially the papa, so thin, so flexible, with his nasty little Austrian-looking green jackets and his beady lascar eyes.

Victoria had recently bought with her earnings from baby-sitting a gift to the house and her father: a china cat to drink the eternal milk from the blue bowl marked "Kitty." The professor did not put the cat in the drawer. He believed it to be worthy of the house, as the Bendsky family had never been. It was a finely modelled little figure, glazed tortoiseshell on white. Curled on the hearth rug at twilight in the ruddy glow of the flames (red cellophane and a penlight bulb), it looked very comfortable indeed. But since it lay curled up, it could never go into the kitchen to drink from the blue bowl; and this was evidently a trouble or burden to the professor's unconscious mind, for he had not exactly a dream about it, one night while he was going to sleep after working late on a complex and difficult piece of writing, a response he was to give to a paper to be presented later in the year at the A.A.A.S.; not a dream but a kind of half-waking experience. He was looking into or was in the kitchen of the inner house. That was not unusual, for when fitting the cabinets and wall panelling and building in the sink, he had become deeply familiar with the proportions and aspects of the kitchen from every angle, and had frequently and deliberately visualized it from the perspective of a six-inch person standing by the stove or at the pantry door. But in this case he had no sense of volition; he was merely there; and while standing there, near the big wood-burning stove, he saw the cat come in, look up at him, and settle itself down to drink the milk. The experience included the auditory: he heard the neat and amusing sound a cat makes lapping.

Next day he remembered this little vision clearly. His mind ran upon it, now and then. Walking across campus after a lecture, he thought with some intensity that it would be very pleasant to have an animal in the house, a live animal. Not a cat, of course. Something very small. But his precise visual imagination at once presented him with a gerbil the size of the sofa, a monstrous hamster in the master bedroom, like the dreadful Mrs. Bhoolabhoy in *Staying On,* billowing in the bed, immense, and he laughed inwardly, and winced away from the spectacle.

Once, indeed, when he had been installing the pull-chain toilet — the house and its furnishings were generally Victorian; that was the original eponymous joke — he had glanced up to see that a moth had got into the attic, but only after a moment of shock did he recognize it as a moth, the marvellous, soft-winged, unearthly owl beating there beneath the rafters. Flies, however, which often visited the house, brought only thoughts of horror movies and about professors who tampered with what man was not meant to know and ended up buzzing at the windowpane, crying vainly, "Don't! No!" as the housewife's inexorable swatter fell. And serve them right. Would a ladybug do for a tortoise? The size was right, the colors wrong. The Victorians did not hesitate to paint live tortoises' shells. But tortoises do not raise their shells and fly away home. There was no pet suitable for the house.

•

Lately he had not been working much on the house; weeks and months went by before he got the tiny Landseer framed, and then it was a plain gilt frame fitted up on a Sunday afternoon, not the scrollwork masterpiece he had originally planned. Sketches for a glassed-in sun porch were never, as his dean would have put it, implemented. The personal and professional stresses in his department at the university, which had first driven him to this small escape hatch, were considerably eased under the new chairman; he and Julia had worked out their problems well enough to go on; and anyway the house and all its furnishings were done, in place, complete. Every armchair its antimacassars. Now that the Bendskys were gone, nothing got lost or broken, nothing even got moved. And no rain fell. The outer house was in real need of reroofing; it had required three attic buckets this October, and even so there had been some damage to the study ceiling. But the cedar shingles on the inner house were still blond, virginal. They knew little of sunlight, and nothing of the rain.

I could, the professor thought, pour water on the roof, to weather the shingles a bit. It ought to be sprinkled on, somehow, so it would be more like rain. He saw himself stand with Julia's green plastic half-gallon watering can at the low table in the book-lined alcove of the living room; he saw water falling on the little shingles, pooling on the table, dripping to the ancient but serviceable domestic Oriental rug. He saw a mad professor watering a toy house. Will it grow, Doctor? Will it grow?

That night he dreamed that the inner house, his house, was outside. It stood in a garden patch on a rickety support of some kind. The ground around it had been partly dug up as if for planting. The sky was low and dingy, though it was not raining yet. Some slats had come away from the back of the house, and he was worried about the glue. "I'm worried about the glue," he said to the gardener or whoever it was that was there with a short-handled shovel, but the person did not understand. The house should not be outside, but it was outside, and it was too late to do anything about it.

He woke in great distress from this dream and could not find rest from it until his mind came upon the notion of, as it were, obeying the dream: actually moving the inner house outdoors, into the garden, which would then become the garden of both houses. An inner garden within the outer garden could be designed. Julia's advice would be needed for that. Miniature roses for hawthorn trees, surely. Scotch moss for the lawn? What could you use for hedges? She might know. A fountain? . . . He drifted back to sleep contentedly planning the garden of the house. And for months, even years, after that he amused or consoled himself from time to time, on troubled nights or in boring meetings, by reviving the plans for the miniature garden. But really it was not a practicable idea, given the rainy weather of his part of the world.

He and Julia got their house reroofed eventually, and brought the buckets down from the attic. The inner house was moved upstairs into Victoria's room when she went off to college. Looking into that room toward dusk of a November evening, the professor saw the peaked roofs and widow's walk sharp against the window light. They were still dry. Dust falls here, not rain, he thought. It isn't fair. He opened the front of the house and turned on the fireplace. The little cat lay curled up on the rug before the ruddy glow, the illusion of warmth, the illusion of shelter. And the dry milk in the half-full bowl marked "Kitty" by the kitchen door. And the child gone.

URSULA K. LE GUIN

Sur

A Summary Report of the Yelcho Expedition to the Antarctic, 1909–10

(FROM THE NEW YORKER)

ALTHOUGH I HAVE NO INTENTION of publishing this report, I think it would be nice if a grandchild of mine, or somebody's grandchild, happened to find it some day; so I shall keep it in the leather trunk in the attic, along with Rosita's christening dress and Juanito's silver rattle and my wedding shoes and finneskos.

The first requisite for mounting an expedition — money — is normally the hardest to come by. I grieve that even in a report destined for a trunk in the attic of a house in a very quiet suburb of Lima I dare not write the name of the generous benefactor, the great soul without whose unstinting liberality the Yelcho Expedition would never have been more than the idlest excursion into daydream. That our equipment was the best and most modern — that our provisions were plentiful and fine — that a ship of the Chilean government, with her brave officers and gallant crew, was twice sent halfway round the world for our convenience: all this is due to that benefactor whose name, alas!, I must not say, but whose happiest debtor I shall be till death.

When I was little more than a child, my imagination was caught by a newspaper account of the voyage of the *Belgica*, which, sailing south from Tierra del Fuego, was beset by ice in the Bellingshausen Sea and drifted a whole year with the floe, the men aboard her suffering a great deal from want of food and from the terror of the unending winter darkness. I read and reread that account, and later followed with excitement the reports of the rescue of Dr. Nordenskjöld from the South Shetland Islands by the dashing Captain Irizar of the *Uruguay,* and the adventures of the *Scotia* in the Weddell Sea. But all these exploits were to me but forerunners of the British National Antarctic Expedition of 1901–04, in the *Discovery,* and the wonderful account of that expedition by Captain Scott. This book, which I ordered from London and reread a thousand times, filled me with longing to see with my own eyes that strange continent, last Thule of the South, which lies on our maps and globes like a white cloud, a void, fringed here and there with scraps of coastline, dubious capes, supposititious islands, headlands that may or may not be there: Antarctica. And the desire was as pure as the polar snows: to go, to see — no more, no less. I deeply respect the scientific accomplishments of Captain Scott's expedition, and have read with passionate interest the findings of physicists, meteorologists, biologists, etc.; but having had no training in any science, nor any opportunity for such training, my ignorance obliged me to forgo any thought of adding to the body of scientific knowledge concerning Antarctica, and the same is true for all the members of my expedition. It seems a pity; but there was nothing we could do about it. Our goal was limited to observation and exploration. We hoped to go a little farther, perhaps, and see a little more; if not, simply to go and to see. A simple ambition, I think, and essentially a modest one.

Yet it would have remained less than an ambition, no more than a longing, but for the support and encouragement of my dear cousin and friend Juana ———. (I use no surnames, lest this report fall into strangers' hands at last, and embarrassment or unpleasant notoriety thus be brought upon unsuspecting husbands, sons, etc.) I had lent Juana my copy of *The Voyage of the "Discovery,"* and it was she who, as we strolled beneath our parasols across the Plaza de Armas after Mass one Sunday in 1908, said, "Well, if Captain Scott can do it, why can't we?"

It was Juana who proposed that we write Carlota ——— in Valparaíso. Through Carlota we met our benefactor, and so

URSULA K. LE GUIN

obtained our money, our ship, and even the plausible pretext of going on retreat in a Bolivian convent, which some of us were forced to employ (while the rest of us said we were going to Paris for the winter season). And it was my Juana who in the darkest moments remained resolute, unshaken in her determination to achieve our goal.

And there were dark moments, especially in the spring of 1909 — times when I did not see how the Expedition would ever become more than a quarter ton of pemmican gone to waste and a lifelong regret. It was so very hard to gather our expeditionary force together! So few of those we asked even knew what we were talking about — so many thought we were mad, or wicked, or both! And of those few who shared our folly, still fewer were able, when it came to the point, to leave their daily duties and commit themselves to a voyage of at least six months, attended with not inconsiderable uncertainty and danger. An ailing parent; an anxious husband beset by business cares; a child at home with only ignorant or incompetent servants to look after it: these are not responsibilities lightly to be set aside. And those who wished to evade such claims were not the companions we wanted in hard work, risk, and privation.

But since success crowned our efforts, why dwell on the setbacks and delays, or the wretched contrivances and downright lies that we all had to employ? I look back with regret only to those friends who wished to come with us but could not, by any contrivance, get free — those we had to leave behind to a life without danger, without uncertainty, without hope.

On the seventeenth of August, 1909, in Punta Arenas, Chile, all the members of the Expedition met for the first time: Juana and I, the two Peruvians; from Argentina, Zoe, Berta, and Teresa; and our Chileans, Carlota and her friends Eva, Pepita, and Dolores. At the last moment I had received word that María's husband, in Quito, was ill and she must stay to nurse him, so we were nine, not ten. Indeed, we had resigned ourselves to being but eight when, just as night fell, the indomitable Zoe arrived in a tiny pirogue manned by Indians, her yacht having sprung a leak just as it entered the Straits of Magellan.

That night before we sailed we began to get to know one another, and we agreed, as we enjoyed our abominable supper in the abominable seaport inn of Punta Arenas, that if a situation arose of such urgent danger that one voice must be obeyed without present question, the unenviable honor of speaking with that voice should fall first upon myself; if I were incapacitated, upon Carlota; if she, then upon Berta. We three were then toasted as "Supreme Inca," "La Araucana," and "The Third Mate," amid a lot of laughter and cheering. As it came out, to my very great pleasure and relief, my qualities as a "leader" were never tested; the nine of us worked things out amongst us from beginning to end without any orders being given by anybody, and only two or three times with recourse to a vote by voice or show of hands. To be sure, we argued a good deal. But then, we had time to argue. And one way or another the arguments always ended up in a decision, upon which action could be taken. Usually at least one person grumbled about the decision, sometimes bitterly. But what is life without grumbling and the occasional opportunity to say "I told you so"? How could one bear housework, or looking after babies, let alone the rigors of sledge-hauling in Antarctica, without grumbling? Officers — as we came to understand aboard the *Yelcho* — are forbidden to grumble; but we nine were, and are, by birth and upbringing, unequivocally and irrevocably, all crew.

Though our shortest course to the southern continent, and that originally urged upon us by the captain of our good ship, was to the South Shetlands and the Bellingshausen Sea, or else by the South Orkneys into the Weddell Sea, we planned to sail west to the Ross Sea, which Captain Scott had explored and described, and from which the brave Ernest Shackleton had returned only the previous autumn. More was known about this region than any other portion of the coast of Antarctica, and though that more was not much, yet it served as some insurance of the safety of the ship, which we felt we had no right to imperil. Captain Pardo had fully agreed with us after studying the charts and our planned itinerary; and so it was westward that we took our course out of the Straits next morning.

Our journey half round the globe was attended by fortune. The little *Yelcho* steamed cheerily along through gale and gleam, climbing up and down those seas of the Southern Ocean that run unbroken round the world. Juana, who had fought bulls and the far more dangerous cows on her family's *estancia*, called the ship *la vaca valiente*, because she always returned to the charge. Once we got over being seasick, we all enjoyed the sea voyage, though oppressed at times by the kindly but officious protectiveness of the captain and his officers, who felt that we were only "safe" when huddled up in the three tiny cabins that they had chivalrously vacated for our use.

We saw our first iceberg much farther south than we had looked for it, and saluted it with Veuve Clicquot at dinner. The next day we entered the ice pack, the belt of floes and bergs broken loose from the land ice and winter-frozen seas of Antarctica which drifts northward in the spring. Fortune still smiled on us: our little steamer, incapable, with her unreinforced metal hull, of forcing a way into the ice, picked her way from lane to lane without hesitation, and on the third day we were through the pack, in which ships have sometimes struggled for weeks and been obliged to turn back at last. Ahead of us now lay the dark-gray waters of the Ross Sea, and beyond that, on the horizon, the remote glimmer, the cloud-reflected whiteness of the Great Ice Barrier.

Entering the Ross Sea a little east of Longitude West 160°, we came in sight of the Barrier at the place where Captain Scott's party, finding a bight in the vast wall of ice, had gone ashore and sent up their hydrogen-gas balloon for reconnaissance and photography. The towering face of the Barrier, its sheer cliffs and azure and violet waterworn caves, all were as described, but the location had changed: instead of a narrow bight, there was a considerable bay, full of the beautiful and terrific orca whales playing and spouting in the sunshine of that brilliant southern spring.

Evidently masses of ice many acres in extent had broken away from the Barrier (which — at least for most of its vast extent — does not rest on land but floats on water) since the *Discovery*'s passage in 1902. This put our plan to set up camp on the Barrier itself in a new light; and while we were discussing alternatives, we asked Captain Pardo to take the ship west along the Barrier face toward Ross Island and McMurdo Sound. As the sea was clear of ice and quite calm, he was happy to do so and, when we sighted the smoke plume of Mt. Erebus, to share in our celebration — another half case of Veuve Clicquot.

The *Yelcho* anchored in Arrival Bay, and we went ashore in the ship's boat. I cannot describe my emotions when I set foot on the earth, on that earth, the barren, cold gravel at the foot of the long volcanic slope. I felt elation, impatience, gratitude, awe, familiarity. I felt that I was home at last. Eight Adélie penguins immediately came to greet us with many exclamations of interest not unmixed with disapproval. "Where on earth have you been? What took you so long? The Hut is around this way. Please come this way. Mind the rocks!" They insisted on our going to visit Hut Point, where the large structure built by Captain Scott's party stood, looking just as in the photographs and drawings that illustrate his book. The area about it, however, was disgusting — a kind of graveyard of seal skins, seal bones, penguin bones, and rubbish, presided over by the mad, screaming skua gulls. Our escorts waddled past the slaughterhouse in all tranquillity, and one showed me personally to the door, though it would not go in.

The interior of the hut was less offensive but very dreary. Boxes of supplies had been stacked up into a kind of room within the room; it did not look as I had imagined it when the *Discovery* party put on their melodramas and minstrel shows in the long winter night. (Much later, we learned that Sir Ernest had rearranged it a good deal when he was there just a year before us.) It was dirty, and had about it a mean disorder. A pound tin of tea was standing open. Empty meat tins lay about; biscuits were spilled on the floor; a lot of dog turds were underfoot — frozen, of course, but not a great deal improved by that. No doubt the last occupants had had to leave in a hurry, perhaps even in a blizzard. All the same, they could have closed the tea tin. But housekeeping, the art of the infinite, is no game for amateurs.

Teresa proposed that we use the hut as our camp. Zoe counterproposed that we set fire to it. We finally shut the door and left it as we had found it. The penguins appeared to approve, and cheered us all the way to the boat.

McMurdo Sound was free of ice, and Captain Pardo now proposed to take us off Ross Island and across to Victoria Land, where we might camp at the foot of the Western Mountains, on dry and solid earth. But those mountains, with their storm-darkened peaks and hanging cirques and glaciers, looked as awful as Captain Scott had found them on his western journey, and none of us felt much inclined to seek shelter among them.

Aboard the ship that night we decided to go back and set up our base as we had originally planned, on the Barrier itself. For all available reports indicated that the clear way south was across the level Barrier surface until one could ascend one of the confluent glaciers to the high plateau that appears to form the whole interior of the continent. Captain Pardo argued strongly against this plan, asking what would become of us if the Barrier "calved" — if our particular acre of ice broke away and started to drift northward. "Well," said Zoe, "then you won't have to come so far to meet us." But he was so persuasive on this theme that he persuaded himself into leaving one of the *Yelcho's* boats with us when we camped, as a means of escape. We found it useful for fishing, later on.

My first steps on Antarctic soil, my only visit to Ross Island, had not been pleasure unalloyed. I thought of the words of the English poet,

> Though every prospect pleases,
> And only Man is vile.

But then, the backside of heroism is often rather sad; women and servants know that. They know also that the heroism may be no less real for that. But achievement is smaller than men think. What is large is the sky, the earth, the sea, the soul. I looked back as the ship sailed east again that evening. We were well into September now, with eight hours or more of daylight. The spring sunset lingered on the twelve-thousand-foot peak of Erebus and shone rosy-gold on her long plume of steam. The steam from our own small funnel faded blue on the twilit water as we crept along under the towering pale wall of ice.

On our return to "Orca Bay" — Sir Ernest, we learned years later, had named it the Bay of Whales — we found a sheltered

nook where the Barrier edge was low enough to provide fairly
easy access from the ship. The *Yelcho* put out her ice anchor,
and the next long, hard days were spent in unloading our supplies and setting up our camp on the ice, a half kilometre in
from the edge: a task in which the *Yelcho*'s crew lent us invalu-
able aid and interminable advice. We took all the aid gratefully,
and most of the advice with salt.

The weather so far had been extraordinarily mild for spring
in this latitude; the temperature had not yet gone below $-20°F$,
and there was only one blizzard while we were setting up camp.
But Captain Scott had spoken feelingly of the bitter south winds
on the Barrier, and we had planned accordingly. Exposed as
our camp was to every wind, we built no rigid structures above-
ground. We set up tents to shelter in while we dug out a series
of cubicles in the ice itself, lined them with hay insulation and
pine boarding, and roofed them with canvas over bamboo poles,
covered with snow for weight and insulation. The big central
room was instantly named Buenos Aires by our Argentineans,
to whom the center, wherever one is, is always Buenos Aires.
The heating and cooking stove was in Buenos Aires. The stor-
age tunnels and the privy (called Punta Arenas) got some back
heat from the stove. The sleeping cubicles opened off Buenos
Aires, and were very small, mere tubes into which one crawled
feet first; they were lined deeply with hay and soon warmed by
one's body warmth. The sailors called them coffins and worm-
holes, and looked with horror on our burrows in the ice. But
our little warren or prairie-dog village served us well, permit-
ting us as much warmth and privacy as one could reasonably
expect under the circumstances. If the *Yelcho* was unable to get
through the ice in February and we had to spend the winter in
Antarctica, we certainly could do so, though on very limited
rations. For this coming summer, our base — Sudamérica del
Sur, South South America, but we generally called it the Base
— was intended merely as a place to sleep, to store our provisions, and to give shelter from blizzards.

To Berta and Eva, however, it was more than that. They were
its chief architect-designers, its most ingenious builder-excava-
tors, and its most diligent and contented occupants, forever
inventing an improvement in ventilation, or learning how to
make skylights, or revealing to us a new addition to our suite of

rooms, dug in the living ice. It was thanks to them that our stores were stowed so handily, that our stove drew and heated so efficiently, and that Buenos Aires, where nine people cooked, ate, worked, conversed, argued, grumbled, painted, played the guitar and banjo, and kept the Expedition's library of books and maps, was a marvel of comfort and convenience. We lived there in real amity; and if you simply had to be alone for a while, you crawled into your sleeping hole head first.

Berta went a little farther. When she had done all she could to make South South America livable, she dug out one more cell just under the ice surface, leaving a nearly transparent sheet of ice like a greenhouse roof; and there, alone, she worked at sculptures. They were beautiful forms, some like a blending of the reclining human figure with the subtle curves and volumes of the Weddell seal, others like the fantastic shapes of ice cornices and ice caves. Perhaps they are there still, under the snow, in the bubble in the Great Barrier. There where she made them, they might last as long as stone. But she could not bring them north. That is the penalty for carving in water.

Captain Pardo was reluctant to leave us, but his orders did not permit him to hang about the Ross Sea indefinitely, and so at last, with many earnest injunctions to us to stay put — make no journeys — take no risks — beware of frostbite — don't use edge tools — look out for cracks in the ice — and a heartfelt promise to return to Orca Bay on February 20th, or as near that date as wind and ice would permit, the good man bade us farewell, and his crew shouted us a great goodbye cheer as they weighed anchor. That evening, in the long orange twilight of October, we saw the topmast of the *Yelcho* go down the north horizon, over the edge of the world, leaving us to ice, and silence, and the Pole.

That night we began to plan the Southern Journey.

The ensuing month passed in short practice trips and depot-laying. The life we had led at home, though in its own way strenuous, had not fitted any of us for the kind of strain met with in sledge-hauling at ten or twenty degrees below freezing. We all needed as much working out as possible before we dared undertake a long haul.

My longest exploratory trip, made with Dolores and Carlota,

was southwest toward Mt. Markham, and it was a nightmare —
blizzards and pressure ice all the way out, crevasses and no view
of the mountains when we got there, and white weather and
sastrugi all the way back. The trip was useful, however, in that
we could begin to estimate our capacities; and also in that we
had started out with a very heavy load of provisions, which we
depoted at a hundred and a hundred and thirty miles south-
southwest of Base. Thereafter other parties pushed on farther,
till we had a line of snow cairns and depots right down to Latitude 83° 43', where Juana and Zoe, on an exploring trip, had
found a kind of stone gateway opening on a great glacier leading south. We established these depots to avoid, if possible, the
hunger that had bedevilled Captain Scott's Southern Party, and
the consequent misery and weakness. And we also established
to our own satisfaction — intense satisfaction — that we were
sledge-haulers at least as good as Captain Scott's husky dogs. Of
course we could not have expected to pull as much or as fast as
his men. That we did so was because we were favored by much
better weather than Captain Scott's party ever met on the Barrier; and also the quantity and quality of our food made a very
considerable difference. I am sure that the fifteen percent of
dried fruits in our pemmican helped prevent scurvy; and the
potatoes, frozen and dried according to an ancient Andean Indian method, were very nourishing yet very light and compact
— perfect sledding rations. In any case, it was with considerable
confidence in our capacities that we made ready at last for the
Southern Journey.

The Southern Party consisted of two sledge teams: Juana, Dolores, and myself; Carlota, Pepita, and Zoe. The support team
of Berta, Eva, and Teresa set out before us with a heavy load of
supplies, going right up onto the glacier to prospect routes and
leave depots of supplies for our return journey. We followed
five days behind them, and met them returning between Depot
Ercilla and Depot Miranda. That "night" — of course, there was
no real darkness — we were all nine together in the heart of the
level plain of ice. It was November 15th, Dolores's birthday. We
celebrated by putting eight ounces of pisco in the hot chocolate,
and became very merry. We sang. It is strange now to remember

how thin our voices sounded in that great silence. It was overcast, white weather, without shadows and without visible horizon or any feature to break the level; there was nothing to see
at all. We had come to that white place on the map, that void,
and there we flew and sang like sparrows.

After sleep and a good breakfast the Base Party continued
north and the Southern Party sledged on. The sky cleared presently. High up, thin clouds passed over very rapidly from southwest to northeast, but down on the Barrier it was calm and just
cold enough, five or ten degrees below freezing, to give a firm
surface for hauling.

On the level ice we never pulled less than eleven miles (seventeen kilometres) a day, and generally fifteen or sixteen miles
(twenty-five kilometres). (Our instruments, being British-made,
were calibrated in feet, miles, degrees Fahrenheit, etc., but we
often converted miles to kilometres, because the larger numbers
sounded more encouraging.) At the time we left South America,
we knew only that Mr. Ernest Shackleton had mounted another
expedition to the Antarctic in 1907, had tried to attain the Pole
but failed, and had returned to England in June of the current
year, 1909. No coherent report of his explorations had yet
reached South America when we left; we did not know what
route he had gone, or how far he had got. But we were not
altogether taken by surprise when, far across the featureless
white plain, tiny beneath the mountain peaks and the strange
silent flight of the rainbow-fringed cloud wisps, we saw a flutter-
ing dot of black. We turned west from our course to visit it: a
snow heap nearly buried by the winter's storms — a flag on a
bamboo pole, a mere shred of threadbare cloth, an empty oilcan
— and a few footprints standing some inches above the ice. In
some conditions of weather the snow compressed under one's
weight remains when the surrounding soft snow melts or is
scoured away by the wind; and so these reversed footprints had
been left standing all these months, like rows of cobbler's lasts
— a queer sight.

We met no other such traces on our way. In general I believe
our course was somewhat east of Mr. Shackleton's. Juana, our
surveyor, had trained herself well and was faithful and methodical in her sightings and readings, but our equipment was mini-

mal — a theodolite on tripod legs, a sextant with artificial horizon, two compasses, and chronometers. We had only the wheel meter on the sledge to give distance actually travelled.

In any case, it was the day after passing Mr. Shackleton's waymark that I first saw clearly the great glacier among the mountains to the southwest, which was to give us a pathway from the sea level of the Barrier up to the altiplano, ten thousand feet above. The approach was magnificent: a gateway formed by immense vertical domes and pillars of rock. Zoe and Juana had called the vast ice river that flowed through that gateway the Florence Nightingale Glacier, wishing to honor the British, who had been the inspiration and guide of our Expedition; that very brave and very peculiar lady seemed to represent so much that is best, and strangest, in the island race. On maps, of course, this glacier bears the name Mr. Shackleton gave it: the Beardmore.

The ascent of the Nightingale was not easy. The way was open at first, and well marked by our support party, but after some days we came among terrible crevasses, a maze of hidden cracks, from a foot to thirty feet wide and from thirty to a thousand feet deep. Step by step we went, and step by step, and the way always upward now. We were fifteen days on the glacier. At first the weather was hot — up to 20°F — and the hot nights without darkness were wretchedly uncomfortable in our small tents. And all of us suffered more or less from snow blindness just at the time when we wanted clear eyesight to pick our way among the ridges and crevasses of the tortured ice, and to see the wonders about and before us. For at every day's advance more great, nameless peaks came into view in the west and southwest, summit beyond summit, range beyond range, stark rock and snow in the unending noon.

We gave names to these peaks, not very seriously, since we did not expect our discoveries to come to the attention of geographers. Zoe had a gift for naming, and it is thanks to her that certain sketch maps in various suburban South American attics bear such curious features as "Bolívar's Big Nose," "I Am General Rosas," "The Cloudmaker," "Whose Toe?," and "Throne of Our Lady of the Southern Cross." And when at last we got up onto the altiplano, the great interior plateau, it was Zoe who

called it the pampa, and maintained that we walked there
among vast herds of invisible cattle, transparent cattle pastured
on the spindrift snow, their gauchos the restless, merciless
winds. We were by then all a little crazy with exhaustion and the
great altitude — twelve thousand feet — and the cold and the
wind blowing and the luminous circles and crosses surrounding
the suns, for often there were three or four suns in the sky, up
there.

That is not a place where people have any business to be. We
should have turned back; but since we had worked so hard to
get there, it seemed that we should go on, at least for a while.

A blizzard came, with very low temperatures, so we had to
stay in the tents, in our sleeping bags, for thirty hours — a rest
we all needed, though it was warmth we needed most, and there
was no warmth on that terrible plain anywhere at all but in our
veins. We huddled close together all that time. The ice we lay
on is two miles thick.

It cleared suddenly and became, for the plateau, good
weather: twelve below zero and the wind not very strong. We
three crawled out of our tent and met the others crawling out
of theirs. Carlota told us then that her group wished to turn
back. Pepita had been feeling very ill; even after the rest during
the blizzard, her temperature would not rise above 94°. Carlota
was having trouble breathing. Zoe was perfectly fit, but much
preferred staying with her friends and lending them a hand in
difficulties to pushing on toward the Pole. So we put the four
ounces of pisco that we had been keeping for Christmas into the
breakfast cocoa, and dug out our tents, and loaded our sledges,
and parted there in the white daylight on the bitter plain.

Our sledge was fairly light by now. We pulled on to the south.
Juana calculated our position daily. On the twenty-second of
December, 1909, we reached the South Pole. The weather was,
as always, very cruel. Nothing of any kind marked the dreary
whiteness. We discussed leaving some kind of mark or monument, a snow cairn, a tent pole and flag; but there seemed no
particular reason to do so. Anything we could do, anything we
were, was insignificant, in that awful place. We put up the tent
for shelter for an hour and made a cup of tea, and then struck
"90° Camp."

Dolores, standing patient as ever in her sledging harness, looked at the snow; it was so hard frozen that it showed no trace of our footprints coming, and she said, "Which way?"

"North," said Juana.

It was a joke, because at that particular place there is no other direction. But we did not laugh. Our lips were cracked with frostbite and hurt too much to let us laugh. So we started back, and the wind at our backs pushed us along, and dulled the knife edges of the waves of frozen snow.

All that week the blizzard wind pursued us like a pack of mad dogs. I cannot describe it. I wished we had not gone to the Pole. I think I wish it even now. But I was glad even then that we had left no sign there, for some man longing to be first might come some day, and find it, and know then what a fool he had been, and break his heart.

We talked, when we could talk, of catching up to Carlota's party, since they might be going slower than we. In fact they used their tent as a sail to catch the following wind and had got far ahead of us. But in many places they had built snow cairns or left some sign for us; once, Zoe had written on the lee side of a ten-foot sastruga, just as children write on the sand of the beach at Miraflores, "This Way Out!" The wind blowing over the frozen ridge had left the words perfectly distinct.

In the very hour that we began to descend the glacier, the weather turned warmer, and the mad dogs were left to howl forever tethered to the Pole. The distance that had taken us fifteen days going up we covered in only eight days going down. But the good weather that had aided us descending the Nightingale became a curse down on the Barrier ice, where we had looked forward to a kind of royal progress from depot to depot, eating our fill and taking our time for the last three hundred–odd miles. In a tight place on the glacier I lost my goggles — I was swinging from my harness at the time in a crevasse — and then Juana broke hers when we had to do some rock-climbing coming down to the Gateway. After two days in bright sunlight with only one pair of snow goggles to pass amongst us, we were all suffering badly from snow blindness. It became acutely painful to keep lookout for landmarks or depot flags, to take sightings, even to study the compass, which had to be laid down on the snow to steady the needle. At Concolorcorvo Depot, where there was a particularly good supply of food and fuel, we gave up, crawled into our sleeping bags with bandaged eyes, and slowly boiled alive like lobsters in the tent exposed to the relentless sun. The voices of Berta and Zoe were the sweetest sound I ever heard. A little concerned about us, they had skied south to meet us. They led us home to Base.

We recovered quite swiftly, but the altiplano left its mark. When she was very little, Rosita asked if a dog "had bitted Mama's toes." I told her yes — a great, white, mad dog named Blizzard! My Rosita and my Juanito heard many stories when they were little, about that fearful dog and how it howled, and the transparent cattle of the invisible gauchos, and a river of ice eight thousand feet high called Nightingale, and how Cousin Juana drank a cup of tea standing on the bottom of the world under seven suns, and other fairy tales.

We were in for one severe shock when we reached Base at last. Teresa was pregnant. I must admit that my first response to the poor girl's big belly and sheepish look was anger — rage — fury. That one of us should have concealed anything, and such a thing, from the others! But Teresa had done nothing of the sort. Only those who had concealed from her what she most needed to know were to blame. Brought up by servants, with four years' schooling in a convent, and married at sixteen, the poor girl was still so ignorant at twenty years of age that she had thought it was "the cold weather" that made her miss her periods. Even this was not entirely stupid, for all of us on the Southern Journey had seen our periods change or stop altogether as we experienced increasing cold, hunger, and fatigue. Teresa's appetite had begun to draw general attention; and then she had begun, as she said pathetically, "to get fat." The others were worried at the thought of all the sledge-hauling she had done, but she flourished, and the only problem was her positively insatiable appetite. As well as could be determined from her shy references to her last night on the hacienda with her husband, the baby was due at just about the same time as the *Yelcho*, February 20th. But we had not been back from the Southern Journey two weeks when, on February 14th, she went into labor.

Several of us had borne children and had helped with deliveries, and anyhow most of what needs to be done is fairly self-evident; but a first labor can be long and trying, and we were all anxious, while Teresa was frightened out of her wits. She kept calling for her José till she was as hoarse as a skua. Zoe lost all patience at last and said, "By God, Teresa, if you say 'José!' once more, I hope you have a penguin!" But what she had, after twenty long hours, was a pretty little red-faced girl.

Many were the suggestions for that child's name from her eight proud midwife aunts: Polita, Penguina, McMurdo, Victoria . . . But Teresa announced, after she had had a good sleep and a large serving of pemmican, "I shall name her Rosa — Rosa del Sur," Rose of the South. That night we drank the last two bottles of Veuve Clicquot (having finished the pisco at 88° 60' South) in toasts to our little Rose.

On the nineteenth of February, a day early, my Juana came down into Buenos Aires in a hurry. "The ship," she said, "the ship has come," and she burst into tears — she who had never wept in all our weeks of pain and weariness on the long haul.

Of the return voyage there is nothing to tell. We came back safe.

In 1912 all the world learned that the brave Norwegian Amundsen had reached the South Pole; and then, much later, we heard the accounts of how Captain Scott and his men had come there after him but did not come home again.

Just this year, Juana and I wrote to the captain of the *Yelcho*, for the newspapers have been full of the story of his gallant dash to rescue Sir Ernest Shackleton's men from Elephant Island, and we wished to congratulate him, and once more to thank him. Never one word has he breathed of our secret. He is a man of honor, Luis Pardo.

I add this last note in 1929. Over the years we have lost touch with one another. It is very difficult for women to meet, when they live as far apart as we do. Since Juana died, I have seen none of my old sledgemates, though sometimes we write. Our little Rosa del Sur died of the scarlet fever when she was five years old. Teresa had many other children. Carlota took the veil in Santiago ten years ago. We are old women now, with old husbands, and grown children, and grandchildren who might

some day like to read about the Expedition. Even if they are
rather ashamed of having such a crazy grandmother, they may
enjoy sharing in the secret. But they must not let Mr. Amundsen
know! He would be terribly embarrassed and disappointed.
There is no need for him or anyone else outside the family to
know. We left no footprints, even.

BOBBIE ANN MASON

Graveyard Day

(FROM ASCENT)

HOLLY, SWINGING HER LEGS from the kitchen stool, lectures her mother on natural foods. Holly is ten.

Waldeen says, "I'll have to give your teacher a talking to. She's put notions in your head. You've got to have meat to grow."

Waldeen is tenderizing liver, beating it with the edge of a saucer. Her daughter insists that she is a vegetarian. If Holly had said Rosicrucian, it would have sounded just as strange to Waldeen. Holly wants to eat peanuts, soyburgers, and yogurt. Waldeen is sure this new fixation has something to do with Holly's father, Joe Murdock, although Holly rarely mentions him. After Waldeen and Joe were divorced last September, Joe moved to Arizona and got a construction job. Joe sends Holly letters occasionally, but Holly won't let Waldeen see them. At Christmas he sent Holly a copper Indian bracelet with unusual marks on it. It is Indian language, Holly tells her. Waldeen sees Holly polishing the bracelet while she is watching TV.

Waldeen shudders when she thinks of Joe Murdock. If he weren't Holly's father, she might be able to forget him. Waldeen was too young when she married him, and he had a reputation for being wild, which he did not outgrow. Now she could marry Joe McClain, who comes over for supper almost every night, always bringing something special, such as a roast or dessert. He seems to be oblivious to what things cost, and he frequently brings Holly presents. If Waldeen married Joe, then Holly would have a stepfather — something like a sugar substitute, Waldeen imagines. Shifting relationships confuse her. She doesn't know what marriage means anymore. She tells Joe they must wait. Her ex-husband is still on her mind, like the lingering aftereffects of an illness.

Joe McClain is punctual, considerate. Tonight he brings fudge ripple ice cream and a half-gallon of Coke in a plastic jug. He kisses Waldeen and hugs Holly.

Waldeen says, "We're having liver and onions, but Holly's mad 'cause I won't make Soybean Supreme."

"Soybean *Delight*," says Holly.

"Oh, excuse me!"

"Liver is full of poison. The poisons in the feed settle in the liver."

"Do you want to stunt your growth?" Joe asks, patting Holly on the head. He winks at Waldeen and waves his walking stick at her playfully, like a conductor. Joe collects walking sticks, and he has an antique one that belonged to Jefferson Davis. On a gold band, in italics, it says Jefferson Davis. Joe doesn't go anywhere without a walking stick, although he is only thirty. It embarrasses Waldeen to be seen with him.

"Sometimes a cow's liver just explodes from the poison," says Holly. "Poisons are *oozing* out."

"Oh, Holly, hush, that's digusting." Waldeen plops the pieces of liver onto a plate of flour.

"There's this restaurant at the lake that has Liver Lovers' Night," Joe says to Holly. "Every Tuesday is Liver Lovers' Night."

"Really?" Holly is wide-eyed, as if Joe is about to tell a long story, but Waldeen suspects Joe is bringing up the restaurant — Sea's Breeze at Kentucky Lake — to remind her that it was the scene of his proposal. Waldeen, not accustomed to eating out, studied the menu carefully, wavering between pork chops and T-bone steak and then suddenly, without thinking, ordering catfish. She was disappointed to learn that the catfish was not even local, but frozen ocean cat. "Why would they do that," she kept saying, interrupting Joe, "when they've got all the fresh channel cat in the world right here at Kentucky Lake?"

During supper, Waldeen snaps at Holly for sneaking liver to the cat, but with Joe gently persuading her, Holly manages to eat three bites of liver without gagging. Holly is trying to please him, as though he were some TV game show host who happened to live in the neighborhood. In Waldeen's opinion, families shouldn't shift memberships, like clubs. But here they are, trying to be a family. Holly, Waldeen, Joe McClain. Sometimes Joe spends the weekend, but Holly prefers weekends at Joe's house because of his shiny wood floors and his parrot that tries to sing "Inka Dinka Doo." Holly likes the idea of packing an overnight bag.

Waldeen dishes out the ice cream. Suddenly inspired, she suggests a picnic Saturday. "The weather's fairing up," she says.

"I can't," says Joe. "Saturday's graveyard day."

"Graveyard day?" Holly and Waldeen say together.

"It's my turn to clean off the graveyard. Every spring and fall somebody has to rake it off." Joe explains that he is responsible for taking geraniums to his grandparents' graves. His grandmother always kept the pot in her basement during the winter, and in the spring she took it to her husband's grave, but she had died in November.

"Couldn't we have a picnic at the graveyard?" asks Waldeen.

"That's gruesome."

"We never get to go on picnics," says Holly. "Or anywhere." She gives Waldeen a look.

"Well, okay," Joe says. "But remember, it's serious. No fooling around."

"We'll be real quiet," says Holly.

"Far be it from me to disturb the dead," Waldeen says, wondering why she is speaking in a mocking tone.

After supper, Joe plays rummy with Holly while Waldeen cracks pecans for a cake. Pecan shells fly across the floor, and the cat pounces on them. Holly and Joe are laughing together, whooping loudly over the cards. They sound like contestants on *Let's Make a Deal*. Joe Murdock wanted desperately to be on a game show and strike it rich. He wanted to go to California so he would have a chance to be on TV and so he could travel the freeways. He drove in the stock car races, and he had been drag racing since he learned to drive. Evel Knievel was his hero. Waldeen couldn't look when the TV showed Evel Knievel leaping over canyons. She told Joe many times, "He's nothing but a showoff. But if you want to break your fool neck, then go right ahead. Nobody's stopping you." She is better off without Joe Murdock. If he were still in town, he would do something to make her look foolish, such as paint her name on his car door. He once had WALDEEN painted in large red letters on the door of his LTD. It was like a tattoo. It is probably a good thing he is in Arizona. Still, she cannot really understand why he had to move so far away from home.

After Holly goes upstairs, carrying the cat, whose name is Mr. Spock, Waldeen says to Joe, "In China they have a law that the men have to help keep house." She is washing dishes.

Joe grins. "That's in China. This is *here*."

Waldeen slaps at him with the dish towel, and Joe jumps up and grabs her. "I'll do all the housework if you marry me," he says. "You can get the Chinese to arrest me if I don't."

"You sound just like my ex-husband. Full of promises."

"Guys named Joe are good at making promises." Joe laughs and hugs her.

"All the important men in my life were named Joe," says Waldeen, with pretended seriousness. "My first real boyfriend was named Joe. I was fourteen."

"You always bring that up," says Joe. "I wish you'd forget about them. You love *me*, don't you?"

"Of course, you idiot."

"Then why don't you marry me?"

"I just said I was going to think twice is all."

"But if you love me, what are you waiting for?"

"That's the easy part. Love is easy."

In the middle of *The Waltons*, C. W. Redmon and Betty Mathis drop by. Betty, Waldeen's best friend, lives with C.W., who works with Joe on a construction crew. Waldeen turns off the TV and clears magazines from the couch. C.W. and Betty have just returned from Florida and they are full of news about Sea World. Betty shows Waldeen her new tote bag with a killer whale pictured on it.

"Guess who we saw at the Louisville airport," Betty says.

"I give up," says Waldeen.

"Colonel Sanders!"

"He's eighty-four if he's a day," C.W. adds.

"You couldn't miss him in that white suit," Betty says. "I'm sure it was him. Oh, Joe! He had a walking stick. He went strutting along — "

"No kidding!"

"He probably beats chickens to death with it," says Holly, who is standing around.

"That would be something to have," says Joe. "Wow, one of the Colonel's walking sticks."

"Do you know what I read in a magazine?" says Betty. "That the Colonel Sanders outfit is trying to grow a three-legged chicken."

"No, a four-legged chicken," says C.W.

"Well, whatever."

Waldeen is startled by the conversation. She is rattling ice cubes, looking for glasses. She finds an opened Coke in the refrigerator, but it may have lost its fizz. Before she can decide whether to open the new one Joe brought, C.W. and Betty grab glasses of ice from her and hold them out. Waldeen pours the Coke. There is a little fizz.

"We went first class the whole way," says C.W. "I always say, what's a vacation for if you don't splurge?"

"I thought we were going to buy *out* Florida," says Betty. "We spent a fortune. Plus, I gained a ton."

"Man, those jumbo jets are really nice," says C.W.

C.W. and Betty seem changed, exactly like all people who come back from Florida with tales of adventure and glowing tans, except that they did not get tans. It rained. Waldeen cannot imagine flying, or spending that much money. Her ex-husband tried to get her to go up in an airplane with him once — a $7.50 ride in a Cessna — but she refused. If Holly goes to Arizona to visit him, she will have to fly. Arizona is probably as far away as Florida.

When C.W. says he is going fishing on Saturday, Holly demands to go along. Waldeen reminds her about the picnic. "You're full of wants," she says.

"I just wanted to go somewhere."

"I'll take you fishing one of these days soon," says Joe.

"Joe's got to clean off his graveyard," says Waldeen. Before she realizes what she is saying, she has invited C.W. and Betty to come along on the picnic. She turns to Joe. "Is that okay?"

"I'll bring some beer," says C.W. "To hell with fishing."

"I never heard of a picnic at a graveyard," says Betty. "But it sounds neat."

Joe seems embarrassed. "I'll put you to work," he warns.

Later, in the kitchen, Waldeen pours more Coke for Betty. Holly is playing solitaire on the kitchen table. As Betty takes the Coke, she says, "Let C.W. take Holly fishing if he wants a kid so bad." She has told Waldeen that she wants to marry C.W., but she does not want to ruin her figure by getting pregnant. Betty pets the cat. "Is this cat going to have kittens?"

Mr. Spock, sitting with his legs tucked under his stomach, is shaped somewhat like a turtle.

"Heavens, no," says Waldeen. "He's just fat because I had him nurtured."

"The word is *neutered!*" cries Holly, jumping up. She grabs Mr. Spock and marches up the stairs.

"That youngun," Waldeen says with a sigh. She feels suddenly afraid. Once, Holly's father, unemployed and drunk on whiskey and 7-Up, snatched Holly from the school playground and took her on a wild ride around town, buying her ice cream at the Tastee-Freez, and stopping at Newberry's to buy her an *All in the Family* Joey doll, with correct private parts. Holly was eight. When Joe brought her home, both were tearful and quiet. The excitement had worn off, but Waldeen had vividly imagined how it was. She wouldn't be surprised if Joe tried the same trick again, this time carrying Holly off to Arizona. She has heard of divorced parents who kidnap their own children.

The next day Joe McClain brings a pizza at noon. He is working nearby and has a chance to eat lunch with Waldeen. The pizza is large enough for four people. Waldeen is not hungry.

"I'm afraid we'll end up horsing around and won't get the graveyard cleaned off," Joe says. "It's really a lot of work."

"Why's it so important, anyway?"

"It's a family thing."

"Family. Ha!"

"Why are you looking at me in that tone of voice?"

"I don't know what's what anymore," Waldeen wails. "I've got this kid that wants to live on peanuts and sleeps with a cat —

and didn't even see her daddy at Christmas. And here *you* are, talking about family. What do you know about family? You don't know the half of it."

"What's got into you lately?"

Waldeen tries to explain. "Take Colonel Sanders, for instance. He was on *I've Got a Secret* once, years ago, when nobody knew who he was. His secret was that he had a million-dollar check in his pocket for selling Kentucky Fried Chicken to John Y. Brown. *Now* look what's happened. Colonel Sanders sold it but didn't get rid of it. He's still Colonel Sanders. John Y. sold it too and he can't get rid of it either. Everybody calls him the Chicken King, even though he's governor. That's not very dignified, if you ask me."

"What in Sam Hill are you talking about? What's that got to do with families?"

"Oh, Colonel Sanders just came to mind because C.W. and Betty saw him. What I mean is, you can't just do something by itself. Everything else drags along. It's all *involved.* I can't get rid of my ex-husband just by signing a paper. Even if he *is* in Arizona and I never lay eyes on him again."

Joe stands up, takes Waldeen by the hand, and leads her to the couch. They sit down and he holds her tightly for a moment. Waldeen has the strange impression that Joe is an old friend who moved away and returned, years later, radically changed. She doesn't understand the walking sticks, or why he would buy such an enormous pizza.

"One of these days you'll see," says Joe, kissing her.

"See what?" Waldeen mumbles.

"One of these days you'll see. I'm not such a bad catch."

Waldeen stares at a split in the wallpaper.

"Who would cut your hair if it wasn't for me?" he asks, rumpling her curls. "I should have gone to beauty school."

"I don't know."

"Nobody else can do Jimmy Durante imitations like I can."

"I wouldn't brag about it."

On Saturday Waldeen is still in bed when Joe arrives. He appears in the doorway of her bedroom, brandishing a shiny black walking stick. It looks like a stiffened black racer snake.

"I overslept," Waldeen says, rubbing her eyes. "First I had insomnia. Then I had bad dreams. Then — "

"You said you'd make a picnic."

"Just a minute. I'll go make it."

"There's not time now. We've got to pick up C.W. and Betty." Waldeen pulls on her jeans and a shirt, then runs a brush through her hair. In the mirror she sees blue pouches under her eyes. She catches sight of Joe in the mirror. He looks like an actor in a vaudeville show.

They go into the kitchen, where Holly is eating granola. "She promised me she'd make carrot cake," Holly tells Joe.

"I get blamed for everything," says Waldeen. She is rushing around, not sure why. She is hardly awake.

"How could you forget?" asks Joe. "It was your idea in the first place."

"I didn't forget. I just overslept." Waldeen opens the refrigerator. She is looking for something. She stares at a ham.

When Holly leaves the kitchen, Waldeen asks Joe, "Are you mad at me?" Joe is thumping his stick on the floor.

"No. I just want to get this show on the road."

"My ex-husband always said I was never dependable, and he was right. But *he* was one to talk. He had his head in the clouds."

"Forget your ex-husband."

"His name is Joe. Do you want some juice?" Waldeen is looking for orange juice, but she cannot find it.

"No." Joe leans on his stick. "He's over and done with. Why don't you just cross him off your list?"

"Why do you think I had bad dreams? Answer me that. I must be afraid of *something*."

There is no juice. Waldeen closes the refrigerator door. Joe is smiling at her enigmatically. What she is really afraid of, she realizes, is that he will turn out to be just like Joe Murdock. But it must be only the names, she reminds herself. She hates the thought of a string of husbands, and the idea of a stepfather is like a substitute host on a talk show. It makes her think of Johnny Carson's many substitute hosts.

"You're just afraid to do anything new, Waldeen," Joe says. "You're afraid to cross the street. Why don't you get your ears pierced? Why don't you adopt a refugee? Why don't you get a dog?"

"You're crazy. You say the weirdest things." Waldeen searches the refrigerator again. She pours a glass of Coke and watches it foam.

It is afternoon before they reach the graveyard. They had to wait for C.W. to finish painting his garage door, and Betty was in the shower. On the way, they bought a bucket of fried chicken. Joe said little on the drive into the country. When he gets quiet, Waldeen can never figure out if he is angry or calm. When he put the beer cooler in the trunk, she caught a glimpse of the geraniums in an ornate concrete pot with a handle. It looked like a petrified Easter basket. On the drive, she closed her eyes and imagined that they were in a funeral procession.

The graveyard is next to the woods on a small rise fenced in with barbed wire. A herd of Holsteins grazes in the pasture nearby, and in the distance the smokestacks of the new industrial park send up lazy swirls of smoke. Waldeen spreads out a blanket, and Betty opens beers and hands them around. Holly sits down under a tree, her back to the gravestones, and opens a Vicki Barr flight stewardess book.

Joe won't sit down to eat until he has unloaded the geraniums. He fusses over the heavy basket, trying to find a level spot. The flowers are not yet blooming.

"Wouldn't plastic flowers keep better?" asks Waldeen. "Then you wouldn't have to lug that thing back and forth." There are several bunches of plastic flowers on the graves. Most of them have fallen out of their containers.

"Plastic, yuck!" cries Holly.

"I should have known I'd say the wrong thing," says Waldeen.

"My grandmother liked geraniums," Joe says.

At the picnic, Holly eats only slaw and the crust from a drumstick. Waldeen remarks, "Mr. Spock is going to have a feast."

"You've got a treasure, Waldeen," says C.W. "Most kids just want to load up on junk."

"Wonder how long a person can survive without meat?" says Waldeen, somewhat breezily. Suddenly, she feels miserable about the way she treats Holly. Everything Waldeen does is so

roundabout, so devious, a habit she is sure she acquired from
Joe Murdock. Disgusted, Waldeen flings a chicken bone out
among the graves. Once, her ex-husband wouldn't bury the dog
that was hit by a car. It lay in a ditch for over a week. She
remembers Joe saying several times, "Wonder if the dog is still
there?" He wouldn't admit that he didn't want to bury it. Waldeen wouldn't do it because he had said he would do it. It was a
war of nerves. She finally called the Highway Department to
pick it up. Joe McClain, at least, would never be that barbaric.

Joe pats Holly on the head and says, "My girl's stubborn, but
she knows what she likes." He makes a Jimmy Durante face that
causes Holly to smile. Then he brings out a surprise for her, a
bag of trail mix, which includes pecans and raisins. When Holly
pounces on it, Waldeen notices that Holly is not wearing the
Indian bracelet her father gave her. Waldeen wonders if there
are vegetarians in Arizona.

Blue sky burns through the intricate spring leaves of the maples
on the fence line. The light glances off the gravestones — a few
thin slabs that date back to the last century and eleven sturdy
blocks of marble and granite. Joe's grandmother's grave is a
brown heap.

Waldeen opens another beer. She and Betty are stretched out
under a maple tree and Holly is reading. Betty is talking idly
about the diet she intends to go on. Waldeen feels too lazy to
move. She watches the men work. While C.W. rakes leaves, Joe
washes off the gravestones with water he brought in a camp
carrier. He scrubs out the carvings with a brush. He seems as
devoted as a man washing and polishing his car on a Saturday
afternoon. Betty plays he-loves-me-he-loves-me-not with the
fingers of a maple leaf. The fragments fly away in a soft breeze.

From her Sea World tote bag, Betty pulls out playing cards
with Holly Hobbie pictures on them. The old-fashioned child
with the bonnet hiding her face is just the opposite of Waldeen's
own strange daughter. Waldeen sees Holly secretly watching
the men. They pick up their beer cans from a pink, shiny tomb-
stone and drink a toast to Joe's great-great-grandfather Joseph
McClain, who was killed in the Civil War. His stone, almost
hidden in dead grasses, says 1841–1862.

"When I die, they can burn me and dump the ashes in the lake," says C.W.

"Not me," says Joe. "I want to be buried right here."

"*Want* to be? You planning to die soon?"

Joe laughs. "No, but if it's my time, then it's my time. I wouldn't be afraid to go."

"I guess that's the right way to look at it."

Betty says to Waldeen, "He'd marry me if I'd have his kid."

"What made you decide you don't want a kid, anyhow?" Waldeen is shuffling the cards, fifty-two identical children in bonnets.

"Who says I decided? You just do whatever comes natural. Whatever's right for you." Betty has already had three beers and she looks sleepy.

"Most people do just the opposite. They have kids without thinking. Or get married."

"Talk about decisions," Betty goes on. "Did you see *60 Minutes* when they were telling about Palm Springs? And how all those rich people live? One woman had hundreds of dresses and Morley Safer was asking her how she ever decided what on earth to wear. He was *strolling* through her closet. He could have played *golf* in her closet."

"Rich people don't know beans," says Waldeen. She drinks some beer, then deals out the cards for a game of hearts. Betty snatches each card eagerly. Waldeen does not look at her own cards right away. In the pasture, the cows are beginning to move. The sky is losing its blue. Holly seems lost in her book, and the men are laughing. C.W. stumbles over a footstone hidden in the grass and falls onto a grave. He rolls over, curled up with laughter.

"Y'all are going to kill yourselves," Waldeen says, calling to him across the graveyard.

Joe tells C.W. to shape up. "We've got work to do," he says.

Joe looks over at Waldeen and mouths something. "I love you"? Her ex-husband used to stand in front of the TV and pantomime singers. She suddenly remembers a Ku Klux Klansman she saw on TV. He was being arrested at a demonstration, and as he was led away in handcuffs, he spoke to someone off-camera, ending with a solemn message, "I *love* you." He was

acting for the camera, as if to say, "Look what a nice guy I am."
He gave Waldeen the creeps. That could have been Joe Murdock, Waldeen thinks. Not Joe McClain. Maybe she is beginning
to get them straight in her mind. They have different ways of
trying to get through to her. The differences are very subtle.
Soon she will figure them out.

Waldeen and Betty play several hands of hearts and drink
more beer. Betty is clumsy with the cards and loses three hands
in a row. Waldeen cannot keep her mind on the cards either.
She wins accidentally. She can't concentrate because of the
graves, and Joe standing there saying "I love you." If she mar-
ries Joe, and doesn't get divorced again, they will be buried here
together. She picks out a likely spot and imagines the headstone
and the green carpet and the brown leaves that will someday
cover the twin mounds. Joe and C.W. are bringing leaves to the
center of the graveyard and piling them on the place she has
chosen. Waldeen feels peculiar, as if the burial plot, not a diamond ring, symbolizes the promise of marriage. But there is
something comforting about the thought, which she tries to explain to Betty.

"Ooh, that's gross," says Betty. She slaps down a heart and
takes the trick.

Waldeen shuffles the cards for a long time. The pile of leaves
is growing dramatically. Joe and C.W. have each claimed a side
of the graveyard, and they are racing. It occurs to Waldeen that
she has spent half her life watching guys named Joe show off
for her. Once, when Waldeen was fourteen, she went out onto
the lake with Joe Suiter in a rented pedal boat. When Waldeen
sees him at the bank, where he works, she always remembers
the pedal boat and how they stayed out in the silver-blue lake
all afternoon, ignoring the people waving them in from the
shore. When they finally returned, Joe owed ten dollars in over-
time on the boat, so he worked Saturdays, mowing yards, to pay
for their spree. Only recently in the bank, when they laughed
over the memory, he told her that it was worth it, for it was one
of the great adventures of his life, going out in a pedal boat with
Waldeen, with nothing but the lake and time.

Betty is saying, "We could have a nice bonfire and a wienie
roast — what *are* you doing?"

Waldeen has pulled her shoes off. And she is taking a long, running start, like a pole vaulter, and then with a flying leap she lands in the immense pile of leaves, up to her elbows. Leaves are flying and everyone is standing around her, forming a stern circle, and Holly, with her book closed on her fist, is saying, "Don't you know *anything*?"

WRIGHT MORRIS

Victrola

(FROM THE NEW YORKER)

"SIT!" SAID BUNDY, ALTHOUGH the dog already sat. His knowing
what Bundy would say was one of the things people noticed
about their close relationship. The dog sat — not erect, like
most dogs, but off to one side, so that the short-haired pelt on
one rump was always soiled. When Bundy attempted to clean it,
as he once did, the spot no longer matched the rest of the dog,
like a cleaned spot on an old rug. A second soiled spot was on
his head, where children and strangers liked to pat him. Over
his eyes the pelt was so thin his hide showed through. A third
defacement had been caused by the leash in his younger years,
when he had tugged at it harder, sometimes almost gagging as
Bundy resisted.

Those days had been a strain on both of them. Bundy developed a bad bursitis, and the crease of the leash could still be
seen on the back of his hand. In the past year, over the last eight
months, beginning with the cold spell in December, the dog was
so slow to cross the street Bundy might have to drag him. That
brought on spells of angina for Bundy, and they would both
have to stand there until they felt better. At such moments the
dog's slantwise gaze was one that Bundy avoided. "Sit!" he
would say, no longer troubling to see if the dog did.

The dog leashed to a parking meter, Bundy walked through
the drugstore to the prescription counter at the rear. The pharmacist, Mr. Avery, peered down from a platform two steps
above floor level — the source of a customer's still-pending law-
suit. His gaze to the front of the store, he said, "He still itching?"

Bundy nodded. Mr. Avery had recommended a vitamin supplement that some dogs found helpful. The scratching had been replaced by licking.

"You've got to remember," said Avery, "he's in his nineties. When you're in your nineties, you'll also do a little scratchin'!" Avery gave Bundy a challenging stare. If Avery reached his nineties, Bundy was certain Mrs. Avery would have to keep him on a leash or he would forget who he was. He had repeated this story about the dog's being ninety ever since Bundy had first met him and the dog was younger.

"I need your expertise," Bundy said. (Avery lapped up that sort of flattery.) "How does five cc.'s compare with five hundred mg.'s?"

"It doesn't. Five cc.'s is a liquid measure. It's a spoonful."

"What I want to know is, how much vitamin C am I getting in five cc.'s?"

"Might not be any. In a liquid solution, vitamin C deteriorates rapidly. You should get it in the tablet." It seemed clear he had expected more of Bundy.

"I see," said Bundy. "Could I have my prescription?"

Mr. Avery lowered his glasses to look for it on the counter. Bundy might have remarked that a man of Avery's age — and experience — ought to know enough to wear glasses he could both see and read through, but having to deal with him once a month dictated more discretion than valor.

Squinting to read the label, Avery said, "I see he's upped your dosage." On their first meeting, Bundy and Avery had had a sensible discussion about the wisdom of minimal medication, an attitude that Bundy thought was unusual to hear from a pharmacist.

"His point is," said Bundy, "since I like to be active, there's no reason I shouldn't enjoy it. He tells me the dosage is still pretty normal."

"Hmm," Avery said. He opened the door so Bundy could step behind the counter and up to the platform with his Blue Cross card. For the umpteenth time he told Bundy, "Pay the lady at the front. Watch your step as you leave."

As he walked toward the front Bundy reflected that he would rather be a little less active than forget what he had said two minutes earlier.

"We've nothing but trouble with dogs," the cashier said. "They're in and out every minute. They get at the bars of candy. But I can't ever remember trouble with your dog."

"He's on a leash," said Bundy.

"That's what I'm saying," she replied.

When Bundy came out of the store, the dog was lying down, but he made the effort to push up and sit.

"Look at you," Bundy said, and stooped to dust him off. The way he licked himself, he picked up dirt like a blotter. A shadow moved over them, and Bundy glanced up to see, at a respectful distance, a lady beaming on the dog like a healing heat lamp. Older than Bundy — much older, a wraithlike creature, more spirit than substance, her face crossed with wisps of hair like cobwebs — Mrs. Poole had known the dog as a pup; she had been a dear friend of its former owner, Miss Tyler, who had lived directly above Bundy. For years he had listened to his neighbor tease the dog to bark for pieces of liver, and heard the animal push his food dish around the kitchen.

"What ever will become of him?" Miss Tyler would whisper to Bundy, anxious that the dog shouldn't hear what she was saying. Bundy had tried to reassure her: look how spry she was at eighty! Look how the dog was overweight and asthmatic! But to ease her mind he had agreed to provide him with a home, if worst came to worst, as it did soon enough. So Bundy inherited the dog, three cases of dog food, balls and rubber bones in which the animal took no interest, along with an elegant cushioned sleeping basket he never used.

Actually, Bundy had never liked biggish dogs with very short pelts. Too much of everything, to his taste, was overexposed. The dog's long muzzle and small beady eyes put him in mind of something less than a dog. In the years with Miss Tyler, without provocation the animal would snarl at Bundy when they met on the stairs, or bark wildly when he opened his mailbox. The dog's one redeeming feature was that when he heard someone pronounce the word *sit* he would sit. That fact brought Bundy a certain distinction, and the gratitude of many shop owners. Bundy had once been a cat man. The lingering smell of cats in his apartment had led the dog to sneeze at most of the things he sniffed.

•

Two men, seated on stools in the corner tavern, had turned from the bar to gaze out into the sunlight. One of them was a clerk at the supermarket where Bundy bought his dog food. "Did he like it?" he called as Bundy came into view.

"Not particularly," Bundy replied. Without exception, the dog did not like anything he saw advertised on television. To that extent he was smarter than Bundy, who was partial to anything served with gravy.

The open doors of the bar looked out on the intersection, where an elderly woman, as if emerging from a package, unfolded her limbs through the door of a taxi. Sheets of plate glass on a passing truck reflected Bundy and the notice that was posted in the window of the bar, advising of a change of ownership. The former owner, an Irishman named Curran, had not been popular with the new crowd of wine and beer drinkers. Nor had he been popular with Bundy. A scornful man, Curran dipped the dirty glasses in tepid water, and poured drops of sherry back into the bottles. Two epidemics of hepatitis had been traced to him. Only when he was gone did Bundy realize how much the world had shrunk. To Curran, Bundy had confessed that he felt he was now living in another country. Even more he missed Curran's favorite expression, "Outlive the bastards!"

Two elderly men, indifferent to the screech of braking traffic, tottered toward each other to embrace near the center of the street. One was wearing shorts. A third party, a younger woman, escorted them both to the curb. Observing an incident like this, Bundy might stand for several minutes as if he had witnessed something unusual. Under an awning, where the pair had been led, they shared the space with a woman whose gaze seemed to focus on infinity, several issues of the *Watchtower* gripped in her trembling hands.

At the corner of Sycamore and Poe streets — trees crossed poets, as a rule, at right angles — Bundy left the choice of the route up to the dog. Where the sidewalk narrowed, at the bend in the street, both man and dog prepared themselves for brief and unpredictable encounters. In the cities, people met and passed like sleepwalkers, or stared brazenly at each other, but along the sidewalks of small towns they felt the burden of their

shared existence. To avoid rudeness, a lift of the eyes or a muttered greeting was necessary. This was often an annoyance for
Bundy: the long approach by sidewalk, the absence of cover,
the unavoidable moment of confrontation, then Bundy's abrupt
greeting or a wag of his head, which occasionally startled the
other person. To the young a quick "Hi!" was appropriate, but
it was not at all suitable for elderly ladies, a few with pets as
escorts. To avoid these encounters, Bundy might suddenly veer
into the street or an alleyway, dragging the reluctant dog behind
him. He liked to meet strangers, especially children, who would
pause to stroke his bald spot. What kind of dog was he? Bundy
was tactfully evasive; it had proved to be an unfruitful topic. He
was equally noncommittal about the dog's ineffable name.

"Call him Sport," he would say, but this pleasantry was not
appreciated. A smart aleck's answer. Their sympathies were
with the dog.

To delay what lay up ahead, whatever it was, they paused at
the barnlike entrance of the local van-and-storage warehouse.
The draft from inside smelled of burlap sacks full of fragrant
pine kindling, and mattresses that were stored on boards above
the rafters. The pair contemplated a barn full of junk being
sold as antiques. Bundy's eyes grazed over familiar treasure and
stopped at a Morris chair with faded green corduroy cushions
cradling a carton marked "FREE KITTENS."

He did not approach to look. One thing having a dog had
spared him was the torment of losing another cat. Music (surely
Elgar, something awful!) from a facsimile edition of an Atwater
Kent table-model radio bathed dressers and chairs, sofas, beds
and love seats, man and dog impartially. As it ended the announcer suggested that Bundy stay tuned for a Musicdote.

Recently, in this very spot — as he sniffed similar air, having
paused to take shelter from a drizzle — the revelation had come
to Bundy that he no longer wanted other people's junk. Better
yet (or was it worse?), he no longer *wanted* — with the possible
exception of an English mint, difficult to find, described as curiously strong. He had a roof, a chair, a bed, and, through no
fault of his own, he had a dog. What little he had assembled and
hoarded (in the garage a German electric-train set with four
locomotives, and three elegant humidors and a pouch of old

pipes) would soon be gratifying the wants of others. Anything
else of value? The cushioned sleeping basket from Abercrombie
& Fitch that had come with the dog. That would sell first. Also
two Italian raincoats in good condition, and a Borsalino hat —
Extra Extra Superiore — bought from G. Colpo in Venice.

Two young women, in the rags of fashion but radiant and
blooming as gift-packed fruit, brushed Bundy as they passed,
the spoor of their perfume lingering. In the flush of this encounter, his freedom from want dismantled, he moved too fast,
and the leash reined him in. Rather than be rushed, the dog
had stopped to sniff a meter. He found meters more life-en-
hancing than trees now. It had not always been so: some years
ago he would tug Bundy up the incline to the park, panting and
hoarsely gagging, an object of compassionate glances from elderly women headed down the grade, carrying lapdogs. This
period had come to a dramatic conclusion.

In the park, back in the deep shade of the redwoods, Bundy
and the dog had had a confrontation. An old tree with exposed
roots had suddenly attracted the dog's attention. Bundy could
not restrain him. A stream of dirt flew out between his legs to
splatter Bundy's raincoat and fall into his shoes. There was
something manic in the dog's excitement. In a few moments, he
had frantically excavated a hole into which he could insert his
head and shoulders. Bundy's tug on the leash had no effect on
him. The sight of his soiled hairless bottom, his legs mechani-
cally pumping, encouraged Bundy to give him a smart crack
with the end of the leash. Not hard, but sharply, right on the
button, and before he could move the dog had wheeled and the
front end was barking at him savagely, the lips curled back. Dirt
from the hole partially screened his muzzle, and he looked to
Bundy like a maddened rodent. He was no longer a dog but
some primitive, underground creature. Bundy lashed out at
him, backing away, but they were joined by the leash. Uninten-
tionally, Bundy stepped on the leash, which held the dog's snarl-
ing head to the ground. His slobbering jowls were bloody; the
small veiled eyes peered up at him with hatred. Bundy had just
enough presence of mind to stand there, unmoving, until they
both grew calm.

Nobody had observed them. The children played and shrieked in the schoolyard as usual. The dog relaxed and lay flat on the ground, his tongue lolling in the dirt. Bundy breathed noisily, a film of perspiration cooling his face. When he stepped off the leash the dog did not move but continued to watch him warily, with bloodshot eyes. A slow burn of shame flushed Bundy's ears and cheeks, but he was reluctant to admit it. Another dog passed near them, but what he sniffed on the air kept him at a distance. In a tone of truce, if not reconciliation, Bundy said, "You had enough?"

When had he last said that? Seated on a school chum, whose face was red with Bundy's nosebleed. He bled too easily, but the boy beneath him had had enough.

"O.K.?" he said to the dog. The faintest tremor of acknowledgment stirred the dog's tail. He got to his feet, sneezed repeatedly, then splattered Bundy with dirt as he shook himself. Side by side, the leash slack between them, they left the park and walked down the grade. Bundy had never again struck the dog, nor had the dog ever again wheeled to snarl at him. Once the leash was snapped to the dog's collar a truce prevailed between them. In the apartment he had the floor of a closet all to himself.

At the Fixit Shop on the corner of Poplar, recently refaced with green asbestos shingles, Mr. Waller, the Fixit man, rapped on the glass with his wooden ruler. Both Bundy and the dog acnowledged his greeting. Waller had two cats, one asleep in the window, and a dog that liked to ride in his pickup. The two dogs had once been friends; they mauled each other a bit and horsed around like a couple of kids. Then suddenly it was over. Waller's dog would no longer trouble to leave the seat of the truck. Bundy had been so struck by this he had mentioned it to Waller. "Hell," Waller had said, "Gyp's a young dog. Your dog is old."

His saying that had shocked Bundy. There was the personal element, for one thing: Bundy was a good ten years older than Waller, and was he to read the remark to mean that Waller would soon ignore him? And were dogs — reasonably well-bred, sensible chaps — so indifferent to the facts of a dog's life? They appeared to be. One by one, as Bundy's dog grew older,

the younger ones ignored him. He might have been a stuffed
animal leashed to a parking meter. The human parallel was too
disturbing for Bundy to dwell on it.

Old men, in particular, were increasingly touchy if they confronted Bundy at the frozen-food lockers. Did they think he was
spying on them? Did they think he looked *sharper* than they did?
Elderly women, as a rule, were less suspicious, and grateful to
exchange a bit of chitchat. Bundy found them more realistic:
they knew they were mortal. To find Bundy still around,
squeezing the avocados, piqued the old men who returned from
their vacations. On the other hand, Dr. Biddle, a retired dentist
with a glistening head like an egg in a basket of excelsior, would
unfailingly greet Bundy with the words "I'm really going to miss
that mutt, you know that?" but his glance betrayed that he
feared Bundy would check out first.

Bundy and the dog used the underpass walkway to cross to the
supermarket parking area. Banners were flying to celebrate
Whole Grains Cereal Week. In the old days, Bundy would leash
the dog to a cart and they would proceed to do their shopping
together, but now he had to be parked out front tied up to one
of the bicycle racks. The dog didn't like it. The area was shaded
and the cement was cold. Did he ever sense, however dimly, that
Bundy too felt the chill? His hand brushed the coarse pelt as he
fastened the leash.

"How about a new flea collar?" Bundy said, but the dog was
not responsive. He sat, without being told to sit. Did it flatter
the dog to leash him? Whatever Bundy would do if worst came
to worst he had pondered, but had discussed with no one — his
intent might be misconstrued. Of which one of them was he
speaking? Impersonally appraised, in terms of survival the two
of them were pretty much at a standoff: the dog was better
fleshed out, but Bundy was the heartier eater.

Thinking of eating —of garlic-scented breadsticks, to be spe-
cific, dry but not dusty to the palate — Bundy entered the market to face a large display of odorless flowers and plants. The
amplitude and bounty of the new market, at the point of entrance, before he selected a cart, always marked the high point
of his expectations. Where else in the hungry world such a
prospect? Barrels and baskets of wine, six-packs of beer and

bran muffins, still-warm sourdough bread that he would break and gnaw on as he shopped. Was this a cunning regression? As a child he had craved raw sugar cookies. But his euphoria sagged at the meat counter, as he studied the gray matter being sold as meat-loaf mix; it declined further at the dairy counter, where two cartons of yogurt had been sampled, and the low-fat cottage cheese was two days older than dated. By the time he entered the checkout lane, hemmed in by scandal sheets and romantic novels, the cashier's cheerfully inane "Have a good day!" would send him off forgetting his change in the machine. The girl who pursued him (always with pennies!) had been coached to say "Thank you, sir!"

A special on avocados this week required that Bundy make a careful selection. Out in front, as usual, dogs were barking. On the airwaves, from the rear and side, the "Wang Wang Blues." Why wang wang? he wondered. Besides wang wang, how did it go? The music was interrupted by an announcement on the public-address system. Would the owner of the white dog leashed to the bike rack please come to the front? Was Bundy's dog white? The point was debatable. Nevertheless, he left his cart by the avocados and followed the vegetable display to the front. People were huddled to the right of the door. A clerk beckoned to Bundy through the window. Still leashed to the bike rack, the dog lay out on his side, as if sleeping. In the parking lot several dogs were yelping.

"I'm afraid he's a goner," said the clerk. "These other dogs rushed him. Scared him to death. He just keeled over before they got to him." The dog had pulled the leash taut, but there was no sign that anything had touched him. A small woman with a shopping cart thumped into Bundy.

"Is it Tiger?" she said. "I hope it's not Tiger." She stopped to see that it was not Tiger. "Whose dog was it?" she asked, peering around her. The clerk indicated Bundy. "Poor thing," she said. "What was his name?"

Just recently, watching the Royal Wedding, Bundy had noticed that his emotions were nearer the surface: on two occasions his eyes had filmed over. He didn't like the woman's speaking of the dog in the past tense. Did she think he had lost his name with his life?

"What was the poor thing's name?" she repeated.

Was the tremor in Bundy's limbs noticeable? "Victor, " Bundy lied, since he could not bring himself to admit the dog's name was Victrola. It had always been a sore point, the dog being too old to be given a new one. Miss Tyler had felt that as a puppy he looked like the picture of the dog at the horn of the gramophone. The resemblance was feeble, at best. How could a person give a dog such a name?

"Let him sit," a voice said. A space was cleared on a bench for Bundy to sit, but at the sound of the word he could not bend his knees. He remained standing, gazing through the bright glare at the beacon revolving on the police car. One of those women who buy two frozen dinners and then go off with the shopping cart and leave it somewhere let the policeman at the crosswalk chaperon her across the street.

JULIE SCHUMACHER

Reunion

(FROM CALIFORNIA QUARTERLY)

IT WASN'T TILL YEARS AFTER the operation that I realized my mother would never have died from it. She came from a long line of unscrupulously healthy women who had dedicated their entire lives to surpassing each other in maturity. They no longer counted their age in years, but in reunions, and nothing under fifty was counted at all.

My mother lived for the reunions. Every year and a half she would dress us up and lead us, trembling and fearful, to the skirts of our grandmothers, great-grandmothers and great-aunts. They towered over us at an impressive height, their legs thickly swathed in flesh-colored stockings. My sister and I were left to ourselves during the ceremonies; we looked wistfully on while the women were photographed, smiling and blowing out huge numbers of birthday candles, more set against the idea of death every day. Their pictures still hang on our living room wall, so close together a finger can't fit between the frames.

It was the first time that any woman in the family had gone into a hospital. My cousins wouldn't even go there to give birth for fear people would suspect them of going for something else. Naturally my mother was questioned, cajoled and warned against the dangers of lost reputation, but she went anyway, taking the largest of the reunion photographs in her suitcase. It was a newspaper clipping of her great-grandmother's sisters seated around a silver trophy bearing the slogan of the American Longevity Association. Their names were listed in order of age in the caption.

My mother left on Thursday. The only thing she said before she shut the door was, "Take care of your father." She always worried about him.

"What for?" said my sister. She and I were the only ones home with him and didn't know how to take care of a fifty-five-year-old man. We didn't want her to go away; at a distance she would seem more vulnerable. Anything that happened to her would be our fault, anything we did wrong was bound to cause her pain.

My father took it harder than any of us. He hadn't really expected her to go, and just the day before he'd made her angry by pointing out that "hospitalization" would go down on her work record. He wasn't trying to hurt her; he only wanted to know where the pain was.

"Is it something to do with your . . . being female?" he asked, spotting me in the doorway.

She told him it wasn't, that it was something much less serious than he could imagine, and that certainly didn't deserve to be on a permanent record.

"Why should I have to imagine? Why don't you tell me so I don't have to imagine?"

"I'm much stronger than you might think." She was already making arrangements to take her Christmas vacation in August.

"What will I do while you're gone? What will the kids do? What will they think?" His voice warbled.

"They know there's nothing wrong with their mother." She smiled at me and I thought of all the times I'd stepped on the sidewalk cracks and then gone back to erase them, rubbing the soles of my shoes sideways along the pavement. "And I've already provided for your food."

When she wouldn't tell him the name of the hospital he accused her of making it all up.

"Why are you bothering with all this?" he asked her.

She was silent so he turned to me.

"Your mother isn't like anyone else," he said.

When we told him she'd gone he called all the hospitals until he tracked her down at Northern Memorial, but the operator said my mother's number was unlisted.

"What room is she in?" he asked.

"I'm not allowed to give out that information," said the operator.

"Well how big is your hospital?"

"Thirty-six floors."

My father was dumbfounded. "Do you know what she's in for?" he asked.

The operator said she didn't know.

My mother called the next day, but wouldn't give us her room or phone number. She said she was fine. She didn't want any visitors, and told us not to send flowers, the room was full of them from the families of other patients. (The flowers we'd already sent were later returned in a cellophane bag, a note taped to the outside with the message: "Put these in the dining room — big yellow vase ¾ full of sugar water.") She asked about my father and we told her he was angry about the unlisted number and didn't want to talk. She sighed, told us to watch that he didn't get upset.

My father was furious.

"She didn't even *ask* to talk to me?"

"No, she just asked how you were. She told us to watch out for you."

He didn't want to know anything more about it. He had the extension wired for the next time she called so that he could hear without being heard, and he would answer all her questions while laughing to himself that she didn't know he was listening.

Once in a while the woman who shared my mother's room would call for her, explaining that my mother was busy — getting signatures on a petition for fresh vegetables on the lunch trays. We didn't know what to say to the woman, but felt obligated to talk to her since my mother had asked her to call.

"What are you in for?" we asked her.

"I'm a kidney patient," she said.

"Kidneys?" said my father, shouting into the dead mouth-piece.

"Your mother's a very nice person. She talks to everyone," said the woman.

"What does she say?"

"She talks about sports and politics, you know."

"Well tell her we said hello."

"Tell her we don't want to talk to any more kidney patients," said my father.

When my mother called back she wanted to know how my father was doing. "Does he ask about me very often?" she said.

I looked at my father's back in the hallway. He was sitting on the floor with the extension to his ear, his legs spread straight in front of him. He looked like a bear in a picture I'd seen once. "All the time," I said, and I saw him shift the extension to his other ear.

One day I found him staring at the space left on the wall where my mother had taken the picture.

"Something's missing," he told me.

"She took it with her," I said.

"There are no men on this wall," said my father, ignoring me.

I looked. There were no men on the wall. The men in my mother's family weren't important; no one knew anything about them except who they were married to, and as soon as they'd produced a few children they seemed to disappear. On the other hand it was well known that my maternal grandmother had once set fire to her own home rather than see it knocked down, and at the height of the blaze, jumped out a second-story window to the ground, her eighty-three-year-old legs sturdy as a cat's when she landed. My great-grandmother came to America on a freight ship, disguised as a sailor, and before reaching shore had been promoted to first mate.

"I guess the women live to be older," I said.

"It looks like a family of clones," he said. "Not a man in the group. There's no pictures of your mother either."

I looked. Everyone in the pictures was at least sixty-five. "She's probably not old enough," I said.

He searched the house until he found a picture of my mother, and then he put it on the coffee table. It showed her gardening, leaning over the tomato bushes in the back yard, perspiration stains up and down the back of her shirt. It was a good likeness. She seemed about to stand up, and the way she bent over the tomatoes made her look even stronger than usual. She could have been an advertisement for vegetables. Photographs always had a way of immortalizing her; even when she was standing next to me I'd imagine her in a different pose. I had a collection of them in my head, and she was different in every one.

My great-grandmothers brought us casseroles and desserts, dropping them off on the step after dark so the neighbors wouldn't see them and start asking questions. They must have been communicating with my mother in spite of their disapproval; one dish of manicotti came over with a tiny envelope on its lid, and the note inside said: "I never use ricotta cheese, it's too expensive. Cottage cheese is just as good and I'm sure they won't know the difference. M." We passed it once around the table and let the dog lick the dishes. My father got angry because we didn't leave enough on our plates.

"Jesus Christ, what's the dog supposed to live on?" he shouted.

It was obvious the strain was affecting him. He still refused to talk to my mother on the phone, but he started giving us lists of questions to ask her: whether the doctors were men or women and how old they were, how many people shared her room, how many times a day she got to eat . . . Sometimes he would sit with the receiver to his ear for hours after she'd hung up, and whenever I walked by him in the hallway he would block my path with his legs and ask me another question.

The next time my mother called she said we shouldn't expect her to call so often, that she wouldn't be calling for two or three days. She said she'd be having an operation, a small one, but that everything was fine, there was no reason to worry.

My father almost tore the extension from the wall. He started shouting into the receiver saying she'd promised it wasn't serious, saying she had to come home immediately. She could hear his voice from the echoes bouncing into the kitchen, and she shouted back, "I'm fine Frederick, they're just going to fix me up a little." When the echoes subsided she said, "Tell your father I'll be fine."

He didn't believe it. He told us all the horror stories he'd ever heard about hospitals.

"During the war there was a man," he said, "a Polish general, who was so weak he couldn't eat. By the end of a month he was shrunken beyond recognition. They'd starved him almost to death, and it was up to his wife to get him out of the country. She had to wrap him in blankets and pull him across the border in a toy wagon."

"You mean she disguised him as a baby and nobody could tell he was really an old man?" we asked.

"He wasn't supposed to look like a baby," said my father. "How could a sixty-year-old man look like a baby? You're missing the whole point."

"Well what does it have to do with Mommy's operation anyway?"

He shook his head as if we were being stupid.

The day of the operation I found him hanging a picture in the empty space on the wall. It was a photograph of an old man wearing a brown coat and a bland expression.

"Who's that?" said my sister.

"My Uncle Jack. He lived to be eighty-seven."

"That doesn't sound very old," we said.

"Just by comparison. No one in your mother's family ever dies. People in my family die early."

"What do they die of?" we asked.

"That's beside the point." He walked to the opposite wall, took a picture of my mother out of his wallet, and tucked its edges into the corner of a reunion photograph, smoothing it down with his thumb. "Way beside the point." It was a newspaper clipping of my mother on the median strip of a highway, a white flag tied to the antenna of her broken-down VW. The picture was taken by a helicopter during the worst traffic jam of the year, and my mother was looking up and waving just when the camera clicked. She was just big enough so that I could recognize her.

"What does all this have to do with Mommy's operation anyway?"

"You don't like the picture?" said my father.

"That's not the point," I said.

"No, I guess it isn't," he agreed.

She came home on a Saturday. The front yard was covered with blackbirds fighting over crusts of pizza we'd thrown out the night before, and as my mother walked over the grass she shooed them away, picking up the crusts and bringing them in the house. "What have you been eating all this time?" she asked, waving the mutilated crusts in front of her. My father took her by the hand and sat her down on the couch. She had a long red scar across the front of her neck.

He was speechless. This had never happened before; it was the first scar in the family, the end of an era.

"Did it hurt?" he asked, finally.

She got up and walked over to the mirror. The scar went straight across the front of her throat, but wasn't obvious unless she tipped her head back. She tilted her head carefully, still looking in the mirror, and ran her fingers over the bluish-red skin, pulling lightly down with one finger and up with another.

"Does it hurt now?" asked my father.

"No." She turned and saw the picture of Uncle Jack on the wall. "Who's this?"

"No one," said my father.

"Why is he hanging on the wall then?"

"He's the one they dressed up as a baby," my sister told her.

"He was *not* dressed up as a baby," shouted my father. "That was *not* the reason for the toy wagon."

He turned to my mother, who had just discovered her own picture. She took it down and put it between the encyclopedias.

"Are you sure it doesn't hurt?" he asked again.

We worried about her from then on. She slept a lot. My father rented a mechanical bed for the living room and we took turns raising and lowering her legs. We never pushed the button that moved her neck even when she said it didn't hurt.

When she started talking about the next reunion, and said she wanted to be in the picture, my two great-grandmothers came over to talk her out of it. They saw the mechanical bed and looked politely away.

"You're not even gray yet," they said. They saw the picture of Uncle Jack and squinted.

"I want to be in the picture," said my mother.

"Aunt Gladys thought you were dead and buried."

"I want to be in the picture," she repeated.

They sighed. "Do you have something with a high neck?"

My mother nodded.

Two months later it was on the living room wall. Uncle Jack had been taken down, and in his place stood my mother, dressed in a blue turtleneck. The scar was completely hidden. Since she was off to one side it was hard to tell whether she was meant to be in the picture or if she'd just walked in by accident. But she looked beautiful, and my sister and I imagined her in blue for a long time.

Aunt Gladys had come up after the candles were blown out. "I thought you were dead and buried," she said, clutching my mother's arm. "What a relief."

Eventually the scar lost its color and settled into a fold in my mother's skin. She said the doctors told her not to drive; the bones in the back of her neck will always be weak.

It wasn't till years afterward that I realized my mother would never have died from it. At night she still stands by my bed in the dark, telling me not to worry. Whenever she leaves the house, or pulls the car out of the garage, I tell myself, my mother is stronger than anyone else's.

I see her driving down the highway, she waves to me and my heart swells. I see her crashing into the car just in front, her whole neck giving away, her head faltering, my mother, the car crossing over the median and bursting into . . . No. It was only a small accident, she's all right, it didn't hurt for a minute. There's my mother standing on the median, safely out of the wreck, thumbing a ride. I know she won't slip, the trucks going by won't even come near her, and soon, someone will roll down their window and offer to take her home. She waves once more and the helicopter pulls back, snaps another picture, another, farther and farther away until she's just a normal woman on a highway, no one's mother, no scar on her neck at all. Cars speed past in both directions, here she is by my bed, her hands cool on my back in the dark. We can sleep peacefully, knowing my mother is immortal. There she is on the highway, there in the yard, leaning over tomato bushes in the garden, and I can bring her back whenever I need her.

SHARON SHEEHE STARK

Best Quality Glass Company, New York

(FROM PRAIRIE SCHOONER)

WHEN I REACH THE DUNKLETOWN EXIT on I-78, I am not thoroughly astonished to be there. Familiar roads, routine trips, have a way of sopping up time, removing the driver from his tired distances, so that he arrives and has not traveled farther from his mind than its side porch or, if you will, the palm of the Hand holding him to the road. Ordinarily, having left my law office but milliseconds before, I arrive at this far point stunned with a sense of sudden, violent dislocation. When did I pass the brewery? What happened to Breene? New Lorraine? Time and space seize up on me, cover my tracks.

As I said, this does not happen today. All the way home I have counted off the landmarks, cursed the exits for not showing their tedious faces sooner. More than the western terminus of a daily habit, a conditioned reflex — today, at least, home is a destination.

The difference is I don't know what I'll find when I get there. Either Wilda's car will be there or it won't, and in either event it will come as a great surprise to me. There! she'd say, further evidence that I don't know my wife at all. Shouldn't I, after sixteen years, have developed a sense of her? Her style, her patterns, her limitations? Would she leave me for more than a day? Other times she went off in a cloud of dust and was back before the dust settled, looking contrite and ashamed, for leaving or for coming back. But lately she's different, lives closer to the windows, stops with her teeth in the apple to listen, walks on tiptoe: *Was that the phone? Is somebody at the door?* An outward leaning, as if there is . . . she might finally have somewhere to go.

And there is something else to be settled, a second surprise, so to speak, and that's how I'm apt to feel about the first one. I'll come up over my long, freshly paved, licorice-smooth driveway, crest at the paint shed and look down through the pines to the house. Either my heart will leap up or sink to new levels. Or I'll go about my business as usual. And I haven't a clue as to which possibility might engage which response. Last night I wanted to kill her. Who knows about today? Last night I smashed lithographs and mirrors instead of her skull. Today I am mild as this late March drizzle — a harmless fellow, looking for home.

Her dirty white Vega, that worthless piece of junk she refuses to trade in because "it's done nothing wrong," is not in the driveway, nor in the garage, nor in the turnaround behind the rose garden. So intent am I that I fail to notice right away what *is* there: a cruiser car smack dab in front of the house and two people, the state trooper and my son, running around kicking at the cellar windows.

I am not alarmed. Rather I feel quickened in the face of a question more intriguing even than the Wilda problem. Seeing me, the cop comes over to the car. He motions with the flat of his hand. *Stay where you are.* With his fingers, he makes circles in the air. *Roll down your window.* I say, "Yeah? What's the story?"

"Not to worry, sir, but you've got an intruder in there who won't come out."

"Won't come out?"

"Your boy here discovered him in the basement."

"Justin's always been a little . . . uh, mystical."

"Not this time. Saw him with my own eyes through the hole in the floor."

"Oh."

"Do yourself a favor." He scratches under the visor of his cap. "Your girl's down at the neighbor's. Kid's just showing me the layout here. Take him down and wait till you hear from me. Got a call in for reinforcements. This guy could be, well he could be anything."

My boy is reluctant to go with me. He wants to hang around and "do his part."

"We can't be responsible," the cop says, and Justie gets in beside me. He is twelve, thirteen maybe. His limbs just hang there, taking on bones. On the way down to Sprecher's he tells me what happened:

They'd heated up some leftover chile for supper. Bridget made some Pillsbury crescent rolls. (Bridget is smaller but older by two years.) I didn't ask why they hadn't bothered to wait for me. Apparently, she went upstairs after supper and then the phone rang. Justin answered it, hoping to hear his mother's voice. It was the Beisel Book salesman with a message for me he can't recall just now. Just before hanging up he noticed the light coming from the hole in the floor near the staircase around the corner from the basement door. Puzzled, he went over and looked down. To his horror he saw a face staring back at him from the room that was once a coal cellar. "I just wanted to get the heck out of there," he says. But then he remembered Bridget, innocent and unadvised on the third floor. (The kids live in the attic. With the completion of their rooms we ended seven years of renovations to the old place.) He found her on the john, memorizing the map of Africa. Shoeless and shaking, she followed him to the second-floor bathroom, out the window, onto the porch roof and down the smooth trunk of the syca-more. Fearing the length and openness of the driveway, they took the shorter but steeper footpath that runs down over the densely wooded hillside to the township road below. The thaw-ing ground was wet and cold, slippery in spots. Bridget cried, "My toe, my foot!" It rained softly through the bare trees. They had almost reached Sprecher's bungalow when Bridget realized she wore only a pair of blue jeans and a persimmon-colored bra. They called the police from Sprecher's.

Again, I have arrived at a point and missed the passage there. I am stung with strangeness. Even my boy Justie seems to have slipped off his own center and I hardly know him. I try to visualize my house, those downstairs rooms I paint with dedi-cated regularity, the floor beneath which the intruder bides his time. Is he living down there? Other houses crowd my brain, laying out criss-crossing floor plans. The hole in the floor? Of course! That opening in the black varnished wood through which the water pipes rise to the upper floors. The metal collar won't stay put, keeps riding up, exposing the gap. Of course!

I see better the rooms where we fought last night — the bedroom, bathroom, the guest room, the hall. She secretes her fatal flaw up there, where nobody sees but me: the defiant banners of her carelessness waving from chests and drawers, towel racks and doorknobs; the beds unmade.

She wanted to talk. I, of course, wouldn't let her. I know that once we get down to syllogism, I'm a beaten man. I took a crap and pretended it was a rough one. I hid behind a book, behind a transcendental calm, behind closed eyelids; I can sleep at the drop of a truth-seeking syllable. She said she couldn't bear to see herself reflected in my eye. I said, "My eyes are closed." She said, "Your eyes behold me darkly. I have no sharp lines, no illumination."

Justin says, "Did you hear from her today?"

"Did you?"

"No."

Sprecher lets us in, nodding gravely. These are the worst of times. His house is small and the air thick with the accessories of his dotage: liniments, salves, mothballs, cheap wine. On the stove in a dented aluminum saucepan, a glob of cold oatmeal, gray and unthinkable as a massing of cancer cells. My daughter sits with her hands loosely joined on the white enamel table top. Her usual dignity has not deserted her, despite the fact that she's wearing Sprecher's long-underwear shirt.

"They got him?" Bridget wants to know.

"We told him to come out of there with his hands up and all, but he didn't even answer. Cop called the barracks for more guys."

"Why'd he do that, Just, when he had you helping flush the guy out?"

"Shut it," Justin says without real malice.

Sprecher suffers their banter in silence, his hands tucked under the bib of his overalls. But he's got that squarish, bulldozer look he gets just before his patience runs out. "I never wanted them people in the first place," he finally breaks in.

I am afraid to ask. "And what people might *they* be?"

Red-rimmed eyes grab at me; his tones beat after my ignorance, whipping his basic Pennsylvania German into a frenzy of
high flat quacking like a duck. We finally understand him to be
cursing the state school up the road.

Justin's eyes widen. They are depthless blueberry blue, like
Wilda's. "That's gotta be it. Retards! Ya shoulda seen him, Dad,
the way he looked up at me." Throwing his head back, he dem-
onstrates an empty, upward stare; mouth a slack wet gaping
hole, eyes vacant.

Bridget shivers openly and Sprecher starts to quack again. "I
knowed it!"

Sprecher is an angry old man, staying alive on oatmeal and
rage and the summer work we throw his way. He mows our
lawns, prunes the orchard, helps Wilda in the gardens. Most of
the time he's furious with us, too: the kids fooling with his
equipment, leaving baseball mitts and lawn games in the path
of his garden tractor; the dog stealing his molasses cake; Wilda
forgetting to buy grass seed. But mainly his anger takes broader
aim. He hates earthen dams and Russians, injustice, the medical
profession (because it refused to save Jenny) and the government. When he was still farming, they made him destroy a
hundred head of tubercular dairy cows, the same government
that today brings us cretins in the basements of honest working
country folk.

"Can't keep aholt of them kind. Too gotdem dumb to stay
put . . . saaaaay, where's the missus?" Just because he squints
and smiles slyly, does that mean he suspects me of something?

I look to Bridget to see what she's told him, but I should know
better; she's close-lipped as I. We are hoarders of secrets. Her
face has no key. I decide to take the humorous route: "She's
hunting small game with the daughters of Diana." Sprecher
likes a joke.

"Ooooooo-ah," he laughs. "And ott of season! Ooooo-ah.
Yeah, well, tell her there's a bigk squirrel in her cellah."

The first year Sprecher worked for us he stopped by one
morning. When Wilda answered his knock, he told her they just
announced over KVNR the start of World War III.

She said, "They already gave it a name?" Then she asked the
agitated old farmer in for fruitade and waited for the first
bombs to fall.

Maybe it's crazy Wilda in the cellar because she had nowhere to go after all. Wilda, maddened with hunger, loneliness and talklessness, reduced to a twisted nubbin of her former self. Still shell-shocked, maybe, from last night.

She'd wanted things settled one way or another. Would I let her go then, if I could not love her? For the sake of her soul, no less. She knows I can't be led kicking to the well of such alternatives. Am I obligated to be her liberator as well as her looking glass? "My, my," I said, "if you're so perfect, when was the last time you put the toilet paper roll on the holder? Why is there a jar of basil on the highboy?" This time she wasn't so dumb as to answer these questions. She pressed on. I kept saying, "Listen to yourself!" and she started getting tongue-tied and talked anyhow, tied of tongue. I gave her the customary warning shot: a couple of snapped pencils, a magazine whipped to the floor. Nothing seemed to sink in. She just stood there oozing pop culture verbiage like a toothpaste tube shot full of holes: honest emotion, psychic pain. "I'm suffering," she said. "*I'm* suffering," I said and closed the subject. One by one I took her Curriers from the bedroom wall — *Mother's Pet, Little Ella, Birth of Our Savior, James K. Polk.* Against the walnut newel post at the top of the stairs I dashed them to smithereens. Shattering glass comforts and composes me, soothes my beleaguered butt. But I needed more: a spotty water glass, the jar of basil, then the old gesso mirror from above the dresser in the guest room. Down the hall Wilda stood with her head in her arms. The kids were up, defending her, too. I took the mirror to her like an offering, held it up to her barricaded face. "Behold!" I said and read the yellowed paper label peeling off the back: "Best Quality Glass Company, New York." Then I marched triumphantly down to the newel post. Silvered shards didn't fly but clinked heavily around my feet, down the first few steps. It wasn't at all the impressive display I had in mind.

"Oy — look it!" says Sprecher from the window. We all go over and watch two more patrol cars glide by like flickering ships through the mist of the early darkness. We follow the path of their lights, blurred red disembodied balls, plucking from oblivion the entrance to our grounds, the lane's upward turnings.

"Poor dumb guy!" Leave it to Justie to pity the intruder. So like his mother who feels sorry for cars. Dreamy, absent-minded pair. Boy with her face, malleable, unsettled features. No-color blonds, eyes against the pallor are dark stains. Given the nature of things, that each fathering requires an act of blind faith, and even having made that act — when I really think about him, spawned by my seed but untouched by my genes, I can stop loving him for the space of that considered injustice. He, another her! But his awkward stride, the down on his neck. I know no other son and am condemned to drown a little daily in the largeness of unspoken love.

Your children are your children, but a wife is just a smoke. They come and they go, wives. Dry-eyed they fill plastic buckets with splinters of glass on their way to the heart and bright fragments flashing a trillion angles of domestic aftermath. So the children don't cut their feet, they clean first, run the Kirby and then pad off into a soft spring night that doesn't sweep them right back in. Nights are not tides.

"How are your feet?" I ask Bridget. She shrugs. Her right toe is cut. Are the woods full of glass, too?

Then they hunker down in your cellar, scaring your kids senseless, settling into the dungeon life while you're still getting used to the broad light of day.

The only light in Sprecher's kitchen is a pink scalloped wall fixture above the table and the illuminated dial of the clock on the stove. The house is chilly. Sprecher must have turned off the heat for the year. In the event of a late March cold snap, he'd just layer on the flannels.

"Mebbe one of them smaht aleckys from up they-ah," he says, stabbing a finger toward the blackness outside the window over the sink.

Bridget screws up her face. "Camp Rockbottom?"

"That place for them little city coluheds, chust abott in my back yawd."

"No way! Face I saw wasn't black. Nobody's up there in March anyhow."

"Besides, they're just kids," says Bridget in tones meant to shame and enlighten. "They're not one bit different . . ."

"Don't tell me no different. They ain't like me! Do I tramp donn an oldt man's sugah peas?" He starts stomping savagely on the cracked linoleum, his finger in Bridget's face. Quack, quack. "Do I tease his poor oldt dogk, break goot limbs off his poor oldt cherry trees?"

"Mr. Sprecher," Bridget says softly, "why don't you show us some of those pictures you've got of Jenny?"

"Well, I don't know — ah," he sulks but almost immediately goes back to the bedroom through a faded blue chenille curtain. I shoot Bridget a look to tell her grandchildren about; she lowers her head demurely.

Justin pulls up a chair; he's a sucker for nostalgic old men. We draw curlicues with our fingernails on the table top, stare at the linoleum, cleave to our private images of the stranger.

"What hole?" I say suddenly to Justin. "What light?"

He looks up. "Huh?"

"There's no hole in the floor by the cellar steps." How had his horror story planted my memory with nonexistent details, added plumbing, so to speak? There are no pipes coming up through openings cut in the floor, not for a long time. That old dark varnish had been covered five years ago with thick plush carpeting, Aztec gold. "And no damn light in the coal cellar either," I tell him.

"Sure there is, Dad, tonight there is. Maybe he has a flashlight. He must have drilled the hole, right through the carpet."

I nod, letting him fill my head again with earnestly proposed preposterousness: visions of fiendish little men wielding tiny noiseless implements, or worse, commandeering my Craftsman toolbox while I spend myself in the marketplace each day. Wilda couldn't drill her way out of a Post Toasties box.

Sprecher comes out with the album, wearing his triumphant little-boy look, the one where he tries not to smile. Wilda calls him the old young man, because in his broad cheeks, deckle-edged bangs, his toe-spragging petulance, she sees something of the eternal Katzenjammer kid, give or take several generations of Berks County stoutishness. She keeps coming down here with her bags of fruit and pumpkin breads though it means near-certain entrapment with Our Family Album. Got caught three or four times myself over the years, but I'm better at bowing out, gracefully and otherwise.

He starts as he always does at the very beginning, with snapshots of the first grasses, tender and atremble, at the dawn of creation. Eventually comes Pappy Follweiler caught in the act of coveting his neighbor's barn and attendant hex signs, taking a moment off from the business of begetting mankind and more particularly Jenny who is soon seen next to her boss at the Rudy Stoudt Shirt Factory and then caressing the fender of a wood-paneled huckster wagon, in the Age of Travel and Technology.

Now, sepia-washed and self-conscious in a lacy Victorian lady's chair, Jenny, the farmer's daughter, waits to become the farmer's wife. "Chenny," Sprecher points, "chust before the weddingk." He gathers himself in the way he does preceding a weighty declaration. "She wass settin right there," he says, nodding toward Justin, "when it happened. Her eyes wass closed, but she sedt, 'Hoyt,' she sedt, 'what will happen to me?' I said, 'Why I don't know-ah.'" Quick pecking glances from one to the other. If his story has a point, he wants us to get it. His eyes are moist, but whether from rheum or tears it's hard to tell.

Justie walks to the window and comes back. I'm wondering if they use tear gas and if the damn stuff lingers. Poor Jenny, you don't ask a guy like Sprecher a rhetorical question with your dying breath.

Bridget, leaning across the table, points to a snapshot. "Who's that, Mr. Sprecher?"

"Oy," he says, "that's Mahlon Herber's youngest." He laughs, blue-gummed and toothless, remembering. "Oy, that young fella wass badt." He has difficulty turning pages with his rough, spatulate thumbs. Bridget turns for him.

When he comes to the farm pictures, I figure it's my turn to check the window. Nothing but the night and the fog. This is the part where he gets mad at us all over again. Jenny and Boots, the German shepherd, in the north field; Sprecher by the giant oak. Sprecher and Jenny planting raspberry bushes. The childless couple in the Primeval Garden.

Out of parodial sequence perhaps, but true to the metaphor lodged in the old man's brain where all evil began on the day he sold the farm, half to Rockbottom, half to the Fergusons who sold it to me.

"Them wass goot burries. All ruint now. Canes busted up. Thistles all arount. And my chicken hoss — that hurts me. Swelt up like a det man's belly, bordts sprung-it loose. Next bigk snow, the roof busts in — gootbye chicken hoss!"

I know I should apologize for not taking better care of his raspberry bushes and chicken coop, but the sanctity of my home has been violated. I polish the window with my handkerchief and peer out, polish and peer again. Can't he see I am much vexed?

"Barn needs work too. Every gotdem time the wint blows, sheets of tin come shookin' donn off the roof." Let him blow over, I think, hearing the tin come off his rafters. He is all raw, splintery anger, quackety quack.

"Mistuh," he calls, "who tolt ya to up and rip donn the grape arbor?"

"Wilda did." (Even as I say it, I see her face, begging for the life of those old vines.) "She said the grapes were little and sour. They made lousy jelly."

As I turn toward him, my first thought is he's going to hit someone. His fists are clenched at his sides, but I can't stop. It's like snapping pencils and breaking glass. "It's *my* land," I say.

He looks to the kids, to me and out toward Rockbottom. His body keeps starting out and coming back. Then he gathers up his album, crookedly, with trembling hands. Photographs pop loose from their corners and flutter to the floor. Bridget and Justin flit after them and hand them back.

"She chust don't know how to make chelly," he says in subdued tones.

While he's shuffling around in the back of the house, Bridget says, "I'm not imposing on his hospitality one second longer," and she pushes us out into the night.

"What hospitality?" I ask. We are three abreast across Sprecher's cement front stoop. "Did he as much as offer us a glass of water?"

"He gave me his undershirt, Dad." She starts to cry before thinking better of it. "And what makes you think the land is yours, man?"

Sensing a trap, I answer anyhow, lamely, "I bought it."

"Well he paid for it," she says through chattering teeth. I want to put my arm around her but I give her my suit coat instead.

Justin is the first to spot their headlights filtering down through the tumbling bank of fog in front of us.

"They're back," Bridget says tiredly.

"I hope they didn't have to shoot him," Justie says. We run through Sprecher's gate to meet the first patrol car. It's the officer I spoke with earlier, and he's alone. "He's in one of the other cars?" I ask, straining to see through the murk into the vehicles pulled up behind. He shakes his head no.

My God, it *is* Wilda! They wiped the soot from her brow, tweaked her mouth into tremulous little smiles and left her propped up in bed eating ice cream and watching Baryshnikov on PBS.

He clears his throat and fidgets and reaches into his pocket. "Here's your culprit," he says at last.

I don't understand at first when he holds out his hand, and then, oh no, I think, oh no you don't, if that's supposed to replace the conjurings of the past hours, the whole waxworks of rogues and retards and wild-eyed Wilda babe . . .

"I can hardly believe it myself," he's saying and hands me a piece of glass, of mirror to be exact, shaped roughly like the state of Nevada. "Was nestled in the nap of the rug as cozy as you please." Since I don't say a word, he feels obligated to go on. "Do yourself a favor, sir. Don't blame the boy. It's a hell of a thing. Had me fooled. Officers Bansky and Heller, too. Didn't figure it out till after we went down there after him. *Him?* Ha! Hell of a thing."

When we get home I offer to scramble the kids some eggs. Justie never turns down food. Bridget stands at the dining area side of the kitchen island, elbows on the rim of the sink. "Not hungry," she says, but makes no move to go up to bed.

There's a silence that needs to be broken, otherwise I can't swallow my eggs, not even with ketchup. I scrape the skillet onto two plates, giving Justie the larger share. "I hope you guys re-alize," I say, "that if we ever *really* need Pennsylvania's finest, they'll never believe us."

"The kid that cried wolf — is that it, Dad?"

"You got it, son."

"I don't want any eggs," he says. There's a sharp pelleting sensation on the back of my head and a sudden cold trickle down my neck. I spin around and take the shot full in the face. Bridget's lips form a silent curse. She drops the spray nozzle in the sink, where it rests a moment before beginning to crawl slowly back down its hole. Then they both run out of the kitchen.

When the upstairs has gone quiet and the light leaves the branches beneath the kids' window, I go to see for myself. From my pocket I extract the bit of glass: the state of Nevada, the state of matrimony. The living room lights are unchanged since early evening. I press it down hard into the untrampled Aztec gold pile here by the baseboard. Immediately there appears a miniature pool of radiance, seemingly lit from below. More difficult than I would have thought, I lean cautiously forward until I see what I came to see: the bug-eyed toad; the leering, drooling, demented fool below.

Quickly I draw back out of his view, subterranean wretch! He has always been before me and I have always been on my way here. How is it I forgot? It'll take a while to get my bearings. Believing itself soundless, the night sneaks past my eardrums, but I keep hearing her car — or is it Wilda chanting antiphons to herself as seen in a lover's eye?

She doesn't know the half of it. Sprecher owns my land; the children turn on me like thankless hounds; the devil's in the basement staring peepholes in my heart.

I make myself a drink, take off my shoes and wait for my wife to come home.

ROBERT TAYLOR, JR.

Colorado

(FROM THE OHIO REVIEW)

SUCH A TIME. WHERE TO BEGIN. With his mother's displeasure or his father's crazed joy, his sister's bitterness or his own young emptiness. It was long ago, that is for certain. He remembers the road signs, how you wait for them and then for the towns they prophesy. Always the anticipation of the mountains. The car, a 1952 two-toned blue De Soto hardtop, was air-conditioned, chilly as a movie theater inside.

He was twelve years old and so his father would have been forty. His mother, six months younger than his father, was pretty. He had taken a picture of her standing by the blue De Soto. In that photograph she wore the very short shorts so popular in those days, her legs long and slender, the ankles nicely set off, he saw later, by the high, wedge-heeled sandals. She looked like a much younger woman, not anything like his friends' mothers, shapeless and gray figures whose sole purpose in life was surely only to be a mother. His mother had an air about her that suggested she was cut out for something else — just what exactly, he couldn't have said, not in those days, but the special quality certainly did not escape him. She did exercises every night on the carpeted floor of the living room, rolled, stretched, twisted, jiggled, crouching, kneeling, sitting, standing, or sometimes lying flat on her back or belly, while he sat in the love seat with his homework in his lap. His father would be in the office, a room several years ago added onto the other side of the garage, a small and separate place, its many shelves cluttered with yearbook samples, order forms, catalogs of rings, company bulletins, copies of *Popular Mechanics* and *Reader's Digest*, musty-smelling books on how to sell, how to succeed, how to win, how to manage, their dust jackets illustrated with photographs of smiling men-in-bow-ties whose hair, only slightly thinning, faintly graying, was always parted in the middle. There was a big desk with a crooked-neck fluorescent lamp that hummed like a radio between stations and made the desk glow with the whitest light you've ever seen, the rest of the room bathed in a darkness so soft that the teeming shelves might have been shadowy altars, the narrow bed beneath the windows a pew. Hunched over the desk, his father took a tiny brush and dipped it into one of a multitude of small jars ranged before him just at the edge of the light and touched that brush to paper, just so, touching, it seemed, with the least motion possible, then laying that brush aside, gently, without breaking his concentration on the fine, graceful lines appearing before him on the paper, and taking another brush as delicate as the other and dipping it into the mouth of another jar and touching it too on the bright and smooth surface of the paper.

His father was a salesman, yes, but an artist too. He could have been much better, but there was never the opportunity to attend an art school. In high school, he said, mechanical drawing had ruined him. The boy never knew, not then, what his father meant by that statement about mechanical drawing. It seemed to him that his father's talent was far from ruined; it was immense. The rings he drew, golden and bejeweled, were fit for the hands of movie stars, too marvelous surely for the awkward fingers of those high school students they were designed for, their subtleties beyond the appreciation of even a graduating senior.

Pretending to do homework, sitting on the narrow couch behind the desk until told to go in and get ready for bed, he watched his father draw. Then he went to the love seat in the living room and watched his mother do her exercises. On the divan opposite, Carolyn and Janie kept their eyes on the big round-screened Zenith console, arguing only during commercials.

That was all long ago.

•

One warm spring night his father came in and, instead of scolding them all for still being up, said, We're going to take a real vacation this year. We're going to Colorado.

His mother, her back erect and her arms jiggling, did not comment.

Where's Colorado, said Janie.

Stupid, said Carolyn. It's a long ways.

We're going to spend two weeks in the mountains, his father continued. No sales conference. A real vacation in the mountains. Colorado. There was a peculiar smile on his father's face, as though the word gave pain as well as pleasure. His eyes glistened and he held his cigar before him as if it were a special pencil for marking on the air.

Colorado. The word hummed, glowed. Made you feel good to say it. It was where the Rocky Mountains rose from the Great Plains. The Rockies were not like those mountains of Tennessee he had seen two summers ago at the sales conference. Those mountains had lacked snow-capped peaks. They were not majestic mountains. He wanted his mountains majestic.

When can we leave, he asked his father.

We'll see. We'll see.

I want to go tomorrow, Janie said.

Stupid, said Carolyn. What about school.

I'd rather go to Colorado. I don't like school.

A second-grader and she didn't like school. Whatever would become of her, so many years to go. Not enough recess, she said. Dumb games. Mrs. Martin doesn't like me. He believed in doing what you were told to do. It was a lot less trouble. The point was to get through. Next year he'd be in the eighth grade, the first seven years over and done with, only five more to go, and then — then he could do whatever he wanted. Nothing was going to ruin him.

I want to go right away, said Janie.

Want, want, want. Was there ever a family with so many wants. His father wanted to go to Colorado. His mother wanted to stay home. A vacation, she said, was only extra work for her. Carolyn wanted to bring a friend along. Couldn't Janie sit in the front seat. Janie wanted to sit where Carolyn sat, by the window. Why should she always have to sit in the middle. Who wants to sit in the middle.

I want you, his mother said to him, to take your accordion.

He wanted to leave it. He was tired of it. At the recital in the Bethany Church he had played *The Washington Post March* by memory, hating every note of it. Wasn't that enough.

The accordion would go, but not Carolyn's friend, who because of Janie wasn't invited. Little brat, said Carolyn. She always gets what she wants.

Do not!

Do too!

Off they went, wanting, wanting, wanting. It was June, it was 1954. Oklahoma City was big, but not so big as it is now. Out on the Northwest Highway there were no tall buildings yet, neither insurance tower nor condominium nor Baptist Hospital. There were houses, though, new ranch-style ones made of brick, with spacious, as yet treeless, lawns, and thick-shingled roofs and two-car garages. After a while there was Lake Hefner over on the right, a motorboat or two whining across its brownish gray surface with water-skier behind. Then you could look back and see the way the city was spread all across the flat but slightly tilted land, in the distance the twin skyscrapers downtown like monuments and all around them lesser roofs and clustered treetops, grayish in the early morning haze.

First came Okarche, hardly a town at all, a street past a few brick storefronts with a school at the other end, then Kingfisher, a bigger version, then Watonga, where you had to make a sharp turn before the highway again opened out across the broad land and yielded, miles later, to the patient and persistent, another town, Woodward. This one had a longer Main Street. We'll have lunch here, his father said, and pulled up into a gravel lot alongside a bright Dairy Queen. Where were the trees though. And the grass. The grass beyond the gravel was sparse, growing in weedy-looking clumps with lots of sandy-red dirt all around. The wind kept whipping up this dirt into little pinkish puffs. And what was that blowing across the highway? Tumbleweeds, his father said. They spun around in bursts of speed, round as wheels, and there seemed to be nothing to stop them. Standing at the window of the Dairy Queen was a tall man in a black cowboy hat. He wore a black vest, string tie, and a thick and elaborately tooled belt, its big silver buckle shaped like the head of a longhorn steer. Receiving his cone of soft ice cream, the man grinned, and his teeth were small blackened stubs, rounded at the edges. Hello, boys and girls, he said, and headed for his pickup, a shiny pink Ford with big dice dangling from the rearview mirror, a rifle rack in the rear window. In the back of the pickup sat a big gray metal box.

That, said Janie, was a cowboy, Daddy, wasn't it.

No. A welder.

A hayseed, said Carolyn, who liked to watch old musicals on television.

It was a quiet drive. Carolyn and Janie rode as though in a spell. After they had gone beyond the suburban developments of Oklahoma City, their wants seemed to have disappeared. It was perhaps magic, he thought, this journey a charmed one, the way to Colorado toward peace, harmony. Janie slept a lot, her head inching towards his shoulder and finally resting there. He didn't mind. He felt very brotherly toward her. He would certainly protect her if she were challenged by bullies, though he knew he would be beaten up badly. He wasn't little, but he was skinny. Slender, his mother said. Whichever, he had no muscle to speak of. The chest expander he'd secretly sent away for, a thick slice of black rubber with metal handles at either end, never affected, as far as he could tell, a single muscle, and after three and a half weeks of nightly pullings he rolled it up and put it in the back of the drawer beneath his underwear, hoping his mother might, if she happened to see it, take it for a sock.

Still he would protect little Janie. Stand up for her. Perhaps the fierceness of his efforts, the fury with which he swung and leaped and darted, would stun his opponent even if the blows themselves caused no harm.

As for Carolyn, well, only a year younger than he was, she was old enough to take care of herself. She was skinny like him, but it was all right for girls not to be muscular. Besides, nobody picked on her. Even with her teeth in braces, she looked tough, seldom smiling, her dark eyes clear and unblinking. She could outrun many a boy, and her girlfriends called her *Care*. When they came over, she made them laugh a lot. He could hear their giggles from his room while he tried to practice his accordion. It was distracting. Not that he wanted them to listen, no, but still they might try to make a little less noise. It would be, as his mother would say, only common courtesy. Oh, Care, they were always saying. Care, really.

He used to sing duets with her. For the grandparents they sang *The Tennessee Waltz* and *Your Cheatin' Heart.* Aunt Ethel, a choir director up from Dallas for a holiday, said, My, don't they sound like the Andrews Sisters. Then his voice began to change and he lost interest in singing. It was understood that soon he would have to begin music lessons of some sort. His mother hoped he might consider the piano because he had such long fingers. She was certain that his fingers were those of a piano player, a *pianist.* He resisted her encouragement, assuring her only that someday he would know what he wanted to play. Maybe it would be the piano, but he wasn't yet ready to decide. Then several of his friends began to take accordion lessons. The accordions rested in dark cases lined with red velvet. There were rows of black buttons on one side and, on the other, keys like on the piano only much whiter. In between was what made the sound possible, the bellows. The bellows of his best friend's accordion had an X-shaped design on them, white on black, that changed into a intricate pattern of Z's continuously expanding and contracting when the music was played. Another set of keys, smaller and fewer, gleamed above the white piano keys. These, his friend told him, for changing the tone of the note you played. You could make a sound like a clarinet, an oboe, an organ, a piccolo. It was wonderful. Mother, he said, I know now. And it was done. His friends, after the first year, had quit their lessons, but he kept on. Strapped to his shoulders, his black Polina accordion was heavy and cumbersome, but he was fond enough of the music that came from it, the spirited marches and mazurkas that his teacher, a small plump young woman affiliated with many churches, taught him how to play. Sometimes he played for hours, in his room among hanging Spitfires and Flying Tigers, vigorously but smoothly pulling and pushing the bellows, pressing the tiny buttons that he had come to know by touch alone while the fingers of his right hand slid across the piano keys in a motion gentle enough to be taken, he liked to fancy, for stroking. For *Lady of Spain* he learned to shake the bellows. His ambition was to master *Malagueña*. Sometimes his mother opened the door and said, That was beautiful. I loved hearing that. Her favorite was a hymn, *Whispering Hope*.

But it was changing. He found it easy to play less. It was spring and there were other things to do. He wanted to get a job so that he could save his money for a motor scooter, preferably a Cushman Eagle. He wanted to climb up high in the tree in the backyard and watch the horizon. He wanted to ride his bicycle to the shopping centers, Lakewood and Lakeside and Village, and sit at the fountains of the air-conditioned drugstores sipping cherry limeades. He wanted to read novels that were going to be made into movies, then see those movies. He wanted a girlfriend to take to them.

Have you practiced today, his mother asked.

Well, when are you going to practice.

Do you want to quit taking lessons.

The accordion grew heavier, the straps, he now noticed, biting deep into his shoulder blades, clear to the bone. But he wouldn't stop the lessons. He had to go on with the lessons. It would have disappointed his teacher if he quit now, and his mother, and it would have meant that he was not so different from his friends after all.

Of course the accordion would have to go with them to Colorado. He brought it to the trunk while his father was packing. It's all right, he said, if it won't fit in. I can leave it here. The trunk seemed bulging with suitcases and garment bags and fishing gear. It'll fit, his father said. Leave it there. I'll find a place to put it. Don't you worry. It'll go.

II

Here we are!

His father stood in the middle of a small room filled with chests of drawers and straight wood chairs dark as dirt and a huge high bed with a sharply arched and ornately carved headboard. There was a musty smell though the room was very light, its three windows extending from high up on the walls nearly to the floor, the curtains white and lacy. The linoleum-covered floor creaked and the ceiling above the bed had on it a large brownish stain, whale-shaped if you looked at it close enough, the wallpaper alongside shining with what might have been its own light, pale but steady, the pattern of pink hearts dangling in the stalks of yellowish lilies like faintly glowing bulbs in a tightly coiled cord, the background gray as shadow.

This is where we're going to stay? asked Carolyn.

It's dirty, said Janie.

There were three rooms, the one room, dark and small, between this one and the kitchen, where he and his sisters would sleep, they in a double bed that filled a good third of the space, he in a cot alongside. Every wall bore a calendar, each for a different year, none more recent than 1949. This one, the 1949 calendar, hung in the small room above the bed. It had a picture of a pink lady wearing the meagerest of underwear and a large purple plume in her tightly curled yellow hair. She smiled and looked, he thought, pleasant enough, as though she would be glad to talk to you if, seeing her, say, in a restaurant, you spoke to her. The other calendars had ladies on them too. The one in the 1948 calendar looked a little like his accordion teacher — in the eyes, that is.

It's cozy, said his father.

It's small, all right, said his mother.

He slept well that night, though wakened once by a strange sound that he realized must have been his father calling from a nightmare. It had been a long day. Mountains galore! Hadn't he seen the mountains, the snow-capped peaks he'd always wanted to see? They had been all around, the road winding through them, twisting along their timber-thick bases, following their swift-flowing streams, crest after crest. Look, his father would say, what a vista. That's what I call a spectacular vista.

You watch, his mother said, the road.

The road was often narrow, twenty of the last forty miles unpaved. Slumgullion Pass, his father told them. We're on Slumgullion Pass. Smell that mountain air. But it was really very dusty and his mother was right to insist on keeping the windows up, even though the air conditioner had been turned off to keep the car from overheating on the steep grades. Up the grades they went, the engine whining, his father saying, Come on, Bessie, you can make it, Bess. And then down, to the popping of ears and the whispering of his mother, I've had enough of vistas. You keep your eyes on the road. She sat stiff, both arms extended to the dashboard, her palms pressed against the glove compartment as if to keep something valuable from falling out. On these downgrades Janie shouted, Faster, Daddy, faster! Carolyn was pale, quiet, a paper bag in her lap in case she should be sick to her stomach. There was no stopping on this road, this Slumgullion Pass.

Not long before coming into the town, they came to a historical marker commemorating a man named Packer, who, trapped and starving in a nearby cave during a fierce snowstorm, ate his companions and survived. Very educational, his mother said. I'm sure the children got a lot out of that.

It was late in the afternoon of the second day of the trip when they came down from the Pass and followed a stream into the town, hardly a town, only a couple of streets and a handful of houses. There was a grocery, a bar, a sporting goods store, and set away from the main street, a group of tiny resort cabins. The mountains rose high on either side of the town and made such abiding shadows that it seemed hours later than it really was, almost night. As for the mountains themselves, well, they were surely *majestic,* their gray peaks now round, now pointed, stretching forth from the dark trees as if to boast of what they might do if they chose to, become sharp or smooth, jagged or straight, rising in fact like spectacular muscles, as firm and as proud. They could be sky, but preferred remaining rock.

Janie wanted to stay in the resort cabins, which, though tiny, were made of logs that had been varnished and polished to a bright yellowish sheen.

We're all set up, his father said, and drove them straight to a little house, the middle one, in a row of three houses at the end of the town's Main Street. Beyond the street a mountain began, this one somewhat shorter than the others, a weathered-looking church at the base of it, abandoned, they soon discovered, with neither pews nor altar inside.

The owner of their house, their father told them, was a retired sheriff. They found him sitting in a dark room in the last house, a magazine spread open on his lap. He said: Key's on the nail, top of the jamb. He wore furry house slippers and woolen trousers. The chair he sat in was draped in many blankets and the room was very warm, the walls covered with pictures clipped from magazines, desert scenes with palm trees, jungle scenes, photographs of movie stars, horses, luxurious automobiles, and all around him stacks of magazines stood like pedestals awaiting busts, each stack the same height as all the others, about three feet, some with tin ashtrays on top, the butts in them still long, bent so that they resembled fingers. The place smelled of tobacco and dust and something else, familiar but not so easily placed, what was it, burnt toast, butter, gasoline? His mother waited in the car.

Well? she asked.

We're all set, his father said.

Did you get the key?

I said we're all set.

I don't see any key.

Taking the key from the nail, his father smiled. It broke off in the keyhole, but the door swung open.

Here we are!

Evenings he played his accordion at the Last Chance Saloon. An old man played the piano. The duet was arranged by his father, who met the piano player in the sporting goods store. The barroom was only faintly lit by a pair of what seemed to be old lanterns attached to the wall at either side of the broad mirror that the bartender stood in front of, a steady stream of cigar smoke coming from his mouth. It was a long narrow room. The piano, a massive dark upright with yellowed keys, began where the bar left off. Along the wall opposite ranged cozy booths above which had been taped travel posters of Colorado, pictures of skiers in midflight, the white mountainside behind them like a great smooth cloud they had just sprung from, and of fishermen knee-deep in swift streams, casting or tugging their lines, of the fish themselves, silvery and plump and streaked or speckled with yellow, green, and blue, of Pike's Peak and the pink Garden of the Gods.

He didn't like to fish. This was a disappointment for his father, he knew. Dutifully he had gone with his father to the streams, was shown how to cast, how to reel, how to bait a hook, and, when sooner than he had hoped he pulled one in, a small one with tiny black eyes, how to remove the hook. It seemed somehow silly, a little like playing baseball. He tried to like it, wanted to like it, if only for his father's sake, but it was no use.

He wanted to climb the mountains, stand at the top of a peak, see what he would see, and take a picture of it.

You can climb that one, his mother said, pointing to the small one with the abandoned church on its slope. Leave the others alone.

He remembers watching his mother in the kitchen of the little house, the fish in the sink before her. He catches them, she said, I clean them. And she slit their slick bellies and gutted them while his father on the back porch cleaned the mud from his hip boots. His father was up early every morning, well before the rest of the family, in fact when it was still dark. He came back at noon, removing the trout from his creel and dropping them into a bucket of water, eating a quick lunch and then driving off again. He drove back deep, he told the family, up the gravel road toward Silverton, then parked the De Soto and walked the streambed until coming to a good spot, a still eddy where the fish rested, drowsy and hungry.

He's crazy, his mother said, slapping a big fish in the cornmeal batter. It's an obsession. He can't relax. I might as well stay at home. *This* is my fun. Vacation! No vacation for me.

The fish sizzled and popped in the big black skillet, and when they were served his father pronounced them delicacies, the likes of which would not be found in stores or restaurants. He caught twice the limit every day.

A lot of bones, Carolyn said, but she said it softly.

His father, disbelief so strong in his voice that it might have had a smell, said it was fine if he would rather climb the small mountain than fish the swift streams for rainbow trout. He'd like to have someone along, but if no one else was interested, why, he guessed he'd just go it alone.

The days were long and warm. His mother walked with them down to the store, no more than a room really, that store, with high shelves and, his mother informed them, high prices. The road to the store was dusty and the peaks of the mountains glistened back of the trees. You could hear the water running over the rocks in the streambeds.

I don't like Colorado, Janie said. I want to go home.

His mother said little. She wore dark glasses and her mouth seemed fixed forever on the verge of a frown. Once his father said to him: You must understand this about your mother, and it is true of all women. They have times when there's no talking to them. Whatever you say is wrong. You mustn't take it personal. You just have to realize that they have these times and it's always been that way and always will be and we just have to live with it and hope we live through it.

This must have been one of those times. There was a crispness to her walking, her steps swift and sure. We must make the best of what's given to us, she told Janie. When you're home again, you'll wish you were here. Think of it that way.

No, said Janie.

He and Carolyn and Janie climbed the small mountain. The girls didn't slow him down much. The way wasn't so steep, after all. It would be different on other mountains. The top of this mountain was broad and flat and grassy, the grass not so thick though, growing in clumps, yellow and knee-high, bending in the stiff cool wind. The three of them sat on a rock — a boulder, he would call it — and looked down on the little town, the house where his mother sat inside alone, and on the stream where, farther up than they could hope to see, his father stalked rainbow trout.

Here we are, he said.

It's like we're on top of the world, Janie said.

I'm the Queen of the World, said Carolyn, and this is my throne. You should thank me for letting you sit on it.

I'm the Queen, said Janie. You're just a princess.

They both tried to look very queenly when he took their picture, holding their heads high and folding their arms in front of them and crossing their legs daintily.

Lately he was thinking a lot about women. Not girls, but women. He was noticing that there was a difference. Running down the mountainside, Carolyn and Janie screaming behind him, he found it pleasing to think that at the bottom of the mountain a woman, somewhat like the waitress at the Last Chance, watched him. You're quite the mountain climber, she might say, and they would embrace. Kissing her would be like — oh, but he couldn't imagine what that would be like — like nothing else in the world, that's for sure! I'm glad, she would say, you don't like fishing.

You better not drop the camera! Carolyn shouted.

The waitress at the Last Chance looked at him while he, with as much feeling as he could muster, played on his accordion *The Stars and Stripes Forever.* She was even nicer, he thought, than the lady in the 1949 calendar that hung on the wall above his cot. She stood in the wide doorway between the bar and the dining room, her arms folded across her chest, leaning against the doorjamb in her white uniform, smiling faintly, as though just for him, her lips red, red, he would say, as strawberries, as new plums, some tart red fruit, how could he have said which, lacking the taste of them. Soon he would be thirteen years old, a teenager. When she asked him how old he was, he said fifteen, then felt his cheeks warm. She smiled a very understanding smile. She was nineteen, a grown woman. He saw the futility of it, but loved her all the same. Maybe she would have mercy. He could play the accordion, and he did, there in the dim light, *Lady of Spain* and, one of his mother's favorites, *Blue Moon.* There's a lot more to it, the old piano player said, than just the notes. You have to put feeling into the music. This was hard. He was learning just how hard that was. He believed he had the feeling, but how did you get it in the music?

The piano player, a tall man, a lanky man, sat hunched over the keys, his great gray head hanging low, as though the better to put his feeling into the music, his long and tobacco-yellowed fingers dancing atop the keys, now at one end of the keyboard, now the other. Sometimes he sang as well as played. When there were no words, as in the fast polkas, he hummed or whistled. I like the old tunes best, he said, like this one. And he played *Sentimental Journey,* the bass notes languorous and steady. His name was John. Some, he said, called him Johnny.

Carolyn and Janie were allowed to stay until 9:30. Then his mother took them back to the little house, sometimes returning later by herself. The owner of their house, the retired sheriff, sat at the bar, a shotglass and bottle before him. He looked small, though holding his shoulders erect and his head high, and he squinted into the mirror, never looking toward the music. There weren't many others in the bar. It's still early in the season, John explained. Later in the summer we'll have the crowds all right. You won't be able to turn around in here.

John drank his wine from a coffee mug, sipping it between tunes.

Watch your step, he said, with women. You got to be real careful.

He had a wife once, he said, and a family, but now he was free. A single man could do most anything he wanted to. You had to watch out for the women though.

The waitress touched John on the shoulder when she poured more wine into his cup, and John winked at her and the piano music seemed suddenly to hop or leap into something new. Feeling, you bet. The waitress's name was Dolores. He found he was thinking of her constantly. Oh, to be twenty — no, twenty-five would be even better, an older man — and muscular and musical with feeling.

During the long days he climbed the small mountain, sometimes alone. He sat on the rock and looked down on the little town. Some afternoons he walked back and forth in front of the Last Chance, hoping accidentally to meet Dolores. Almost every evening his mother cooked fish, but still she could not keep up with his father. What they didn't eat, his father took to the freezer at the sporting goods store. We'll pack them in dry ice, he said. They'll keep all the way home. We'll be eating trout next winter.

Until we're blue in the face, his mother said.

Walking back to the house from the Last Chance, his father and mother held hands. They walked ahead of him, dark and romantic in the stillness, the mountains like strange shadows. His accordion in its velvet-lined case was heavy, but he imagined that he carried it as a demonstration of his love for Dolores and that muscles quietly were taking shape under his shirt. He watched his parents. Someday, he thought, I will have a wife and family. I will not let anything ruin me.

Later he was awakened.

In the next room his mother was saying No. Please, no. Please let me sleep. Please, can't you understand I want to sleep.

An old story, was what he thought he heard his father say before the stillness came round again.

MARIAN THURM

Starlight

(FROM THE NEW YORKER)

ELAINE AND HER MOTHER HAD SPENT the day shopping, going from one department store to the next — from Lord & Taylor to Saks to Jordan Marsh to Burdines. It was Elaine's third day in Florida, and they had been looking for gifts for her two boys: Jesse, who was nine, and Matthew, who was eleven. Elaine hadn't seen either of them in months, and she hoped the shirts and sweaters she had bought were the right sizes. The last time she saw them was in early December, when she left their house in New Jersey with three large suitcases crammed with her winter clothes. At first she had felt an overwhelming grief when the boys told her they preferred to live with their father; the humiliation had come later, along with a sudden, cold anger. She got over her anger soon enough — how could you be angry at children who were too young to know they had hurt you? The grief stayed with her much longer, but she was finally over that, too. It was the humiliation that lingered. As her mother and father had said more than once since Elaine's arrival, "Who ever heard of young children like that just coming right out and picking their father over their mother, no two ways about it?"

Even Peter, Elaine's husband, had been amazed at the boys' decision. He hadn't been all that pleased about it, either. Keeping Jesse and Matthew meant keeping the house and finding someone to take care of things until he got home from work. It wasn't anything like what he had envisioned for himself. He didn't go into details, but Elaine knew that whatever it was he wanted was going to be harder to get now that there were two

children to be looked after. When he first told her why he
wanted out, she stared at him in disbelief. She was boring, he
said. Nothing she did or said or wanted was interesting anymore. They were on their way back from the city, where they
had had dinner with a friend of Peter's from college — a criminal lawyer who specialized in defending celebrities who'd been
arrested on drug charges. He had asked them to a big party he
was giving, where there was sure to be plenty of really good
dope, and Elaine wanted to know why Peter had said they'd love
to come, why he'd said it sounded like a great way to spend an
evening. We're not college kids anymore, she yelled at him in
the car as they crossed the George Washington Bridge. You
really are a drag, he said quietly, and he didn't let up until they
pulled into the driveway of their house. They sat in the car for
what seemed to be hours, Elaine shivering as they talked. What
did he want her to do? she asked him. Take up skydiving? Get
a job as a trapeze artist? Put a ring through her nose? That's
when he told her he wanted out and gave his reasons. Her own
reasons, at least, made sense; it was impossible to love someone
who criticized her at every opportunity, who belittled her in
front of her children, her friends, strangers, the whole world.
After thirteen years, she had had enough. Even so, Peter had
the last word. Whenever Elaine heard a book or a movie or a
TV program described as boring, her skin prickled with goosebumps, as if she were in danger.

"You had a phone call," her father said. He had just unlocked
the apartment's four locks to let Elaine and her mother inside.

"Who was it?" her mother said.

"Sweetie, did I say I was talking to you?" her father said.

"Who was it, Daddy?" Elaine said.

"It was Peter. He said the airport in Newark was snowed in,
and the kids wouldn't be down until tomorrow. Or maybe the
day after. It all depends on the weather."

"Was he civil to you, at least?" Elaine's mother said. She and
Elaine put their shopping bags down in the foyer. The apartment was the perfect size for two people, with an L-shaped
living room and a kitchen that could only take a small, round
table. Elaine had been sleeping in the second bedroom her par-

ents used as a den, but once the boys arrived she'd have to camp
out in the living room. The three of them went out onto the
screened-in terrace. The terrace overlooked the Intracoastal
Waterway; just as they sat down, a motorboat went by, buzzing
so loudly neither of them caught her father's answer. "Well, was
he or wasn't he?" her mother said.

"Bastards," her father said. "I wish those creeps would stay
out of my back yard."

"What else did he say?" Elaine asked her father.

"Peter? He was very polite. He asked how all of us were. He
said the boys were very disappointed about the trip's being post-
poned. They can't wait to see all of us. Especially you, Lainie
Bug, needless to say."

"Needless to say." Elaine knew her father was lying — his
voice sounded unnaturally hearty, as if he were speaking to
someone too old or too young to be told anything close to the
truth.

"Well," her mother said, "disappointed though we all may be,
you can't do anything about the weather, and that's that."

"Thank you, Mother, for your wit and wisdom in these trying
times," Elaine's father said.

"Please don't talk to her like that," Elaine said.

"Your mother knows I like to kid around. That's the way I
am."

"I don't mind. Or most of the time I don't. After forty
years —"

"Well, you should mind," Elaine said. She stood up and
looked out over the water at the condominiums that seemed to
take up every last square foot of land. Just across the way, a
hundred yards in the distance, she could see men and women
lounging around a long rectangular swimming pool, and a diver
poised on the board, ready to take off. She watched as he flew
into the water and disappeared. It was a mistake to have come
to Florida, she realized. But the boys had never been here before, and she had wanted to meet them on neutral ground, to
vacation with them far enough from home so that she wouldn't
have to worry about their calling for their father to come and
get them in the middle of the night. And she had wanted to be
among allies, people she could count on for comfort if things

went disastrously with her children. What she hadn't counted
on was her parents' making her feel worse than she'd felt all
winter long. Her father was especially hard to take. Since his
retirement, he'd mellowed, but she never knew what to expect.
It was easy enough to be fond of him from a distance; living
with him in such close quarters these past few days, she'd begun
to wonder if she'd last the week or end up running out to find
herself a motel.

The telephone rang.

Her mother said, "Arthur?"

"Don't look at me," her father said. "I'm just sitting here
enjoying the view from my terrace."

"If it's for you, I may just hang up."

"Suit yourself."

Her mother picked up a phone that was on the terrace floor,
next to a seven-foot-tall cactus. "Brenda," she said after a moment. "It's not bad news, is it?" She carried the phone past the
sliding glass door into the living room, rolling her eyes as she
went.

"Who's Brenda?" Elaine said, running her hand along the
spines of the cactus.

"One of your mother's friends from O.A."

"I give up," Elaine said. Her fingertips were bleeding; she put
them in her mouth.

"Overeaters Anonymous. Your mother can be on the phone
day and night with those people. If any of them feel like they're
about to go stuff their faces with a nice Sara Lee cake, for
example, they call someone in this network they've got set up
and talk their heads off instead of finishing the cake. Mommy
lost fifteen pounds, by the way. Looks great, doesn't she?"

"Terrific." Elaine turned around in her chair so she could see
her mother. "Wonderful," she said.

"You, on the other hand —"

"I'm fine."

"Feel like talking your head off to your old father?"

"About what?"

"Whatever. How about what you're going to do to get the
boys back."

"This is the last time I'm going to repeat this," Elaine said, "so pay attention: They're perfectly happy where they are. Perfectly."

"They can't be. Children belong with their mother. That's the way it works in this world."

"It seems to me I've heard that before — twice yesterday and once the day before that."

"Does it sound any better today?"

"Worse," Elaine said.

Her mother came back out onto the terrace, eating the largest carrot Elaine had ever seen, and she was reminded of Jesse and Matthew, aged three and five, dressed in their Popeye pajamas, holding carrots in their hands as they sat on their knees in front of the television set watching some dopey program — *Gilligan's Island,* she thought it was. They were young enough then that their heads smelled sweet when she bent to kiss them. She hadn't noticed when the sweetness disappeared; one day, it was simply gone.

She couldn't explain why her children had done what they had. The morning after she and Peter had driven home from the city, they had just finished breakfast and Jesse and Matthew were about to leave the table when Peter said, "Sit still a minute." They listened to him talk, staying silent until Peter said it was all up to them, whatever they wanted to do was fine. "Think carefully. Take your time," Elaine started to warn them, but already Matthew was saying he would stay with his father and Jesse was nodding his head up and down, saying that was what he wanted, too. They shrugged their shoulders when she questioned them, and she didn't have the heart to press the issue. If they had been daughters, it might have been different; she just didn't know. After she left, she settled herself into an apartment in Fort Lee and found a job as a secretary in a private school in Manhattan — the first job she'd ever had. She stayed away from the house in Fair Lawn and talked to Peter briefly now and then. She spoke to Matthew and Jesse only once; she was near tears throughout the conversation, and couldn't wait to hang up. They talked about school — book reports, and new gym uniforms, and the science teacher who made Matthew come in at the end of the day and stare at the clock on the wall for half an hour as punishment for talking in class. The boys talked easily, as if it had been hours rather than months that had passed since they heard her voice. At the end, she told them she missed them, then hung up before she could hear their response.

It was spring vacation and she was ready to see them, finally; to see what would happen. She wouldn't expect too much of them — if they were stiff as strangers at first, she was prepared to draw back and let them approach her at their own pace. Maybe, after their week together in Florida was up, they would decide to see each other every weekend, or every other weekend. Beyond that, she couldn't speculate. She certainly wasn't about to ask them to come and live with her, to set herself up for being kicked in the teeth again. That was what it had felt like this winter — a swift, hard blow that left her so weak she could hardly move.

Her parents kept wanting to know what she had done. It's easy enough to be a lousy mother, her mother told her. You think you're doing everything right and then one day it turns out you were all wrong.

Elaine knew what her mother had done wrong. She had been a mother who couldn't wait for her children to grow up. Elaine and Philip, her younger brother, were always treated like adults; whenever there was trouble, they were expected to act calmly and reason things out. Once, at the train station, when they were on their way to the city to see *My Fair Lady*, Philip, who was terrified of escalators, couldn't bring himself to put one foot in front of the other and step onto the moving stair. "Just get a grip on yourself," their mother had shouted, while Elaine, who was twelve, ran down the other escalator to Philip and took his hand. It was the middle of the winter, but Philip's hand was moist and warm. Elaine promised him that it didn't matter whether they ever got to the city to see *My Fair Lady* that day, she only wanted him to stop crying. After the train left without them, their mother came down from the platform. "Get away from him," she said to Elaine. "I don't want you feeling sorry for him. The whole world knows how to deal with escalators. What's so special about him?" Elaine watched her brother lick tears from the corners of his mouth, and she wanted to lift him off the ground and fly him high above the escalator all the way to the city, leaving her mother behind with a look of absolute

astonishment on her face. But Philip finally made it up the
escalator and was forgiven. It was her mother who was never
forgiven — not by Elaine, anyway.

"Do I care that Brenda has to put her mother into a nursing
home?" her father was saying. "Does Elaine care?"

"What?" Elaine said.

"Tell your mother you couldn't care less."

"All right, I get the picture," her mother said.

"Can't we talk about something pleasant for a change?"

"What should we talk about? The weather? Even that kind of
talk gets me in trouble."

"Talk to your daughter. Find out what's on her mind."

"I'm going to take a nap," Elaine said. "That's what's on my
mind."

"Are you tired?" her mother said. "I'm not surprised. A long
day of shopping can be very exhausting."

"I'm a people watcher," Elaine's mother announced in the airport coffee shop the following afternoon. During breakfast,
they'd got a call from Peter saying the boys would be arriving at
three-fifty-five. After the call, Elaine had gone alone to the
beach in Fort Lauderdale, taken a quick swim, then slept in the
sun for an hour, and returned to the apartment feeling fairly
self-possessed. (It was the one time she'd been away from both
her parents — the one time she'd successfully avoided them.)
Now it was almost three-thirty, and she was close to panic.

"People fascinate me. I could look at them for hours," her
mother went on. "Look at the couple over there." She motioned
toward a man wearing a cowboy hat and a big red mustache,
and the black woman who sat opposite him. Their baby was
asleep in a plastic infant seat they had placed on the table. "Now,
what do you think motivates people like that?"

"What do you think motivates your mother?" Elaine's father
asked. He smiled at her. "Plain old-fashioned nosiness?"

Elaine smiled back, but her hand shook as she reached for
her water glass.

"Go ahead and laugh," her mother said. "I guarantee you
ninety-nine percent of the people in this world would understand my point."

"I think," her father said, "the time has come for me to make my speech."

"If it's the one about mothers and children and who belongs with whom, you can cancel it," Elaine said.

"Give me a chance," her father said. "I just want to give you a little piece of advice, that's all. You listen to what I'm going to say to you and you'll have those children eating out of the palm of your hand one-two-three."

"Excuse me," Elaine said, and pushed back her chair.

"You can't afford to make any more mistakes, Lainie Bug," her father called after her as she headed for the rest rooms at the back of the coffee shop.

Inside, she rushed past a teen-age girl who was tweezing her eyebrows in front of a large mirror over a row of sinks. She locked herself into a stall, dropped the seat cover, and sat down on the very edge. She closed her eyes. The stall reeked of strawberry-scented deodorizer; still, it was easier to breathe now that she was alone.

In the dark, she told herself who she was: a grown woman scared to death of two little boys. Her own children. She had always wanted to be a mother, had always wanted babies. You couldn't go wrong with babies; there was no possibility of disappointment. You could hold them as close as you needed to, tell them all day long how much you loved them, and never feel foolish.

One night last summer, already suspecting her marriage was lost, Elaine had led the boys into her darkened bedroom, and in their pajamas Jesse and Matthew stretched themselves out on the floor and stared in amazement at the hundred glow-in-the-dark stars and planets she had stuck on her ceiling that afternoon — a whole galaxy that shimmered endlessly above them. Peter was away in Japan on a business trip, on the other side of the world; there was no one to question what she had done with her day. After the boys were settled, Elaine got down on the floor, concentrating on nothing except the perfect faces of her children. When she awoke two hours later, her neck was stiff and the boys were gone. There was a light summer blanket covering her; someone, Jesse or Matthew, or maybe both of them, had bent over her while she slept.

"We thought you fell in and drowned," her father said when Elaine made her way back to the table. "Like that time at the World's Fair when you and your friend What's-Her-Name disappeared into the bathroom for a nice relaxing smoke. I couldn't imagine what you two were doing in there for so long. Of course, as soon as I got a whiff of you I knew what it was all about."

"You all right?" her mother said. She touched her lips to Elaine's forehead. "Nice and cool."

"Do you want a Coke or something?" her father said.

"Not me," Elaine said. "We really should get a move on. I don't even know why I sat down again."

They got to the gate just as the first passengers from Newark appeared. Matthew and Jesse were right up front, dressed identically in tweed jackets, tan pants with cuffs, and Weejuns. Jesse was wearing glasses and had a flesh-colored patch over his right eye. Elaine ran to him. "What's the matter with your eye? When did you start wearing glasses?" she said. She kissed him and then she kissed Matthew. Neither of them kissed her back, though Jesse hugged her and Matthew shook her hand.

"Can't you give your mother a kiss?" her mother said.

"I'm in seventh grade," Matthew said. "I shake hands."

"And what about your brother?"

"Me?" Jesse said. "I hug, but I don't kiss."

Elaine said, "What's the patch for? Tell me what's wrong." She sat down in a padded chair opposite the check-in counter. Everyone else stood around her.

"It's just a lazy eye," Jesse said cheerfully. "It won't do any work unless I force it to. With a patch over the other eye, the lazy eye has to do all the work. You understand what I'm saying?"

"Why didn't your father tell me?" Elaine said. "Why didn't you tell me?"

"He says 'Hi,' " Matthew said. "I forgot all about it."

"You know what? His girlfriend bought us Star Wars costumes, even though it wasn't Halloween," Jesse said.

"God, what a jerk." Matthew put his hand over his brother's mouth.

"It's all right." Leaning forward, Elaine took Matthew's hand away from Jesse and held it. "Your father can have as many girlfriends as he wants. It makes no difference to me whatsoever."

"Well, he doesn't have one anymore. She dumped him."

Jesse said, "She used to make breakfast for us a lot on Saturdays and Sundays. She'd be there real early in the morning, like seven o'clock. She was a real early bird, Dad said."

"This kid is unbelievable," Matthew said.

Quickly Elaine's mother said, "Who would like to go for a midnight swim tonight? The water will be nice and warm, and we'll have the whole pool to ourselves."

"If it's really summertime here, can we have a barbecue?" Jesse asked.

"Sorry, guys," her father said. "No barbecuing allowed. Those are the rules of the condominium."

Jessie tried again. "Instead of a barbecue, can we go to Disney World?"

"You don't want to go to Disney World," her father said. "It's a four-hour drive each way. And you've already been to Disneyland, haven't you?

"Are we going to have fun on this trip, or what?" Matthew said. "What did we come down here for?"

"What do you mean? You came down here to be with your mother," Elaine's mother said. "That's the main thing."

Elaine studied her shoes, yellow espadrilles that she had bought just for the trip. The little toe on each foot had already worn holes through the canvas, she noticed. When she looked up, Jesse was dancing, shifting his weight back and forth from one foot to the other, his arms in the air, his elbows and wrists bent at right angles. Some sort of Egyptian dance, Elaine thought.

"Look at me. I'm Steve Martin," Jesse yelled. " 'Born in Arizona, moved to Babylonia. King Tut.' "

"Terrific," Elaine said, and clapped her hands.

"Oh Jesus," Matthew said.

Ignoring her mother's warning and her father's dire predictions, Elaine took the boys everywhere they wanted to go: Monkey Jungle, Parrot Jungle, and the Seaquarium. The boys

seemed excited and happy, though often they would run ahead
of her, too impatient to stay by her side. Once, from a distance,
Elaine saw Jesse casually rest his arm on his brother's shoulder
as the two of them stood watching a pair of orangutans groom
each other; she kept waiting for Matthew to shake Jesse off, but
it never happened. Two nights in a row, they went to see the
movie *Airplane!* A couple of nights, they played miniature golf.
At the end of each day, Jesse and Matthew told Elaine they had
had "the best time." She supposed that this meant the trip was
a success, that they would have nothing to complain about to
their father when they went back home. She had kept them
entertained, which was all they seemed to have wanted from
her. She might have been anyone — a camp counsellor, a
teacher leading them on class trips, a friend of the family put in
charge while their parents were on vacation. There was plenty
of time to talk, and they told her a lot — long, involved stories
about the fight Jesse had recently had with his best friend, the
rock concert Matthew had gone to with two thirteen-year-olds,
the pair of Siamese fighting fish with beautiful flowing fins
they'd bought for the new fish tank in their bedroom — all
about the things that had happened to them in the four months
they had been out of touch. But she still didn't know if they
were really all right, if they loved their father, loved her. You
couldn't ask questions like that. When, several years ago, her
brother had started seeing a shrink, he'd complained that his
parents were always asking him if he was happy. It's none of
their business, the shrink told him — if you don't feel you want
to give them an answer, don't. As simple as that.

It was nearly midnight; the boys had just gone to bed. Elaine
went into her parents' room, where her mother and father were
sitting up in their king-size bed watching *Columbo* on a small
color TV. Dick Van Dyke was tying his wife to a chair. He took
two Polaroid pictures of her and then he picked up a gun. His
wife insisted he was never going to get away with it; he aimed
the gun at her and pulled the trigger.

"Wait a minute," Elaine's mother said. "Is this the one where
Columbo tricks him into identifying his camera at the —"

"Thanks a lot," her father said. "You know how I love Peter
Falk."

"Who knows, maybe I'm wrong."

"You're not," Elaine said. "I saw this one, too."

"Well, it's nice to be right about something."

Elaine lay down on her stomach at the foot of the bed, facing the TV set. She yawned and said, "Excuse me."

"All that running around," her mother said. "Who wouldn't be tired?"

"It's not necessary to run like that all day long," her father said. "Didn't those two kids ever hear of sleeping around the pool, or picking up a book or a newspaper? Maybe they're hyperactive or something."

"They're kids on vacation. What do they want to read the newspaper for?" her mother said.

Elaine sat up and swung her legs over the side of the bed. "It's my fault," she said. "I couldn't bring myself to say no to them about anything."

"Did you accomplish anything all those hours you were running?" her mother asked. "Do you feel like you made any headway?"

Elaine was watching an overweight woman on TV dance the cha-cha with her cat along a shining kitchen floor. "What?" she said.

"Of course, if they really are just fine there with Peter and his sleep-over girlfriends, that's another story," her father said.

"Quiet," her mother said. "Look who's here."

Jesse stood in the doorway, blinking his eyes. "There's a funny noise in my ears that keeps waking me up," he said. He sat down on the floor next to the bed and put his head in Elaine's lap. "You know," he said, "like someone's whistling in there."

Elaine hesitated, then kissed each ear. "Better?"

"A little."

"More kisses?"

Jesse shook his head.

"Let me take you back to bed." Elaine walked him to the little den at the other end of the apartment, where Matthew was asleep on his side of the convertible couch. Jesse got onto the bed. On his knees, he sat up and looked out the window. "I can't go to sleep right now," he said quietly. Beneath them the water was black; above, the palest of moons appeared to drift by. There were clouds everywhere, and just a few dim stars.

"Did you want to tell me something?" Elaine waited; she focused on the sign lit up on top of the Holiday Inn across the Waterway.

"We're getting a new car. A silver BMW," Jesse said dreamily. "We saw it in the showroom." He moved away from the window and slipped down on the bed. "We might drive it over to Fort Lee and come and see you. And when Matthew has his license, the two of us will pick you up every day and take you anywhere you want to go."

Elaine still faced the window; she did not turn around. "To the moon," she said. "Will you do that for me?"

Jesse didn't answer for a long time. "We can do that," he said finally, and when she turned to look at him he was asleep.

JOHN UPDIKE

Deaths of Distant Friends

(FROM THE NEW YORKER)

THOUGH I WAS BETWEEN marriages for several years, in a disarray that preoccupied me completely, other people continued to live and die. Len, an old golf partner, overnight in the hospital for what they said was a routine examination, dropped dead in the lavatory, having just placed a telephone call to his hardware store saying he would be back behind the counter in the morning. He owned the store and could take sunny afternoons off on short notice. His swing was too quick, and he kept his weight back on his right foot, and the ball often squirted off to the left without getting into the air at all, but he sank some gorgeous putts in his day, and he always dressed with a nattiness that seemed to betoken high hopes for his game. In buttercup-yellow slacks, sky-blue turtleneck, and tangerine cashmere cardigan he would wave from the practice green as, having driven out from Boston through clouds of grief and sleeplessness and moral confusion, I would drag my cart across the asphalt parking lot, my cleats scraping, like a monster's claws, at every step.

Though Len had known and liked Julia, the wife I had left, he never spoke of my personal condition or of the fact that I drove an hour out from Boston to meet him instead of, as formerly, ten minutes down the road. Golf in that interim was a great haven; as soon as I stepped off the first tee in pursuit of my drive, I felt enclosed in a luminous wide bubble, safe from women, stricken children, solemn lawyers, disapproving old acquaintances — the entire offended social order. Golf had its own order, and its own love, as the three or four of us staggered and shouted our way toward each hole, laughing at misfortune and applauding the rare strokes of relative brilliance. Sometimes the summer sky would darken and a storm arise, and we would cluster in an abandoned equipment shed or beneath a tree that seemed less tall than its brothers. Our natural nervousness and our impatience at having the excitements of golf interrupted would in this space of shelter focus into an almost amorous heat — the breaths and sweats of middle-aged men packed together in the pattering rain like cattle in a boxcar. Len's face bore a number of spots of actinic keratosis; he was going to have them surgically removed before they turned into skin cancer. Who would have thought that the lightning bolt of a coronary would fall across his plans and clean remove him from my tangled life? Never again (no two snowflakes or fingerprints, no two heartbeats traced on the oscilloscope, and no two golf swings are exactly alike) would I exultantly see his so hopefully addressed drive ("Hello dere, ball," he would joke, going into his waggle and squat) squirt off low to the left in that unique way of his, and hear him exclaim in angry frustration (he was a born-again Baptist, and had developed a personal language of avoided curses), "Ya dirty ricka-fric!"

I drove out to Len's funeral and tried to tell his son, "Your father was a great guy," but the words fell flat in that cold bare Baptist church. Len's gaudy colors, his Christian effervescence, his game and futile swing, our crowing back and forth, our fellowship within the artificial universe composed of variously resistant lengths and types of grass, were tints of life too delicate to capture, and had flown.

A time later, I read in the paper that Miss Amy Merrymount, ninety-one, had at last passed away, as a dry leaf passes into leaf mold. She had always seemed ancient; she was one of those New Englanders, one of the last, who spoke of Henry James as if he had just left the room. She possessed letters, folded and unfolded almost into pieces, from James to her parents, in which she was mentioned, not only as a little girl but as a young lady "coming into her 'own,' into a liveliness fully rounded." She lived in a few rooms, crowded with antiques, of a great inherited country house of which she was constrained to rent out the larger portion. Why she had never married was a mystery that sat upon her lightly in old age; the slender smooth beauty that sepia photographs remembered, the breeding and intelligence and, in a spiritual sense, ardor she still possessed must have intimidated as many suitors as they attracted and given her, in her own eyes, in an age when the word *inviolate* still had force and renunciation, a certain prestige, a value whose winged moment of squandering never quite arose. Also, she had a sardonic dryness to her voice and something restless and dismissive in her manner. She was a keen self-educator; she kept up with new developments in art and science, took up organic foods and political outrage when they became fashionable, and liked to have young people about her. When Julia and I moved to town with our babies and fresh faces, we became part of her tea circle, and in an atmosphere of tepid but mutual enchantment maintained acquaintance for twenty years.

Perhaps not so tepid: now I think Miss Merrymount loved us, or at least loved Julia, who always took on a courteous brightness, a soft daughterly shine, in those chill window-lit rooms crowded with spindly, feathery heirlooms once spread through the four floors of a Back Bay town house. In memory the glow of my former wife's firm chin and exposed throat and shoulders merges with the ghostly smoothness of those old framed studio photos of the Merrymount sisters — three, of whom two died sadly young, as if bequeathing their allotment of years to the third, the survivor sitting with us in her gold-brocaded wing chair. Her face had become unforeseeably brown with age, and totally wrinkled, like an Indian's, with something in her dark eyes of glittering Indian cruelty. "I found her rather disappointing," she might say of an absent mutual acquaintance, or, of one who had been quite dropped from her circle, "She wasn't absolutely first-rate."

The search for the first-rate had been a pastime of her generation. I cannot think, now, of whom she utterly approved, except Father Daniel Berrigan and Sir Kenneth Clark. She saw them both on television. Her eyes with their opaque glitter were failing, and for her cherished afternoons of reading while the light died outside her windows and a little fire of birch logs in the brass-skirted fireplace warmed her ankles were substituted scheduled hours tuned in to educational radio and television. In those last years, Julia would go and read to her — Austen, *Middlemarch,* Joan Didion, some Proust and Mauriac in French, when Miss Merrymount decided that Julia's accent passed muster. Julia would practice a little on me, and, watching her lips push forward and go small and tense around the French sounds like the lips of an African mask of ivory, I almost fell in love with her again. Affection between women is a touching, painful, exciting thing for a man, and in my vision of it — tea yielding to sherry in those cluttered rooms where twilight thickened until the pages being slowly turned and the patient melody of Julia's voice were the sole signs of life — love was what was happening between this gradually dying old lady and my wife, who had gradually become middle-aged, our children grown into absent adults, her voice nowhere else harkened to as it was here. No doubt there were confidences, too, between the pages. Julia always returned from Miss Merrymount's, to make my late dinner, looking younger and even blithe, somehow emboldened.

In that awkward postmarital phase when old friends still feel obliged to extend invitations and one doesn't yet have the wit or courage to decline, I found myself at a large gathering at which Miss Merrymount was present. She was not quite blind and invariably accompanied by a young person, a round-faced girl hired as companion and guide. The fragile old lady, displayed like peacock feathers under a glass bell, had been established in a chair in a corner of the room beyond the punch bowl. At my approach, she sensed a body coming near and held out her withered hand, but when she heard my voice her hand dropped. "You have done a dreadful thing," she said, all on one long intake of breath, like a draft rippling a piece of crinkly cellophane. Her face turned away, showing her hawk-nosed profile, as though I had offended her sight. The face of her young companion, round as a radar dish, registered slight shock; but I smiled, in truth not displeased. There is a relief at judgment, even adverse. It is good to know that somewhere a seismograph records our quakes and slippages. I imagine Miss Merrymount's death, not too many months after this, as a final serenely flat line on the hospital monitor attached to her. Something sardonic in that flat line, too — of unviolated rectitude, of magnificent patience with a world that for over ninety years failed to prove itself other than disappointing. By this time, Julia and I were at last divorced.

Everything of the abandoned home is lost, of course — the paintings on the walls, the way shadows and light contended in this or that corner, the gracious warmth from the radiators. The pets. Canute was a male golden retriever we had acquired as a puppy when the children were still a tumbling, pre-teen pack. Endlessly amiable, as his breed tends to be, he suffered all, including castration, as if life were a steady hail of blessings. Curiously, not long before he died, my youngest child, who sings in a female punk group that has just started up, brought Canute to the house where now I live with Jenny as my wife. He sniffed around politely and expressed with only a worried angle of his ears the wonder of his old master reconstituted in this strange-smelling home; then he collapsed with a heavy sigh onto the kitchen floor. He looked fat and seemed lethargic. My daughter, whose hair is cut short and dyed mauve in patches, said that the dog roamed at night and got into the neighbors' garbage, and even into one neighbor's horse feed. This sounded like mismanagement to me; Julia's new boyfriend is a middle-aged former Dartmouth quarterback, a golf and tennis and backpack freak, and she is hardly ever home, so busy is she keeping up with him and trying to learn new games. The house and lawn are neglected; the children drift in and out with their friends and once in a while clean out the rotten food in the refrigerator. Jenny, sensing my suppressed emotions, said something tactful and bent down to scratch Canute behind one ear. Since the ear was infected and sensitive, he feebly snapped at her, then thumbed the kitchen floor with his tail in apology.

Like me when snubbed by Miss Merrymount, my wife seemed more pleased than not, encountering a touch of resistance, her position in the world as it were confirmed. She discussed dog antibiotics with my daughter, and at a glance one could not have been sure who was the older, though it was clear who had the odder hair. It is true, as the cliché runs, that Jenny is young enough to be my daughter. But now that I am fifty everybody under thirty-five is young enough to be my daughter. Most of the people in the world are young enough to be my daughter.

A few days after his visit, Canute disappeared, and a few days later he was found far out on the marshes near my old house, his body bloated. The dog officer's diagnosis was a heart attack. Can that happen, I wondered, to four-footed creatures? The thunderbolt had hit my former pet by moonlight, his heart full of marshy joy and his stomach fat with garbage, and he had lain for days with ruffling fur while the tides went in and out. The image makes me happy, like the sight of a sail popping full of wind and tugging its boat swiftly out from shore. In truth — how terrible to acknowledge — all three of these deaths make me happy, in a way. Witnesses to my disgrace are being removed. The world is growing lighter. Eventually there will be none to remember me as I was in those embarrassing, disarrayed years while I scuttled without a shell, between houses and wives, a snake between skins, a monster of selfishness, my grotesque needs naked and pink, my social presence beggarly and vulnerable. The deaths of others carry us off bit by bit, until there will be nothing left; and this too will be, in a way, a mercy.

GUY VANDERHAEGHE

Reunion

(FROM SATURDAY NIGHT)

IT WAS A VIVID COUNTRYSIDE they drove through, green with new wheat, yellow with random spatters of wild mustard, blue with flax. The red and black cattle, their hides glistening with the greasy shine of good pasture, left off grazing to watch the car pass, pursued by a cloud of boiling dust. Poplar bluffs in the distance shook in the watery heat haze with a crazy light, crows whirled lazily in the sky like flakes of black ash rising from a fire.

The man, his wife, and their little boy were travelling to a Stiles family reunion. It was the woman who was a Stiles, had been *born* a Stiles rather. Her husband was a Cosgrave.

The boy wasn't entirely certain who he was. Of course, most times he was a Cosgrave. That was his name. Brian Anthony Cosgrave, and he was six years old and could spell every one of his names. But in the company of his mother's people, somehow he became a Stiles. None of them saw anything but his mother in him: hair, eyes, nose, mouth — all were so like hers they might have been borrowed, relatives exclaimed. Since his father had no people (at least none that mattered enough to visit), Brian Anthony Cosgrave had never heard the other side of the story.

"For God's sake, Jack," Edith Cosgrave said, "stay away from the whisky for once. It's a warm day. If they offer you whisky, ask for a beer instead. On a hot day it isn't rude to ask for a beer."

"Yes, mother dear," her husband said, eyes fixed on the grid road. "No, mother. If you please, mother. Christ."

"You know as well as I do what happens when you drink whisky, Jack. It goes down too easy and you lose count of how many you've had. I don't begrudge you your beers. It's that damn whisky," she said angrily.

"It tastes twice as good when I know the pain it costs a Stiles to put it on the table."

"Or me to watch you guzzle it."

"Shit."

The Cosgrave family had the slightly harried and shabby look of people who, although not quite poor, know only too well and intimately the calculations involved in buying a new winter coat, eyeglasses, or a pair of shoes. Jack Cosgrave's old black suit was sprung taut across his belly, pinched him under the armpits. It also showed a waxy-white scar on the shoulders where it had hung crookedly on a hanger, untouched for months.

His wife, however, had tried to rise to the occasion by dressing up a white blouse and pleated skirt with two purchases: a cheap scarlet belt cinched tightly at her waist and a string of large red beads wound round her throat.

The boy sat numbly on the back seat in a starched white shirt, strangled by a clip-on bow tie and itching in his one pair of "good" pants — heavy wool trousers.

"They're not to be borne without whisky," Cosgrave muttered, "your family."

"And you're not to be borne with it in you," she answered sharply. But relented. Perhaps it did not pay to keep at him today. "Please, Jack," she said, "let's have a nice time for once. Don't embarrass me. Be a gentleman. Let me hold my head up. Show some respect for my family."

"That's all *I* ask," he said, speaking quickly. "*I'd* like a little respect from *them*. They all look at me as if I was something the goddamn cat dragged in and dropped in the front parlor." Saying this, he gave an angry little spurt to the gas pedal for emphasis and the car responded by slewing around in the loose gravel on the road, pebbles chittering on the undercarriage.

So like Jack, she thought, to be a bit reckless. A careless, passionate man. It was what drew her to him in the beginning.

His recklessness, his charming ways, his sweet cunning. So different from what she had learned of the male character from observing her brothers: slow, apple-faced men who plodded about their business, the languor of routine steeped deep into their heavy limbs.

Edith Cosgrave glanced at her husband's face. A face dark with furious blood, dark as a plum. He was right in believing her family didn't think much of him. A man meant to work for wages all his life, that was how her brothers would put it. She only wished Jack had not failed in that first business. It had been his one chance, bought with the little money his father had left him. He was unsuited to taking orders, job after job had proved that. Now he found himself a clerk, standing behind a counter in a hardware store, courtly and gallant to women, patient with children, sullen and rude to men. Faithful to his conception of what a man owed to pride.

"It's not as bad as all that," she said. "Don't get your Irish up."

He smiled suddenly, a crooked, delighted grin. "If one of them, just one of them, happens to mention — as they always do, the bastards — that this car is getting long in the tooth, why, my dear, that Stiles sleeps tonight cold in the ground with a clay comforter. I swear. Who gives a shit if my car is nine years old? I don't. Nineteen forty-six was a very good year for Fords. A good year in general, wasn't it, mother?"

"You're a fool," she said. It was the year they had married. "And whether it was a good year or not depends on how you look at it." Still, she was glad to see his dark mood broken, and couldn't help smiling back at him with a mixture of relief and indulgence. The man could smile, she had to grant him that.

"How long is this holy, blessed event, this gathering of the tribe Stiles, to continue?" he asked, with the heavy irony that had become second nature whenever he spoke of his in-laws.

"I don't have the faintest. When you're ready to leave just say so."

"Oh no. I'm not bearing that awful responsibility. I can see them all now, casting that baleful Stiles look, the one your father used to give me, certain that I'm tearing you against your will out of the soft warm bosom of the family. Poor Edith."

"Jack."

"What we need is a secret signal," Cosgrave said, delighted as always by any fanciful notion that happened to strike him. "What if I stamp my foot three times when I want to go home? Like this." He pounded his left foot down on the floorboards three times, slowly and deliberately, like a carnival horse stamping out the solution to an arithmetic puzzle for the wondering, gaping yokels.

Brian laughed exuberantly.

"No, no," his father declared, glancing over his shoulder at the boy, playing to his audience, "that won't do. If I know your mother she'd just pretend to think that my foot had gone to sleep and ignore me. I know her ways, the rascal."

"Watch the road or you'll murder us all."

"What if I hum a tune? That would be the ticket. Who'd catch on to that?"

" 'Goodnight Irene,' " his wife suggested, entering into the spirit of the thing. "You used to sing it to me when you left me on the doorstep when we were going out." She winked at Brian. He flung his torso over the front seat, wriggled his shoulders, and giggled.

"Mind your shirt buttons," his mother warned him, "or you'll tear them off."

"My dear woman, you must have me confused with what's his name, Arnold Something-or-other. He was the type to croon on doorsteps. I was much more forward. If you remember."

"Jack, watch your mouth. Little pitchers have big ears."

"Anyway," he carried on, " 'Goodnight Irene' isn't it. How about 'God Save the Queen'? Much more appropriate to conclude a boring occasion. Standard fare to bring to an end any gathering in this fair Dominion. After all, it's one of your favorites, Edith. I'll pay a little vocal tribute to Her Majesty, Missus the Duke, by the Grace of God, etcetera. How does that strike you, honey?"

He was teasing her. For although the Stileses' hardheaded toughness ran deep in his wife, she had a romantic weakness for the royal family. There was her scrapbook of coronation pictures, her tears for Group Captain Townsend and the Princess. And, most treasured of all, a satin bookmark with Edward VIII's abdication speech printed on it. She had been a girl when he relinquished the crown and it had seemed to her that Edward's love for Mrs. Simpson was something so fine, so beyond earthly considerations, that the capacity for such feelings had to be the birthright of kings. Only a king could love like that.

"Don't tease, Jack," she said, lips tightening.

Brian flung himself back against the back seat, sobered by the knowledge she meant business. The game, the lightheartedness, was at an end.

"Oh, for Christ's sake," his father said testily, "now we're offended for the bloody Queen."

"You never know when enough is enough, do you? You've always got to push it. So what if I feel a certain way about the Queen? Or my family? Why can't you respect that?"

The car rushed down into a little valley where a creek had slipped its banks and puddled on the hay flats, bright as mercury. The Ford ground up the opposing hills. Swearing and double-clutching, his father had to gear down twice to make the grade. A few miles on, a sign greeted them. Brian, who read even corn-flakes boxes aloud, said carefully: "Welcome to Manitoba."

The town was an old one judged by prairie standards and had the settled, completed look that most lack. Where Brian lived there were no red-brick houses built by settlers from Ontario, fewer mountain ashes or elms planted on the streets. The quality of the shade these trees cast surprised him when he stepped from the car. It swam, glided over the earth. It was full of breezes and sudden glittering shifts of light. Yet it was deeper, cooler, bluer than any he could remember. He threw his head back and stared, perplexed, into a net of branches.

His mother took him by the hand, and, his father following, they started up the walk to what had been her father's house and now was her eldest brother's. A big house, two storeys of mustard-colored stucco, white trim, and green shingles, it stood on a double lot. The lawn was dotted with relatives.

"They must have emptied the jails and asylums for the occasion," his father observed. "Quite a turnout."

"Jack," Edith said perfunctorily, as she struggled with the gate latch.

Brian could sense the current of excitement running in his
mother's body and he felt obscurely jealous. To see the familiar
faces of aunts, uncles, brothers, and the cousins with whom she
had idled away the summers of childhood had made his mother
shed the tawdry adult years like a snake sheds an old and worn
skin. Every one of them liked her. She was a favorite with them
all. Even more so now that they felt sorry for her.

"Edith!" they cried when they hugged and kissed her. Brian
had his hair rumpled and in a confusion of adult legs his toes
stepped on once. An uncle picked him up, hefted him judi-
ciously, pretended to guess his weight. "This is a big one!" he
shouted. "A whopper! A hundred and ninety if he's a pound!"

Jack Cosgrave stood uncomfortably a little off from the small
crowd surrounding his wife, smiling uneasily, his hands thrust
in his pockets. He took refuge in lighting a cigarette and appearing to study the second-storey windows of the house. He
had spent one night up there in the first year of their marriage.
But never again. That same year he had come to his father-in-
law with a business proposition when the shoe store failed. A
business proposition the miserable old shit had turned down
flat. None of the rest of those Stileses needed to think things
wouldn't have been different for Jack Cosgrave if he had got a
little help when he really needed it. If he had, he'd have been
in clover this minute instead of walking around with his ass
practically hanging out of his pants and nothing in his pockets
to jingle but his balls.

"Brian," said Edith, her arm loosely circling a sister-in-law's
waist, "you run along and play with your cousins. Over there,
see?" She pointed to a group of kids flying around the lawn,
chanting taunts to one another as they played tag. *"Can't catch
me for a bumble bee!"* squealed a pale girl with long, coltish legs.

"Just be careful you don't get grass stains on your pants, okay,
honey?"

The boy felt forlorn at this urging to join in. His mother,
returned to her element, sure of the rich sympathies of blood,
could not imagine the desolation he felt looking at those children's strange faces.

"Bob, dear," said Edith, turning to a brother, "keep an eye on
Jack, won't you? See that he doesn't get lonely without me."

They all laughed. Among the stolid Stileses Edith had a reputation as a joker. Jack Cosgrave, looking at his wife's open, relaxed face, seeing her easiness among these people, felt
betrayed.

"Sure, sure thing, Edith," replied her brother. He turned to
Cosgrave, seemed to hesitate, touched him on the elbow. "Come
along and say hello to the fellows, Jack." He indicated a card
table set under a Manitoba maple around which a group of men
were sitting. They started for it together.

"Jack," said Bob, "these are my cousins from Binscarth, Earl
and George. You know Albert, of course." Jack Cosgrave knew
Albert. Albert was Edith's youngest brother and the one who
had the least use for him. "This here is Edith's husband, Jack
Cosgrave."

"Hi, Jack, take a load off," said one of the men. Earl, he
thought it was. Cosgrave nodded to the table, but before he took
a seat his eye was caught by his son standing, arms dangling
hopelessly as he watched his cousins race across the grass. The
boy was uncertain about the etiquette of entering games played
by strangers in strange towns, on strange lawns.

"Pour Jack a rye."

"You want 7-Up or Coke?" asked Albert, without a trace of
interest in his voice.

"What?" The question had startled Cosgrave out of his study
of his son.

"Coke or 7-Up?"

"7-Up." He sat down, took the paper cup, and glanced at the
sky. The blue had been burned out of it by a white sun. No
wonder he was sweating. He loosened his tie and said the first
thing that came to mind. "Well, this'll make the crops come,
boys."

"What will?" asked Albert.

"This here sun," said Jack, turning his palm up to the sky.
"This heat."

"Make the weeds come on my summer fallow. That's what it'll
do," declared Earl.

"Don't you listen to Earl," confided Bob. "He's got the cleanest
summer fallow in the municipality. You could eat off it."

"Is that so?" said Jack. "I'd like to see that."

"Go on with you," said Earl to no one in particular. He was pleased.

The conversation ran on, random and disconnected. There was talk of the hard spring, calf scours, politics, Catholics, and curling. Totting up the score after four drinks, Jack concluded hard springs, calf scours, politics, and Catholics weren't worth a cup of cold piss. That seemed to be the consensus. Curling, however, was all right. Provided a fellow didn't run all over the province going to bonspiels and neglect his chores.

Jack helped himself to another drink and watched the tip of the shadow of a spruce advance slowly across the lawn. It's aimed at my black heart, he thought, and speculated as to when it would reach it.

"I would have got black," said Albert of his new car with satisfaction, "but you know how black shows dust. It's as bad as white any day."

"Maybe next year for me," said George. "An automatic for sure. I could teach the wife to drive with an automatic."

"Good reason not to get it," said someone.

"Albert's got power steering," Bob informed Jack. "I told him he was crazy to pay extra for that. I said, 'The day a man hasn't got the strength to twist his own steering wheel . . .' well, I don't know." He shook his head at how the very idea had rendered him speechless.

"What you driving now, Jack?" Albert asked smoothly, leaning across the table.

You conniving, malicious shit, thought Cosgrave. Still doing your level best to show me up. "The same car I had last year, and the year before that, and the year before that. In fact, as I said to Edith coming down here, I bought that car the year we got married." He stared at Albert, defiance in his face.

"I wouldn't have thought it was that old," said Albert.

"Oh yes it is, Bert," said Cosgrave. "That car is *old*. Older than dirt. Why, I've had that car almost as long as you've had the first nickel you ever made. And I won't part with it. No, sir. I'd as soon part with that car as you would with your first nickel."

"Ha ha!" blurted out cousin Earl. Then, embarrassed at breaking family ranks, he took a Big Ben pocket watch out of his trousers and looked at it, hard.

Jack Cosgrave was drunk and he knew it. Drunk and didn't

care. He reached for the whisky bottle and, as he did, spotted Brian sitting stiffly by himself on the porch steps, his white shirt blazing in the hot sunshine.

"Brian!" he called. "Brian!"

The boy climbed off the steps and made his way slowly across the lawn. Cosgrave put his arm around him and drew him up against his side. His father's breath was hot in the boy's face. The sharp medicinal smell repelled him.

"Why aren't you playing?"

Brian shrugged. Shyness had paralyzed him; after a few halfhearted feints and diffident insults that had been ignored by the chaser, he had given up.

Jack Cosgrave saw that the other boys were now wrestling. Grappling, twisting, and fencing with their feet, they flung one another to the grass. He pulled Brian closer, put his mouth to the boy's ear, and whispered: "Why don't you get in there and show them what a Cosgrave can do? Whyn't you toss a Stiles on his ass, eh?"

"Can't," mumbled Brian in an agony of self-consciousness.

"Why?"

"Mum says I have to keep my pants clean."

"Sometimes your mother hasn't got much sense," Cosgrave said, baffled by the boy's reluctance. Was he scared? "She's got you all dressed up like little Lord Fauntleroy and expects you to have a good time. Give me that goddamn thing," he said, pulling off the boy's bow tie and putting it in his pocket. "Now go and have some fun."

"These are my good pants," Brian said stubbornly.

"Well, we'll take them off," said his father. "It's a hot day."

"*No!*" The child was shocked.

"Don't be such a christly old woman. You've got boxer shorts on. They look like real shorts."

"Jesus, you're not going to take the kid's pants off, are you?" inquired Albert.

Cosgrave looked up sharply. Albert wore the concentrated, stubborn look of a man with a grievance. "I am. What's it to you?"

"Well, Jesus, we're not Indians here or anything to have kids roaming around with no pants on."

"No, I don't want to," whispered Brian.

"For chrissakes," said Jack. "You've embarrassed the kid now. Why'd you do that? He's only six years old."

"It wasn't him that wanted to take his pants off, was it? I don't know how you were brought up, or dragged up maybe, but we were taught to keep our pants on in company. Isn't that so, Bob?"

Bob didn't reply. He composed his face and peered down into his paper cup.

"Bert," said Jack, "you're a pain in the arse. You're also one hell of a small-minded son of a bitch."

"I don't think there's any need —" began Bob.

"No, no," said Albert. He held his hand up to silence his brother. "Jack feels he's got things to get off his chest. Well, so do I. He thinks I'm small-minded. Maybe I am. I guess in his books a small-minded man is a man that lets a debt go for four years without once mentioning it. A man that never tries to collect. Is that a small-minded man, Jack? Is it? Because if it is, I plead guilty. And what do you call a man who doesn't pay up? Welcher?"

"*I* never borrowed money from you in my life," said Cosgrave thickly. "What *she* does is her business. I told her not to write and ask for money."

"You're a liar."

"Hey, fellows," said Bob anxiously, "this is a family occasion. No trouble, eh? There's women and kids here."

"I told her not to write! I can't keep track of everything she does! I didn't want your goddamn money!"

"In this family we know better," said Albert Stiles. "We know who does and doesn't hide behind his wife's skirts. We know that in our family."

Edith Cosgrave came down the porch steps just as her husband lunged to his feet, snatched a handful of her brother's shirt, and punched clumsily at his face. Albert's folding chair tipped and the two of them spilled over in an angular pinwheel of limbs. It was only when sprawled on the grass that Jack finally did some damage by accidentally butting Albert on the bridge of the nose, sending a gush of blood down his lips. Then they were separated.

By the time Edith had run across the grass, ungainly on her
heels, Bob was leading Albert to the house. Albert was holding
his nose with his fingers, trying to stanch the blood that dripped
on his cuffs and saying, "Son of a bitch, they're going to have to
cauterize this. Once my nose starts bleeding . . ."

A few women and children were standing some distance off,
mute, staring. Jack was trying to button his suit jacket with trembling fingers. "That'll hold him for a while, loud-mouthed —"
he began to say when he saw his wife approaching.

"Shut up," she said in a level voice. "Shut your mouth. Your
son is listening to you, for God's sake." She was right. Brian was
listening and looking, face white and curdled with fright. "And
if you hadn't noticed, the others are politely standing over
there, gawking at the wild colonial boy. You're drunk and you're
disgusting."

"I'm not drunk."

She slapped him hard enough to make his eyes water, his
ears ring. "Christ," he said, stunned. She had never hit him
before.

"You're a drunken, stupid pig," she said. "I'm sick of the sight
of you."

"Don't you ever hit me again, you bitch." He wiped his lips
with the back of his hand.

"Don't you ever give me reason to again. Stop ruining my
life."

"You don't want to hear my side. You never do."

"I've heard it for nine years."

"He was yapping about that hundred dollars you borrowed. I
said it wasn't any of my affair. I want you to tell him I didn't
have anything to do with it."

"Nothing at all. No, you didn't have anything to do with it.
You just ate the groceries it bought."

"I didn't ask him for anything. I wouldn't ask him for sweet
fuck all."

"Don't fool yourself. You don't like being hungry any better
than I do. Don't pretend you didn't want me to ask him for the
money. Don't fool yourself. You needed my brother because
you couldn't take care of your family. Could you?"

Cosgrave straightened himself and touched the knot of his

tie. "We're going," he said, as if he hadn't heard her last words. "Get the boy ready."

"The hell we are! I want you to apologize to Albert. Families don't forgive things like this."

"It'll be a frosty fucking Friday in hell the day I apologize to Albert Stiles. We're leaving."

"No we aren't. Brian and I are staying. This is my day and I'm having it."

"All right, it's your day. Welcome to it. But it sure isn't mine. If you don't come now don't expect me back."

His wife said nothing.

It was only when he turned up the street and headed for the beer parlor, his shoulders twisted in his black suit, feet savage on the gravel, that Brian trotted after him, uncertainly, like a dog. The short legs stumbled; the face was pale, afflicted.

His father stopped in the road. "Go back!" he shouted, made furious by his son's helplessness, his abjectness. "Get back there with your mother! Where you both belong!" And then, without thinking, Cosgrave stopped in the street, picked up a tiny pebble, and flung it lightly in the direction of his son, who stood in the street in his starched white shirt and prickly wool pants, face working.

By nine o'clock that night the last dirty cup had been washed and the last Stiles had departed. Edith, Brian, Bob, and his wife went out to sit in the screened verandah.

It was one of those nights in early summer when the light bleeds drowsily out of the sky, and the sounds of dogs and children falter and die suddenly in the streets when darkness comes. In the peace of such evenings, talk slumbers in the blood, and sentences grow laconic.

Edith mentioned him first. "He may not be back, you know," she said. "You may be stuck with us, Bob."

"His car's still in the street."

"What I mean is, he won't come to the house. And if he sits in the car I won't go to him."

"It's your business, Edith. You know you're welcome."

"He's always lied to himself, you know," she said calmly. "It's that I get tired of mostly. Big ideas, big schemes. He won't be

what he is. I don't complain about the other. He doesn't drink
as much as people think. You're mostly wrong about him, all of
you, on that count."

Brian sat, his legs thrust stiffly out in front of him, eyes fixed
on the street where the dark ran thickest and swiftest under the
elms.

"You should cry," suggested her sister-in-law. "Nobody would
mind."

"I would. I did all my crying the first year we were married.
One thing about him, he's obvious. I saw it all the first year.
Forewarned is forearmed. But if he blows that horn he can go
to hell. *If he blows it.* I never hit him before," she said softly.

They sat for a time, silent, listening to the moths batter their
fat, soft bodies against the naked bulb over the door. It was
Brian who saw him first, making his way up the street. "Mum,"
he said, pointing.

They watched him walk up the street with the precarious
precision of a drunk.

"He won't set foot on this place. He's too proud," said Edith.
"And if he sits in the car I won't go to him. I've had it up to
here."

Cosgrave walked to the front of the property and faced the
house. For the people on the verandah it was difficult to make
him out beneath the trees, but he saw his wife and son sitting in
a cage of light, faces white and burning under the glare of the
light bulb, their features slightly out of focus behind the fine
screen mesh. He stood without moving for a minute, then he
began to sing in a clear, light tenor. The words rang across the
lawn, incongruous, sad.

"Jesus Christ," said Bob, "the man's not only drunk, he's
crazy."

Edith leaned forward in her chair and placed her hand
against the screen. The vague figure whose face she could not
see continued to sing to her across the intervening reaches of
night. He sang without a trace of his habitual irony. Where she
would have expected a joke there was none. The voice she
heard was not the voice of a man in a cheap black suit, a man
full of beer and lies. She had, for a fleeting moment, a lover
serenading her under the elms. It was as close as he would ever

come to an apology or an invitation. Jack Cosgrave was not
capable of doing any more and she knew it.

> God save our gracious Queen,
> Long live our noble Queen,
> God save the Queen:
> Send her victorious . . .

Edith Cosgrave was not deluded. Not really. She was a Stiles,
had been born a Stiles rather. She got to her feet and took Brian
by the hand. "Well," she said to her brother, "I guess I can take
a hint as well as the next person. I think the bastard is saying he
wants to go home."

DIANE VREULS

Beebee

(FROM SHENANDOAH)

WHEN HE WAS SIX WEEKS OLD his mother gave him back. The identity bracelet was still on his wrist: Baby Boy Brewster, known from the start as Beebee. The hospital sent him to the county orphanage. The following winter it burned to the ground. He was then placed in five foster homes in succession and only once adopted — by a couple killed in a plane crash two months after signing the papers. "I'm good at being orphaned," he likes to tell me. Sometimes he writes that in the blank that asks "Profession." Sometimes he prints FOSTER SON.

His second decade was spent in reform school and homes of detention. He was your model juvenile delinquent back in the days boys earned the label for truancy, stealing cars, a little breaking and entering — nothing mean; you can tell Beebee's never been mean. More the kind of quiet that's taken for insolence, with a grace that combined with his small stature is felt by clumsy men — cops, judges, wardens — to be sly. When his juvenile years were numbered and the penalties grew stiff, he looked for another line of work. Having been trained to hand-tool leather, sweep shops, pick locks and beans, after lying his way quickly in and out of the army, he decided to be an actor. At twenty he landed a part in an off-Broadway show he won't forgive me for having missed, though he knows I was just a kid at the time and living in Simpson, Illinois, a place that didn't even get films to speak of. "Are you sure you didn't see me?" he asks. Most of his parts have been smaller since.

We met four summers ago when I started work at the nursery. As I marched twenty four-year-olds in pairs down the block to the park one Friday morning, he fell in with my step, walked me back to the school and then home to my apartment. He's been my partner since, more or less. More when he's waiting for work. Less when he's out on the road with second-string touring companies of last year's Broadway hits. It's an arrangement I try not to chafe at. I was attracted to him because he was so unlike the boys I grew up with, because he promised a future that cancelled my past in a way that wouldn't erase me in the process. It's what we all hope for, no? Truth is, he's been trying to get me to leave him from the first. His means are restricted. He will not argue, would never strike me, won't even contradict. But I know he's waiting for me to close the show. When he returns from a gig out of town he will not engage a cab until he's called from the Port Authority and checked with me first. He can't risk coming unasked. For God's sake, Beebee, I say. Prolonged courtesy is an insult; you can't help but wonder what rage it conceals. Look, I say, if you don't want to come back, don't. Then he always tells me he loves me — too easy, I think.

He has been in love only once. He was twelve and her name was Stella. Stella McNult. For her he learned every Stella poem in the western world lending library, or at least every branch he's been near. The Herrick Memorial Library in Wellington, Ohio, the Muhlenberg Branch of the NYPL, the dusty shelves of army bases in Alabama and Tennessee. He knows twenty-three poems to Stella, of which twelve are written by him. When he wants to tell me a love poem, I get one to Stella. He changes the name, but I know: the rhyme scheme is off.

She was his fourth foster mother, the only one he remembers aloud. She lived in the country with her husband, Bud, and the kids she took in to make ends meet: five or six day-boarders and Beebee full-time, on the state. He was proud of that, of being the only one of the lot truly residential. He had his own bed and chest in the glassed-in sun porch she used for sewing, and though she sometimes napped the babies there when the cribs were full, she always referred to it as Beebee's room and asked his permission first. Being the oldest, he helped with the other kids, could do diapers and bottles and toss and tickle the bawlers and walk the toddlers and work the Busy Boxes on the cribs.

He could run the washer and dryer and put on snowsuits, stuffing arms and legs in the proper casings as well as Stella did, and fix broken zippers and push their trikes and pull them in coaster wagons around the puddles out by the barn. On days she looked peaked, he stayed home from school and took over, while she baked and phoned and sometimes dozed on the sofa till Bud returned. The note she sent back to Beebee's teacher next day always said "He got sick in the night." When he missed so much school they refused to pass him in June, "night disease" he claims was the reason they gave on his report card, but the fact was he dropped seventh grade due to running a baby farm with Stella in Wakeman, Ohio.

She was younger than I am now, had married Bud out of high school. They were so dumb they thought they had to marry after Homecoming, but later she found out she wasn't pregnant at all.

"She told you that? At twelve?"

She told him everything, sipping her Mogen David with ice cubes in it, talking to him as if he were her mother, while she ironed, while she polished the silver-plate coffee service she kept on the oak buffet, while she dusted Venetian blinds or shelled garden peas or poured hot Jell-O into custard cups every day after lunch. The way he looks at me Sunday mornings when I'm making pancakes, I know he sees Stella, his first woman in a housecoat, hair uncombed, her broad flowered back to him as she stands at the stove, tending a life her husband and he can rise to, her cooking heat steaming the room. No matter how early I wake, she's there before me.

He asks me to tie up my hair as she must have worn hers. He buys me blue-flowered robes. He is still as she formed him, his hair cut short despite all changes of fashion, giving his long face an immaculate look of surprise. Cuts down your roles, I tell him, that hair, that demeanor of Fifties nostalgia that can't play forever, but he picks up a part in a commercial — the antihero, Brand X — just often enough to justify his looks. In fact, the residuals from his perennial performance as Vapor Lock are enough to land us in Darien, make burghers of us both. But Beebee won't buy that.

He comes into the kitchen fully dressed, wearing the lumber

jacket she gave him for Christmas. He mumbles a soft good
morning so she won't be startled and burn herself, but she always jumps, regardless, scattering grease. "You're up early,
Beebee," she says more sharply than he deserves, and he hurries
to help her wipe up the floor with paper towels from the
sink.

He has tried to delay. He has pulled on his clothes slow motion, dallied making the bed, tucking the army blankets in one
by one. Then, already trained not to sit on beds, he'd hunched
at the sewing machine, snapping the catch on the cover, pulling
out drawers in the stand. Or he'd peered through the blinds to
check on the progress of dawn, found the yard dark, the street-
lamp down where the road met the county highway, the only
thing lit for miles. He'd listened for animals, then, knew they
were out there in the yard, feeding not far from his windows —
he'd see their small tracks later in the snow — but all he could
hear was the scrape of breakfast plates pulled from shelves in
the kitchen, the chime of cups set into saucers, the clang of
something metal dropped in the sink. He'd feared, then, that
he had been dreaming, that he had lost all track of time, that he
would run into the kitchen and find the food cold on his plate,
Bud gone to work, Stella doing the dishes, and the cars that
brought the babies already turning into the drive. This has
never happened, but he is terrified it might.

"Did you wash?" Stella asks.

He nods. The daily lie. Bud is in the bathroom, how could he
have washed? It's something he's never been able to figure out
through four foster homes: how to get a turn in the john. He
was too shy to share the room as they did in some families; if he
managed to enter alone, he worried he might be forcing someone to wait. The one other place he'd slept on a porch, he'd
simply used the yard, but here the door was nailed shut year
round and stuffed with weather stripping. So he'd trained himself to wake late at night and feel his way down the hall, hoping
his hands would push the right door, while floor plans of earlier
houses whirled in his brain. He was less afraid of the dark than
of his own noises: of stumbling into furniture, brushing objects
off a hall table, releasing a doorknob too quickly and waking the
sleepers with the sudden recoil of its spring. By the time he

stayed with Stella, he'd become expert at prowling at night. It can't have been good for his growth, this chronic lack of sleep. I see it in some of the kids I work with — a fatigue that thins the skin, shrinks the frame, gives them a fitful precocity; one moment they're wired, the next the fuse has blown. Beebee's sallow still.

"Sleep well?" Stella asks, as she does every morning. He always says yes.

He sits at the table and waits for Bud. She won't serve till he comes, stacks the pancakes upright in an old metal dishrack she's set in an oven, where they'll keep crisp. Beebee is fascinated by this trick, by all her kitchen skills, the twist of the wrist that dollops out batter exactly into pancakes that spread to identical size on the grill, the body rhythm that measures how long something's broiled or perked or simmered so that she never need glance at a clock or lift a lid to tell if it's done. He watches her intently. She doesn't notice or doesn't mind if she does, chatters brightly at him as she moves around the room. But she is tense this morning, tight-lipped. She doesn't even acknowledge his sitting there until she leans to an old roller tray by the stove and turns on the TV. She never has it on when she's alone.

Bud enters without a greeting, face raw from the razor, his movements stiff and painful as if he were injured in his sleep. He's a small man and so thin you wouldn't think he could put away the stacks of pancakes she puts at his place. Beebee inches his chair from the table to give the man space. In the seven months he's been there, they've barely spoken, he and Bud. It wasn't a matter of resentment or suspicion, he knew even then, but only a simple shyness on both sides. Beebee eats with his eyes to his plate but monitors Bud's presence so acutely that he can describe to this day the way his hair, sculptured high in a wave, parts and falls onto his forehead whenever he bends to his food, how the wet wool of his collar and cuffs (he must dress before he washes and not bother to roll up his sleeves) emits a smell which, mixed with that of coffee, seems as male to Beebee as musk. That morning he senses in Bud something acrid as well, metallic. He thinks back on the previous evening. The babies were gone by five-thirty, Bud came home at six. At dinner Stella talked about her day. After Beebee'd washed up the

plates, he retired to the porch to do homework. If they'd argued, he hadn't heard them. Yet what Bud says next sounds
like the clincher.

"You can shove it. I'm not going back."

Stella, leaning against the counter, answers directly to the TV:
"Suit yourself."

"Fat chance," he says.

"What's that supposed to mean?"

"This wasn't *my* idea. Things are bad enough as it is."

"Well, we have to start sometime, don't we?"

"Not now."

"Then when?"

He doesn't answer. She watches an ad, switches channels,
turns to the sink. Bud balls up his napkin and stuffs it into his
juice glass. He sets the glass inside his coffee cup, then slow as a
child building blocks he centers his cup in his saucer, sets the
saucer on his plate and crosses knife and fork along the rim. He
regards his construction a moment, then with a nod of satisfaction he pushes back his chair and leaves the room. Minutes later
the front door clicks. The truck door slams. Stella doesn't let on
she's been listening to gears shift, the truck break the ice in the
drive, then turn down the road and out of hearing until she
says "He forgot his lunch."

The first baby arrives. It's Beebee's signal to leave, to strike
out for the highway where he'll wait half an hour for the bus.
He'd rather wait out there today, sets off without asking for
milk money, afraid that in the time it will take her to remember
where she left her purse, he might decide to stay behind and
help.

On the road he's passed by women driving babies. He loathes
them. The way they fuss when they hand the kids to Stella, butts
propping open the storm door to let in the icy cold. The way
they whine out needless instructions and complaints of the jobs
they'll run off to. Worst of all the lingering mamas who step
inside to undress their children. You know at once the kid's got
strep and they'll all take sick within the week.

"Not fair," I interrupted.

"What's not?"

"About the mothers. Why blame them?"

"Come to think of it," he shrugged, "I didn't catch things, from the babies or anyone else." When he was a recruit at Fort Rucker, the entire camp came down with dysentery; it was his luck to stay hale, to man the bedpans and buckets. When he was a busboy in the Berkshires, a fish fry poisoned the hotel. One of the few remaining upright, he had to dash from room to room with burned toast. His resistance, he claimed, is total and dates from an early orphanage where a fever got you slapped in isolation — a sickbay the size of a gym where you lay in a sea of white beds, forgotten till the next state inspection. I doubt his stories, of course, but it's true he's never ill. And is good at tending those who are. He's nursed me through the usual flus, as caring as any mother.

"Get on with the story," I said.

"Where was I?"

Jones Road and Route 80. He studies white letters on green signposts he's sure no one's noticed but him: locals know the roads too well to look for markers and who else would ever drive by? Six other children use this bus stop, all from a family called Welling who live a quarter mile up Jones Road. Appalachians, says Stella, and too dumb to count their own kids. They treated Beebee with the scorn that any pack reserves for a stray. To dodge them, he chooses not to wait. Besides, he can't take the wind. It comes from Canada, he explained. Down three states every morning, looking just for him. He walks the two miles to the junior high backwards, counting his steps in the drifts. He arrives at school exhausted; the heat puts him instantly to sleep. He wakes for roll call, for lunch, for a film. In between he's so perfectly propped (chin on palms, face towards book) his teachers' reports on his conduct commend his as "well behaved."

He was never caught sleeping, he says. I think he was the one child in ten that studies show teachers overlook. I understand why the tenth was Beebee. Say we've made plans to meet at a drugstore or gallery or entrance to a park; even when the place is deserted Beebee isn't easily seen. Once I pick him out of the landscape like the face hidden in a print, I wonder why I didn't spot him sooner. Must be a psychic form of coloration, which would also explain why at auditions producers don't often select him — they can't single him out of the crowd. Let me stay with this a moment; it seems to explain other things. His attraction, for one. It is not as my former roommate supposes, that he appeals to my suppressed maternal instinct. (*How* suppressed? I work at a nursery, she seems to forget.) No, it's his habit of eluding definition, of inviting you to see him as you will and then — and this trait is even rarer — of conforming absolutely to your needs. How can you ditch someone like that? To reject him is to abandon your own invention. At times it's eerie, though, his camouflage. There are days when I've come home from work and haven't known he's in the apartment until I'm about to flop on the sofa and there he is, sprawled with a book.

When Beebee returned from school, he could hear the wail of babies from the drive. One step inside, he was hit by a wall of noise, the smell of urine and worse. The living room was an aural fever ward: babies shaking the rails of their playpens, toddlers buried beneath sofa pillows, sobbing as remorselessly as they breathed. At his entrance they stopped for a moment, then resumed in more desperate pitch. Stella was nowhere in sight. He attended them one by one, changing diapers, gagging their screams with cookies and bottles of juice. When their mothers came to collect them, they were sleeping in front of the TV. It wasn't till seven that Stella emerged from the bedroom. "How'd it go?" she asked. Then: "Oh, I thought you were Bud."

He made them toasted cheese sandwiches with mustard, and undiluted tomato soup.

"You're a good cook, you know that? I mean, when you think how most men can't take care of themselves at all, you're way ahead, Beebee, you really are."

She didn't eat a bit of what he'd made.

"They called. Twice. Bud never went to work."

Bud worked in a local sandstone quarry; had to, Stella once explained, since they'd sold off the land from the farm and sunk all their cash into a garage. The garage had failed. Not Bud's fault — he was a good mechanic, she said, but so were half the men in the county. From time to time, he'd look for other jobs, would be gone two days, come back drunk as a loon. This had not happened since Beebee moved in. "You can't blame him," she said. "He hates the quarry but there's no one else hiring now."

"When will he be back?" Beebee asked.

"When he's out of cash. He can't have much on him. Maybe tonight."

But it wasn't that night, though they thought they could hear the truck a dozen times over. Whenever a car passed the house, Stella would jump up from the couch, part the drapes of the picture window to watch the taillights burn down the road. Then she'd return to the TV set and lower the volume a twist — as if hearing the next car sooner would cause it to turn up the drive. By the time Beebee went to bed, she was watching a silent screen.

Next morning she woke him stirring buttons. A soft clatter, pause, then a long spill. He reached for his bed light; she was kneeling at the sewing table across the room. In one hand she held a man's shirt, from the other buttons poured into the drawer like coins into a chest.

It was the first of her Saturday projects. While Beebee did the regular cleaning she shampooed the living room rug. She emptied shelves, put down new paper, sponged fingerprints off of door frames. He tried to stay out of her way, but she filled the house with a heat lightning he knew wasn't aimed at him but seemed dangerous anyway. When she baked, she was better, calmer. Watching butter on a slow melt, she began to relax, even hum in her tuneless way. He curled up in a chair to wait for pans to lick. But she had other ideas.

"Bud might not be back for a while, maybe not for days. We'd better get in food." So he was sent with a list and a sled to the nearest grocery, a crossroads affair with a gas pump a mile away. It was a nasty trip — wind and a stinging snow blowing into his face and, coming back, grocery sacks bumping off the sled. If Bud's such a good mechanic, he thought, they should have a car as well as a truck. From all the wrecks Bud towed into their fields, couldn't he have built a single working car? Suppose Bud stayed away for a long time? They could eat from the freezer for months, but milk was required almost daily. He made a plan. He would board the school bus next Monday and, with Bud's old rifle from the barn, force the driver to stop at the town IGA, raid the shelves, and return to Stella with a busful of cola and steaks. The thought warmed him all the way back to the farm.

"Well, we just can't sit around waiting," she said. "It's Saturday night." She combed out her curlers, put on lipstick, fried up popcorn and laid out Scrabble.

Games depressed Beebee. Once over an orphanage Christmas he'd played Monopoly for four days, caught in a marathon the older boys wouldn't let him quit. Down $550,000, he shook the dice, paused, picked up the board by the corners and proceeded to fold it in half, scattering money, hotels, houses, onto the floor of the rec room. The others were so stunned Beebee almost made the door before they attacked him. But Scrabble was different, Stella maintained. As Bud didn't like it, she hadn't played much lately, which was a shame. It increased your word power, helped you read books. Stella was strong on anything literary. She had a glass bookcase in the front room ("She always said *front room* for *living room*," Beebee noted) filled with Reader's Digest Condensed Books. "Perfect," I said, but he wouldn't hear the put-down. She was the first person he'd met who bought hardbound books.

The game lasted five hours. Stella took twenty minutes a turn. She made *nadir. Beautify. Empathy. Poleax* with the *x* on a triple. "The most important *acquisition* you can have," she said, "is a first-rate vocabulary. Crossword puzzles are *utile*, but you can't beat Scrabble for words." He didn't stand a chance. It didn't matter. He liked watching her squint at her letters, busily rearrange her tiles, then triumphantly slap down a seven-letter creation. "Never mind, it's just a game," she said with a delight that showed they both knew different. They celebrated her victory by toasting marshmallows over the stove. She stared into the gas ring, her eyes glowing. "You know what I always wanted to be?" she confided. "A stewardess. It's corny, I know. Just a waitress, really. But think of the places you visit."

"Where would you go?"

"St. Louis, for starters. That's where my sister lives." Beebee wasn't impressed. "How 'bout a singer?" he suggested. He thought she looked, at that moment, exactly the way Patsy Cline sounded late at night on the truck radio.

"Beebee," she laughed, "you've heard me sing! Once I tried out for choir in high school because my best friend was in it. I wanted to be a soprano so I could stand next to Marge. You know what they made me? Utility alto — you ever heard of that?"

Beebee shook his head.

"Me neither," she said. "So I quit. But you know, I bet there's lots of things I could do, things I haven't thought of yet." She was doing a kind of dance on the kitchen floor, marshmallow dangling from the end of her fork. "One thing — I'm smart. I really think I am."

She was happy all of Sunday. For breakfast she made them Humpty-Dumpty eggs — fried bread with a hole cut out for the eggs — and squeezed oranges for juice. "You call it today," she commanded as they ate. He knew what she usually had in mind for Sunday — the mall that had opened twenty minutes away. He and Bud hated the place, always found something that needed attention back in the barn just when she said they should go, left her to sit in the cab of the truck, honking the horn till they came. It was her weekend spa. "It's like this place I once saw in a museum," she explained to Beebee, trying to get him to see it her way. "The Main Street of Yesterday. A whole street of stores and things, only all indoors, you know? And people walking around, like villages in Europe. People out strolling, meeting their friends." The fact that she never saw a familiar face didn't daunt her; she loved watching families marching down the concourse (to Beebee they all looked fat); liked seeing what women wore (gabardine slacks and bowling jackets, says Beebee) and the special exhibits of high school art hung on beaverboard screens she made him study (fifty sailboats, Beebee remembers, twelve ballerinas, and dogs). "Can't go to Westgate," he said in a voice he hoped sounded stricken. "No truck."

"I was thinking of something here," she said. "Looks almost warm out."

"We could build an igloo," he suggested, then felt like a fool. He never was sure just how old Stella was; when he tried to act his most adult to impress her, he felt she was bored; on the other hand, his rare lapses into childishness annoyed her. "Cut it, Beebee," she'd say, "I can't take one more baby today." But she considered the igloo with a gravity that surprised him, made sketches, calculating the size of the blocks, how many they'd need to cover them when they stood, how wide the fire pit should be. It suddenly seemed like a lot of work, another whole house to attend to. He thought that would be the end of it, that she'd bury herself in some sewing or maybe a book — she was an indoor person at heart and hated the cold. Still he risked suggesting a walk, hoping the novelty would intrigue her: she knew only the geography of the truck. "Sure thing," she said. "On with the wraps." He loved that word, *wraps*. Only grade school teachers used it ("Put on your wraps, boys and girls") — and Stella.

"That's another thing you could do," he said as they headed across the pasture, stepping light on the icy crust that coated the snow. "You'd be a good teacher." "You think so?" She stopped, surprised and clearly flattered. Then, in a teasing voice: "And what would you say I could teach?" Her tone, not the question, abashed him. She laughed, gave him a jab. He lost his balance, fell backwards, broke through the crust of ice. In a moment he found himself sitting, mired shoulder-deep in the snow. Once the shock of falling was past, he discovered he liked it there. It was an oddly pleasant place, like a lake that you've sat down in when you're tired of keeping afloat and won't leave because it's warmer than the wind. Or a bed, vast as the pasture, muffled in down. "Come on," he heard her shout across the glare of the sun-struck snow. Through squinted eyes he could just make out her red scarf flying, mittens rowing the air as she plunged deeper and deeper into the snow until as last she gave up and dove in too. He lay back and closed his eyes.

He heard doors slamming and voices. He turns over, is roused again, falls back into nightmare. At the sound of his name he bolts up, fully awake.

The man and the woman stand at the living room drapes. He remembers the curtains as lighted from behind so that the figures appear in silhouette, but it must have been pitch black out, so that can't have been the case. What he's sure of is that the man was striking the woman over and over across the side of her face, across the chest, then back up to the face with some-

thing that looked like a bottle but bent on impact, something
that would not break. What seemed odd was not the man's
steady and unimpassioned violence but the way the woman simply stood there, arms at her sides, while the man continued to
hit her with such force that she was knocked off balance, had to
steady herself against the drapes, against the back of the sofa;
not once did she even try to move from his reach.

Neither one saw — or acknowledged — his presence. If she
had cried out to him for help, she gave no sign now of wanting
assistance. Yet it must have been she who had called into his
sleep. He ran into the kitchen and phoned the police.

For what seemed like hours, he crouched by the phone,
straining for sounds from the other room, the blood in his ears
pounding with such a roar he only saw but did not hear the
men who entered. "You called?" He led them into the front
room.

The two were standing exactly where they had been before
but were now turned awkwardly to face the intruders.

For a moment no one spoke. Beebee studied Stella. Her face
was beginning to swell. When she held her sleeve to her nose he
thought he saw blood.

"What the hell are you doing here, Cochrane?" Bud walked
towards the men, careful — Beebee could tell — not to sway,
not to lurch. His voice held more command than Beebee had
ever heard him summon. His hands, Beebee noticed, were
empty.

"We received a call . . ." the man named Cochrane began. He
stopped. Jammed his hands into his pockets, shifted uncomfortably. The other had pulled out a pad, was clicking a ballpoint
pen in and out with his thumb.

"What you writing, Beeler?"

Beeler looked over at Bud, shrugged, and gazed around the
room. It was in perfect order, still smelled of ammonia and wax
from yesterday's cleaning. He cast his eyes to his boots and
noticed the puddle of melting snow that was staining the
rug.

"Nobody called you," said Bud.

Cochrane and Beeler both looked at Stella, the first time since
they'd entered. "That so?"

She nodded. "Beebee might've." Her voice was muffled behind her sleeve.

"How's that?"

She withdrew her arm; there was no sign of blood.

"Beebee. He sometimes has nightmares."

Beeler put away his pad. Cochrane said they had to check out
every call but they wouldn't file a report unless someone might
want to press charges. This last was addressed to no one, least
of all Stella. Bud said there was no chance of that. He was sorry
they'd had to come out on such a bad night and wouldn't they
like a shot before hitting the road? They said no.

While Bud saw the men to the door, Stella made her way
around to the front of the sofa and, gripping the armrest, lowered herself to the cushions. Her face was enormous now; her
eyes had almost disappeared, but the look she gave Beebee was
clear: pure contempt.

"Cute," she told him. "That was real cute."

Beebee's going away again, I found out last night. I'd heard him
banging around the apartment, dropping things. He often quits
the bed to pace in the dark, his way lit only by the small glow of
clocks or the quick shaft of icebox light as he reaches for food.
He's usually so quiet I don't hear him till he returns, carefully
folding himself back between the sheets. I'll stir then, roused
when another's breathing alters my own. Last night, however,
he switched on the overhead light and asked if I knew where
he'd put his rubber boots.

"Is it raining?" I said with the narrow logic of one who is
wakened from sleep.

"I'll need them; I'm taking that job on the coast."

"What job?"

"Oh, didn't I tell you?" He's joining a rep group in Seattle,
leaves in two days.

"For how long?"

"Three months."

"And then?"

"And then?" He looks blank.

He'll be back, of course. We'll go on as we always have. He's
got to engineer things so that I finally send him away. Or take

leave myself. I'm not ready to do that yet. On the other hand, once I'm awake I almost never go back to sleep.

"I've been thinking," I began. "It's four years since we met. And though I'm leery of long-term commitments, it might be good to settle some things."

"Like what?"

"Like my employment. I'm sick of Head Start. I'm sick of raising other people's kids."

"Wait a minute, you lost me," he said.

"Figure it out."

He was concerned. "Jesus, not now."

"Then when? Come on, Beebee. Orphans want big families, didn't you know? Besides, think of all that practice you had with Stella."

That's when he filled me in on that weekend and other details of his life in Wakeman, Ohio, most of which he'd mentioned at one time or another but never in sequence. It was a long account and took us to dawn.

"And what happened then?" I asked.

"I'll tell you in the morning."

"It's morning now."

The first thing he stole from her was a silver charm bracelet. Then the tongs to the coffee service on the buffet. He took them with him to school, found no place to stash them, finally tossed them into a culvert down their road. He still stayed home several days a week to help with the babies, but Stella remained withdrawn: she wasn't unfriendly, exactly; more preoccupied. Since she didn't seem to need him as much as before, he kept to the yard, isolated in an extended recess he soon wearied of. Bud went back to work at the quarry and seemed to settle. He was around more, helped Stella, even warmed up to Beebee, teaching him to bowl on the weekends and shoot rabbit. Beebee went through a padded blue box Stella kept on her dresser. He stole what he thought was a genuine diamond brooch. A week later, the earrings to match. After a storm in late June, the farmer who owned their fields was repairing fences down by the creek and found the tongs and brooch caught on weeds. His wife thought they might just belong to Stella McNult. "It isn't that you stole, Beebee, you know that," she said as they drove him back to the county home. Well, it could have been lots of things. His flunking seventh grade. The caseworker's obvious disapproval during her frequent visits that spring. Stella's pregnancy, which he'd only noticed when she suddenly changed her style of clothes. Or physical changes of his own that — he'd read in the pamphlets they'd passed out in health class — signified he was becoming a man, a condition he supposed disqualified him once and for all from adoption. Whatever it was, he didn't ask and she didn't explain. But she did hug him and tell him to come out to see them and added she was sorry he couldn't stay.

LARRY WOIWODE

Firstborn

(FROM THE NEW YORKER)

CHARLES TRIED TO SETTLE HIMSELF where he sat on the edge of the bed. It was a bed they had bought from the couple who had lived in the apartment before them — merely mattresses on a bare metal frame equipped with casters (concealed by a dust ruffle Katherine had sewn), with a loose headboard that had to be wedged against one wall in order to stand upright, and a footboard that kept falling off; too low and unpredictable an affair to sit comfortably on. But comfort had never been an asset to him in any crisis, he thought. Actually, the opposite. Lack of it kept you alert.

He looked up from the book between his knees, his place held in it with his index finger, to the clock on the top of her oak secretary. 5:15.

The clock was rectangular, white plastic, a revenant of Katherine's single life, with a crack down its face and her maiden name written across its back in her slanting exuberance, with a marking pen, as if the hand that didn't bear his ring would always deny that marriage had made them one, proving her to be as divided as he was on this. He looked over his shoulder at her: still on her side, turned away, the covers up over her hair, her knees drawn up, one arm flung out over the other edge of the bed, her hand hanging limp from its swollen wrist. As far as they were able to tell, she was in labor. Their first child.

Faint beginnings of morning light appeared as milky blueness at the windows in the turret off the street side of their bedroom — one window oblong, one circular, one square, with a balanced

shapeliness to them that he hadn't noticed before now, never
having been up at this hour. Drapes that matched the mahogany
of the dust ruffle, drawn back in great swags from the ceiling,
framed the alcove of the turret, where an ivory telephone sat
on a steamer trunk below the windows. It was September. The
crown of the pin oak outside, which he could begin to make out
in outline, was shrunken and insubstantial from shedding its
leaves.

He'd been reading to her from *War and Peace,* a last straw in
the whorl, or a raft in it, and she'd fallen asleep. That quick.
But he'd gone on to the end of the section, after Andrei has
learned of Natasha's attempt to elope with Anatole Kuragin
and, like anybody afraid of his anger, has sent a go-between,
Pierre, to return to her her portrait and her letters, signifying
the end of their betrothal, and Pierre, who can't think that this
is final, plans to lecture her for falling prey to his frivolous
brother-in-law, but finds himself so moved by her and her state
that he says if he were not himself but the handsomest, dearest,
best man in the world, and free, then he'd be down on his knees
asking her to marry him (the first intimation of what is to come),
and then goes out in "twenty-two degrees of frost" and sees
from his sledge the comet of 1812 arrayed among the stars
across the sky above Moscow: a comet that is supposed to por-
tend all sorts of disasters but for him speaks to "his own softened
and uplifted soul, now blossoming into a new life."

The residue of the moment and Pierre's emotion still troubled
the room; the shapes of the three windows sparkled as if out of
that night and its moment of change. Which came at the middle
of the book, indicating the swing the story would take in the
opposite direction from that point, as if pulled by celestial powers, and now he looked down at the parted pages, as if to measure their ability to affect him like this. He'd begun the book the
month they were married, when they first moved into the apartment, and she had picked it up; she'd completed a major in
Russian but had never read *War and Peace.*

They dropped everything and let the apartment lie in disorder around them during three days of immersion in this Russia
that bore the many-dimensional stability of Tolstoy's moral
stamp. And just as they looked up from the end of the book,

blinking still (or so it seemed now), the Soviet film of it appeared, and they sat through the eight-hour extravaganza of that. (Just as when they'd met, two years ago, he'd finished *Doctor Zhivago* to appease her, and then the movie of *that* appeared.) He was appalled at the paucity of his imagination within Tolstoy's world, or at the timidity of it, so far as it went — leagues removed from the actual opulence of that life as it was lived on the grand scale, as depicted in the movie (or was this partly propaganda?) — and she was furious that it was dubbed. She kept shifting in her seat, as fitful as the images reflected over her, he noticed with uneasiness, and when they went out for dinner during the break provided, to an expensive restaurant he'd chosen with her in mind, she said, "I wish this place were old-style Roman, so we could lie down and eat, I'm so sick of sitting through those Britishy accents. *Ugh!*"

"Vomitorium?" he asked. It was at about this time that they'd become a kind of comedy team, with him responding to her puzzling pronouncements in these quirky, semi-sequitur twitches.

His reading now was meant to recall those early days to her — a form of reconciliation, and the closest he could come to being open with her, lately. She was pregnant when they were married, four months ago. He assumed that the child was his since they'd been planning to "legalize their status" whenever circumstances seemed right for them both, and she assured him it was. And then recently, in the center of this same bed, hysterical, her hair down over her newly ample nakedness, she'd confessed to another liaison while "finishing" the relationship she was involved in when he met her, meanwhile insisting that the child had to be his, or she wouldn't have married him. As if she'd broken through to logic at last.

He started for the telephone, to call a lawyer about a divorce, but since he didn't carry through on the impulse, could never mention the possibility to her, though he still considered it. Then, as they were leaving a neighborhood party about two weeks ago, and he was stepping down the stairs with that practiced carefulness that too many drinks can bring on, her provocative backside suddenly seemed packed with such shifting and separated willfulness he kicked at it, and, when he could next

see, saw her spread out and thumping like a child down the last
stairs of the flight. He'd been in a remorse that gripped under
his ribs like talons ever since: for the danger to the child, the
bruises she still bore, and his lengthening vision of the sick fits
that a marriage (even theirs, which he'd suspected might be one
of the best) could find itself thrashing within as if for life.

They'd had arguments, loud shouting ones that had caused
the neighbors below to pound on the ceiling with the handle of
a mop or a broom — and these got worse, until his senses felt
stuffed and worn raw with an endless colloquy of his rights and
wrongs, as if the halves of his brain were in conflict. He'd always
thought that one of the most fatuous statements he used to hear
was "I don't see how she puts up with it," meaning injustice in a
marriage, since it never considered a woman's ability to turn
around and walk off, but he saw now how it applied to them,
and was grateful that she hadn't left yet.

He stared at the clock and then through it, in the outpouring
of his impulse still to crush and break, and was drawn back by
the thought that it was up to him to time these intervals. 5:17.
She'd seen the secretary in an antique shop on Montague, the
Madison or Third Avenue of Brooklyn Heights, depending
upon which side of the street you were on, within which block,
and he'd walked over one Saturday afternoon and talked to the
dealer until they'd arrived at a price he considered bearable;
and then, after he'd paid, in cash (the only medium that satisfied
his sense of anonymity in the city), the dealer said that the price
of course didn't include delivery. So he came back the five blocks
to their apartment, got one of the burlap carrying straps the
movers had left behind when they'd brought up the heaviest
pieces, returned to the shop, and carried the secretary all the
way home on his back, in the bent-over shuffle he'd watched the
black movers adopt, and had been so invigorated by the look on
the dealer's face, and the flex of strength returning to muscles
only partly used for years, he hadn't once set it down. He'd been
a high school athlete, a quarterback of the sort who would spend
so much time trying to outthink the opposition, from the coach
on the sidelines to the tackle hurtling toward him, that he'd have
insights he never should have had in the middle of a pass, or
become impulsive, led by his imagination, "like a *girl*," his coach
would growl — unpredictable.

The secretary was solid oak. He scraped and sanded and worked on it for days, from its squat turned legs to the fragile basswood of its pigeonholes, and now yellow-gold striations rose in relief from the wide plain sweeps of blackish grain in the growing morning light. It had become her niche, or nest; her nature was to be in control, to the penny, to the framing of the proper response in writing at the proper moment, and she worked on their accounts here, running down his cash outlays; and sometimes sat for hours composing letters to her family or to friends, most of which she never sent. Or, when she sent them, remained unanswered. None of them knew that she was pregnant. Nobody in his family did. Both of them had come to the city separately, far from those connections, largely to sever them, for their own reasons. He was from the Western Upper Plains, she was from the Northwest (two unrelated regions that in New York came under the category of "the Midwest") — Wests they wanted to forget and be free of: be *Eastern,* as was true of most people their age that they met here. He'd worked before as a performer and announcer — "live talent," in the creeping jargon of the medium — and could do that again, but for now preferred a shadowy role; he sold time for an FM station, his hours his own.

"Katherine," he said, sure that she'd moved, and turned and put a hand on the covers, over the thigh he'd bruised, he realized, and quickly lifted it away. He'd thought he'd felt something there, but there were unpredictable swellings to her now, extra padding in unexpected spots, new curves over the familiar ones, as if the body that he'd charted so many times were being withdrawn inside this other. "Katherine, did you fall asleep?"

There was no answer; then a wash of the covers as she moved. A contraction, as she and her OB, Harner, called it? He'd begun to shy from their technical vocabulary at about the time she came home from a visit to Harner and stripped and lay down on the bed to demonstrate her "Braxton-Hicks contractions." 5:22.

He turned. "Are you awake?"

No answer.

"Are you" — he couldn't quite get out "contraction" but didn't want to say "labor pain" — "feeling another again?"

Nothing.

"Would you like something to eat?"

"No! I'd puke it all up!"

"Do you want me to go on with the chapter?"

"No!"

It was as well. Her attitude had eroded any equilibrium left in him, and after this night his nerves were worn to visionary frailty; she'd hear that in his reading voice. She was stronger than he'd suspected — it was all he could do to keep her nails from his face during some of their arguments, as they rolled over the bed or the floor — and stoic, usually, shifting without a pause into the next situation and moving through it at her regular speed, her eyes ahead, as if she'd been raised in the absence of any expectations and whatever arrived, no matter how troublesome or perverse, was a gift to get open and out on her desk and put in its place. And seemed able to shake off circumstances as she shook off her umbrella: entirely, so that she didn't have to leave it open in the apartment to dry. After she'd recovered at the bottom of those stairs, wiping a hand under her eyes, smearing her running mascara, she looked up at him and smiled, and said, "I deserved that."

But through yesterday and the night, into this morning, she'd been absent from the level where the commerce of life went on, as if the child in her had taken hold and were drawing her down under. He'd never pretended to be able to enter her inner life, but he was usually able to reach her; or she was able to reach to him out of her concentration that became so pure she could take on the aspect of stone. Artists and photographers came up to her and asked her to pose. She gathered her intellect like an essence deep in herself, unreachable, and its concentrated power drew your eye over a harmony of lines of untouched womanhood, or that was her impact, at any rate, and she'd begun to get work as a model, which was her work now. And these last months she'd withdrawn to even deeper recesses of solitary silence, into an intensity of beauty that left its mark on every eye (or negative; she continued to work), until he feared she'd be refined away into oblivion. As now. As it seemed to him.

They had gone to the city the day before to look at a lamp she

liked which might as well have been a chromium sculpture, it
was that expensive, and on the way back, on the subway, as he
rocked in a semi-trance on the seat beside her, as content as he'd
ever been, in spite of her recent revelation, she took his hand
and said into his ear in a breathy moistness, "You'll never believe this. I think I've lost control of an essential function."

"Faction?"

He tried to study her, as full now of interior movement as the
car shaking around them over its rails; lately any reference to
her body took on this evasive and almost clinical cast. There was
a sunken expression of fear in her eyes, which had widened so
much over the last few weeks he felt he was looking into a
different, diminished face overtaken by their pooling, liquid
presence. But her face was broader, too, and her nose and nos-
trils were, as if every cell in her were making accommodation
for the child; even the arch of each nostril had heightened,
along with an accompanying loose turn he could feel in her
limbs, present now in her hand, which made him wonder with
uneasiness whether the cartilaginous parts of her weren't being
somehow secretly consumed.

She drew him closer, so he couldn't stare, and, in the pretext
of putting her head on his shoulder, whispered, "It seems to
have really given out this time — ah, I mean, you know, my
bladder, that is."

"You're joking."

"You know how improvident I've become."

"Incontinent?" he asked, somehow in time and tune to the
train, so that the syllables seemed shaken from him, not voiced,
and once out of him not really spoken.

"Well, neither, literally," she said, and settled against him as
if to sleep. "Neither, but both. Sometimes it's an affront to reason to be at the mercy of a body you don't know." Then it was
their stop. "Get up before I do," she whispered. "Walk one step
behind."

He obeyed and noticed only what might be a spot of rain at
the back of her raincoat. He kept his position across the platform and up the ramp to the elevators, and in the September
sun outside the hotel, in that rich spill of autumn copper over
car tops and bricks, he felt a rush of renewed hope for

their marriage, as if it had just begun. He looked across the street and up the block to their corner, at the ornamental iron fence whose scrolling yet jagged lines were like his impatience for this newly perceived future, and was about to say, *Let's get home.*

"How do I look?" she asked.

"Great!"

"No, I mean" — she tipped her head as if glancing into a mirror, and her hair swung wide in a whitish shine — "there."

"Oh, fine. Wonderful. Nothing."

"Good, then let's go to the store." She took his arm. "We haven't shopped for days. It's time to. What a weakling I've become."

"And me?" he said, and saw that she didn't catch this as an effort to reach her. He was relieved. When she planned to do something, she always carried it through, shifting the expected order of things into an altered state resonant of her, until the doing itself took on the distinctiveness of her touch — a new aspect he kept trying to compare with what once was, but never could, since it was gone. That quick. He was happy to be merely a witness to her effects.

But at the supermarket, as she lingered over every item in her new, slow, considering inwardness, which he'd forgotten about, as if she were agonizing over every detail on each label, he wandered off. His impulses had become as unpredictable as hers, and when the fatherly, middle-aged internist who saw them both suggested that this younger crop of American husbands had a tendency to enter into couvade at the very onset of pregnancy, long before birth, and they'd returned home holding the word like a sweet on their tongues, and had looked it up in the dictonary, and then looked at one another, they both had to nod.

The man's name was Weston, and he was a forensic expert and a student and collector of first editions of nineteenth-century philosophy, and a dispenser of it — one of their few real friends in the city, in their consideration, even though they had to pay to see him. He was a willing participant and player in the tragedy (as they saw it) of their daily, domestic unease within the dedicated depths of their love. As they saw it. How were they to go on, given that imbalance? There were some good discussions, they felt, or dialogues, as Weston called them; he was so well read in current literature, also, that his mintings of last month were this season's jargon. He kept careful records, and whenever they stepped into his inner office after an exam, into the sunlight from French windows looking out on a balcony with a stone balustrade, and found Weston at his desk in a suit jacket already exchanged for his smock, every hair in place, jotting down notes, they couldn't help smiling; the thickness of his file folders on them was that reassuring. *Home,* Charles almost sighed. They were entities as particular as family in the city, kept under the care of this scrupulous man, who knew absolutely what he was up to, and who, with his Century Club manner and correct, Manhattan dapperness, was valued highly, they knew, among people in the places that matter most.

When they'd got their apartment decorated to the degree that they felt suggested a newly married couple on their own in the city and making it, they had a party, and the first person they invited was Weston; though of course he didn't come. They invited all the tenants in their building, but only the couple from the apartment below showed up, as if to observe first hand the kind of degenerates who could cause such resounding bedlam, and on their way out, after a quick drink, suggested putting padding and carpet down in all of the rooms. "Bathroom?" Charles asked, as they started down the hall. "Let me know with a bang of the mop if the thickness isn't suitable to you, O.K.?"

"Yardstick," the man said, and turned on him in a sudden, reddening fury. "I use a yardstick!"

A can of imported corned beef caught at an urge, and he looked around to ask her about it. She was at a freezer case with her back to him, her head held as if listening, and he saw her, with a shock of surprise, as separate from him, an abstract, pregnant woman, and then felt a chill, as if from the case where she stood: a clear liquid, like the pure line of a song, was pulsing in a threadlike stream down her tanned and shining inner calf. The top of her tennis shoe was wet. As he hurried over to her, he saw a wet track on the floor behind her, where she'd taken a step. He put a hand on her shoulder.

"We better go," she said, and wouldn't look at him. "Get what you want."

•

At the apartment she dropped her coat and pulled off her dress
— a lime-colored shift imprinted with miniature flowers, which
she'd removed the belt loops from and wore wherever they
went, drawing the line at maternity outfits, or "advertising costumes," as she called them — and got into the shower. He
picked up her coat and hung it in their closet and paced around
as if pursued and then went into the bathroom and drew the
shower curtain aside; she was soaped, soaping, and when her
weight shifted in a certain direction he could see the liquid dart
in a pulse through the suds. "Kath!" he cried. "That's not —"
And didn't know whether to use "urine" or a commoner term.

"What are you doing in here?" she asked, the sunken
fear again in her face, and covered her stomach with her
hands.

They called Harner, her obstetrician. He'd been recommended
by Weston, who said that a woman's response to her obstetrician
was apt to be "chemical," so Katherine might like this man and
might not, and if she didn't she was to ask Weston to recommend another; Harner was his wife's OB, he said, but his
daughter couldn't stand him. "He's fairly brilliant, I believe,
but a bit impulsive." Katherine was vague about him, as she
recently was about so much, and seemed to stay on with him
mostly to keep from calling into question the taste of Weston's
wife.

Charles had met Harner at her first interview, and Harner
had appeared to him too ready to pass off their questions with
a humor that didn't seem natural, as if he'd learned it somewhere, or with his authority, which didn't rest lightly on him.
He was young, portly, going bald on top, and his remaining hair
looked combed back in haste with heavy oil, which offended
Charles. He promised them that Charles could be with her all
through labor, right up to delivery, which was what they
wanted, and then went off with her to perform an examination.

Over the phone, as Charles sat on the steamer trunk and
stared at her across from him on the bed, with a towel around
her after her shower, Harner said, "Well, we'll soon know
whether it's the amniotic fluid or not."

"How's that?" (*Herr Harner,* as Charles thought of him, be-

cause of his smiling Germanic demeanor, which Charles could
picture even over the phone.)

"She'll go into labor. If she does, call me right back."

"But this is only her seventh month."

"I'm quite aware of that, you can rest assured. We'll have to
handle the situation as it develops."

"Isn't there anything I can do? I mean, wouldn't it be better
if we went to the hospital now, and — "

"Oh, no, I don't think that will be necessary — not till we see
where this is headed. Unless you're afraid. Give her some hard
liquor, if you like — it's marvellous for premature or false labor
—and keep her in bed, on her back. If things stabilize, I'll have
her in in a day or two for a checkup. These things happen. Give
me a call otherwise, O.K.?" He hung up.

She'd been in bed ever since, and when it seemed to them
that labor had begun, in the middle of the night, Harner said,
"You might be getting a reaction to losing some of the fluid.
Don't call me again unless the contractions get real hard — it's
unmistakable — and about ten minutes or so apart, O.K.? Time
them." He hung up.

Charles had gone over to the St. George and persuaded a
bartender to sell him a bottle of Old Bushmills, her favorite
whiskey, but after a couple of sips she set it aside, as if it were a
placebo she wasn't about to be taken in by. He'd poured it
straight over ice cubes, and its pale remains now sat on a wooden
chair beside the bed where her arm was outstretched. He hesitated to touch her, and then did.

"Kath, do you want to leave for the hospital now?"

"I can't believe this is happening to me! I'm worn out just
from the movement inside! My stomach's like a rock!"

He tried to modulate calm into his voice. "Well, Harner said
if — "

An arm struck him as she rolled and drew up with the force
of another struggle, starting to pant, and he knew why this was
called labor — for the effort it was — and why travail; he was
sure he'd never be the same as he watched her features flatten
as if by extragravitational force into a face that wasn't hers, and
then she began going "*Gur, gur, gurr,*" and then "Ah! Ah! Ah!"
as every shade of color emptied from her.

"Katherine! We have to go!"

"Ah! Ah! All right!" she got out, and her tight-shut eyes fluttered open on unfocused depths. "Just — *stay* with me *through* this!"

He took her hand, icy, its veins going vivid in wheyey paleness, held on tight. Her fine blond hair was whitened from bleach and entire afternoons spent sunbathing on their roof (*ghostly* came to him, as he stared down on its snowy disarray), except for an area over her crown in the shape of a skullcap, coming in in her natural blond, an effect he'd noticed from their windows one day when she'd gone out alone. Now it seemed the place where the power of her will was concentrated, vulnerable. He placed his other hand over it, wondering how he'd let her go off alone that day, and she said, "Thanks. Thanks. Oh, thank you a lot."

All he wanted was for this to be over and her herself again. But he knew she didn't want to admit that matters were already beyond her control. He didn't even care about the child anymore, for her sake; the child seemed the cause, and didn't women die in childbirth that came too soon and sudden, like this?

"Put your hand here!" she said, still fighting for air, and pulled it with both of hers over her stomach. Her skin was extraordinarily sensitive, delicate as the back of a baby's neck over her entire body, but here more so — nearly a profanation to touch — and now stretched over a hump like a stone. An elbowish bulge revolved under his palm from beneath, and he started to pull his hand away. Then felt the sensation spread from there and concentrate in an unsettling, thrilling tickling under his chin and down his throat.

"Must be his *head*," she got out. "Currents from it."

What? He didn't dare ask. They were so convinced it was a boy they'd named him Nathaniel.

Then her eyelids, shiny and purplish, closed down, but not completely, and her lashes went flickering over crescents of white. And then it was over, as if a wave had passed.

"All right," he said. "That's it. Get ready. We're going."

Once something like this gets off the tracks, he thought as he ran down the street, his throat still tickling, it keeps plowing into places that get worse. There weren't any cabs in sight in the early-morning quiet of the streets. There weren't any at any of the hotels he ran to. He took off for Fulton Street, and the rattle of being winded brought up a picture of her alone and fighting for breath, which sent a shock through him he couldn't contain, and then he was on the curb at Fulton, beside a chain-link fence clogged along its weedy bottom with paper and wrappings like the leavings of the bulldozed lot it enclosed, aware of the cold and of being in shirtsleeves and probably looking like a burnt-out derelict suffering his ultimate vision of absolute destruction — the worst sort of prospect to pull over a cab at this hour. And couldn't keep from jumping off and on the curb, and then wading out into the street, as if to bodily stop one. Finally, an old Checker swerved over, and he was in the back, spilling his situation to the driver, who seemed incredulous to be hearing this, already enmeshed in it.

He was an older man, with twists of gray in his tangled curls, which he pulled at, wide-eyed, as if to pull them out, and his rumpled clothes were aromatic of the long nervous hours, or days, spent in them. Charles directed him down the narrow streets and around to theirs, lined with cars under the slim oaks and maples on both sides — it was too early for the alternate-side-of-the-street parkers to have started their morning shuffle — and just broad enough for the bulky Checker body to squeeze its way down. He'd hoped she'd be outside their building, waiting, but she wasn't. "Here," he said, and hopped out before they were stopped. "It'll just be a second."

"Why, you haven't paid — "

Which the door clopped off. But he was reminded to get money as he went up the steps to the vestibule in two bounds, and was inside. He'd forgotten his keys. He rang the buzzer. No response. Then he remembered their signal and repeated it several times. There was another mind-dimming shock he couldn't contain, and then the lock went into its rattly vibrations, and he took the steps in leaps and swung around on their landing to see the door ajar. He hit it with his shoulder and felt it stop against something inside: shoes. Her tennis shoes. Their soles were facing him, their laces loose, and she was on her elbows and knees, her head down, a splash of hair over the carpet, her spilled makeup and open compact beside her, its mirror shining up at him, rocking on her haunches and crying, "*Ahh!* Oh, aggaaah!"

He tried to lift her up.

"No!" she screamed. Then got control of her voice. "No, wait —till this is over. Can't *talk* when — "

He hurdled her and was in the spare room, which was to be the child's but wasn't fixed up yet — dammit! — and where a plain door was laid across stacked milk cases filled with ring binders and station logs: his desk. Under this he jerked open the drawer of a file and fumbled out his manila folder of cash, and noticed at a glance, as he stuffed the bills into his pocket, well over a hundred dollars. Then he sprang into the bedroom to their closet and jerked on a suit jacket, coat hangers clashing, and with an emerging hand swept up the watery whiskey from the chair and knocked it back (seeing an image from somewhere of a well-dressed man down on his knees, his head thrown back, draining a percolating bottle) — a mistake; he'd need every ounce of clearheadedness and nerve he could summon, the convulsion of his stomach insisted. And from the altered angle it took to drain the dregs his eyes rolled around to fix on the bed: it was disordered, gray with damp over this half, and like slashes across the center of that were rusty streaks of blood.

She was at the table, her hands pressed on its top, leaning so far forward her hair hid her face in a whitish cloud. Her lime dress looked stained. He put his hands around her from behind. "Do you think you should wear this?"

"It was all I could do to get it on and it's all I've got on and I mean *all!*"

He went down on his knees and started tying her shoes from behind and realized what a blur his haste had built to, and then was watching his trembling hands attempting the turns of this simple task, with its folding intricacy and —

"Oh, this is absurd!" she cried, identifying for him the feathery ascension troubling his throat, and then they were gripping one another for support at the laughter that broke out of them both in a diabolical barking they couldn't stop.

The cab was gone. No. The man had parked at the hydrant a few cars down. Charles helped her into the back with the pre-

monition that they'd never make it, and felt this undercut by
the wholly practical realization that the cab needed new shocks.
They pulled away, and she closed her eyes against the lurching
and uncushioned impacts; her lips drew down. He put an arm
around her but felt at such a distance that he wanted to lift her
into his lap. Then she said "Move over," and as he slid to the
other side she turned and lay back, dropping her head into his
lap so hard it hurt, as though she'd read his thought, but in
part. He lifted away filaments of hair caught in her eyelashes
and over her lips, and smoothed it back. Her forehead, with bits
of perspiration glittering in its pores, was as icy as her hands,
and as they yawed around a corner and she groaned, he cried,
"Hey, can you speed it up?"

"Who'll pay the tickets?"

"I will."

There was a surge of acceleration, and then the purling of
the bridge's grid beneath the adhering and separately tracking
tires, and he sensed their rising suspension over water, a chasm
he felt open under him in fear, seeing the idiot uprights of gray-
black stone ahead, with their paired, churchlike arches, apparently in the process of sinking, both still to be passed through,
while the swoop and rushed stutterings of the cables out the
windows were like projections of his nerves in strumming on-
slaughts across the buildings of the city beneath. Then he saw
his keys on the grain of their table, next to her outspread hands,
forgotten again, and felt his focus narrow in and fix on them as
on a vision: he'd held the keys that would have opened up an
easy passage for her through this, and had let them drop. Every
lie he'd ever told and every person he'd ever hurt had led to
this, the keys pointed to, and he started pulling at his hair, like
the driver, as if to tear his thoughts loose from the tangle that
this implied.

"Take it easy," she said, and smiled crosswise below. "It'll be
all right. Can you move over more?"

"I'm against the side."

This time she chewed at her lips in her attempt not to cry out,
as her body went into its arch, sending her darkening crown in
a crush against his privates, like an assault on the cause. Then
she raised her knees, gripped them, and pressed down on him

with her entire force. "Ow!" he cried as they slid underneath a red light somewhere and he had to grapple with her and an armrest to keep them from striking the seat ahead, and then realized that there were cars with people in them around on all sides and horns going off.

A man at a wheel an arm's length away, out her window, looked over and did a take, his eyes widening, and Charles wished he had a pistol to blow the pervert away, for taking advantage of her as he was in her helplessness. He gave the fellow the finger as they squalled off, and then reached up and dropped a twenty-dollar bill down on the driver's seat.

Inside the emergency entrance, he was told he'd have to check her in before they could go up to the maternity ward. "But she's fainting!" he said, because she appeared to be; he had to support her — her legs were giving way. The nurse was young, with blond hair up in a French roll — exactly as Katherine wore hers whenever they went out, to look older — and now touched an arranging hand to some wisps at her neck at his attention; she'd been summoned by phone and had appeared pushing a wheelchair. "I'm sorry," she said, and looked appealing and flustered. "It's procedure here." But then as Katherine grew worse, so that he had to lock his arms under her breasts to hold her up, the nurse said, "All right, I'll take her up and go ahead and prep her, if you'll admit her right away. Then come right on up with her papers. O.K.?"

The procedure took a half hour, sending him to the opposite end of the building, where he had to fill in a four-page form in the forgotten cramp of a student's writing chair, and then a woman behind a counter, at a teller's window he was directed to, wondered if it could be true that they actually didn't have any hospitalization insurance. "We pay for everything by bank draft or cash," he said, and pulled out what he had in his pocket.

"Oh," she said, and stared at the bills as if in distaste, while covertly trying to tally them, it appeared, and then paged through a floppy book of computer printouts, turned her back and made a phone call, and finally said, "We require a three-hundred-dollar deposit for maternity."

He counted out a hundred and said he'd bring the rest later.
"We will have to have it before three this afternoon," she said.
"What will you do if you don't?" he asked. "Kick her out?"

Then it took time to get to the seventh floor and find the
correct "suite." A graying nurse in half-glasses, at a desk inside
the swinging doors, accepted the papers and said he'd have to
wait; Katherine was being prepped, she said — whatever that
was. He felt the cold caul of air conditioning grip his scalp; a
fluorescent-lit anteroom swung off behind the nurse in lines
that verged on circularity, with doors leading off it all around,
as in a maze, and with a huge column at its center encircled by
a desk partitioned into pie shapes with slabs of glass. Nobody
was at the desk. Heads of bolts showed in uprights and ceiling
beams and through the metal panels of the walls, as if he were
in the interior of a ship, and horizontal strips of chromium
reflected the unsettling curves of the place back upon itself. On
him.

A stretcher banged through a pair of metal doors and went
wheeling along the opposite wall, the young blond nurse pushing, and he saw by the swinging drape of hair and profile that
the sheet-covered figure on it was Katherine. The nurse at the
desk cried "Sir, *sir*" as he took off, but the blond one beckoned.
And an overweight Latin attendant in a white suit who had
come through the doors behind her and was forced by her pace
into a tripping step that had him out of breath, while a stethoscope jogged in wild loops from one ear, gave an O.K. sign, so
Charles joined the entourage as it went banging through a single door.

Into a tiny room, a cubicle, really, hardly large enough for
them all and the stretcher on the other side of the elevated bed,
which had bars up on both sides — a place that also seemed
made of metal, trimmed with the same chromium, like a miniature hold within the ship; or, worse, like a quadrant at the outer
perimeter of a centrifuge just starting into its spin. For now
Katherine rose as if in protest, white as the smock she had on,
then swayed away; the sheet flew up, the bars on that side of the
bed banged down, and he reached across as if to pull her up
from drowning but missed her grasping hand. She was reaching
back at the attendant, who had her under the arms, so that his

big belly pressed her head forward, forcing a cry from her cramped throat.

"Hey!" Charles yelled. "What the hell — "

"*Please,* sir," the blonde said. "Or you'll have to leave. You may help with her feet, if you would."

He leaped around and took Katherine's ankles while the nurse, placing one hand below his shoulder blade, over his ribs, passed with a taut swish across his backside, and eased away the attendant, who acted so inept he must be new. The fellow gestured apologetically at Charles and gave a dog's overacted gape of shame. Then sudden sweat seemed to strip his pudgy face to its essence, grainy fat, and ran in streaks around his eyebrows, dripping from them and from the manicured band of his mustache. They got Katherine on the bed and Charles saw indentations left by his grip in her ankles, then hurried around to the other side, to be out of their way, and reached over the bars and took her hand, and in the light from the window above saw her closed eyes pouring tears.

"Where's Harner?" he asked, with a fear that collapsed his voice into breathlessness.

"He should be here any minute." The blonde. "He was almost in from the Hamptons when he responded to his beeper. You know they're vacationing there." An intimacy had been touched on; her eyes widened, and then she blinked this away. "We're paging him right now. Dr. Ramirez is our resident on duty. He'll fill in till then." She wheeled the stretcher out.

P. Ramirez, M.D., Charles saw on the plastic clip above the stethoscope pocket of the "attendant." The man now drew the sheet down from Katherine and then pulled up her smock, jerking at it, and Charles was shocked to see the clenched bulge of movement across her shining abdomen, and the shine below that of being shaved clean. He draped her there with the sheet and discovered himself caught in a kind of contest with the resident, who was trying with his stethoscope to keep up with the strumming sidewise roll of the bulge. The man's eyes bugged; he pressed his hearing piece so hard it became buried and left red hoops, and Charles, as if from a deafening distance, watched her arch against it and cry out and saw the exposed swath of her as this man must, as meat.

The bulge revolved in reverse, and now a three-way conflict began as she pushed at the resident's hands, one of which Charles was trying to restrain while the other dug into the scoop of her hip as the man leaned close and continued to try to listen. She cried and coughed to get her breath, and her lips, usually so blood-infused they didn't need makeup, blued, and then she went limp and her eyes rolled up.

"Holy God, she's passed out!" Charles cried. "Watch it!"

The man swung to the head of the bed and fumbled at the wall with equipment there, his hands shaking, and got loose an oxygen mask and set it over her face, the strap awry and in the way, and then reached back and fiddled with some knobs. There was a hiss and he picked up the mask and listened to it, shook it, then sniffed it. "Hol' dis," he said putting it down in the same way, and Charles lifted the strap free, up onto her hair, and pressed the mask in place. "Say 'Breeze deep,' " Ramirez said.

"Kath, please, breathe."

An outside force seemed to seize her ribs and pull them up in shuddering white bands, and he saw water pool over her lashes as her eyes squeezed. "Ahhhh!" she cried, so loud he had to gasp with joy at the noise of it. "Hurts me!"

"Breeze deep," the man commanded, and then, beginning to pant himself, pointed and said, "You. Tell hor." And in quick squeaking strides was out the door. In a frantic scrambling to reconstruct the moment, to make sense of it, Charles realized the man had pointed at a sign before he'd left: NO SMOKING. Did the fellow think he would here? Now? With all that was in the balance?

She was awake and trying to focus on him. She shook her head and flung the water in the sockets of her eyes free. "Oh, hurts," she said, under the mask, and her voice came to him as over the telephone, distantly metallic, with most of its overtones abstracted into a miniature, nasal, girlish version of her — a child with a cold. She took his hand that held the mask.

"Don't leave me," she said, in the same tinny girlishness, which he heard as through a disc at his ear.

"Don't worry, I won't."

"What happened?"

"You needed air."

"Am I in delivery now?"

"No."

"Everything exploded in slow motion, all blue. The Battle of Borodino."

The window above, oblong and blank, appeared to pulse, and he saw through to the moment she meant: choreographed columns of uniformed men going down to death through billowing smoke. Then Ramirez walked in with a thing like a trike horn strapped to his forehead, with the blond nurse at his back, her face set, carrying something like ice tongs, as if to protect him. On their side of the bed they lifted the smock Charles had drawn back down, the nurse more sensitive in her sisterly attuning to abasement, and used the tongs, or calipers, to take a measurement, then covered Katherine except for the active bulge. Ramirez inserted listening tubes into his ears and bent down to force the trike horn into the now relaxing mass. Katherine pushed the thing away. "Not that," she said under the mask in her tiny, metallic voice. "Hurts!"

The man's shoulders went up and his hands out as if to say, "What can you do?" to the nurse, whose face had got the naked red of a blonde, and she slipped on her own stethoscope and moved it over the area of the bulge with a cold agility. "Try here," she said, and placed two fingers flat. Then she gripped the horn and guided it as the resident hunched over with his eyes rolled up in the swarthy polish of his face. He listened, and when she let go shoved so deep that Katherine began to kick and arch, the sheet flapping aloft, and then again was unconscious, in spite of the mask.

"Dammit!" Charles said, letting the mask go and grabbing the horn and lifting the man upright with it. "Stop that crap!"

All three of them stilled, frozen in shocked confrontation, and then as Charles bent to get the mask back in place he heard in his ears what he thought was his swelling heartbeat, but it was footsteps, and Harner, pulling loose his tie, came through the door. "What?" he said, and stopped, startled, studying each with birdlike concern, in a trim tan summer suit, with a burn or blush reddening his wrinkled head, and looked locked in a conflict to establish his control. "What the — " This came out half-cocked. "What's going on here? Answer me at once."

"She's ten *sahn*-timeters dilated, Doctor," the nurse said, all professional, as if to obscure some complication with jargon.

"What!" he said. "Well, good God, why didn't somebody give me an idea of the problem?"

The blonde let this pass and in a swoop got the mask from Charles and over Katherine's blue-spotted face.

Harner pointed a finger, surprisingly small and delicate, at Charles' forehead, only inches away in the cramped space, and said, "What the hell is *he* doing here?"

"But you said I — "

"And where's his sterile gown and cap, for God's sake?" Harner asked the nurse, ignoring him, so that the "*he*" stung worse.

"Katherine specifically asked me — "

"This is an emergency. Get out!"

"But my wife asked me not to — "

"Get out! Do you understand English? Get the hell out!"

Charles turned, nearly colliding in the doorway with the resident, who apparently felt Harner also meant him, and in the anteroom found himself fighting an anger so fierce it seemed brighter than the fluorescent tubes flashing past overhead as he walked, as in the aftermath of a stunning concussion in football, when criticism from a coach, as much as the injury, could throw his entire body off balance. The nurse at the desk smiled as if she'd overheard the scene, and said, "Why don't you wait in the lounge, down the hall to your left?" And then plucked at his coat sleeve as he passed, so he had to turn to her. "I could never see the sense of those gowns in the labor rooms anyway," she confided. "Since we go in in what we've been wearing all day. But that's what I was trying to tell you when you ran off. And then Dr. Harner — well, he can be so touchy." She wrinkled her nose at him.

The lounge was lined with chairs upholstered in primary colors, stilled in a compression of sunlight through windows that went from ceiling to knee-level along the length of the far wall. Empty. To sit, to him, was to concede to the hierarchical unreality closing around Katherine like the structure of the hospital itself, until it seemed she might disappear. So he went to the wall of plate glass and stood like a sentinel for her on the real world. His knees, which were at the level of the ledge of black material below, had been magically unlocked, he felt, and would suddenly begin bending in both directions. He was staring down at the river they'd crossed, here in its muddied surge against the city's sculpted edge, cut as fine at this juncture as if by a razor, and the growing sound, like voices at the fringes of his understanding, was, he saw, from the moving traffic building into its morning patterns over the streets below — a tentative stir that reached him also like the beginning billows of an unexpected, unpredictable wind.

The grayish cavern of a basement under construction — a further addition to the building — opened into the ground directly below, and he could make out reinforcing rods, like wires bent awry, rising at him out of the lines of future walls, and felt his exact place in relationship to them brought home with such an anesthetizing impact everything in him was blanked except a central sexual core, expanding and pulsing upward, so that he had to battle the perverse pull to throw himself down.

The still sheen of the glass with bands of gold sun resting deep in its thickness as if in insets in it — Then there was a spraylike dispersion within him (release? his limit?), and he felt it spill outside his boundaries through the window, hesitating in the air beyond, and then he was blinking back tears as he tried to remember how it was that Pierre had done this to him, when —

He couldn't get his breath and felt afloat as he watched his own unfeeling hands slapping over him for cigarettes, and finally got them out and lit one as if to anchor himself with it. Then fought visions of the glitter and gore of an operating room where he had Harner strapped down and was hacking at him with every instrument he could get his hands on.

He had to talk to somebody.

He'd cut off his family, as he'd wanted to, since none of them appeared to approve of Katherine to the degree that he thought they ought to. What could his father, or a brother, for instance, say about this if he called, not even knowing that she was pregnant? Katherine's father he scarcely knew. Maybe he could talk to Weston. Sure he could, certainly he could; he might even meet Weston in the halls. Weston taught here.

He caught a reflection coming toward him and turned. It was Harner, who halted at his look, taking on an air of also being afloat, in a ballooning green gown cinched at the waist and a cap like a housepainter's cap but without the bill, which gave the grin he put on a sillier aspect. Then Harner came up and put a hand on his shoulder, and Charles felt a response there like the sparking at a battery's terminal; he didn't care to be touched by any man. "Say, I'm sorry," Harner said. "I guess I blew my top back there. Nobody likes to walk in on a situation like that."

Charles looked into his eyes and encountered only an evasive fear — as if Harner had had glimpses of his operating-room assault — and managed to keep from saying anything but "How is she?"

"Well, it was a precipitate delivery, a classic case of it."

"Is that bad?"

"It's not so common that it didn't have us thrown a bit, you'll have to admit that." He tried to smile, and Charles felt that they were high school enemies who'd met on a street corner and decided to be mature and civil, and with that illumination Harner's smile came clear: the slack-lipped grin that cowards get, of having secretly eaten something tasty, just before they're socked. "It's not from anything either of you might have done, but unfortunate coming this early in her final trimester. Also, she's pretty badly edematous."

"What's that?"

"Gathered fluid. The swelling you see in her extremities. I wish you had told me about that."

"I did, over the phone."

"Oh, I guess you did, yes," he said, and looked down to recover himself, then up with a professional reserve. "I just want to reassure you that as far as we can tell it's very doubtful that anything that you or she might have done yesterday or the day before could have caused this. Certainly nothing that happened a week or more ago. Rest your mind on that. These things happen."

He'd seen the bruises.

Then that wiggly smile appeared again, and he said, "We'll want to keep a close eye on her, though, after this, and next

time might recommend some conjugal restraint over her last
trimester." His eyebrows bobbed. "In certain cases, that seems
to trigger contractions."

"Precipitate?"

"Yes, it's precipitated by God knows what and comes on like
a bugger. It takes a fraction of the time of usual labor and
delivery, once it gets going, and there's no way of knowing what
to expect next. We'll have to watch that, too, the next time
around."

"You mean Katherine —"

"Oh, she's great, you have a wonderful wife there! You're a
lucky guy! She came through it like an old pro, wide awake all
the way. The sedative didn't even have time to take hold before
it was over."

"It's over?"

"Well, yes — that is, the birth is, yes."

And now Charles had to wait while the enemy, who seemed
to have been priming for this, underwent a surge that appeared
in his eyes, like awe, before disclosing his ultimate dirty secret.
"You had a boy. We have one of our best pediatricians with him
right now. There's no use falsely getting your hopes up. He's
very small and very weak, almost two months early, and this has
been a terribly severe trauma for him. His respiratory system
isn't responding as it should be. He's fighting for his life right
now."

"What about an incubator, for God's sake!"

They both flinched at the tone of this.

"We're giving him oxygen. We've done all we can, actually,
medically."

"I want to see my wife." Needlelike intrusions started stitching
underneath his lids and at the corners of his eyes.

"She'll be in the recovery room soon. There are a few more
things we'd like to check out, and then I have to tidy her up a
bit."

He put a hand on Charles again, this time over his flexed arm
muscle, as if to intercept any violence, and wrinkled his nose
(had the nurse talked to him?) and said, "There are some restaurants and some little" — he waved his hand at the window —
"some little *places* across the street. Why don't you make it an
hour, say." This seemed a command.

"I'll wait right here."

But a few minutes later, when Harner came back and told him the child was dead, he walked out.

The bartender was scattering violet sweeping compound over the floor of one of the little places that had recently opened. Charles took his bottle of beer to a table, to be alone, though nobody was there but the bartender. Low morning light came through the open door at an angle that didn't quite reach to his shoes; the sprinkled boards beneath them gave off cold and damp. The door faced the river, with the regular storied height of the hospital between, and half of the pedestrians wore white, as if to claim their affinity with the constant newness of the business that they hurried toward.

He was too terrified to feel remorse. He had sensed that this would happen and knew that when it did he'd be off at a distance, apart from her, the expendable party. No recourse. No help. He'd had complete freedom most of his life, he realized now, or he'd taken it, even after they were married, but this he'd never be free of. This was on him, and he didn't know how he'd ever get out from under it. He was the cause. He'd take the responsibility for it upon himself. He'd tell her that. There was no possibility of divorce now, for him. He couldn't exist with this if he didn't have her side of it, or her portion of the experience, under him in support. She'd done all she could, given the circumstances. He was lucky to have her, as Harner said, and lucky she was alive. From this moment, their relationship would have to be as open as that door. He'd tell her that, and how the thought had come to him, like further sunlight through the door, but first he had to ask for and have her forgiveness. The way had to be cleared with that, or they couldn't take the first step together to begin again. He'd do what he could to make it from day to day after that, for her sake. No promises. No —

A raying silence spread from his center, like the silence that invades a house in a driving rain. He would not sit and imagine what it would have been like to have had a son.

The door darkened, and an elderly woman with a stocking cap pulled over her ears came rocking into the place, carrying a shopping bag in each hand, and sat at the table next to his, talking to herself as she sorted through her bags and smoothed scraps of paper out on the table as if they were dollar bills. Under a sweater, under a number of open coats, she appeared flat-chested above her pot belly, and her wide, white face was kept active by her licking at and worrying a single lower tooth. He thought with an impact which set him back in his chair that his mother would be this age if she were still living. He was about to move from the pall of irritation the woman spread; he'd had enough; this was over; he wanted off; and then heard "Could you get me one of those, sonny?"

He set his face toward the light, in case she was referring to him.

"Hey! Sonny, could you get me —"

"Aggie," the bartender said from behind. "Leave the kid alone."

Charles put down a dollar. "It's all right," he said. "Get her one."

"You know the rules," the voice said. "Not unless she walks in with you. I know Aggie."

There was a silence of restructuring accommodation, as if they were contemplating the movielike beams within the broader band of light, with only the sound of traffic in its passing breezes of accompaniment outside and, as if in answering sweep to that, the broom over the floor behind. Then the woman's talk seemed to stir in a different direction. "You hurt?" she said. "I'm all pain. It's my fault, it's all my fault, that's true. But you think you're the only one that suffers. One-crack mind, one-crack mind. One of these days you're going to wake up with your voice changed and realize you was always queer."

Sensation gave like snowslides in him, and his joints ached from the siphoning draw of dread. There was something terribly wrong with him, he was convinced, that he kept attracting these grotesques. And he must be more than monstrous himself (he had to fend off textbook images of abnormalities at birth), if he was already acclimated to this death, or even acting as if he were. Because what had been dislocating him all along under everything over the past few months was that he'd had an affair at the same time Katherine had had hers, as if they'd been signalling to one another the need to break free at the thought of being bound, and he'd felt he had got a taste of what he deserved when she confessed. But then had feared, first, that the child wasn't his and, second, that it wouldn't live.

"Like you lost your best friend," the woman said, and he turned and found her eyes on him, gray-gold in the light, while she sucked at the tooth as if to extract its essence. "Don't let it get you down. They're always after you. They don't let up. You got an ounce of sympathy yourself? You got sympathy with me?"

"Yes."

"Yeah, you say you do, but they all say that." Customers had come in, and she threw her head back as if to indicate them, and called out in a loud voice, "Ain't that right, Jack?"

"Sure, Aggie," the bartender said.

" 'Sure, Aggie,' he says, like he's my echo. They don't let up no matter what. I said to him, 'You want a mother, a wife and kids, you want a young girlie type, or you want a queer?' "

"What are you after?" Charles asked.

She leaned toward him and smiled a sweet-old-lady's smile, pegged at its corner by the tooth, and said, "A nice big jug of rosé wine. Maybe a hunk of you, Butch."

He took two dollars and dropped them and the other over the papers in front of her on his way out, feeling mistily benevolent; she'd never know the events or the state in him that this pitying generosity had risen from. And then out in the sunlight, blinking as if stunned, he felt he'd been lanced through the spot below his ribs where the talons curled. He couldn't tell Katherine he'd come here. Not while she'd lain alone over there. How could he have listened to Harner? And then he sensed something further hurrying close and heard in a faint whisper at his ear, *Murderer. You'll never quit paying for this.*

The gray-haired nurse got up from the desk as he stepped through the swinging doors; she, too, had her duty to do now. He'd decided to come and see Katherine, and let the rest take its turn from her. The nurse gripped him by his coat sleeve and said, "This time we won't forget," and led him to a line of lockers behind a wall of the curving anteroom — dim atmosphere of high school and the stripped-down purity of physical sports, with their innocence of the actual world, he now knew, in their unvarying perimeters and established rules. Not to mention the assumption that they were training grounds for life. From a shelf over the lockers she got a gown and shook it, to unroll it, and held it out for him; he stepped into it, over his jacket and all. Then, with a hand on him, exhaling something minty, she came around and started tying it at his back, and in the starchy chill of its cloth drawing close he felt he'd entered the hospital at last, and the hospital held Katherine in a state he hadn't seen yet. It held their dead son.

He gulped at the grief that went down his throat like brine and saw sudden darker spots travelling over the front of the gown as though its substance were giving out. "I understand," the nurse said, and pulled on one of the caps, then let her hands rest on his shoulders. "It's terrible to lose the first. God comfort you." She shook him.

He recovered, but in the anteroom, seeing Harner at the column encircled by the desk, in his suit and tie again, motioning him over, felt anger seal off his release. "We have some forms we'd like you to sign," Harner said, and put on his slack-lipped grin again. Two minutes alone with him, Charles thought; just two minutes would do. "It's a formality," Harner said, and his eyes swerved at the freezing cry of a newborn. "Then you can see your wife."

In heavy type on the top sheet on the desk Charles saw "Death Certificate." Farther down, written in: "respiratory failure." "Why should I sign it?" he asked. "I haven't seen him."

"Oh, not that," Harner said, and shuffled the papers until he came up with two others, one of which read "Waiver."

Again Charles said, "I haven't seen him."

"Well, in effect what these say is there's been a birth and then that you'll be making a gift of the case to the hospital. Our research is acknowledged across the United States, and this might be a way of helping out somebody else in a similar situation. We would take care of all matters of disposal, so you wouldn't have to worry yourself about that."

"It's no worry. I want to see him."

"I think perhaps it might be better for you if you didn't." That smile once more, which quivered now at its corners with his authority.

And struck across Charles' own trembling, so that he couldn't ask why it would be better if he didn't, while "disposal" brought to mind the whirring mechanism that could shake a whole sink. Then he saw a miniature casket at the edge of an open grave, with Katherine down beside it, the air all black around her, and wasn't sure he could take that. He was trapped. "I want to talk to Katherine first."

"I don't know if it's something she should have to handle now, seriously. Do you? I know it might feel like a tough decision, but it's pretty much routine, or procedure here, because of our research."

And then Charles saw, as down a corridor darker than the one where the lockers were, a flaking fetus in a jar, on a set of shelves among hundreds of others like it, and heard the refrain from a current folksinger's ballad, that for every child born another man must die, and felt an exact exchange of that sort, with deeper implications, taking place right now, here. While the tick and cluck and shuffle of doors and footsteps and equipment all around seemed to be those actual lives and deaths going in and out, moving through in an endless passage. And the only light of exit at the other end for him came shining out from the promise of seeing Katherine.

He signed the papers.

Harner gave a nod, as if to confirm Charles in his manliness, and then led the way to one of the branches off the anteroom, down a hall, to a door. "She might be resting," he said in a rasping whisper, as if he'd injured his voice. "If she is, maybe you should let her. Just take a peek so you can say you were in. She's been terribly excited about this — maybe overly so for now. We'll give you five or so minutes, and then in a while get her to a room — you'll want a private one for her, I know — and you can spend as much time there with her as you like."

This place was still smaller, with monitoring equipment against one wall and just enough space to pass by the stretcher where it was parked; the blond nurse was facing him, at its foot. "Done," she whispered, her eyes enlarging on him again, and then there was only the door at her back flapping in its frame at her quick retreat. A hypodermic syringe, with a final crystalline drop depending from its needle, lay on a stainless-steel tray on the stainless-steel counter that held the equipment.

Katherine's hair, curled from exertion or moisture, hung less low over the stretcher, and she was moving a hand under the smock, testing her stomach. He stepped around to where she could see him and took her hand, and was confronted by a glossy incandescence in her eyes, which had pooled even wider in their dark liquidity. "It's so flat!" she exclaimed. "It's hard to believe it's so flat! That that's me! I wish you could have been with me through it all. I was totally engulfed by it, by the birth — by him, I mean. I'm sorry I was so out of touch before; I got afraid. Once things were going all right, I kept saying, 'Nathaniel! Nathaniel! I'm here, I'm with you all the way!' I felt his head come out — it was wonderful! — and then I knew something was wrong. The rest was hardly there."

She looked away, toward the machines, and he knew he couldn't tell her what he felt he had to until this, which must be the ecstasy of birth, had subsided or passed over her. She turned back, with the incandescence in her eyes at another level. "Suddenly he was entirely himself and left such feeling with me. Only I really understand it right now, but you will, you will! My only regret is how I failed you."

"You came through it like a pro, I heard."

"No. He's gone. I know. I lost him. They told me. He died."

"You haven't failed me, I'm the —"

"I've failed you. You wanted him so badly."

He realized now that he had. "You haven't failed me. It's my fault."

"I was afraid you'd say that; I knew you would. Don't, please, for me. Please. I wanted to see him, but Harner wouldn't let me. 'I guess he just couldn't wait,' he said. All I wanted was to see him. It wouldn't have bothered me. If I could only have seen even his hands. But maybe it's better. Maybe I'd have nightmares. They rushed him away, and then I saw Harner and another doctor, across the room by the windows, working with him. Their backs were to me. I couldn't see him. The nurse was so great. She —"

"The blond one?" He wanted to get this all straight, as if for the terrible recompense that was to come.

"Yes, she was great! Back in the recovery room, well, here, I said, 'I just wanted to see him. I don't care how ugly he was.'

And she said, 'There wasn't a thing the matter with him. He wasn't ugly. He was a beautiful baby. He was simply too tiny.' Can you imagine how intelligent he must have been to have done this?"

"What?" The talons in him flexed with a catch.

"He wanted to bring us closer together, and this was his only way. He knew that. He was so much like you, really — ready to give up everything to make things right."

"Kath."

"I'm in a different perspective after the feeling he left. Now I know that time and events can never destroy actual love. It's something you can't understand just by reading about it. I had to learn that, and he knew it. We both had so much to learn from him!"

She laughed with a freer and deeper openness than he'd heard in her before, and he began to shrink from this and from her growing vision of events; he was diminishing by degrees, he felt, until he had to take hold of the stretcher at her head to keep himself from being drawn into her completely, as he feared, consumed. And then she pulled him down to her and kissed him on the mouth, and whispered with the intimacy of their bed, "No doubt about it. We've had our first child."

Then there was the perineal bottle in the bathroom of their apartment, in the stilled and grayish light through frosted glass; the green dress she never wore again, in shadow at the back of their bedroom closet; the barrenness of her secretary, as if she'd cleared it of even the essentials; the crescent-shaped planter of flowers he'd brought to her room in the hospital, with a nineteenth-century figurine in brown pantaloons and a long yellow coat with lace cuffs and lace froth at the collar, fixed in a contemplative pose, standing among the blossoms, which the florist at the last moment had set in place, and which Charles was unable to look at from the first without *Nathaniel* registering in him, followed by a stream of tickling over his throat; the few articles they'd got for the child, chiefly a red-and-blue banner imprinted with stylized Buckingham Palace Guards, which followed them through every move over the years (like the figurine he kept gluing and regluing until one day it was gone, with no explanation from her) and would suddenly appear out of a box, like another presence, striking them speechless; her feeling of betrayal that he'd signed the body away without telling her, and her depression that wouldn't leave for so long, and seemed would never leave, and when it did leave would reappear without warning and set up further silences within her, making her mistrust her ability to work as she once had; his anger at Harner and the hospital, which kept revolving in him and reached its peak in the fall, so that more than once he started toward a lawyer to sue, but found himself foiled each time as if by the season, his favorite, in a release of grief and melancholy — for he was never able to bear the loss with equanimity, or with her wholly physical sense of loss.

And it wasn't until after they'd had not only a second child but a third, and then a fourth, graced by this heritage, and he was leaning under the hood of a pickup on a fall afternoon with gold-red trees all around awash in a wind, and a son underfoot, running off with his tools, that he finally coughed out, "Good God, forgive me." And felt freed into forgiveness, for himself, first, then for her, the rest falling into place — for her because she'd never explained her experience during the birth and what she'd learned from it, as she'd said she would. But he knew now that the child had always been with him, at the edges of his mind and in his everyday thoughts, as much as any of their living children (*more,* he thought, as he set aside the wrench in his hand and watched the tops of the trees above him springing in the wind), and he began then to look out on those children, on this boy with his hair going back in the wind, and on Katherine and on others, with less darkness in his eyes: that is, began at last to be able to begin again to see.

Biographical Notes
Other Distinguished Short Stories
 of 1982
Editorial Addresses

Biographical Notes

BILL BARICH is the author of two books of nonfiction — *Laughing in the Hills* (Viking/Penguin) and the forthcoming *Travelling Light*. His stories and articles appear frequently in *The New Yorker*, and he has also written for *American Poetry Review, Rolling Stone, Playboy, Sports Illustrated*, and other journals and magazines.

CAROL BLY is a rural humanities consultant with the Land Stewardship Project and owner of Custom Crosswords. Her translations, poetry, and fiction have appeared in *New Directions, Poetry Northwest, The New Yorker, American Review, Ploughshares*, and elsewhere. Harper & Row published a book of her essays, *Letters from the Country*, in 1981. She has four children, Mary, Biddy, Noah, and Micah, and lives in Sturgeon Lake, Minnesota.

JAMES BOND is a graduate of Eastern Washington University and, together with wife, daughter, and parents, lives on a ranch sixty miles north of Spokane. His fiction has appeared in *Epoch, CutBank*, and *Willow Springs Magazine* as well as elsewhere.

RAYMOND CARVER's fourth collection of short stories, *Cathedral*, which includes "Where I'm Calling From," is forthcoming this year from Knopf, and *Fires*, a collection of his stories, poems, and essays, was published this spring by Capra Press. Mr. Carver is also the author of three collections of poetry. He teaches in the Creative Writing Program at Syracuse University.

CAROLYN CHUTE, a native Mainer, lives with her family on the Two Goose Farm in Gorham. She has published in *Ploughshares, Shenandoah*,

Agni Review, Ohio Review, and *Grand Street* and has just completed a novel called *The Beans,* which concerns hunger and rage in America.

LAURIE COLWIN was born in New York City, where she now lives. She has published three novels — *Shine On Bright and Dangerous Object* (1975), *Happy All the Time* (1978), and *Family Happiness* (1982) — and two collections of short stories — *Passion and Affect* (1974) and *The Lone Pilgrim* (1981). Her stories have appeared in *The New Yorker, Playboy, Mademoiselle, Antaeus, McCall's, Redbook,* and *Cosmopolitan.* In 1977, she won an O. Henry Award.

JOSEPH EPSTEIN, who is the editor of *The American Scholar,* teaches literature and writing at Northwestern University. He is the author of *Divorced in America, Familiar Territory, Ambition,* and *The Middle of My Tether.*

LOUISE ERDRICH grew up in Wahpeton, North Dakota. She is of German and Chippewa descent, and belongs to the Turtle Mountain Band of Chippewa. Her work has appeared in *Dacotah Territory, North American Review, Redbook, Ms.,* and is forthcoming in *The Atlantic* and *The New England Review.* Her story "The World's Greatest Fishermen" won the 1982 Nelson Algren Award and was published in *Chicago* magazine. *Jacklight,* a book of poetry, will be published by Holt, Rinehart and Winston in the winter of 1984.

URSULA K. LE GUIN was born in California and lives in Oregon. She has published poetry, essays, short fiction, and novels (including *The Left Hand of Darkness, The Dispossessed,* and *A Wizard of Earthsea*), has written film and radio scripts, and has taught at a number of writing workshops and conferences.

BOBBIE ANN MASON is a native of Kentucky. Her collection of stories, *Shiloh and Other Stories,* was nominated for the PEN/Faulkner Award for Fiction, a National Book Critics Circle Award, and an American Book Award. It received the Ernest Hemingway Foundation Award for the most distinguished first-published work of fiction in 1982. Bobbie Ann Mason received a grant from the National Endowment for the Arts in 1983 and a Guggenheim Fellowship for 1984. She is a contributor to *The New Yorker* and *The Atlantic Monthly.*

WRIGHT MORRIS's latest book is *Solo: An American Dreamer in Europe, 1933–34.*

JULIE SCHUMACHER was born in Wilmington, Delaware, and received a B.A. from Oberlin College. She works as an editor, translator, and free-lance writer in New York City.

SHARON SHEEHE STARK grew up in Johnstown, Pennsylvania, and presently resides with her family near Lenhartsville, Pennsylvania, where she is trying to finish a first novel. Her stories have appeared recently in *StoryQuarterly, Antioch Review, Yankee, Playgirl, Missouri Review, South Dakota Review,* and other literary magazines.

ROBERT TAYLOR, JR., was born and reared in Oklahoma City. He attended the University of Oklahoma, San Francisco State University, and Ohio University, and has taught at Bucknell University since 1972. His stories have appeared in *The Agni Review, The Ohio Review, The Georgia Review, Cimarron Review,* and many other literary magazines. *Loving Belle Starr,* his book of outlaw stories, will be published in the spring of 1984 by Algonquin Books.

MARIAN THURM is a graduate of Vassar College and Brown University. Her fiction has appeared in *The New Yorker, The Atlantic, Redbook,* and elsewhere. A collection of her stories will be published by Viking this winter.

JOHN UPDIKE was born in Shillington, Pennsylvania, in 1932. After attending the public schools of that town, he attended Harvard and the Ruskin School of Drawing and Fine Art in Oxford, England. After two years on the staff of *The New Yorker,* he moved to Massachusetts, where he has resided ever since. He is the author of some twenty-five books, including ten novels and eight collections of short stories. This is his seventh appearance in *The Best American Short Stories.*

GUY VANDERHAEGHE was born in Esterhazy, Saskatchewan, in 1951. His short stories have appeared in Canadian literary magazines and anthologies, among them *Best Canadian Stories.* He has published one collection of short stories, *Man Descending* (Macmillan of Canada, 1982), and is at work on a novel.

DIANE VREULS has published a book of poems, a novel, and a children's book. Her stories have appeared in *The Paris Review, The Iowa Review, The New Yorker, Shenandoah,* and elsewhere. She teaches in the Creative Writing Program at Oberlin College. She is married to Stuart Friebert, a poet, and has two children.

LARRY WOIWODE was born in Carrington, North Dakota, in 1941. He now lives and farms in the southwestern corner of that state with his wife and family. He has been a contributor to *The New Yorker* since 1964. His novels are *What I'm Going to Do, I Think* (recipient of the William Faulkner Foundation Award, 1969), *Beyond the Bedroom Wall,* and *Poppa John,* and he has written a book of poetry, *Even Tide.* In 1980, he received an award in literature from the American Academy and National Institute of Arts and Letters.

100 Other Distinguished Short Stories of the Year 1982

SELECTED BY SHANNON RAVENEL

CARVER, RAYMOND
Feathers. The Atlantic Monthly, September.
A Small, Good Thing. Ploughshares, Vol. 8, Nos. 2 and 3.
CHAPPELL, FRED
The Dreaming Orchid. New Mexico Humanities Review, Spring.
CHUTE, CAROLYN
Olive and August. Shenandoah, Vol. 32, No. 3.
CLARK, ELEANOR
The Fortress and Raggedy Ann. The Georgia Review, Spring.
COLLIER, PETER
The Early Sixties. The Seattle Review, Fall.
CORODIMAS, PETER
The Face of London. The Virginia Quarterly Review, Spring.
CURLEY, DAN
The Contrivance. New Letters, Winter.

DAVIS, KATHRYN
Eternity. New England Review & Bread Loaf Quarterly, Fall-Winter.
DAY, ROBERT
Speaking French in Kansas. New Letters, Winter.
DRISKELL, LEON
A Fellow Making Himself Up. Wind/Literary Journal, Vol. 12, No. 44.
DUBUS, ANDRE
The New Boy. Harper's, January.
DUGGIN, RICHARD
A Certain Knowledge. Kansas Quarterly, Summer.

GALLANT, MAVIS
Grippes and Poche. The New Yorker, November 29.
Luc and His Father. The New Yorker, October 4.

GERLACH, JOHN
Night Tale. Ascent, Vol. 7, No. 3.
GRIESEMER, JOHN
Comfort Stations. West Branch, No. 10.

HELLENGA, ROBERT R.
The Mountain of Lights. California Quarterly, Summer.
HELPRIN, MARK
Passchendaele. The New Yorker, October 18.
HIGGINS, JOANNA
Natural Disasters. Passages North, Spring/Summer.
HUMPHRIES, JENNY STONE
The Vegetable Queen. The Greensboro Review, Winter.

JAFEK, BEV
Holograms, Unlimited. Mississippi Review, Fall.
JANOWITZ, TAMA
Ode to Heroine of the Future. Mississippi Review, Fall.
A Visit to Chicken Greiben. The Agni Review, No. 16.
JUST, WARD
Maintenance. New England Review & Bread Loaf Quarterly, Autumn-Winter.

KINGERY, MARGARET
Saved. Confrontation, Winter.

LARSEN, ERIC
Hannah. The Ohio Review, No. 27.
LAVERS, NORMAN
The Sod House. Pequod, No. 14.
LEAVITT, DAVID
Territory. The New Yorker, May 31.
LOUIE, DAVID
One Man's Hysteria — Real and Imagined — in the 20th Century. The Iowa Review, Vol. 12, No. 4.

MASON, BOBBIE ANN
The Retreat. The Atlantic Monthly, July.
Underground. The Virginia Quarterly Review, Spring.

MEINKE, PETER
Getting Rid of the Ponoes. Yankee, January.

MERRILL, RICHARD
The Disappearance. Antaeus, Winter.

MUNRO, ALICE
Mrs. Cross and Mrs. Kidd. The Tamarack Review, Winter.
Visitors. The Atlantic Monthly, April.

NELSON, KENT
Winter Ascent. Southwest Review, Winter.

O'BRIEN, JOHN
The Missionary Has Some Thoughts. Northwest Review, Vol. 20, No. 1.

PAINTER, PAMELA
The Intruders of Sleepless Nights. Ploughshares, Vol. 8, No. 4.

PAUL, JAY S.
Aunt Titus Nusbaum Toots In from Tootsville. Cimarron Review, January.

PETERSON, LEVI S.
The Canyons of Grace. Ascent, Vol. 7, No. 3.

PROULX, E. A.
The Wer-Trout. Esquire, June.

RANKIN, RUSH
Smart Men. TriQuarterly, Spring.

ROBISON, JAMES
Set Off. The New Yorker, September 27.

ROOKE, LEON
Narcissus Consulted. The Malahat Review, No. 61, February.

ROSNER, ANNE F.
Blind Mule. The Antioch Review, Spring.
In the Chinaberry Tree. The Yale Review, Summer.

RUBIN, LOUIS D., JR.
The Man at the Beach. The Virginia Quarterly Review, Autumn.

SCHELL, NIXA
Hairdo. CutBank, No. 18.

SCHINTO, JEANNE
Mr. Swint. Ascent, Vol. 8, No. 1.

SCHUSTER, JOSEPH M.
Destinations. Western Humanities Review, Summer.

SCHWARTZ, LYNNE SHARON
The Wrath-Bearing Tree. Fiction Supplement, Summer.

SCHWARTZ, STEVEN
Society of Friends. Epoch, Summer.

SELZER, RICHARD
Imposter. Antaeus, Winter.

SHACOCHIS, ROBERT
Stolen Kiss. The Paris Review, No. 83, Spring.

SINGER, ISAAC BASHEVIS
The Bond. The New Yorker, June 28.

SMITH, JEWELL
How It Had to Be. The Kenyon Review, Summer.

SPRINGSTUBB, TRICIA
My Mother's Novel. The Ohio Review, No. 27.

STARK, SHARON SHEEHE
The Barlip Run. South Dakota Review, Spring.

TALLENT, ELIZABETH
Refugees. The New Yorker, January 4.

TAUS, BEATRICE
Power. Partisan Review, 3/1982.

TAYLOR, ROBERT, JR.
The James Boys Ride Again. The Georgia Review, Summer.

The Tragedy of Jesse James. Cimarron Review, April.

TOMLINSON, NORMA
Snowbound. Carolina Quarterly, Fall.

TREGER, MARIAN
Gorillas in the Kitchen. Fiction Supplement, Summer.

TRIVELPIECE, LAUREL
The Burying. Stories, November-December.

UPDIKE, JOHN
First Wives and Trolley Cars. The New Yorker, December 27.

VAN WERT, WILLIAM F.
Putting and Gardening. North American Review, June.

VIRGO, SEAN
Through the Eyes of a Cat. The Malahat Review, October.

VON HOFFMAN, NICHOLAS
The Brahms Lullaby. Harper's, February.

WAKSLER, NORMAN
Moral Education. The Greensboro Review, Winter.

WEAVER, GORDON
Home Economics. Western Humanities Review, Winter.

WELLS, SALLY
Polaroid. The New Yorker, April 5.

WHISNANT, LUKE
Watching TV with the Red Chinese. Esquire, March.

WHITNEY, RUTH SAUER
Arrested in Mid-Flight. The Threepenny Review, Fall.

WHITTEN-STOVALL, BONNA
The Great Dance Rattle. Carolina Quarterly, Fall.

WHITTIER, GAYLE
Blood Telling. Ploughshares, Vol. 8, No. 4.

WILLIAMS, JOY
Building. Esquire, January.

WOODMAN, ALLEN
The Lampshade Vendor. Epoch, Spring.

Editorial Addresses of American and Canadian Magazines Publishing Short Stories

Agni Review, P.O. Box 349, Cambridge, Massachusetts 02138

Akros Review, University of Akron, Akron, Ohio 44325

Analog, 380 Lexington Avenue, New York, New York 10017

Antaeus, 1 West 30th Street, New York, New York 10001

Antioch Review, P.O. Box 148, Yellow Springs, Ohio 45387

Apalachee Quarterly, P.O. Box 20106, Tallahassee, Florida 32304

Aphra, RFD, Box 355, Springtown, Pennsylvania 18081

Arizona Quarterly, University of Arizona, Tucson, Arizona 85721

Ascent, English Department, University of Illinois, Urbana, Illinois, 61801

Aspen Journal, P.O. Box 3185, Aspen, Colorado 81612

Atlantic Monthly, 8 Arlington Street, Boston, Massachusetts 02116

Aura Literary/Arts Review, 117 Campbell Hall, University Station, Birmingham, Alabama 35294

Ball State Forum, Ball State University, Muncie, Indiana 47306

Bennington Review, Bennington College, Bennington, Vermont 05201

Black Messiah, Vagabond Press, 1610 North Water Street, Ellensburg, Washington 98926

Bloodroot, P.O. Box 891, Grand Forks, North Dakota 58201

Boston Globe Magazine, The Boston Globe, Boston, Massachusetts 02107

California Quarterly, 100 Sproul Hall, University of California, Davis, California 95616

Canadian Fiction, Box 946, Station F, Toronto, Ontario M4Y 2N9, Canada

Capilano Review, Capilano College, 2055 Purcell Way, North Vancouver, British Columbia, Canada

Carolina Quarterly, Greenlaw Hall 066A, University of North Carolina, Chapel Hill, North Carolina 27514

Chariton Review, Division of Language & Literature, Northeast Missouri State University, Kirksville, Missouri 63501

Chelsea, P.O. Box 5880, Grand Central Station, New York, New York 10163

Chicago, 500 North Michigan Avenue, Chicago, Illinois 60611

Chicago Review, 5700 South Ingleside, Box C, University of Chicago, Chicago, Illinois 60637

Choice, Box Z, State University of New York, Binghamton, New York 13907

Cimarron Review, 208 Life Sciences East, Oklahoma State University, Stillwater, Oklahoma 74078

Commentary, 165 East 56th Street, New York, New York 10022

Confrontation, English Department, Brooklyn Center for Long Island University, Brooklyn, New York 11201

Cosmopolitan, 224 West 57th Street, New York, New York 10019

Crazyhorse, Department of English, University of Arkansas at Little Rock, Little Rock, Arkansas 72204

Creative Pittsburgh, P.O. Box 7346, Pittsburgh, Pennsylvania 15213

Cumberlands (formerly Twigs), Pikeville College Press, Pikeville College, Pikeville, New York 41501

CutBank, Department of English, University of Montana, Missoula, Montana 49812

December, December Press, 6232 N. Hoyne, Chicago, Illinois 60659

Denver Quarterly, University of Denver, Denver, Colorado 80208

Descant, P.O. Box 314, Station P, Toronto, Ontario M5S 2S5, Canada

descant, Department of English, Texas Christian University Station, Fort Worth, Texas 76129

Epoch, 245 Goldwin Smith Hall, Cornell University, Ithaca, New York 14853

Esquire, 2 Park Avenue, New York, New York 10016

Event, Kwantlen College, P.O. Box 9030, Surrey, British Columbia V3T 5H8, Canada

Fantasy & Science Fiction, Box 56, Cornwall, Connecticut 06753

Fiction, c/o Department of English, City College of New York, New York, New York 10031

Fiction International, Department of English, Saint Lawrence University, Canton, New York 13617

Fiction-Texas, College of the Mainland, Texas City, Texas 77590

Fiddlehead, The Observatory, University of New Brunswick, Fredericton, New Brunswick E3B 5A3, Canada

Four Quarters, La Salle College, 20th and Olney Avenues, Philadelphia, Pennsylvania 19141

Gargoyle, P.O. Box 57206, Washington, D.C. 20037

Georgia Review, University of Georgia, Athens, Georgia 30602

Good Housekeeping, 959 Eighth Avenue, New York, New York 10019

Grain, Box 1885, Saskatoon, Saskatchewan S7K 3S2, Canada

Great River Review, P.O. Box 14805, Minneapolis, Minnesota 55414

Greensboro Review, Department of English, University of North Carolina at Greensboro, Greensboro, North Carolina 27412

Harper's Magazine, 2 Park Avenue, New York, New York 10016

Harpoon, P.O. Box 2581, Anchorage, Alaska 99510

Helicon Nine, 6 Petticoat Lane, Kansas City, Missouri 64106

Hudson Review, 65 East 55th Street, New York, New York 10022

Indiana Writes, 110 Morgan Hall, Indiana University, Bloomington, Indiana 47401

Iowa Review, EPB 308, University of Iowa, Iowa City, Iowa 52242

Kansas Quarterly, Department of English, Denison Hall, Kansas State University, Manhattan, Kansas 66506

Kenyon Review, Kenyon College, Gambier, Ohio 43022

Ladies' Home Journal, 641 Lexington Avenue, New York, New York 10022

Lilith, The Jewish Women's Magazine, 250 West 57th Street, New York, New York 10019

Literary Review, Fairleigh Dickinson University, Madison, New Jersey 07940

Little Magazine, Dragon Press, P.O. Box 78, Pleasantville, New York 10570

McCall's, 230 Park Avenue, New York, New York 10017

Mademoiselle, 350 Madison Avenue, New York, New York 10017

Malahat Review, University of Victoria, Box 1700, Victoria, British Columbia V8W 2Y2 Canada

Massachusetts Review, Memorial Hall, University of Massachusetts, Amherst, Massachusetts 01002

Michigan Quarterly Review, 3032 Rackham Building, University of Michigan, Ann Arbor, Michigan 48109

Mid-American Review, 106 Hanna Hall, Department of English, Bowling Green State University, Bowling Green, Ohio 43403

Midstream, 515 Park Avenue, New York, New York 10022

Mississippi Review, Center for Writers, Southern Station, Box 5144, Hattiesburg, Mississippi 39406

Missouri Review, Department of English 231 A & S, University of Missouri, Columbia, Missouri 65211

Mother Jones, 625 Third Street, San Francisco, California 94107

Ms., 199 West 40th Street, New York, New York 10018

MSS, Department of English, State University of New York, Binghamton, New York 13901

Nantucket Review, P.O. Box 1234, Nantucket, Massachusetts 02554

National Jewish Monthly, 1640 Rhode Island Avenue, N.W., Washington, D.C. 20036

New England Review, Box 170, Hanover, New Hampshire 03755

New Laurel Review, 828 Lesseps Street, New Orleans, Louisiana 70117

New Letters, University of Missouri-Kansas City, 5346 Charlotte, Kansas City, Missouri 64110

New Mexico Humanities Review, Box A, New Mexico Tech, Socorro, New Mexico 87801

New Orleans Review, Loyola University, New Orleans, Louisiana 70118

New Renaissance, 9 Heath Road, Arlington, Massachusetts 02174

New Yorker, 25 West 43rd Street, New York, New York 10036

North American Review, 1222 West 27th Street, Cedar Falls, Iowa 50614

Northwest Review, 369 PLC, University of Oregon, Eugene, Oregon 97403

Ohio Journal, Department of English, Ohio State University, 164 West 17th Avenue, Columbus, Ohio 43210

Ohio Review, Ellis Hall, Ohio University, Athens, Ohio 45701

Old Hickory Review, P.O. Box 1178, Jackson, Tennessee 38301

Omni, 909 Third Avenue, New York, New York 10022

Only Prose, 54 East 7th Street, New York, New York 10003

Ontario Review, 9 Honey Brook, Princeton, New Jersey 08540

Paris Review, 45-39 171 Place, Flushing, New York 11358

Partisan Review, 121 Bay State Road, Boston, Massachusetts 02215

Passages North, William Bonifas Fine Arts Center, 7th Street & 1st Avenue South, Escanaba, Michigan 49829

Pequod, 536 Hill Street, San Francisco, California 94114

Phoebe, George Mason University, 400 University Drive, Fairfax, Virginia 22030

Playboy, 919 North Michigan Avenue, Chicago, Illinois 60611

Ploughshares, P.O. Box 529, Cambridge, Massachusetts 02139

Plum, 1121 First Avenue, #4, Salt Lake City, Utah 84103

Prairie Schooner, 201 Andrews Hall, University of Nebraska, Lincoln, Nebraska 68588

Present Tense, 165 East 56th Street, New York, New York 10022

Primavera, Ida Noyes Hall, University of Chicago, 1212 East 59th Street, Chicago, Illinois 60637

Prism International, University of British Columbia, Vancouver, British Columbia V6T 1W5, Canada

Quarry West, Porter College, University of California, Santa Cruz, California 95060

Quarterly West, 312 Olpin Union, University of Utah, Salt Lake City, Utah 84112

RE:AL, Stephen F. Austin State University, Nacogdoches, Texas 75962

Redbook, 230 Park Avenue, New York, New York 10017

Richmond Quarterly, P.O. Box 12263, Richmond, Virginia 23241

St. Andrews Review, St. Andrews Presbyterian College, Laurinburg, North Carolina 28352

Salmagundi Magazine, Skidmore College, Saratoga Springs, New York 12866

San Jose Studies, San Jose State University, San Jose, California 95192

Saturday Night, 70 Bond Street, Suite 500, Toronto, Ontario M5B 2J3, Canada

Seattle Review, Padelford Hall GN-30, University of Washington, Seattle, Washington, 98195

Seventeen, 850 Third Avenue, New York, New York 10022

Sewanee Review, University of the South, Sewanee, Tennessee 37375

Shenandoah, Box 722, Lexington, Virginia 24450

Shout in the Street, Queen's College of the City University of New York, 63-30 Kissena Boulevard, Flushing, New York 11367

South Carolina Review, Department of English, Clemson University, Clemson, South Carolina 29631

South Dakota Review, University of South Dakota, Vermillion, South Dakota 57069

Southern Review, Drawer D, University Station, Baton Rouge, Louisiana 70893

Southwest Review, Southern Methodist University, Dallas, Texas 75275

Sou'wester, Department of English, Southern Illinois University, Edwardsville, Illinois 62026

Stories, 14 Beacon Street, Boston, Massachusetts 02108

StoryQuarterly, P.O. Box 1416, Northbrook, Illinois 60062

Texas Review, English Department, Sam Houston State University, Huntsville, Texas 77341

Threepenny Review, P.O. Box 9131, Berkeley, California 94709

TriQuarterly, 1735 Benson Avenue, Northwestern University, Evanston, Illinois 60201

Twilight Zone Magazine, 800 Second Avenue, New York, New York 10017

U.S. Catholic, 221 West Madison Street, Chicago, Illinois 60606

University of Windsor Review, Department of English, University of Windsor, Windsor, Ontario N9B 3P4, Canada

Vanderbilt Review, 911 West Vanderbilt Street, Stephenville, Texas 76401

Virginia Quarterly Review, 1 West Range, Charlottesville, Virginia 22903

Vision, 3000 Harry Hines Boulevard, Dallas, Texas 75201

Wascana Review, English Department, University of Regina, Regina, Saskatchewan, Canada

Waves, 79 Denham Drive, Thornhill, Ontario L4J 1P2, Canada

Webster Review, Webster College, Webster Groves, Missouri 63119

West Branch, Department of English, Bucknell University, Lewisburg, Pennsylvania 17837

Western Humanities Review, University of Utah, Salt Lake City, Utah 84112

Whispers, 70 Highland Avenue, Binghamton, New York 13905

Wind/Literary Review, RFD Route #1, Box 809K, Pikeville, Kentucky 41501

Wittenberg Review, Box 1, Recitation Hall, Wittenberg University, Springfield, Ohio 45501

Writers Forum, University of Colorado, P.O. Box 7150, Colorado Springs, Colorado 80933

Yale Review, 250 Church Street, 1902A Yale Station, New Haven, Connecticut 06520

Yankee, Yankee, Inc., Dublin, New Hampshire 03444